Little Flowers

DLP BOOKS

Virginia Beach, VA

Also by Kathryn Lively

Pithed: an Andy Farmer Mystery

Little Flowers

KATHRYN LIVELY

DLP
books

PO Box 55071
Virginia Beach, VA 23471
Cover art © 2008 Kathryn Lively

ISBN-13 9781449538491
First DLP Edition – November, 2009
Library of Congress Number 2001087382
Printed in the United States of America

10 9 8 7 6 5 4 3 2 1

Author's Notes

With regard to the layout of the Ghent district of Norfolk, Virginia, and that of Williamsburg, Virginia as described in this story: I have taken a few liberties. There is no women's clinic located near the corner of 21st Street and Granby as written here; nor is there a Norfolk Coffee Company in this particular area (such a place does not exist). There is also no such paper as *The Norfolk Times*. Café Lisieux, as mentioned in this story, is also a fictitious locale, and St. Vincent's and Holy Name Academy are also fictitious names. The Naro Theater and Dog and Burger in Norfolk, however, are real places, as is the Trellis in Williamsburg.

Special thanks to my family for their love and encouragement, for without their support I may never have been able to see this story to completion; to Patricia and Karen Sealy for their help and enthusiasm during the production of the book's original print version; to the members of the Catholic Writers Association for countless missives of support and prayers via the Internet; to Timothy Drake and Dr. Ronda Chervin for their critiques and suggestions; lastly, to my husband, Malcolm, for not feeling embarrassed that his wife carries a spiral notebook everywhere she goes.

This book is dedicated to the memory of Linda Lee Chesney

Ad majoram dei gloriam!

One

The winking blinds of the Mastersons' master bedroom were partially open, allowing the morning sunshine to slice into the room in long, slender fingers. Coming to rest on the bed, the light rays caressed the sleeping face of Doctor Neil Masterson, gently tapping at his eyelids and tempting him to wake. The alarm clock on the nightstand beside him had already failed at that task.

"Mmph." Neil tumbled onto his stomach, in the process tugging at the billowing bed comforter so it exposed his feet to the sun's warmth, which was magnified through the window glass as the February winter continued to prevail. He shifted for a cool spot in the bed, eyes closed only in vain now as he struggled for at least five more minutes of peace before having to rise and face the working world.

He smoothed his hands underneath his pillow and tucked his legs underneath the flap of the comforter, relishing the refuge they offered from the persistent sunlight. Had his bladder not woken up before him, Neil may easily have stolen ten more minutes of sleep.

Quite suddenly a liquid eye popped open for a blurred view of the alarm clock - the time 3:20 lit in digital red blinked back at him. Power outage, he realized.

"Damn!"

As if on fire, Neil sprang from bed and snatched his watch from the highboy dresser across the room, sighing with tense relief on discovering he had only overslept twenty minutes. No big deal, he thought; there were no pressing appointments today, at least, nothing that could not wait, and in this day of precarious health reform, patients were used to waiting long periods of time as it was.

So I'll get to the clinic twenty minutes late, Neil thought as he shifted into his staid morning routine. The patients coming in today will get treated twenty minutes later than hoped, the paperwork will be filled and filed twenty minutes late, and I'll go home twenty minutes late. Problem solved. Carrie would understand, it was not as if he had never worked late before…

Carrie.

Neil jerked his head away from the bathroom mirror and glanced at the bed, noting his wife's section of mattress and pillow appeared unused. It took three seconds for him to remember that she was in Richmond keeping vigil for her sister, who was probably enduring her twenty-seventh consecutive hour of labor. If Carrie's last phone call to him was any indication, their pending nephew or niece was in no hurry to begin mortal life.

Neil had offered to knock off work for a few days and join Carrie and the boys for moral support, but the look on his wife's face at the mere suggestion of it negated the whole proposal. Those simple brown eyes of hers widened in shock, and her small lips twisted downward. A perfect imprint of his wife's face lingered in the back of Neil's mind. Whether it was shame or worry she would not say, though Neil was already aware of Carrie's sister's disdain for his line of work, despite the numerous occasions where he and Carrie attempted to explain fully what exactly it was that he did for a living. It always struck Neil as odd that Carrie seemed to have no problem voicing her pro-choice opinions at social gatherings and in eloquent, albeit sometimes anonymous, letters to the editor, but otherwise she was either apologetic or tight-lipped. What was it about blood relatives that turned his wife's resolve to jelly?

He was not a monster, Neil often assured his sister-in-law. He never held a gun to the heads of the various women, troubled or confident, seeking the aid of his practice. The choice was always ultimately theirs; he was only the doctor in the clinic offering the service.

Carrie's Aunt Barbara was probably going to be there, in Richmond, thought Neil, hunkered down in front of the picture window at the maternity ward, cooing at the babies and shaking her damn rosary like a rattle. Just as well he stayed in Williamsburg, he thought. He didn't need any of Barbara's disapproving stares today.

He nicked his chin with the last pull of the razor blade, and a small spot of blood surfaced and mingled with the last traces of shaving cream on his face. Neil cursed silently as he ran a damp washcloth over his face. If that were the only blood he saw today, he would consider his shift a good one.

Abortions were not among his favorite procedures to perform, but as long as they were legal in the state he had an obligation to offer his services to anyone who wanted it. It was not as if every day at work was, as Barbara called it, a "massacre of life in progress"; the clinic also offered other gynecological services, mainly for women without insurance and who were low on the annual income totem pole.

"Tell that to Barbara," he muttered to himself, shaking his head. She only saw a butcher when she looked at Neil, a butcher with a medical degree. His white coat might as well have been spotted dark red every day.

Padding downstairs into the kitchen, Neil noticed the sun's rays had followed him and strengthened as the morning minutes ticked away. A beautiful day, Neil decided, too beautiful to be wasting away under the dim ultraviolet lights of the clinic, surrounded by antiseptic white. It was too beautiful a day to watch girls just a few years older than his eleven-year-old son tread somberly in and out of the exam rooms, their heads lowered and lips quivering as if they, and not the growing buds inside them, were about to be terminated.

As Neil wrestled with the coffee machine, more inaudible curses escaped his breath. Seventeen years of leaving all household appliances in his wife's capable hands had left him at their mercy. A hot cup of espresso at the shop across the street from the clinic would have to suffice now, he thought, if he still wanted to be only twenty minutes late. He would call Carrie from the office during lunch for the latest update on his sister-in-law, and to tell her that he loved her.

He sighed heavily as he shrugged on his heavy wool coat, quick-stepping to the front door. He told Carrie that he loved her so many times it seemed automatic to him, like blinking an eye. Today, though ...a bitter feeling tugged at his brain. It seemed more urgent to do so, yet he couldn't dally any longer. Twenty-five minutes late, he grumbled to himself with a quick glance at his watch as he turned the knob.

The first bullet was fired as Neil stepped over the threshold; his hand still gripping the outside doorknob as he intended to pull it closed behind him. Instead the door opened wider as the force of the bullet tore into Neil's stomach and pushed him back inside. He backed into the closed closet door and caught his back on the knob before sliding to the floor, landing on a worn pair of pre-teenage cleats and clutching his abdomen.

What the hell happened, he thought. He heard nothing leaving the house, only a stiff buzzing sound filling his ears before impact. Nothing like a gunshot.

Warm blood spread across his gut as if he had spilled tomato juice on his shirt, just before someone thrust a pitchfork in his stomach to twirl his intestines like a strand of spaghetti, it hurt so much. He howled in pain and thought immediately of his family, distraught they were not around to help, yet relieved that they would be spared bullets themselves - this day or any other day. He did not need to see the gunman's face to know who was responsible, and there was certainly no mistake of motive, or that he was the target.

His head wavered from side to side, his breathing grew labored and his body tingled; he knew the feeling once before, when he and his wife donated a pint of blood at a clinic drive a month ago. Carrie told him that it was the closest she ever came to feeling near death.

He pushed his finger deeper into his gut to stifle the flow of blood, which was already forming a crust on his shirt. Quite unexpectedly a laugh bubbled up from his throat - this was a shirt he had ironed himself last night, without so much as a call to Richmond for a consultation. How he was looking forward to showing off to Carrie when she got back. Now look at me, he thought. Look at me...

His gaze floated upward to the chipped almond molding of the front door - a thick cotton spider web filled the cracks of one corner. No warning, he thought, not like on television. No endless weeks of perfunctory phone threats or being pelted with rotten vegetables as he left the building at night, no grotesque postcards of saline-fried fetuses tucked underneath his car windshield wipers bearing a block-printed YOU'RE NEXT notice.

His days as an abortion doctor were, well, until this moment, occasionally disturbed, with only the line of subdued protesters across the street from his building to nudge at his conscience. Could this have been one of them, he wondered. Could one of those people - one of Barbara's friends - brought himself or herself to set down a picket sign long enough to fire a gun?

So lost in thought and light-headed was Neil that he did not detect the presence of the figure in the long dark coat until he was standing practically over him, blocking the sunlight from the open door and introducing a sudden sense of quiet rage. The man wore a Baltimore Orioles baseball cap with the bill pulled over his eyes; he nearly had to tilt his head ninety degrees to look Neil in the face.

Neil eyed the tightened silencer on the muzzle of the man's gun. "Praised be the Lord, Jesus Christ," bellowed a deep bass with an accent dripping of Southern twang; it had to be disguised, Neil guessed, but why would he bother if he were planning to...

"No babies will die in this town today," the man proclaimed, and Neil wondered with the last of his conscious reasoning if his would-be assailant was going to tack on a whooping Rebel Yell after that. His next thought consisted of only two words: *Oh, Jesus!*

"None by your hands, anyway, you asshole." The man cocked the gun, aimed for Dr. Neil Masterson's puzzled face, and fired without blinking.

Two

Peach-glossed lips pursed, then rubbed together to smooth the cracked skin left behind after a day of braving cold wind without a scarf. Laura Merwin applied another thin coat of lipstick and, seeing too much of a shine to her taste, just as quickly snapped a Kleenex from its box and pressed it to her mouth.

"Of all the nights to go to dinner," she grumbled to herself as she turned to her lingerie chest in hopes that a virgin pair of control top pantyhose had materialized there since the last time she went shopping for herself. Wasn't Bush Senior still in the White House, she asked herself with a shrug.

Fumbling through tangles of snagged stockings and knee-length socks, she settled instead on a sheer off-white pair with a finger-long run that ran the length of the seat. She scrunched up both nylon legs to fit over her feet and gingerly stretched the material north, sucking in her gut and begging silently for God's Mercy until the waistband snapped securely above her navel.

"Whew." A deep, expansive sigh of relief followed as she shyly took stock of her figure in her full-length mirror, allowing only a fleeting moment of pride to wash over her. She patted the slight bulge of her abdomen and instinctively straightened her posture so she would not appear any lumpier than she was certain she already was.

Forty-five years of life and bearing five children did not leave her body a complete disaster area, and for that she was grateful. At least some parts of her remained firm when she poked them, instead of folding into long rolls of fluff or succumbing to the pull of gravity and becoming drooping little pendulums of flesh. She checked her fingernails, each one perfectly manicured and polished by her thirteen-year-old daughter, Therese. The girl eagerly volunteered for the task. If only she applied that much zeal to her homework, Laura thought with a quieter sigh. She thrust her shoulders back and saw her breasts rise half an inch.

"Okay," she smirked to the mirror, "now stay that way for the next forty-five years."

Laura's husband Chris barged into the bedroom to find her only in a full slip, hypnotized by her mirror image. "Laura, hon, why aren't you dressed yet?" he cried, fumbling with the button of his dress shirt. To his wife, he looked no more ready to leave than she did; his hair still glistened wet from a quick shower and it pointed in several directions, the cuffs of his shirt were undone and he was barefoot.

"You know Pre can't hold a table past six on a busy night, and if you want to catch that meeting by eight o'clock, it would help if you had a few more layers on!" He brushed past her to the nightstand on his side of the bed, slapping her bottom playfully on the way. Laura squealed and tried to retaliate, but Chris was too quick.

"Five seconds!" she called out, laughing. "That's all I need to throw on my skirt, sweater and shoes and we can be out of here before the kids ask us to solve some last-minute crisis. You want you should time me?" she dared, eyeing the watch Chris buckled onto his wrist.

"The kids," he muttered, "Oh, great, I just remembered. CJ, get in here!" he hollered to the open bedroom door. Chris felt his back pocket and, finding it empty, looked pleadingly at Laura, who pointed automatically to the dresser, where Chris's always elusive wallet lay next to his car keys. These were two items Laura insisted be sewn onto Chris's body lest he misplace them once more. Twenty-two years of familiarity with her husband's quirks and absentmindedness fostered in her a sixth sense that kicked in whenever anyone in the family lost something. World leaders craved such powers of a wife and mother.

"Thanks, hon. I have a twenty in there for the kids to get pizza."

"That's too much for a pizza, don't you think?" she gazed forlornly at the noble portrait of Andrew Jackson on the bill she cradled in her hand. With only Chris working full-time and what little she brought in from her freelance tutoring work, the Merwins had to watch every penny entering and leaving the house. As a result, not much money was left for luxuries, but even when a large bill like a twenty or higher found its way into Chris's wallet, it still did not seem enough to satisfy needs and wants, much less take-out pizza.

Considering how much fast food CJ alone could consume, Laura knew, it was a surprise to see Andrew's face at all these days.

"Too much?" Chris chortled. "I hope it's just enough. Besides, we're going out to eat, and I promised the kids a treat. You know, what with Lent coming up," he ambled on guiltily, fully aware that Laura kept a good supply of price club bulk package frozen burritos, tater tots, and corn dogs in the garage freezer for just such occasions, rare as they were. The same high sodium and cholesterol for only one-third the price!

Within seconds, Chris's loud call brought forth not only their eldest son, seventeen-year-old Chris Junior, but also nine-year-old Judith, resplendent in her favorite hot pink jumpsuit. The baby of the family, six-year-old Joshua, tagged along behind them, a sticky fist locking a headless Barbie doll in a gleeful death grip.

"Mooo-*ooom!*" whined Judith, twirling the missing plastic head by its brunette hair. "Josh won't give back my doll!"

To drive her point home she lunged for the doll, only to send her younger brother shrieking into the hall.

"She said I could have it!" was Joshua's only defense, which launched a war of "Did not/Did sos" until Laura, still in her slip, ushered the two into the bedroom across the hall, which the two shared, to negotiate a quick truce.

CJ rolled his eyes at the scene and casually crossed himself. "God grant me the strength and serenity to make it through this night," he mumbled.

Chris threw him a stern look. "Relax. If you're worth your salt as a babysitter they'll all be finishing their homework quietly and be in bed early, and you'll have so much serenity you'll go nuts from the silence."

"Who knows," he added, piercing his son with a sharp wink, "maybe you could use all that serene free time to practice making a decent Sign of the Cross."

CJ muttered a contrite apology. "Doubt I'll have time to enjoy any peace if that's still going on," he said, hooking his thumb toward the far bedroom shared by Therese and sixteen-year-old Monica, from which the thumping sounds of the Beatles' *White Album* could be heard through the closed door.

Concern spread across Chris's face. "I checked in when I got home and your sister was motionless on her back, listening to that same album. Don't tell me she's still like that. That was two hours ago!"

"I guess she and Jack had another fight."

Chris reddened. Jack Nixon was CJ's classmate, a clean-cut, acne-free wrestling team star, the ideal personification of a high school sweetheart to any parent with a teenaged daughter. Chris liked Jack fine, but viewed his relationship with Monica with scrutiny; as far as he was concerned, Monica was still not ready to date and would not be until long after he was buried.

"Well, if she and Jack decide to sort things out, they do it over the phone. No visitors," he commanded. "That goes for Nina, too." Nina Simmons was CJ's girlfriend, and Chris's views of CJ dating were no different.

"Sure."

"And don't forget to lead the Rosary tonight."

"I won't forget, Dad." The family Rosary, a staple in the Merwin household since Chris carried Laura over the threshold twenty-two years ago, was prayed daily after dinner. The elder Merwins agreed to make up for lost time when they returned home and saw no reason why the tradition should be broken for the children.

"Mrs. Wilkens said she'd be keeping an eye out for strange cars in the driveway," Chris added, tightening the knot of his tie. "I don't want her to have to deliver a report when we get home."

"Dad!" CJ folded his arms, angry. "You've got neighbors spying on us? You don't think Nic and I can pull this off?"

"I trust you completely. It's those legions of hormones raging inside you that make me worry." He noticed the bewildered look on his son's face and added, "Hey, I didn't come of the womb a forty-five-year-old man." Grinning, he clapped his son on the shoulders and eased him back outside, where Laura was waiting for him with twenty dollars and a blossoming headache.

Chris leaned against the doorjamb, smiling at his wife. "Five seconds, huh?"

Three

Café Lisieux was alive with chattering voices and clinking silverware, and as Lola Marquez surveyed the activity from behind the counter, she quietly congratulated herself for letting Pre take the initiative in ordering more wine and beer for tonight. People wanted to live it up on Fat Tuesday, enjoy their final indulgences and forbidden pleasures before the toll of the midnight bell which would herald a forty-day desert of atonement and sacrifice standing between them and Easter morning. The way some people were eating and drinking, it appeared there would be much atonement tomorrow, not to mention new resolutions to diet and exercise.

Lola felt relieved, too, that Pre also had the foresight to stock up on extra desserts. There did not appear to be a table tonight that did not order one of the café's delicious cream-filled pastries, slices of fruit pie or rich chocolate cake. Every place setting sent back to the dishwasher had at least one fork or plate smeared with chocolate icing.

"Some night, huh? Told you we'd get hammered."

Lola's cafe manager Pre Winningham sidled up to the bar with a large round tray of empty beer bottles and glasses. The waiter scheduled to work the closing shift had called to say he would be delayed due to car trouble, and though Lola's son Miguel had left to fetch him, the trip looked to be at least forty-five minutes. Pre elected to bus tables and help in his absence.

"Oh, Pre. Let me help you with something! I feel so bad just leaning against the bar rail watching everyone else work." Lola reached for the tray, but Pre gently slapped her hand and shifted the tray so it now balanced on her hip.

"You'll do no such thing." Pre wiped away a wisp of her blond hair back over her head and gripped the tray firmer. She rounded the bar and entered the kitchen. "You know what the doctor said. You have to rest your foot so the swelling will go down."

Lola gazed down at her right foot, a flesh balloon wrapped in a beige Ace Bandage, and sighed. A few days earlier, she had slipped in a pair of high heels and banged it against the light post outside the café. The stern-faced doctor who attended to her at the local hospital's emergency room wrapped it in gauze, declared it a severe sprain, and ordered her to bed to completely heal. Apparently, Lola thought at the time, this man never owned a restaurant. The only thing Lola had been healed of during the week was wearing high heels.

There was too much to do at the café, and Lola was not about to spend the week in bed worrying about whether or not she would have a place of business by the end of it. Not that she expected her employees to mutiny or steal her blind or convert the small café into a frantic saloon worthy of a boisterous police raid, but Lola was a hands-on businesswoman. She was always the first and last person to walk through the café door each day.

Though she was tempted to give in to Pre's suggestion that the younger manager watch over the business, Lola insisted she at least be present during peak hours. Pre was a gift from God, Lola knew, but Café Lisieux was her baby; she cherished the eatery as much as she did her only child, and she was not going to let a sprained foot turn her into an invalid.

"At least let me seat the Merwins!" Lola called over the din of conversing customers, hobbling over to the main entrance before Pre could emerge from the kitchen and catch her. Chris and Laura were hanging their coats as the slightly pudgy café owner, limping on her bad foot, greeted them.

"So rare to see you two on a school night," Lola kidded them, "but all the same it's wonderful. You're not worried you won't return home to *Animal House*?"

Chris laughed and happily took the menus Lola offered, even though he and Laura knew every item listed. "Oh, our kids know very well that if we come home to less than status quo, they'll be coming home after school and staying put. No dates, no phone calls, no clubs...nothing for at least a month."

"The threat of not being able to see their sweethearts is incentive enough for the older ones, that and losing the phone privileges," Laura added as her husband and Lola nodded in agreement. "They'll be all right."

Lola guided them to a table set for two abutting the café's large storefront window. Chris immediately balked.

"Isn't this table usually taken?" he asked cautiously. Lola looked at him, puzzled, until she realized he was referring to another customer, one who dined at Café Lisieux daily.

"Oh, you mean Rosie." Lola playfully waved a hand. "Rosie won't be eating with us tonight," she revealed to two surprised faces. "She's opted to spend her Shrove Tuesday at home."

"Home? Instead of trying a dish of your famous hot jambalaya and andouille sausage?" Laura cocked her head toward a sandwich board by the door, which advertised that and other Mardi Gras dinner specials. "It's odd not seeing her here, though, she's as much a fixture as the pipes, I'm sure."

"Not to mention the portraits of the Little Flower everywhere," Chris added. He gestured to the small dining area around them, which, on the busiest of days, sat just over fifty customers. Now in its tenth year of operation, Café Lisieux began as a vacant storefront in a newly-built strip mall near Williamsburg's colonial downtown area and the College of William and Mary, a locale rich in Southern beauty and early American history.

Yearning to open a business of their own, while also contributing to the area's Catholic community, Lola and husband Ephraim purchased the last vacancy in the building sandwiched between what would become a florist shop and a dry cleaning operation. Lola fell instantly in love with their slice of property - the mall as a whole did not have the modern, cold appearance most hastily constructed strip buildings possessed. This building was tailored to suit the quaint, quiet community: a light red brick exterior and dark thatched roofing offered the Marquezes a perfect exoskeleton with which to work, and the couple searched antique shops all over the Hampton Roads area for decor.

They selected dark woods, furniture designed with intricate carvings, and other similar fixtures to give their new shop a kitschy look, one attractive to the area college students yet not too brazen as to divert the town's more established citizens. The decor may have brought people inside, but Lola's tempting menus of hot sandwiches, pasta dishes, and rich desserts kept a regular cycle of return customers.

The eatery's name was Ephraim's idea, in honor of his favorite Catholic saint, Therese Martin of Lisieux, known affectionately over the past century as the Little Flower by her admirers. Her story of absolute piety and childlike love for God attracted Ephraim and touched him deeply, and as someone who also experienced the loss of his mother at a young age, as St. Therese did, Miguel believed he had found a kindred spirit in his Catholic faith. Like Therese, Ephraim practiced in life a "little way" approach to prayer, talking to God in fits and spurts, sometimes at points of high stress and anxiety, yet equally faithful and devout with each word.

Miguel decorated Café Lisieux with portraits and drawings of St. Therese, resplendent and angelic in her recognizable brown Carmelite habit, as well as a large framed map of France he obtained from a National Geographic magazine. A two-foot-high concrete statue of Little Flower greeted customers at the front entrance, near a doormat with a rose design. Lola could not resist buying the item when she found it at a local hardware store, it worked well with keeping the restaurant's theme.

Over the years regular customers and visitors added their own personal touches, hanging plastic bead rosaries and woolen scapulars from the light fixtures, or sending the Marquezes picture postcards and personal photographs of popular Catholic pilgrimages such as Fatima, Lourdes, or the Vatican. These images were displayed on two large bulletin boards behind the bar, with plans for a third pending.

For all the reminders of the young nun Pope Pius XI once called "the greatest saint of modern times," nobody involved in the business of Café Lisieux ever expected the last, equally tragic parallel between Therese and Ephraim - an untimely death. Just as Therese succumbed to illness short of living a quarter of a century, so Ephraim Marquez lost a brief battle to cancer short of reaching forty on, strangely enough, the eve of the one hundredth anniversary of Little Flower's passing. All festivities planned at the café were immediately canceled, with a Rosary vigil at the Marquez home taking precedent.

Two years had passed since Ephraim's death, and Lola still mourned, though her pleasant demeanor and cheerful attitude toward her customers masked the pain and emptiness in her heart since the only man she ever loved was taken from her. Throwing herself completely into her work, catering to the needs of special regular diners like the aforementioned Rosie, was her only method of coping. "No tears, only God...and food," was her new motto.

"Is Rosie feeling alright?" asked Chris.

Lola, still lost in thought over her late husband, did not answer immediately until Laura waggled her fingers in a "come back to Earth" gesture.

"Hm? Oh, she's fine," Lola laughed. "She told me after Mass this morning that she wanted to spend the night in prayer, preparation for Ash Wednesday, naturally. Would you believe she actually took me aside to warn me so we wouldn't worry about her not showing up tonight?" This merited another chuckle for Lola; few customers concerned themselves with the feelings of the Café Lisieux staff beyond interaction during meals, not like Rosie.

"There you are!"

Pre approached the group, hands on hips and a stern look directed at Lola. "Why are you out here and not resting that foot? It's never going to heal if you keep walking on it."

She nudged her boss toward the back of the café. "Let's go! Behind the bar." To Chris and Laura she said, "For the first time in my life, I'm beginning to realize what it feels like to be a mother."

"Oh, you won't know that feeling until I start sneaking into the house at three in the morning or 'borrowing' money from your purse without asking," was Lola's gentle retort, prompting laughter all around, even from a few onlookers at other tables.

"We really should apologize, Pre," Laura said. "We should have known better than to let Lola get away from you."

"Ah, don't worry about it. It's not like Lola listens to any of us anyway."

"Now you know what it feels like to be a parent," teased Chris.

Pre smiled sadly, and instinctively Laura kicked her husband under the table.

"Ow!"

"Sweet tea to drink?" Pre asked as Laura and Chris, now rubbing his shin, nodded. "Back in a sec. Jeff will be right over to get your orders," she added, and with that she retreated hurriedly into the kitchen, nearly knocking Lola into the bar.

Four

CJ held the phone to his ear, bracing it with his shoulder. His youngest siblings surrounded him at the kitchen table, shouting a chorus of suggested pizza toppings.

"I don't want pepperoni." Judith stuck out her tongue. "It's too greasy and it causes pimples."

"Like you need to be worrying about that," CJ countered, rolling his eyes. "What I wouldn't give for skin like yours again." He smoothed his free hand over his chin, where fresh acne was destined to erupt any minute.

CJ fingered the buy one, get one free pizza coupon on the table. "How's this? We get a pie with meat, and one with just cheese. If I'm going forty days without meat for Lent, I'm eating pepperoni and sausage tonight."

"But you only can't eat meat on Fridays," pointed out Joshua, who, though quite young, was very much aware of modern Lenten customs, thanks to the detailed home schooling he received from his mother. He knew that while he and Judith were still exempt from meatless fasts, Therese, Monica, CJ and most people over the age of thirteen were not. Older people, like his grandparents, were also exempt from full-day fasts due to health concerns.

"I know I don't have to give up meat the entire forty days, Josh. I'm doing it as my Lenten sacrifice. You know how Mom and Dad choose something they like and go without it from Ash Wednesday to Easter?" CJ playfully tapped his younger brother on the nose. "It's a sign of appreciation for the sacrifice Jesus made for us when He died on the Cross. I want to do the same thing, so this year no more meat, chicken, and pork for the next forty days."

"I'm giving up chocolate," said the ever self-conscious Judith. "That'll give you pimples, too."

"What can I give up then?" Joshua frowned. He never liked to be left out of anything. "I wanna give up something for Jesus!"

"How about giving up bugging your older sisters?" groaned Therese. Judith heartily asserted this suggestion.

"OK, everyone, calm down," commanded CJ, mashing the refresh button on the phone as the disconnect signal blared in his ear. "Let's order the pizza and I'll help you find something to sacrifice for Lent, okay, Josh? Now, where's Nic? How am I supposed to know what she wants on the pizza?"

Therese played with the frayed split ends of her long dishwater blonde hair; she was the lone contrast among her dark haired siblings. "Oh, she's still upstairs moping. She said whatever you order is fine with her."

Another sharp beeping noise emitted from the receiver, and CJ reached over to the phone and punched the reset button again, returning the mellow hum of the dial tone. The younger kids settled on toppings as CJ dialed. Monica would just have to live with what was ordered. It must have been some serious fight with her boyfriend, he thought; the threat of thermonuclear war could not prevent Monica Merwin from voicing her opinion when it came to food.

* * * *

Upstairs, Monica lay on her back upon the bed, staring at the magazine pinups of favorite actors and musicians she had affixed to the ceiling with thumbtacks. Every few seconds her gaze would wander toward the open door of the far closet, which bulged with clothes she and Therese wore and shared. Between dozens of dresses and pantsuits poked a swatch of fine lavender silk - a formal gown-in-progress Laura obtained from an older, taller niece. Alterations of the gown for Monica to wear to the junior/senior prom in May were nearly complete. All Monica had to do was stay the same size for the next four months.

Right, she thought.

Prom night was all Monica discussed with her friends over Christmas break. How many days, she wondered, had she spent poring over dog-eared pages of *Seventeen* and *Cosmopolitan*, studying hairstyles and makeup tips, giggling and ruminating over A-list celebrity fantasy dates with Therese? How often had she tried on the dress during its various stages of alteration, imagining herself already there on the arm of handsome Jack Nixon in his tuxedo? Too many too remember what was happening in the real world, she decided.

Now, nearly two months later, Monica could not even bring herself to smile. Naturally her parents were concerned with the sudden mood swing, but they were determined to see that Monica enjoyed the event regardless of whether or not Jack would still be in the picture. Who can tell such things given the fickle nature of teenagers?

"Fifteen days," she whispered, tears forming in the corners of her eyes. Fifteen days had passed since her period was due. For fifteen mornings she woke and bolted for the upstairs hall bathroom shared by the five Merwin children, expecting to see her underpants stained red, but found nothing. Never before had she so desperately wanted her menstrual cycle to resume. The stomach pains she would have gladly welcomed, as well as the discomfort of using feminine hygiene products.

Tentatively she rolled over to her nightstand and eased her phone off the hook. CJ was ordering pizza. She gently placed the receiver back into the cradle and rolled onto her stomach, burying her face in her pillow. Six hours had passed since she and Jack last spoke, six hours since she last had the opportunity to tell him but changed her mind. She wondered if he would call tonight. Jack called often during the eight months they had been steadily dating, sometimes twice a night, but lately his commitments to wrestling and college hunting slowed the communication between them.

Monica's reluctance to continue to forge the new boundaries of their relationship also made things uncomfortable. Jack was not pleased with this sudden plea for celibacy. A first time to him was supposed to lead to a second, third, and future times.

Quickly she flipped back and sprang from the bed. If she were indeed pregnant, it probably was not good to lay for an extended period of time on her stomach. She might be impeding the health of the new life inside her.

Then again, perhaps if she did nothing but lie on her stomach for the next week or so, she could miscarry. No need to have to say anything to her parents, and perhaps she could eventually convince Jack to resume a more stable, celibate relationship. By then, she might just have the courage to talk about the baby-in-progress and scare him into keeping his pants zipped. Problem solved.

That is, if she were indeed pregnant. Monica was not one hundred percent positive.

She put a hand to her abdomen and sat perfectly still, waiting for a wave of nausea to well up from the pit of her stomach and seize her throat. She felt fine that morning and was relieved to know she was not suffering morning sickness, until the information she found on the Internet during library time informed her that nausea symptoms for some women occurred all day long, while others never experience such symptoms at all! How was she to know what type she was?

The prospect of eating a cheesy, greasy pizza did make her feel sick, and pizza was her favorite dinner, but that sensation she attributed to nerves. Regardless of whether or not she was pregnant, it would still likely come out that she and Jack had been sexually active, and Monica could not decide which was worse in her parents' eyes.

"Oh, Jack, why don't you call?" she whispered, now pacing around her room like a caged cat. She rifled through her collection of compact discs and slid a Van Halen title she borrowed from CJ in her stereo and turned up the volume, letting the loud screeching guitars and thumping bass wash over her and drown out the sounds of her sobs.

Why did I say yes? Monica thought to herself. Why did I cave in after telling myself time and again that it was the right thing, the only thing, to wait until marriage? Why did I believe Jack when he said everyone else in school was doing it, too? In the days since their first, and only, time Monica had spoken frankly to many of her friends, only to discover differently.

She eased herself to the floor and sat cross-legged in the middle of the room. Already her clothes were feeling tighter. She gazed sullenly behind her at her school backpack, which was hanging from the back of her desk chair. Inside the front pocket was an unused home pregnancy test, bought on the sly after classes, which she had to use with her first morning urine to determine if she was about to be an unwed teenage mother. How she was going to be able to complete the test in a house where she and her siblings shared one bathroom without arousing suspicion she was not certain. She thought once about taking the test at school.

"How appropriate. A test I want to fail," she chuckled to herself while in line at the drugstore. There was, however, always the off chance a teacher or one of the nuns might barge into the girls' restroom for a surprise inspection. Either that or another student might see her, and rumors spread so fast and so far, all the way to CJ's and Jack's homeroom and beyond ...

Monica sighed. She would find a way to know for sure. She had to know.

Five

Very few people referred to Barbara Fitzgerald by her name. Everybody just called her the Rosary Lady. Rosie for short.

The monikers came naturally to the silver-haired septuagenarian with the small, thin form and colorful wardrobe. Seldom was she seen in public without a rosary either clutched in her wrinkled hands or hanging around her neck and twisting around the chain of her pewter crucifix as she walked briskly through the main streets of downtown Williamsburg, nodding hello to passersby in between her silent prayers. To see her without a 'rosy' expression coloring her face was equally rare.

She was quite the topic of conversation and idle speculation among the town's tightly knit Catholic community. Appearing literally from out of nowhere three years ago, the Rosary Lady purchased outright a large house on Richmond Road zoned originally to be a bed and breakfast inn, as it was located on a stretch of road known by some as "B&B Row." Rosie herself called it "Holy Row," for Richmond Road was home also to several different houses of worship, including St. Vincent's Catholic Church.

People expecting yet another colonial-style inn to open for seasonal business were surprised when weeks passed with nary a sign or advertisement. Clearly the old woman had other plans.

The Rosary Lady turned the stately two-story house into a home base for her one-woman apostolate: a rosary workshop and prayer support center for anyone and everyone desiring spiritual help. The three bedrooms on the second floor of the house were transformed, with the help of a few volunteer members of St. Vincent's youth group, from romantic getaway bedrooms to storage facilities for the old woman's nearly infinite supply of rosary materials. Plastic and metal crucifixes and medals, nylon cords and coils of nickel wire, and beads of every color, ranging from iota-sized seeds to centimeter thick spheres, took up much of the rooms' space in numerous plastic boxes.

The downstairs den, once used as a community room for guests to convene over hot cocoa or cordials, became the home office. It was stocked completely with a computer and Internet modem, printer, a color scanner, and even a personal copy machine used for duplicating the Catholic apologetics pamphlets the Rosary Lady distributed with her wares. Then there were the rosaries.

So many rosaries!

CJ Merwin had been one of the strong young men moving furniture into the house, and never before had he seen so many sets of prayer beads in one place. They hung in rainbow strands from coat racks and curtain rods and every other place in the living room where there was a free hook. This lady had plastic bead rosaries in a rainbow of colors - tiger's eye rosaries, crystal birthstone rosaries, faux pearl, black onyx, jade, aquamarine, cloisonné, and other semiprecious stones linked together by either tightened cord knots or meticulously created chain links. The roughened calluses on the Rosary Lady's hands suggested to CJ that she did most, if not all, of the handiwork on display.

"You like that one, don't you?" Her vibrant voice filled his ears that day three years ago as he and his friends rested with proffered paper cups of soda. Rosie spied him admiring what looked to be a small chain of fabric beads connected by a medal.

"I've never seen anything like it before, a rosary without a crucifix. It's so small." CJ gingerly fingered the soft beads and flipped over the medal, revealing an image of St. Therese of Lisieux.

"That is the chaplet of St. Therese, my friend, not a traditional Dominican rosary," Rosie said matter-of-factly. "It's the third most popular item that I distribute. I make these beads with rose petals which I dye red to enhance the color, as this dear saint is traditionally represented by the rose." She took the chaplet and pinched the medal between her long fingers. "There are twenty-five beads, twenty-four of which symbolize the years of Therese's earthly life."

The Rosary Lady went on to explain the history behind the devotion and the prayer method. "The way I remember, there was once a priest who was an ardent admirer of the young saint, and he wanted her heavenly intercession that the Lord would grant him aid. This priest started a routine of praying twenty-four Glorias for nine consecutive days and asking for Therese's aid and for her confirmation of prayer with a rose. Sure enough, more than halfway though the novena the priest received a rose from a friend, and his prayers were answered," she said. "Many regard Therese a powerful intercessor in asking the Lord's favors."

CJ mentioned that his younger sister, Therese, was named for the saint; the old woman folded the chaplet into his hand without a second thought. "Then you must give her this," she said. When CJ reached into his back jeans pocket for his wallet, she waved a finger to decline.

"No. I won't accept anything for it."

"But it looks so fancy, ma'am," CJ protested. "It must have cost a lot of money to make it." Though only fifteen and unable to work regularly, CJ garnered his share of mad money from mowing lawns and other odd jobs. What little he had saved up for miniature golf and movies he was willing to pay. Therese's tenth birthday was approaching, and she was excited about her first year in the double-digits. Given the young girl's interest in her faith, CJ knew that the chaplet would be the perfect gift for her.

"Please, let me give you something." CJ opened his billfold. "I don't have a lot of money, but if I could at least cover the cost of the beads-"

Rosie chuckled and stilled the boy's hand, which still clutched a few crumpled dollar bills. "Very well." She backed up and took a small cardboard milk carton from the living room fireplace mantle. "I collect for Catholic Relief Services and other charities." She held up the container as CJ stuffed the bills inside. "Consider your debt paid," she smiled.

As their conversation progressed, CJ also mentioned Café Lisieux, and that night began a three-year tradition of nightly dinners for the Rosary Lady. She came to know Lola, Pre, the wait staff and many regular customers very well over the weeks and soon she and they were on a first name basis. Though Lola and Pre knew her real name by virtue of the personal checks the old woman used to pay for her meals, they like everyone else simply addressed her as "Rosie." Rosie did not want it any other way.

A second fixture in the Rosary Lady's daily routine was morning Mass. Spot on nine, rain or shine, the officiating priest would see the matronly woman in the third pew to the right of the altar, with a black lace mantilla covering her curled hair and a black wooden bead rosary wrapped around her wrist. She sang all hymns and prayer responses in a shrill, melodic voice and received her Eucharist on the tongue. To St. Vincent's small group of daily communicants, she certainly struck an anachronistic appearance as she cycled through the motions of the Mass in pre-Vatican II mannerisms. Some half-expected her to respond to the priest in Latin.

Today, Rosie, clad in a dark blue floral print dress and bright purple sweater underneath her coat, was not ten steps out of the vestibule following the first Ash Wednesday service of the day when she felt a light tap on her shoulder. Lola Marquez, her forehead bearing a deep black cross of ash like the old woman's, held out her gloved hands to her.

"We missed you last night!" Lola chided. "I hope this doesn't become a habit."

Rosie patted the younger woman's hand. "Oh, don't worry. That was but a minor bump in my staid schedule. There will be plenty of dinners at your café to come, and much more money to be taken from my bank account."

Lola's face fell slowly. "Oh, Rosie, I didn't mean to sound-" she began in a hushed tone, but the light laughter of the old woman easily reassured her.

"I know, I know. You missed my smiling face more than my shining silver. Well, to be truthful, I did feel strange not going out to eat last night, but for some reason I felt compelled to stay home."

The two women walked - Rosie walked, Lola limped - along the stone path leading to the curb, where many parishioners like Lola had parked their cars. The Rosary Lady's home was only a block away; both ladies started in that direction.

"I felt as if I were being pushed to pray," Rosie continued. "Like there was a soul out there tragically forgotten who needed an earthly advocate, someone to plead their case to God." She shook her weary head. "I did not get to bed until three this morning. I'm surprised I managed to get through Mass without nodding off, much less walk here on my own."

"Perhaps God had a mission for you that couldn't wait," Lola suggested. "It happens." As one who prayed constantly during the day, she understood the urgency of prayer for those in need. Her own prayer petitions were left to the will of God. "Is there anyone in your family who is ill? Or in financial trouble?"

"My niece Melissa is due to give birth any minute now, but her husband did not let on to any problems when I last called. I had planned to visit them to help, but I changed my mind. I think they'll be busy enough with his family clamoring to see the new addition.

"Of course, I pray that the Lord has seen fit to take the souls of those in my family who left us," Rosie added, looking at Lola. "I certainly pray for the well-being of all my friends and the parishioners here, you and Miguel included, and for the young girls I see entering the clinic."

Lola smiled sadly at this, thinking of the number of young women - some not even women, but children - treading into the women's clinic in nearby Norfolk seeking out advice and aid regarding sex and pregnancy and disease prevention. Such heavy topics coming from people who should be more concerned with homework and just being young, she thought.

Worse yet, Lola knew, there were the girls who entered the clinic not to seek preventive measures but looking for help after the fact. Too scared to turn to their parents, they looked for a quick, painless solution, something not even the most skilled physicians could provide.

A sharp wind whipped through the trees above them, rustling the leaves loudly, and both women drew their coats together and bowed their heads to shield their faces. Lola put a hand on her beret while the older woman cursed herself silently for neglecting to wear her scarf.

They reached Rosie's house. "Come inside for coffee," the old woman offered.

Lola smiled. "Why not? I don't have to be at the café until noon. Thanks for asking," Lola said with a slight nod. She picked up the morning paper left on the porch as her hostess unlocked the door.

Later, as Lola was settled in the living room in a wingback chair facing the fireplace, Rosie brought in a wood tray with two mugs of instant coffee. She noticed the open paper on Lola's lap, in particular a bold black headline that seemed to have her friend's attention.

"Bad news?" Rosie asked.

"Rosie, were you planning to sit in front of the clinic today?"

Rosie sipped her coffee. "That's a silly question. You know Father Welker and I go there every other afternoon to pray the Rosary, and today will be no exception. We keep to ourselves and don't harangue the people who go in and out, unlike some of the more vocal protesters there. They pretty much ignore us, if you think-"

Lola folded the front page into quarters and held it up for Rosie to see. "I don't think you and Father should go there today."

"But why, dear? What happened?" Rosie's eye caught the thick block font in full now, resting atop a color photo of a familiar face smiling with his wife and young children.

"Oh, dear." Instinctively she blessed herself, prompting Lola to do the same out of habit. Rosie read aloud snatches of the article, focusing on words explaining the actual murder of Dr. Neil Masterson and how a neighbor who was out walking his dog that morning discovered his body. The doctor, whom many anti-abortion protestors, including Rosie, had often seen opening and closing the Hampton Roads Women's Clinic and Family Planning Center, suffered two bullet wounds. One was lodged in his stomach, and one struck him between the eyes at so close a range that the top of his skull nearly split in two.

While leads on motives seemed clear, Rosie read, his association with the clinic was not officially declared the primary one. The article did not mention whether or not any of the area's more radical pro-life organizations had claimed responsibility for the death. Too soon to tell, Rosie figured. That the newspaper was able to get the story in the morning's edition so soon after the fact was amazing.

The old woman's finger rested on the photo; she felt a chill rush through her body and her heart pounded harder. "I know him. Or rather, I knew him," she said finally. "I prayed for him and his family daily; they were always the first and last of my regular intentions." Oh, Neil, she asked herself, where are you now? Hell? Purgatory? Are there enough prayers in the world to help you find peace?

"Sometimes when the other protesters weren't beating him down with words, we'd exchange nodding glances from across the street," Rosie continued. "No words, however. Not for a long time."

Lola watched as the old woman sipped from her gray ceramic mug, wondering exactly how well she knew the slain doctor, but deciding not to press the issue. Rosie did not appear to take the doctor's death very well, more so than hearing of another baby lost to abortion.

Rosie wrapped her fingers around the warm mug to keep them from trembling. "Some days he'd stop first at the coffee shop, over where I sit. Very brave of him to do so, if you ask me, since a more raucous person could easily have assaulted him. He'd nod at me and look away quickly - I could never tell if it was indifference or shame. Probably the former."

Rosie pictured the doctor with the serious face, wrinkled with a hundred simultaneous worries, forcing a morning nod toward her and Father Welker as he passed by them on his way to work. His gait always appeared lumbering and depressed to her, as if the years spent terminating pregnancies were starting to take its toll on his emotions. Many times she wanted to pause during a Hail Mary prayer to start a conversation about his job, his family, or the repercussions his actions might have on the fate of his soul. The Lord knew she had tried so many times before to no avail, but lately the words would not come to her, and it seemed unlikely Neil Masterson would have listened anyway. The stubborn old mule, she cursed quietly. She then asked Jesus to forgive her for the ill thought.

Lola leaned over the paper, her hand coming to rest on Rosie's. "You're as pale as a sheet," she observed. "Are you feeling all right?"

Rosie's eyes widened into saucers. "I just keep picturing that poor man lying in a bloody puddle." Her eyes darted heavenward. *Oh, Christ my King, have mercy on his soul and the one who ended his life.* She crossed herself again, quickly this time, and tried to stand.

"As appalled as I was by what Neil Masterson did for a living, to wish him dead is something I never did nor wanted," she added as Lola helped her out of the chair. "I feel dizzy all of a sudden."

"Then don't get up. Rest." Lola gripped her friend by the wrists and lowered her back down. "Do you need any aspirin?"

Rosie checked the wall clock over the mantle and waved her hand. "I'm fine, I don't need anything. Pills can't fix emotions. Besides, Father Welker is due here any minute."

"You don't think he's going to want to go, assuming he's read the paper this morning?" Father Welker, only a few years younger than Rosie, suffered adult onset diabetes as well as high blood pressure and did not need the excitement. Lola was certain Dr. Masterson's murder was going to result in more volatile demonstrations in front of the Norfolk clinic.

But Rosie was eyeing her red scarf, which dangled from an oak hat stand in the foyer, and reminding herself to grab it on the way out. "I have to go, Lola. That place is sorely in need of prayer, now more than ever."

Six

Carrie Masterson left her sons in Richmond, making arrangements with their teachers to take them out of school for an indefinite period of time. Given the circumstances, nobody dared to argue with her. Who knew what was running through the mind of the person who murdered Carrie's husband? Who knew whether or not he or she was contemplating putting two more bullets into the brains of blameless children who, by virtue of relation, were linked to a family planning clinic that offered abortions?

Besides, the last thing Carrie wanted her boys to see was a chalk outline of their father's dead body greeting them at the house. As far as she knew, they still had not heard of the slaying; she and her brother-in-law had managed to shield them from newspapers and news stations while thrusting all of their attentions on the boys' new baby cousin. They were only eleven and nine years old, for goodness sake, she thought. How does one begin to explain what happened?

Neil Junior and Jacob only knew that their father was a doctor and went to work every day to help people feel better. In that respect, Carrie thought, she and Neil were not lying to their children. Neil was a licensed gynecologist, after all. Not every workday involved "butchering babies" with suction hoses and saline, as the more harassing pro-lifers wanted the state and everyone in it to believe.

Neil had been a sympathetic doctor, genuinely caring for the women who sought out his practice in need of affordable medical care. Mammograms, pap smears, pelvic exams, and yes, even pregnancy care for women who held no insurance were handled by her husband. He maintained a roster of regular patients and welcomed walk-ins wanting advice on birth control and good gynecological care. He helped people, damn it! Carrie wanted to shout to anyone who would bother to listen. Why would someone so fervent about protecting life be willing to take one away?

Did not "pro-life" mean all life? What about Neil's life? What about the lives of Neil's children and parents, friends and colleagues?

Carrie rubbed her temples. She probably would not have time to contact everybody before news of his death hit the national wires, as most assassinations of this sort did nowadays. She wished, at the very least, the local media had allowed her some time before broadcasting across the state. Somebody close to Neil was going to learn of his death while enjoying breakfast over CNN because she likely could not contact him or her in time.

She did, however, manage to get a hold of her in-laws and Neil's siblings as soon as the news came to her. She felt like a robot, automatically dialing each phone number, keeping her voice calm and clear with each delivery. She did not know how much longer she could stay in that mode before the cracks started to show.

Mark Skinner, the detective assigned to Neil's homicide, wanted to keep the crime scene - Carrie initially shuddered at the mere thought of her home being referred to as a "crime scene" - secure and make a thorough investigation before allowing the widow to return. She assented; she was not exactly ready to come home, and damned if she was going to taint any evidence needed to catch the killer.

The police confiscated the tapes from the Masterson's answering machine in hopes of finding a recorded threat, but Carrie knew that was to be a wasted effort. Their home address was unlisted and any suspicious letters and messages that slipped by were immediately destroyed before the kids came home from school.

"You never kept track of the people who made threats on your husband's and children's lives? Not even to report them to the police?" Skinner asked her late that morning. They were sitting in the den of the hotel suite Carrie rented indefinitely until she was allowed to return home. Even then, Carrie was not sure if she would be staying there longer. They drank room service coffee and Carrie stared at the bland beige curtains covering the sliding door leading to the balcony.

"We did, for a while," she began. "But it's difficult when your enemies don't leave names on the bricks they hurl through your windows. The police said they really couldn't intervene unless somebody physically entered our home and started beating Neil over the head with a tire iron. Big help they were." If Skinner was annoyed by Carrie's sudden acidity, he did not let it show.

"Anyway, after we moved to our house five years ago, we got an unlisted number, put the kids in a private school and installed a security system that could keep the Navy SEALs at bay," Carrie continued. "Things settled down, until. this ..."

Carrie's face was already streaked red and sore from crying the entire drive from Richmond. Her eyes were rubbed raw with tissues and her nose dripped. She dipped her hand inside her jacket pocket for the wadded ball of Kleenex she had been using since morning and composed herself.

I must be strong, she told herself. Neil needs me to be strong.

"You haven't saved any of your old answering machine tapes, other than what we already have?"

Carrie rolled her eyes. "We didn't think they were of any value! Most of the voices were disguised, and after so many of the same old threats they all sounded alike anyway. Besides, we haven't received any crank calls for at least a few years or so, and don't ask me how the people who did call got our number. We just thought people were trying to scare Neil, not kill him." Her voice broke into pieces with her last few words.

"Mrs. Masterson, I want you to know that I'm very sorry for your loss," Mark sounded sympathetic yet forced to Carrie. He held out a hand to pat her shoulder but slowly retracted it. "I know this is very painful for you, and I imagine the last thing you want to discuss is your husband's dealings with crank calls, but please understand that we want to explore every avenue."

A pause followed to allow her to blow her nose. "We're going to find the person or persons who did this, Mrs. Masterson."

"Carrie, please."

Mark smiled gently. "Okay then, Carrie. We're going to find who's responsible and bring them to justice. Count on that."

Carrie bowed her head, flexing her fingers and tightening the tissue ball in her fist. "Detective Skinner?"

"Mark, please."

"Mark," Carrie began again, her face softening. "I'd like to know, what is your view on abortion?"

The detective appeared surprised by her question and her straight-forwardness. Carrie had been loath to delve into any personal topics upon their first meeting. "Well, to be truthful, I'm not married. I've never given much thought to the issue, but if I had a teenage daughter who got pregnant I certainly wouldn't want her to have one."

"Okay. What if this hypothetical daughter, or even your hypothetical wife, was pregnant and found to be ill?" Carrie asked. "An abortion could save their lives but continuing with the pregnancy and birth might kill them, what would you think then?"

Mark was flustered. "Uh, I really don't see what this has to do with the investigation."

"Then let me just say this," Carrie interrupted. "My husband performed abortions under varying degrees of circumstances. Not every patient was a thirteen-year-old girl or a heartless tramp disposing of an inconvenience the way some people toss a wad of paper in the trash." Anger flushed her cheeks. "There would be nights where my husband would come home upset, nearly devastated after having to console a cancer patient who saw no other choice but to abort her child rather than see it deformed or diseased by her chemotherapy treatments. We're talking about women who *wanted* their babies, Detective!"

"Despite the endless arguments for and against abortion that you have no doubt heard, Detective - Mark - do you believe my husband deserved to die because he was willing to perform them?"

Mark closed his eyes, thought a minute, which lasted years to Carrie, and said, "No. Nobody deserves to die the way your husband did."

"Thank you," she whispered, wondering if that would be the only time somebody would say that to her.

Seven

The murder of Dr. Neil Masterson was the lead story on all the local television news programs the day it happened, starting around noon, with a string of reporters yammering impromptu monologues to their respective cameras before the crowded streets near the clinic. Further televised coverage was made available by way of establishing video shots before a stream of yellow police tape lining the Mastersons' house. A preliminary sweep of the major national cable channels implied that as of Wednesday afternoon the crime had not yet been promoted to nationwide attention.

It would be, thought Roy Jeffries as he mindlessly mashed the channel buttons of his remote control. News programs ate this stuff up, and the local stations had enough sound bites and video clips to appease the tragedy-hungry people of the nation. Pick a channel, any channel, and see tight views of the blood-soaked concrete steps or panoramic shots of warring picketers outside Masterson's clinic. Norfolk was a town torn apart.

"The time has come," he muttered to himself. "Your bastard pals will get the message, Masterson."

Roy was sitting in the living room of his modest two-bedroom house in Newport News. Normally he would be working at his Norfolk antique furniture store, preparing items for delivery and overseeing various restoration projects, but in anticipation of the activity at the clinic he decided to stay home. To discourage suspicion among his staff, he claimed today a paper inventory day; none of his employees argued. His brother Larry, with whom he lived, would be gone until late evening and would be none the wiser as well.

The shades in the house were drawn and the lights were off, and Roy lay stretched across a long brown sofa wearing only a tee shirt and boxer shorts, with a fleece blanket covering his body. He hit the couch after breakfast and seeing Larry off to school.

He rotated between the three local channels. No witnesses had come forward, all of the programs revealed, and no ballistics reports had been made public. Roy smiled. He felt that left him plenty of time to get rid of the gun. That thing would be drifting halfway into the Atlantic Ocean before the cops would even think of checking this way for clues.

The phone rang abruptly. The sharp loud chimes pried Roy from his prone position and he checked the caller ID device attached to the phone. *Unknown name, unknown number* blinked in black digital letters. Probably some telemarketer wanting to hawk a service provided by a pro-choice friendly company. Not a chance in Hell, thought Roy. God only knew how much of his money went to supporting the death mills through the purchase of simple products, and damned if he was going to do it consciously.

He let the phone ring, grateful at least for the reason to finally get off of his rear. A quick shower and hot mug of coffee sounded better with each passing second. There was much to do today anyway.

Eight

"Hey, Pre. C'mere a sec."

Miguel Marquez waved Pre over to the café bar with a strong brown hand. He and a friend were finishing up their lunches when Pre appeared with a tray of empty salt and pepper shakers for refilling.

"This is Jack. He's on the wrestling team with me." Pre and the boy shook hands as Miguel slurped down the last of his root beer. "He hasn't heard the story, you know, about how you got your name."

Pre folded her arms. "It's not much of a story, I don't know why everybody makes such a big deal of it. Why don't you tell it to him?"

"You tell it better, Pre. Besides, would any of us pass up the chance to hear that beautiful voice of yours?" He winked at Pre, who noticed Jack the wrestler was also directing a newly smitten glance at her. Lola had told her some time ago she was certain Miguel was harboring a mild crush on Pre, a notion that amused Pre but did not worry her. In six months Miguel would have his eye on someone closer to his own age. Maybe more than one girl, she warned the boy's mother.

"Okay, but I'll give you the abridged version. I want to get this place cleaned up before we open." She leaned over the bar, conscious that the neck of her sweater did sag down too low to offer a free exhibition. "You ever hear of Steven Prefontaine?"

Jack nodded, and Pre continued. "So did my mother. In fact, she was running track at the University of Georgia around the same time Prefontaine was at Oregon. She held up her own at school, but not enough to make running a career.

"Anyway, Mom had other priorities, namely a fellow teammate who eventually became my father. They married midway through their senior year despite family protests and almost immediately they got pregnant with me."

Pre reached down at the small refrigerator under the bar and grabbed her bottled water. "I was due in the summer of '72, smack dab in the middle of the Munich Olympics. Even though my mom didn't run much while she carried me, she still kept up to date with the college standings and other runners. I guess she was hoping to one day compete again as a professional, I don't know.

"Naturally, she's watching the Olympics when her water breaks." She paused as Miguel stifled a laugh; the story seemed funnier to him every time he heard it. "My dad wants to take her to the hospital, but Mom says no. Pre's event was coming up, and she was his biggest fan. She wasn't about to let a simple thing as childbirth get in the way of watching her favorite runner take gold."

Jack fiddled with his napkin. "So, what, your parents get in this big fight while she's getting ready to have a baby? Over a TV show?"

Pre laughed. "It does sound silly, but you have to remember this was in the days before VCRs and 24-hour cable sports networks that run and rerun events to death. Had she left the house, the race would have gone on without her, along with any chance she had of getting to see it."

"You just said 'had she.' You're not saying ..."

"They stayed," Pre nodded. "The starter pistol fired and Pre took off, just as the contractions got closer and quicker. She ended up giving birth to me on the living room floor as my frantic father watched helplessly. All the while, she was shouting 'Go, Pre!' 'Go, Pre!' like she was more interested in the race than with me."

Miguel elbowed his friend. "Just wait. This is the best part."

Pre cast a stern glance at Miguel for interrupting. "So, my mother's shouting 'Go, Pre!' at the television, and Prefontaine is actually in the lead at the bell lap. As she shouts, my head pokes out from underneath her and my father manages to get a hold of me as I'm being born. I actually crossed the finish line before Prefontaine did. He didn't even medal in the race.

"I'm all red and wrinkled, squirming in a puddle on the floor, and my father looks up at my mom and says, 'Well, her name must be Pre, too. She must of thought you were shouting at her to hurry up."

"So her parents named her Prefontaine! Isn't that a hoot?" Miguel was about to burst. Jack, plagued by visions of childbirth, pushed away the few remaining French fries on his plate and laughed politely.

"Do you run, Pre?" Jack asked, careful to pronounce the name correctly: *pree*.

Pre nodded carefully and swabbed the bar with a damp cloth. "I do, but I'm hardly an Olympian myself. I'm afraid I'm more of a legend in the field of couch-potato lounging."

"And restaurant managing," added Miguel with a touch of pride. "Mom says she's indispensable, like an angel sent from God."

"Let's not get carried away," Pre laughed. "Say, how come you two don't have ashes on? Doesn't your school hold Mass on holy days?"

Jack unconsciously brushed his forehead and smoothed his brown hair away. "Yeah, but the upper grades go in the afternoon, which is cool because we can leave school straight afterwards."

Pre began stacking the dirty utensils and plates before her. A fleck of black ash from the cross on her forehead fluttered down on the pile. "Well, speaking of school, your lunch period is almost over. You better hurry back before Lola gets back from the office supply store and sees you two still warming those stools." She winked at them; even though the school Miguel and Jack attended allowed seniors to lunch off-campus, Lola always preferred her son take a lunch to avoid tardiness.

"Jack, it was nice meeting you. You're welcome back any time for lunch. Usually we're open at this time, but Lola likes to open late on Holy Days. Hope you liked the sandwich."

Jack and Miguel stood up to leave, scooting stools loudly against the hardwood floor and grabbing their packs. "Oh, it was great, Pre. Thanks for having me. I just might bring my girlfriend here Friday for dinner."

"Wonderful. What's her name?"

Jack smiled. "She's the best. Her name is Monica."

Nine

Blue. It was blue.

Oh, God, thought Monica. She fumbled in the trashcan for the empty pregnancy test container. Blue meant what now?

With trembling fingers she extracted a folded paper and read the instructions.

Blue meant pregnant.

"Oh, God. No," she whispered.

Monica was leaning over a porcelain sink, alone in the girls' restroom in the upper school wing. Her only opportunity to test herself came now, during her lunch period. All of her friends were gathered around a stone table in the senior courtyard, laughing about the nuns over peanut butter, gawking at and whispering about the guys at the other tables, and just being teenagers. Monica looked in the mirror and knew those days of carefree life were over. She was already missing them.

"This can't be right," she muttered, wincing at the echo that bounced off the tile walls of the empty three-stall restroom. How could she be pregnant? She and Jack only did it that one time, and to her it did not seem long enough for a sperm to fertilize an egg. Jack had worn a condom, too, and those things were supposed to block sperm and help prevent sexually transmitted diseases. He said it was protected with spermicide to make it more effective. It couldn't possibly have failed.

Could it?

Slowly she sank to the floor and crouched into the far corner, still holding the box. It had to be wrong, Monica decided. The instructions called for use of the first morning's urine, and she had already used the toilet before coming to school. Maybe there was a chance she had tainted the test, or perhaps the test was faulty.

Monica put a hand to her stomach; she still felt no qualms of morning sickness, but her period had yet to make an appearance.

She checked her watch. Ten minutes had passed since she entered the restroom to use the pregnancy test; surely one of her friends would come looking for her. She rose quickly and ran cold water through the faucet, splashing it on her face and drying with a paper towel.

Monica would not see Jack until Ash Wednesday Mass in less than two hours. She would have to tell him then. If the test was correct, Monica knew she could not postpone the news any further.

The door to the restroom squeaked open as Monica screeched, crunching the box in her hands and pitching it into the trashcan. The test stick was still lying in the sink. She managed to grab it and shove it into her sweater pocket before her friend Jennifer approached.

"There you are, Nic!" she chided, apparently not noticing Monica's still damp face. "We all thought you fell in."

Monica straightened her school jumper, reaching underneath it to pull the tails of her blouse straight. "Yeah, sorry. I wasn't feeling too good. I think I flunked that history test, and it's getting to me."

Jennifer shrugged. "Aw, big deal. One F is nothing to get sick over. Maybe it was something you ate."

Or something I did, Monica wanted to add. Instead she responded with, "Yeah, maybe. I guess I have other things to worry about besides a dumb history test."

"Like the dumb math test we have after lunch," laughed Jennifer. "Let's go, your peanut butter sandwich is going stale."

Monica followed Jennifer out into the courtyard, all the while praying silently to God that her one time did not result in one, big mistake.

Ten

"Are you sure you want to lug that around with you today?" Father Welker asked Rosie, pointing to the large canvas tote resting on her lap. Inside the bag was her daily work - several yards of nylon cord, hundreds of multi-colored bugle beads, and a long grooved metal tool she used to tie knots in the cord rosaries she made. Also included was a small box for storing the finished products, rosaries free for the taking to anyone who so desired.

Much of the Rosary Lady's day keeping a protestant vigil outside the women's clinic was spent in meditative prayer, with each bead strung in time to a prayer for the clinic's staff, patients, and the lives-to-be, some of whom ceased to exist after their mothers left. She hoped today would be no different, that the death of Neil Masterson did not cause too much chaos.

"Well, if it looks too iffy out there, I'll leave the bag in the car. Though I don't much like being without a rosary, or not being able to make them. I like to keep my hands busy."

"Somehow I can't believe you could ever be without a rosary, Barbara," Father Welker's eyes crinkled as he smiled. He passed a dented Mustang going into the Hampton Roads Bridge Tunnel toward Norfolk, then shifted his own Escort into overdrive and sped into the darkness. Bland yellow lights blurred past at sixty miles an hour.

"You must have at least seven in your purse," the middle-aged priest added. "One for each day of the week."

"Ha, ha," the old woman, for lack of a wittier retort, answered. She unzipped her purse with a gloved hand; she was prepared this time for the biting wind. A gray wool hat covered most of her head while her scarf dangled from her shoulders; the priest arrived at her house not long after Lola Marquez bade a reluctant farewell, leaving Rosie with no time to change clothes. If only she had begged for a few seconds more to put on some warmer socks - her feet felt as if they had been dipped in ice.

Father Welker's car was freezing and offered little comfort. Probably colder in here than it is outside, she thought. She reached for the heat dial on the dashboard next to the radio.

"Don't bother," Father Welker said as he signaled to shift to the right lane. "The heater finally conked out yesterday, and it probably won't work again until summertime, when the AC will be on the fritz. Besides, we're almost to Ghent. Just think of enduring the cold as part of your Lenten sacrifice to God." The miniature automobile pulled off on the Granby Street exit.

"Oh, please," Rosie huffed. "I sacrificed plenty during that Christmas ice storm. Would the good Lord deny me one breath of warm air from this blasted machine?" She slapped the panel for effect and accidentally turned on the radio, sending an abrupt jazz saxophone solo ringing throughout the enclosed space.

Father shut off the radio. "Are you that cold, Barbara?" he added apologetically. "Because I have an extra coat in the back."

Rosie batted her eyelashes at him. "No, thank you. I inherited my father's hardy constitution. I'll survive. I've seen worse winters than this, and if it gets too much for me I'll slip into the coffee shop and have Chuck fix me something hot."

As the car angled in a right turn toward 21st Street and the clinic, Father Welker and Rosie were met with a thick horde of traffic. Slowing cars funneled into an even thicker crowd of warmly dressed people, all huddled into two opposing camps and shouting incoherently at each other from the sidewalk across the street from the clinic, where one nurse was tentatively making her way up the steps to the entrance.

Father Welker managed to ease the car down the street, parting the people around him. Rosie could feel the angry heat rising from them in short bursts of visible breath.

"Murderer!" cried one protestor from the pack in a deep, grating voice; he held aloft a homemade sign depicting a drawing of a viable fetus sucking its thumb atop the inscription *Before I created you in the womb I knew you*. Rosie blinked, trying to recall where in the Bible she had read that quote.

"Leave her alone," insisted a female voice on the other end of the spectrum amid supportive mutterings. The cry came from a woman in her thirties wearing earmuffs and waving a National Organization for Women placard. "She has the right to work where she pleases, just as any of us have the right to do what we believe is best for our bodies!"

"What about the body growing inside a pregnant woman?" shot back a tall, short-haired woman in among the pro-life group. "What about the rights of that growing child?"

"What child ever asked to be born?"

"What child ever asked to be sucked out of his or her mother's womb with a vacuum cleaner?"

"It!" screeched one red-faced pro-choice sign waver. "It's not a person, it's a lump of tissue. It's not a person until it's born."

"Yeah, right. A lump of tissue with a beating heart and the ability to feel pain," murmured Father Welker to himself from inside the car. Rosie shot a sideways glance at him and noticed his face flushing with frustration. For three years the pair had been coming to pray amid the unsettled crowds, which varied in number over time, for God's mercy and forgiveness. Never before had Rosie seen the priest so agitated.

They prayed for forgiveness for the anger expressed on both sides of the abortion rights issue, forgiveness for the doctors and nurses performing the procedures, forgiveness for the mothers allowing this to happen. Prayers also went out to those young expectant mothers wringing their hands, unsure of how to cope with their situations, that God might encourage them in some way to choose an alternative solution.

Rosie set aside many Divine Mercy chaplets also for those, like the unnamed murderer of Neil Masterson, who believed violence was the only method of stopping violence against the unborn. She knew that was not the proper way to react, as violence makes only a tense situation worse.

As Father Welker steered the car down the street slowly in search of a parking space, Rosie prayed a silent Gloria for Neil Masterson's soul and for the apprehension of his killer.

Two-person camera crews darted in and out of the crowd - the largest both the priest and old woman had seen in the past three years - trailing behind cords attached to video cameras and microphones to their respective mobile television vans. Several faces battled for airtime among the skittish news reporters, all garbling their own opinions of the clinic, Neil Masterson, and abortion in general to unseen audiences.

Due to the increase of cars and human traffic along the narrow avenue which housed the clinic as well as some of the adjoining shops and restaurants in the arty Ghent district of Norfolk, Father Welker was forced to find a space nearly three blocks further south. Within the half-hour they were barreling straight into the hornets' nest, which to Rosie did not appear to have calmed any. She decided, however, to bring along her bag. Perhaps in time some of the curious fringe would lose interest and fade away.

They brushed past a gentleman with shoulder-length brown hair in a turtleneck sweater and jeans; slightly curled locks fell over his eyes as he scribbled hastily in a slim notepad. He stood silently against the stucco wall of an antique shop, drinking in the chaos as if watching it on a movie screen. He caught Rosie's eyes and nodded pleasantly to her, and received a nod in return.

Such a contrast from the cacophony around us, she thought, trying to keep up with the brisk pace of her priest companion, who was halted abruptly by a flash of metal. A brunette woman wearing a tight melon business suit with wide lapels and a white oxford shirt invaded from another angle. She shivered in a blast of wind, and Rosie noticed the woman's fingers, clutching a microphone trailing a long black cord, were turning blue.

"Father! A moment please for Channel 3 News in Richmond?" The reporter's tone was loud and harried over the din of people; she looked as if she had yet to meet any cooperative faces in the crowd. Whether she chose to query the priest for his obvious appearance or assumed expertise in public speaking Father Welker could not tell, but he knew a few good, publicized words for the sanctification of human life could not hurt the cause of the pro-life movement.

"I would be happy to speak on behalf of those who hold all life dear, not just those of the unborn," he told the now relieved reporter. To Rosie, standing just behind him, he said, "I won't be long. I don't really think we should stick around afterward."

"Go right ahead, Father. I'm going to head for my usual spot by the coffee shop." Rosie backed away graciously.

"So, I take this to mean you disapprove of the murder of Dr. Masterson as action against the pro-choice movement, Father?" The reporter stuck the microphone under the priest's chin.

"Of course!" Father Welker replied, horrified to think anyone would believe he could ever endorse the murder of another human being. "The Bible says, 'Thou shalt not kill.' It's stated in the Old Testament and reiterated by Jesus Christ. I've always believed this commandment to apply to anyone, otherwise God would have told us, 'Thou shalt not kill with the exception of ...and insert your preferences here.'" The priest's voice was polite as the reporter eyed him. He wondered if any of his on-camera statements would be edited, mangled, and used out of context during the interview. Some media outlets had been known to put a negative spin on all things Catholic for the sake of ratings.

Rosie leaned against the large picture window of The Norfolk Coffee Company, watching Father Welker. He cut an impressive appearance standing six-three in his clerical clothes and long black trench coat, with a set of black rosary beads dangling from his wrist, as he led the reporter and cameraman to a remote corner of the fracas to continue the interview. The crowd, too preoccupied with tearing each other down and forcing their political placards in view of passersby, neither noticed nor accommodated them.

Rosie stared helplessly at the melee; if she spoke up to calm the crowd, who would hear her? The few policemen assigned to curtail the crowd and prevent the protest from becoming an out and out riot were having a difficult time with their jobs, how could an old lady keep the peace?

Through prayer, she decided.

She spotted the coffee shop manager through the store window; and he waved and made his way outside. "I've had to delay in setting up the patio tables," he said before she could inquire of their absence. "I didn't know how ugly it was going to get out here, and I didn't want anyone seeing them as potential weaponry, know what I mean?"

"Oh, that's okay, Chuck. Mind if I just park here for now?" She jerked her neck toward the low stone sill of the picture window. "I don't think we'll be here much longer anyway. Father Welker doesn't seem too comfortable with my being here." She then pulled out a dollar and two quarters from her coat pocket and asked Chuck for a short vanilla coffee.

"Sure, but there's no need to lean against the shop. Hang on a sec." Chuck darted back inside for a wooden chair and sat Rosie down near the door. "I'll get that coffee for you," he added.

Rosie thanked him profusely and, after he slipped back inside, made the Sign of the Cross. Only a few eyes acknowledged her actions.

"Dearest God, my Father, look at your children. We are behaving so abominably today," she prayed quietly, her head bowed and eyes closed. "Certainly there is nobody here on the street who stands without sin, myself included, but on their behalf, I beg for Your forgiveness and undying Mercy."

"All you saints in Heaven, and dearest Mary, too," she added, "we could certainly benefit from your prayers to God today. Jesus, grant us a calm after this storm. Grant that no further injuries or attacks may arise from this demonstration. Protect the lives, unborn and adult, inside the clinic, and have Mercy on the soul of Your child, Neil Masterson."

She thought a moment, then concluded her prayer, "I pray also for the Masterson family, Carrie and those dear boys, that they may be given the courage and strength to cope with this tragedy. Comfort them, my Lord, and let them know You are not far. Nobody deserves to lose a loved one this way. Let Thy Will be done."

She set her bag beside her and took out the small box of completed rosaries, laying it at her feet just as Chuck returned with her coffee. They numbered more than twenty today, as she spent most of yesterday in prayer and therefore did not make many more before she went to bed. Rosie frowned. She liked to keep at least fifty in the box; they often went fast during the week, she hoped, to be used for prayer rather than for the sake of snatching a freebie, regardless of its nature.

Father's impromptu interview appeared to grow in strength and length as the reporter pressed questions into his face, so Rosie quickly reached for her rosary tool and a coil of precut cord. She wondered if she would have time to make at least one decade before Father became exhausted with constant interrogations. She clasped her hands together and looked to Heaven.

"My Jesus, my Lord and Savior," she prayed to herself. "I begin this Rosary today for the safety of everyone here. Through the intercession of Your beloved mother, I pray for Your Grace. I love You."

Rosie pinched about two inches of the cord from one end, marked the spot with her fingernail, and wrapped the longer end around the slim, grooved tool four times. She slipped the long end of the cord through the groove under the loops, then slid the loops from the tool and pulled both cord ends in opposite directions, forming the first knot. From here Rosie would string ten beads - the first of five decades separated by four single beads used for the Our Father prayer.

Just as she was securing the first set of ten, Rosie turned her head cautiously, detecting the presence of a body standing over her. Father Welker had finally managed to break free from Channel 3 News. Good, she thought. The crowd likely did little for his health. "I'll just finish this knot and we can go if you like, Father," she said, her eyes still on her hands.

No answer.

Rosie strung the Our Father bead and began another knot before lifting her gaze and meeting that of the long-haired man she had seen earlier.

He smiled down at her. "Cold enough for you?"

She looked over at the crowd, spotting Father Welker easing away from the camera crew to end the interview, only to come face to-face with a scowling pro-choice demonstrator. A heated discussion soon ensued.

"Oh, I'm just fine," Rosie answered, tapping the rosary box with her foot. A brisk gush of wind whipped between her and the man, nearly sending a few beads on her lap airborne. She eyed the small gold cross pendant hanging from his neck. "Would you like a rosary?" she asked. "They're all made with sturdy cord, and should last a long time."

"Well, I'm not Catholic-" the man began hesitantly.

"There's no prerequisite for owning a rosary, it's simply a string of beads attached to a crucifix." She selected a string composed of white decades and light blue. "When it is used in prayer, however, it can be a powerful weapon."

She curled the rosary and held it up to him. "Why don't you take this one? I patterned it to match Mother Teresa's habit."

The man took the rosary and folded it into his shirt pocket with his notepad. Rosie offered him instructions and dug deeper into the bag for a pamphlet.

"I think I can figure it out, thanks. How much do I owe you?"

"I don't charge for cord rosaries. Enjoy it with my compliments."

From the corner of her eyes she saw the priest approaching, a weary look highlighting the wrinkles on his face. Hastily she tossed everything into her bag and stood. The longhaired man pulled a crumpled bill from his jeans pocket and tossed it into Rosie's bag, deaf to her protests.

"That's for more supplies. It's nice to meet someone who is willing to devote her time and energy to promoting pro-life in a pacifist way."

"Thank you very much, Mister, uh-"

"Oh, I'm sorry," the man grinned, holding out his hand. "Larry Jeffries."

Eleven

Monica picked at her dinner, taking an occasional bite between her parents' persistent queries about her school day. The ashen cross on her forehead itched and she resisted an urge to wipe it off. Only the fear of smudging the cuff of her blouse with a black stain prevented her from doing so. Chris and Laura preferred everyone leave the ash markings intact until bedtime, anyway, a notion that sometimes baffled Monica. It was a school night, and they rarely left the house then. Who was going to see them?

All around Monica conversation swirled lively and noisily, with the smaller children raising their voices to overlap CJ and their parents. Monica tuned out CJ's explanation of why he wanted to stay at home and attend William and Mary rather than his father's first choice of Franciscan University in Ohio. Laura's idle questioning of Therese's pending Confirmation retreat and little Joshua's banging his fork against his plate buzzed in her other ear.

Monica speared a green pea on her plate and munched on it quietly. She hated peas.

"Josh, knock it off. You're making a mess!" Chris's voice was firm and effective, as Joshua quickly ceased stirring his peas into his mashed potatoes and set down his fork. "You had your turn to speak, now give your brother a chance to talk about his day."

Joshua pouted and shoveled an extra-large forkful of potatoes into his small mouth. Laura cast a warning glance in case the child was contemplating a gesture unbecoming to dinnertime, such as pushing the potatoes through an open smile with his tongue. But the little boy, already familiar with the threat of punishment, quietly chewed the mushy white globule.

Meanwhile Chris leaned over to his eldest and asked him why, after almost two years of assuring everyone he wanted to attend a Catholic college, he was changing his mind. "You'd receive a thorough Catholic education at Franciscan, nothing watered down, that was what you wanted," Chris was saying, "and your chances for advancing to graduate school with an assistantship would be excellent! What about your plans to go to law school, or to pursue social work? Besides, I would think after eighteen years in a crowded house you would be chomping at the bit to get out of here."

"Chris, please. Your voice," Laura chided. She was not exactly looking forward to the day her firstborn fled the nest.

CJ looked up from his fish dinner and smirked, "Can't wait to get rid of me, huh? You already have blueprints for the game room drawn?"

"No, I want your room!" Therese bounced in her seat. "I'm tired of sharing with *Moan*-nica." She cackled loudly, expecting either a playful or annoyed slap on the shoulder from her older sister. She received neither.

"Monica?" she prodded.

Monica only shrugged and muttered, "Whatever." Her focus was on her dinner plate as she pushed loose breadcrumbs into a mashed potato mountain. Her parents exchanged concerned glances.

"Nic, sweetie, are you okay?" her mother asked. "Are you not feeling well, or did something happen at school that we should know about?"

"You didn't flunk that history test today, did you?" Chris sipped his glass of tepid water.

Monica did not answer her father; her eyes were on Laura. Something happened, all right, she thought, but not at school. Try in the back of Jack's car nearly a month ago. "I'm just not feeling well, Mom," she finally answered, in all truth feeling queasy. "Mind if I go upstairs and lie down?"

Nobody objected. Monica let her fork fall to the plate with a loud *clunk* as she excused herself and made her exit, leaving Judith and Joshua to fight over the fish sticks she left behind and Therese to moan about how she had yet to choose an alternate sponsor for her Confirmation.

Monica made sure her door was closed and her face buried in her pillow before letting the day's worth of restrained tears burst as if coming from a dam. All throughout classes after lunch and afternoon Mass she had to blink back tears and sniffled hard, thinking the force would dry her tear ducts, but that could not stop her lip from quivering or for the occasional lone tear to escape in a thin stream down her cheek. To anyone who did ask about her melancholy countenance, she attributed the low mood to her rocky relationship with Jack.

Jack.

Monica slowly turned onto her side. She and Jack shared only one class - Spanish Level Two - which had been cancelled due to the Ash Wednesday service for the upper grades, and because school policy had boys and girls sitting in separate groups in the school hall-cum-chapel, she was unable to speak to him. In fact, for a couple largely regarded by friends and others as "going together," Jack and Monica rarely spoke and kidded around the way they did since their first and only coupling.

Since then, everything else seemed to take precedence. Monica worked on the school yearbook staff and with Spanish Club, while Jack was heavily involved with the wrestling team and his harried college search. A statewide champion, he had been spending more of his free time in conference with college reps courting him to their respective schools with scholarship promises. Then there was Therese's upcoming Confirmation, and Chris and Laura expected nothing less than full family participation in helping her prepare for it.

Soon would come prom, graduation, and a host of pageants, sporting events, birthdays, parties, and exams, and Monica wondered if she would be brave enough to tell anyone, much less Jack, before the baby started preschool!

Abruptly she lifted her head. Black ash was smudged on her pink pillowcase. "Damn it!" she cursed, and reached for a tissue on the nightstand to clean her forehead. What ash was on the pillow she blotted away.

The door of her room opened, startling Monica so that she slipped off the bed. A more subdued Therese poked her head inside. "You feeling better?"

Monica blew her nose. "Yeah," she lied. "I think it's just cramps. You'll know how it feels when you get your period."

Monica hugged the ashen pillow to her closely and rolled over to face the wall.

"Oh, okay. Well, can I listen to some music?"

"I guess. Just use the headphones, please?"

Therese ventured to her side of the room, selected a DC Talk compact disc from the bookshelf, slid it into the stereo and plugged in the bulky headset before cranking the volume to seven.

She caught a glance of herself in the dresser mirror. "Man, I look like Princess Leia," she said to herself. She stretched out the long coiled cord plugged into the stereo and flopped onto her own bed, the muffled sound of Christian rap music seeping into the air. Monica lifted her upper body, watching as her younger sister gestured in air guitar motions and mouthed the lyrics to the music.

Aside from Jennifer and Becky at school, Therese was her closet friend. They shared everything, not just by virtue of being sisters, but because they were close enough to trust each other with their innermost secrets and feelings. What would she think if she knew, Monica thought, if I told her I had sex with Jack and was pregnant? What would she think of me? Would she twist away from me in disgust, call me a slut? Never speak to me again?

Would she just cry, miserable with the knowledge that I let her down, Monica wondered, on the verge of fresh tears. She and Therese were good girls, home schooled until the eighth grade, raised lovingly on Christian values in a stable household that prayed together, stayed together, and loved together. Chris and Laura Merwin did not raise their children to stray from the high morals instilled in them, sex outside of marriage being very high on the list. Yet she did it anyway. Sixteen years...*poof.*

Therese slipped the headset off her ears, squeezing the speakers together to further muffle the sound.

"Hey, Nic?"

"Yeah?"

"Mom just got a call from Aunt Maggie, and she's certain that she won't be able to come up for Easter."

Laura's sister Maggie was first choice to be Therese's Confirmation sponsor. She already was her godmother.

"So who are you gonna get?"

"I was hoping you would do it."

Monica swung her legs around to the edge of the bed.

"You wouldn't have to do much," Therese rejoined. "The instruction's almost done, and I do the retreat with my class. All you have to do is show up."

Monica rolled her eyes. "Well, duh! Like I wasn't already planning to go. I mean, I gave up a date with the Backstreet Boys for this," she said just before a stuffed animal from her sister's side of the room came flying toward her face.

Therese giggled. "Mom suggested I ask you to proxy for Aunt Maggie, but I'd rather you just do it yourself, you know, if you want."

Monica looked at her sister with glassy, smiling eyes. "Are you kidding? I'd love to."

Twelve

Too tired from answering endless questions from police detectives and reporters, Carrie Masterson opted to dine in the clammy discomfort of her hotel room. With her legs stretched across one of the double beds in front of the active television, she unwrapped a fast-food cheeseburger that looked as if it had been trampled by a cattle stampede seeking revenge for their brethren's slaughter. Not her usual fare, but she was too exhausted and grief-stricken to be conscious of her fat intake.

She munched on the sandwich thoughtfully, thinking that her sons would be jealous to know that she was eating one of their favorite foods while she made her sister and brother-in-law promise to feed them healthful meals. No snacks or sweets. She was the bad cop when it came to food, whereas Neil was the Great Compromiser.

She laughed to herself, remembering all the nights when Neil would come home from work with candy bars hidden in his inside coat pockets. He'd hang his coat in the closet, and the boys knew exactly where to go.

She crammed three salty, limp French fries in her mouth, trying not to cry. It hurt her head to cry, and she had taken the last of the aspirin that afternoon. Oh, Neil, she thought, what am I going to do? How am I going to tell our children what happened to you?

Booming bass trumpets signaled the beginning of the evening news, and Carrie tapped the volume button of her remote to hear the top story, indicated by an inset box containing her husband's picture. Neil's stern visage floated above the right shoulder of an anchorwoman with cropped red hair and lips Carrie was certain were enhanced with collagen. Still no word on suspects, no mention of Carrie (thank goodness, she thought, for she already endured a few curious stares while in town today thanks to her constant sniffling and red eyes) or the rest of the family. This station was more keen to rehash a rousing demonstration at the Hampton Roads Clinic.

Carrie watched brief clips of bundled protestors waving signs and mouthing slogans as a soothing voice-over explained the activity, in particular of how people came from as far north as Washington, DC to either decry or praise the right to abort. Reactions to Neil's death were equally mixed.

The camera cut to a tall, gray-haired priest with a hardened jaw. The close-up shot magnified the tired look of his face and the wrinkles around his eyes. "While it is the belief of the Church and myself that abortion is a moral evil, it is certainly a greater evil to put to an end a man's life solely on such a basis." The priest wrinkled his forehead; the dark cross on his forehead appeared to glow. "The murder of Dr. Masterson was a needless, senseless tragedy and clear proof that violence does not solve any problems."

"Amen," said Carrie as the point of view switched angles to a passive group of pro-life demonstrators, many with bowed heads, moving their lips silently to Catholic meditations.

A flash of silver caught Carrie's eyes. She dropped her cheeseburger and scooted to the edge of the bed, leaving a trail of fries behind her, to get a better look at the old woman to the right of the screen, sitting in a simple chair by a storefront window.

"Aunt Barbara?" she whispered.

Thirteen

Pre was never one to condition herself for an early morning jog, particularly in February when the winter chills tended to use their last reserves of energy before giving way to milder spring temperatures. But this morning she was feeling extra punchy, and despite her loath to exercise she felt as if she could run to Richmond and back and not have to stop for air. Because time prevented her from taking on a pace of marathon proportions, she opted instead for Colonial Williamsburg.

She parked her ancient, rusting Toyota in the narrow lot behind Café Lisieux and emerged wearing a bulky green William and Mary sweat shirt with matching shorts over white Lycra tights. Her long, straight hair was secured in a ponytail flowing over a terrycloth green headband which covered her ears. It was eight o'clock and the morning sun was rising in full force. Lola would be along soon to attend morning Mass and visit the bank before opening the eatery. Pre had plenty of time to run and return home for a shower and change.

"Thank You, Lord, for the weather. Please grant us many more days like this," she prayed silently, breathing deep the crisp, cool air as she walked to the end of block. Swinging branches above her speckled the sunlight into many tiny shadows on the ground. Pre watched a pair of squirrels scamper around on a thick tree trunk in the yard of a neighboring bed and breakfast. For a short while she almost forgot why she was there.

Her brisk walk to the corner of downtown escalated into a slow jog as she passed the chained posts blocking Duke of Gloucester Street from vehicular traffic. She quick-stepped past closed gift shops, the Williamsburg Theater, home to showings of classic and contemporary films as well as the seasonal vaudeville program, and a sidewalk full of gourmet restaurants and sweet shops. At the end of the block she crossed the street into the 18th century, quietly huffing along the preserved homes of the town's first residents which had over the past 300 years slowly morphed into idle curiosities for summer tourists.

She would pass a person on occasion dressed in period garb - not an uncommon sight as they were mainly employees of Colonial Williamsburg who operated the walking tours and colonial souvenir shops during the day. As spring and summer would progress, more people would converge on the dirt roads to participate in mock encampments and marches to the delight of visiting shutterbugs. Pre nodded to them as she ran, recalling fondly her own days as local color so many years before. It seemed like forever.

She arrived at The College of William and Mary at eighteen, an impressionable skinny girl with a duffel bag full of Duran Duran cassettes and empty lined journals, all of which she hoped to fill with poetry by the time she had degree in English literature. She took one look at the dogwoods nestled against the brick buildings on campus, strolling coeds lugging books and knapsacks to class, and Pre knew she made the right choice in schools.

Her parents, though pleased that Pre was able to obtain some scholarship money to attend the school, had expressed disappointment over her choice. There were a few universities in the Jacksonville, Florida area where they lived at the time, so surely Pre was not purposely taking courses in Virginia just to get away from them, they surmised. Pre could only laugh; nobody was closer to her parents than she, Pre assured them, but she believed she would have a better chance finding ground as a writer in a new environment.

While Jacksonville had its secluded, shady spots dispersed around the twisting interstates and tall glass downtown buildings, Williamsburg was quiet, quaint and compact. To drive from one end of Jacksonville to the other just to see a movie could take almost two hours depending on traffic for Pre, whereas two hours driving south from one point in Williamsburg could land one nearly in North Carolina.

Unlike what her family had predicted, homesickness never tormented Pre. The Hampton Roads area of Virginia bore so many similarities to North Florida that she often had trouble discerning Norfolk from the Mayport area whenever she drove across the James River Bridge.

Her studies progressed swiftly, with Pre spending every minute of her spare time either in the library or reading in some comfortable spot on campus, usually under a tree if the weather was warm, with a spiral notebook on her lap for jotting down notes and spontaneous bursts of inspiration. Words, images, thoughts and feelings, anything she could use to mold a verse and polish up her poetry went into the notebook.

She wrote about God often, which surprised her, as neither of her parents showed any preference toward religion in general. Out of curiosity she began attending services at a different house of worship every week. At first she felt silly, comparing her spiritual quest to shopping for a new car, but her interest in God was strengthening and becoming more evident in her writing, and she yearned to know Him better.

She enjoyed meeting the friendly faces of the nearby Baptist and Methodist churches, many of whom shared classes and club interests with her, but for some reason their worship services did not appeal to her. One sermon through which she sat, delivered by a guest minister whose stance and gait were as rigid as his beliefs, came off as dry and almost cold. The minister seemed so certain that so many people were going to Hell regardless of how pious and repentant they became; Pre asked herself how anyone could believe in a God that took pleasure in casting people into "the lake of fire," as reiterated by many ministers in passing weeks.

From what she had discerned from her sporadic readings of the New Testament, Jesus's words were being interpreted to whittle all men down to just their little community. Was that really God's Will?

She enjoyed attending the services held at Bruton Parish Episcopal Church, the oldest church in Williamsburg, and the local Lutheran church. She liked the liturgical structure and warmth of the congregations and the haunting sincerity of pipe organs bellowing praise to God. As she attended these churches more and more she brushed up on their histories. From the times of the first churches in America back to the reformations of Martin Luther and

King Henry VIII of England, Pre read voraciously, pinpointing their reasons for splitting with the Catholic Church in Rome, which apparently had always been around, since Christ was alive on Earth.

Pre turned left as she jogged past Bruton, marveling at its noble structure, heading toward the old governor's mansion. From there she would come up the other side of the promenade and finish her whirlwind tour of the old town.

She remembered her first visit to the local Byzantine Catholic Church, an odd choice for her considering its distance from campus. Her studies of early Christianity, however, had taken her to books about the great East/West schism that created the Orthodox faith, and eventually on to information about the few churches which returned to unite with Rome while maintaining Orthodox-style liturgical traditions. Pre found the service to be the most elegant and melodic of those she had attended, with the cantor leading the small parish in almost operatic prayer. She marveled at the ornate iconography decorating the church, depicting Christ the King seated in Heaven and other scenes in His life. There was the Crucifixion, the Resurrection, where the picture also presented Christ helping Adam and Eve from their graves, and another icon depicting something the Orthodox called the Dormition, the "bodily assumption" of the Virgin Mary.

As far as Pre could tell, only the Catholic and Orthodox faiths acknowledged Mary in a highly revered role, not just as the woman who gave birth to Jesus and then disappeared into a throng of Galilean disciples. Both faiths under the umbrella of Christianity recognized in Mary many qualities that were essential of any Christian - her piety, loyalty to God, and unconditional love. Pre liked the notion of the Holy Family: Jesus, Mary and Joseph; she admired how the Catholic Church celebrated them all year, not just at Christmas like other denominations.

Pre began attending Mass at St. Vincent's during her senior year, falling in love with its mysticism and liturgy. In between classes she studied the Bible and catechism and read up on the lives of the saints, devouring the writings of Thomas Aquinas, Teresa of Avila, and John of the Cross. By the fall she began preparing for conversion through RCIA, meeting a kindred soul in her search for

Truth, her catechist Ephraim Marquez, whose wife Lola became her sponsor. In April, before earning her bachelor's degree, Pre received the Sacraments, much to the minor murmuring of her family, who did not think the occasion merited enough importance to attend.

She wheezed past the rest of the stretch down Duke of Gloucester Street and skidded to a halt, walking out the cramps around the dirt cul-de-sac near Josiah Chowning Tavern. She was surprised to see how far she had come in that moment, both spiritually and physically, yet her heart pounded and she gasped for air.

"Oh, Lord, stay with me on the return loop," she prayed silently. "Please give me that extra push."

She kicked her heels into the gravel roads and began a faster pace, thinking that the sooner she reached the drugstore at the other end of the stretch, the sooner she could stop. The soreness that festered in her calves had spread around to her shins and up her thighs. Pre reveled in the burning pain, imagining millions of fat molecules melting into muscle, but she knew it would take more than a lousy mile around Colonial Williamsburg to see those kinds of results.

Her mind chugged along too to the beat of her steps. *Go, Pre. Go, Pre.*

She passed another woman dressed in period clothes, this one pushing a modern baby stroller. Pre laughed to herself; such anachronisms were common around town, though some town board members frowned upon the "cheating," as they wanted to present the most accurate portrayals of colonial life they could to visitors. Pre remembered one protest during her term as a colonial maiden, when a colleague declared that if the women of the Revolution Era knew about disposable diapers there would be have been no question that they would have used them. Two more ladies piped in their five cents about cloth diapers, and within minutes the entire group of colonial matrons launched into a debate about child care in front of the town ticket office as a high school class watched in amusement.

She turned back to catch a glimpse of the inside of the stroller as she passed, her heart melting upon seeing a bundled baby sleeping in the deep pocket, his lips puckered with spittle and his tiny fingers clutched in fists. Not even the rumbling of the stroller's thin rubber wheels over the road's bulky cobblestones could rattle the child awake. He was gone.

Pre re-directed her view in front of her, a large lump swelling at the base of her throat. Why do you keep doing that to yourself, she asked herself, because wishing and praying for a baby isn't going to make ovaries grow back, no matter how many rosaries and chaplets you pray. God may be all-powerful, but Pre knew He probably respected the human physiology He created so much that He was not going to just snap His fingers and present her with a working reproductive system just so she could satisfy her aching desire for a family.

Though it angered and depressed her at times, Pre submitted to God's Will for her, though she could not understand why it had to be she who was to go through life unable to bear children. It seemed every other day she opened up a newspaper or turned on the news to see a story or commentary decrying the rise of teen pregnancy in the United States. Children half Pre's age were taking on sexual responsibilities without caution to the consequences, and were spending their nights at home with swollen wombs while their friends went to movies and dances and took advantage of unencumbered youth. To hear Rosie drone on sadly about more of the same type of girls warily entering the clinic to get their youth back was too much for Pre to hear as well.

How, she asked God over the seven years since her emergency hysterectomy, could it be allowed that legions of women who neither wanted nor could afford to have children became pregnant as easily as opening a bottle of milk. Meanwhile, women with the resources and abundance of love needed to raise a child had so much trouble conceiving, if they could at all. It just was not fair, she thought. Then again, Pre knew she had no right to make such observations because she could not prove them for certain.

She felt a second windfall of energy, and her legs kicked and stomped the dust underneath her. Pre wondered if it was her own frustration that fueled her. If that were true, she thought, it might be best to quit now before running herself into a seizure.

She walked from the cordoned-off downtown area the rest of the way back to the café as a warm-down exercise. Pre could already see a large white truck disappearing into the lot behind the strip mall. Louis had arrived with the weekly delivery of supplies. She wondered if anyone had come to meet him, so Pre quickened her gait, much to the dismay of her sore muscles.

"I've got to get out and do this more," she muttered to herself.

As she rounded the building she saw Bill, the only other full-time employee at Café Lisieux, waving in the back of the truck toward the open back door. Lola, still sporting a bandaged foot, supervised from the threshold with a pen and clipboard.

"Goodness, you look like Mary Decker Slaney just come from two consecutive marathons!" remarked Lola as Pre wheezed up to the cold steel of the dirty white truck and pressed her face against it. "You need some water, Pre?"

Pre sucked in a big gulp of air. "Sure, no need for a glass, though. I'll just take it straight from the hose. Start with my head."

Lola chuckled. "In this cold? It'll freeze right on you." She moved out of the way as Bill and Louis carried inside several cylindrical cola syrup containers for the carbonated drink machine. Lola put an arm around Pre's damp shoulder, careful not to get too sticky. "Have a good run?"

Pre smiled, still breathing rather wildly. "Quite. A very emotional experience, like I ran through my entire life."

Lola did not know what to make of that.

Fourteen

"Yo, bro."

Larry Jeffries held a sealed envelope to the light above the kitchen table and squinted at it.

"Yo yourself." Roy flipped an almost fried egg over in a buttered skillet.

"You know what Dorothy Parker once said were the two most beautiful words in the English language?"

"I dunno. Free beer?"

"Uh-uh. Check enclosed," Larry said matter-of-factly as he slid his forefinger under the loosened flap of the letter sent to him by *The Norfolk Times* newspaper. "And this, my ever understanding landlord, is today's contribution to the Larry Jeffries Rent Fund."

Roy turned from the stove and examined the paycheck. He whistled. "Look at all those zeros," he remarked sarcastically. "What was this for?"

Larry shrugged. "Some book reviews, plus a guest commentary for the religion page."

"That piece you did on those local schools trying to start Bible clubs?" Ray was practically his younger brother's editor; he read every word the master's student wrote and often offered constructive criticism and praise. Though he had very little writing experience short of what he picked up in business school, Roy read voraciously, and Larry figured him at best a good guinea pig for his work.

Larry nodded. "If I play my cards right, I just might secure a permanent job with the paper after graduation. Man, it would be nice to get on with a retirement package and health benefits." The internship with the newspaper had its perks, but Larry did not consider it a real job, nor did many of the regional newspapers to which Larry applied for work previously. Experience to them meant a permanent nameplate somewhere, and not an internship, even if it was paid.

Roy dropped the check on the table and finished making breakfast. "Make sure you endorse that before you leave. You expecting any more?"

"Not for a month. *Catholic Monthly* won't pay me until my piece is published. Even then, it could take weeks before a check it cut and sent here."

Roy raised an eyebrow. *Catholic Monthly*? That was an odd choice of publication for his brother. Not that Roy had anything against the Catholic Church - he actually knew very little about the faith and was not interested enough to learn - but he had always figured Larry would lend his talents towards general Christian publications more in sync with their own views.

"What piece was that?"

Larry poured two glasses of orange juice. "Oh, I revamped that profile of the pregnancy counseling center in Portsmouth to include some quotes from area clergy to add Catholic relevance." He took a quick sip. "We got any cinnamon left?"

Roy pointed to a cabinet near the refrigerator, nearly shuddering from the chill running down his spine. "I didn't know you were doing that," he said coolly.

"I know. I figured since you'd read it before that I'd go ahead and send it in. There are no major changes to the text, just added some quotes." Larry coated a slice of toast with semi-soft butter and cinnamon before devouring it in three bites.

"Oh." Roy still did not feel comforted. He never liked to be left out of anything where Larry was concerned.

"You opening the store early today, Roy?"

Roy held the sizzling skillet over his brother's plate and pared off his share of eggs. He glared at the enormous ring of keys resting on the kitchen counter next to the microwave. "Yeah. I figure the excitement's died down enough for me to get in there. Make up for some lost time." Roy's antique furniture shop was located on Granby Street in the Ghent area, not too far away from the women's clinic.

"Actually, the cops did a good job keeping the protest concentrated in one area," Larry said. "You probably could have gone in yesterday, and don't tell me you did because I ran into George at Taco Bell. He told me everything."

Roy chuckled. "I should know better to keep secrets from an investigative reporter," he said. "I just didn't want you thinking your older brother was a slacker."

"You're not a slacker. I don't blame you for staying home, though. It's your business."

Roy sat down at the table and immediately speared a triangle of egg white from his own plate. "Ah, I needed the break anyway. Besides, a lot of my business is phone and paperwork, which I did here. But I might just stay open late to make up for lost delivery time."

Larry broke the yolk of his egg and dabbed at it with another slice of toast. "Speaking of phone work, I need to get on the horn today. I got an idea for another *Catholic Monthly* piece and I need to call some churches around Williamsburg."

"What for?"

"There was a priest at the demonstration yesterday and he was with some elderly lady who was sitting near the coffee shop, just praying and making rosaries," he explained. "Some other people I talked to said‹"

Roy abruptly dropped his fork. "You mean you actually went down to that near riot? I thought you were just talking about watching the TV coverage!"

"Relax, bro. There was no riot, just a few hours of bickering at high volume. Didn't you see it on the news?"

Roy stiffened. "I'm…I'm sorry, I just worry about you doing things like that. Sometimes I wonder if that journalistic instinct of yours will get you killed."

Larry rolled his eyes. "I was just curious, thought I could get a simple project out of going, Roy. I didn't storm the beach at Normandy."

Roy raised his hands in defeat and finished his breakfast as Larry continued. "Anyway," he said, "it turns out that this old lady is there all the time. She and the priest are regular pro-life demonstrators. She gave me this."

Larry produced the plastic bead rosary from his pants pocket. "She just sits in a chair outside the clinic and makes these and gives them away. I thought it'd make a good human interest profile. If I can find her, and if she's willing to talk to me, I plan to interview her."

"Yeah, it might work. I've seen that lady before, when I go to lunch around there," Roy responded quietly. "Good luck."

The brothers finished eating and cleaned up in silence, with only the clattering of the plates and forks in the sink filling the air with noise. Larry endorsed the check, grabbed his pre-made lunch by the refrigerator and darted into the living room, where a stack of books waited for him on a bureau by the front entrance.

"Hey, I'm going to the paper after class today, so don't wait for me at dinner," Larry called from halfway out the door. He was already to his car before Roy could acknowledge the call.

Roy watched his brother drive away from an open slit in the vertical blinds covering the front window. Outside the sun shone over a row of similarly built homes in their middle-class neighborhood; small children in bulky coats lumbered toward the designated bus stop as the wind toyed with their hats and scarves.

Larry was going to be a great reporter, of that Roy was certain. He was going to make people think and open their eyes to the horrors of the modern world, a world that seemed to think nothing of ending life at its conception, before its potential could ever be realized. All for the sake of convenience - sick, sick, *sick*.

Larry is going to change things for the better, Roy thought. So am I.

He opened a small drawer on the bureau desk, extracting a rosary of nylon cord and black beads, not unlike the one Larry showed him earlier. Yes, Larry's going to be a great writer, thought Roy. All he needs is that one breakthrough story.

Fifteen

As the Merwin family flitted in and out of rooms, up and down the stairs, speeding through their individual morning rituals before school and work, Therese nibbled on a toaster pastry and sat at her desk. Already dressed and groomed, she bent over her desk and scribbled in her prayer journal.

Dear Therese, was how she began today's entry. Most days her journal entries numbered from just one to as many as seven to ten, depending on how badly Therese thought she needed spiritual aid. Every intention, every prayer request, every gripe, compliment and grievance that came to mind went straight into her journal; most letters she addressed to Christ, while a few requests she reinforced through separate entries begging for the intercessory prayers of the Virgin Mary and assorted saints.

Today, Therese decided, she would address the one for whom she was named, Marie Therese Martin, better known as St. Therese of the Child Jesus and the Holy Face, the Little Flower of God.

Therese had further acquainted herself with the saint through her thin yet inspiring autobiography, *The Story of a Soul*, commissioned by St. Therese's older sister, Pauline, who served as the younger's mother superior during the saint's brief tenure as a Carmelite nun in late-nineteenth century France. That the book was written while Therese of Lisieux was in her early twenties amazed the young girl; the words chronicling the saint's lifelong devotion to God appeared too serious, too mature to have been written by the pen of someone so young.

If only I had the creativity to record my thoughts and memories as you did, Therese wrote, *would my prayers by answered any quicker? Would God be more inclined to bestow His grace on me?*

I am so grateful to the Lord for everything I have - my wonderful family, the clothes on my back, the food on my plate, and every blessing seen and unseen. I'm still worried about my sister, Monica, though. She still seems sad, and I wonder if there is more behind her constant discomfort, and maybe a possible break-up with Jack. Who really knows for sure?

Therese chewed her pen cap and checked her watch. She had exactly one minute to finish the entry before her mother rounded up the older children to take to school. Judith and Joshua would ride along, but return home for a day of home schooling. Therese bent over her journal again and wrote faster.

Anyway, Therese, she penned, *today is day three of my novena for your intercession to God. My requests remained unchanged: I pray for my sister's well-being. Whatever pain she is experiencing, whatever problems she suffers, it is my hope that you will be my advocate in Heaven and ask Jesus to comfort Monica. Help to let her know that she is not alone in her troubles ...*

Fifteen seconds to go. Therese could hear her mother's footsteps thumping up the stairs.

Send me a rose so I'll know Jesus has granted my request. In His name I pray, she quickly scribbled with a flourish, slapping her journal shut and slipping it under her pillow before her door opened.

"Hey, Big T! Let's go!" Laura called from the other side of the door. "You got all your books and papers and what not?"

Therese slung a stuffed backpack over her shoulder and trudged behind her mother down the stairs and out the door. "Yes, Mom," she sighed.

Once stuffed in the family minivan between CJ and Judith, Therese closed her eyes and prayed her novena prayer, which she had memorized from her father's tattered paperback prayer book. *O Little Therese of the Child Jesus, please pick for me a rose from the heavenly gardens and send it to me as a message of love...*

Sixteen

Father Welker suggested they distance themselves from the clinic until the furor over Dr. Masterson's murder calmed, and Rosie reluctantly agreed. There would always be people there to defend the rights of the unborn through prayer and vocal activism, but she felt she might be doing a disservice to the patients of the clinic who strongly needed to see a friendly face. Rosie wanted to remind them that regardless of their decisions in life, God would certainly not abandon them.

"Barbara, your prayers are valid anywhere. They will be just as effective in the safety of your own home as they were in the shivering cold on a sidewalk in Ghent," the good priest told her over a cup of morning coffee following Mass. They were sitting in his cubicle of the small parish office, which was relatively quiet save for the clicking of the secretary's typewriter as she transcribed notes for the next month's newsletter.

"I realize that, Gary. It's just that I want to be kept abreast of what is happening down there. The media will only be involved until Masterson's killer is apprehended or something else horrendous and newsworthy occurs, God forbid." She blessed herself quickly. "And I don't have to tell you that not everyone in the media industry is sympathetic to our cause. I just want to be there for myself."

Father Welker shuffled some papers stacked on his desk. "You will be there. We will. I would just prefer that the climate is safer before we venture that way again."

"Oh, Father! Where's that fighting spirit of faith?" Rosie's eyes twinkled. "St. Teresa of Avila used to roam the dirt roads of her home town hoping to become a martyr for Christ. She believed it was the best thing she could do for Him."

"She was a child then," Father Welker said, standing slowly, gripping his lower back as he straightened. "I'm afraid I'm just a bit too old for anything adventurous."

"Gary, you're seven years younger than I am!"

"In age only, not in spirit," the priest chuckled. Outside the clacking stopped with the shrill ring of a phone. Seconds later, the parish secretary, a brunette closing in on forty with a smiling, chubby face informed the priest he had a call. At this, Rosie stood to leave.

"I shouldn't keep you from your work," she said as Father Welker took her hand. "But we will discuss this later? I shouldn't have to tell you that I don't mind asking someone else for a ride to Norfolk."

"Then I hope you'll let me know before you do." The priest's eyes clouded with worry for his friend. He saw her to his door before taking the call.

Rosie was already outside and on the sidewalk when Father Welker exclaimed loudly into his phone receiver, "Why, yes, I do. You just missed her, as a matter of fact."

Seventeen

If any of the teachers at Holy Name Academy were able to teach the morning's classes without having to stifle several cliques of secret conversations and intercept traveling notes, it would indeed have been a miracle. Sister Mary Grace, the upper school principal, sounded so vague and distant during the morning prayers and announcements. The news of the special homerooms for individual visits to the upper room classes by the principal surprised everyone, especially the teachers, who had not been given advanced warning. From the second the intercom switched off, voices in every classroom rumbled in low murmurs, speculating on the purpose of the visits. A note passed to Monica by her friend Jennifer read, *You think the MG's going to retire?*

Monica tucked the paper into her history textbook before it could be spotted by their teacher, and she answered Jennifer, sitting next to her, with a silent shrug. Rumors of Sister Mary Grace's pending retirement had been circulating around campus for at least two years, and given that the old nun was in her late seventies and talking more and more about missing her native Ireland, Monica pondered the possibility of that being the reason for the assemblies. Normally the old nun's voice was light-hearted and gay, nothing like the drone that crackled over the intercom this morning.

Then again, she thought, why would the MG, as the nun was known among the students, visit each class in the upper grades and not the elementary school as well? Would not a full school assembly in the auditorium have made more sense?

Therese and the cluster of students seated around her were debating that same point in hushed whispers as Sister Mary Regina scratched out an algebra problem on the chalkboard. Other theories - a surprise inspection by some diocese official, a sudden death among the student body, a motherly lecture about the evils of drugs - were bandied about but ultimately rejected with doubtful glances.

The MG entered Therese's classroom, prompting everyone to stand and chime, "Good morning, Sister Mary Grace," in singsong unison. Therese sighed in relief as she sat; she hated being kept in suspense and wished the announcement would be quick and painless. Sister Mary Regina ceded the class to the diminutive principal, who stood straight in the simple habit worn by all the school's Sisters of Mercy - crisp white blouse and calf-length navy skirt with a matching veil covering the old nun's short gray hair. The large silver crucifix that hung around her neck twisted as she moved to the front of the class, and a beam of light filtered from an open window cast a tiny reflection on the *corpus*.

"Good morning, class. I will be brief so as not to divert you too much from your studies," began the nun as a few scattered groans erupted. Normally such a reaction would have elicited a smile from Mary Grace, but today her face remained stone.

"No doubt you are curious as to why I'm making these rounds, so I will get to the point. Yesterday afternoon, one of our custodial staff was in the process of cleaning the restrooms in this wing when she discovered a most disturbing object, which she immediately brought to my attention."

Therese half-expected to see something unalarming like a makeup compact or a crushed cigarette pack - things considered almost commonplace for teens these days but absolutely taboo to the faculty. She wondered if any of the nuns gasped in shock to see a female student brandishing nail polish.

Instead the nun produced from her skirt pocket a plastic sandwich bag containing an empty pregnancy test container and held it high for the class to see. "You can imagine my shock at seeing something like this in our school. It is especially disconcerting since the bathroom where this was found is used by students only, and it pains me to think a young girl - at seventeen, fifteen, or, Heaven forbid, thirteen - would see the need to use such a device.

"We were unable to find the actual test, so I will assume the owner of this," Sister waved the container over her head, "still has it in her possession. Now, I'm not here to make any accusations. I think by now all of you are aware of the beliefs of this faculty and the of the Church in general with regards to pre-marital, ahem," she searched for a discreet word, "relations."

Therese saw a patch of red color the nun's cheeks.

"I just want to say," Sister continued, "that if the person or persons responsible for this test are in this room, that I am not here to judge you. I'm here to help. It is my hope that someone will come forward to the principal's office with information, and that the mystery of this, this..." Sister put the evidence back in her skirt pocket, unable to bring herself to say *pregnancy test*, "this box will be solved soon. If not by the school, then by the parents of the student or students in question."

Sister Mary Grace made a move toward the door; some students moved to stand for the customary class farewell but she stifled them with an open palm. "If this was yours, please know you have no reason to be afraid," she added before exiting, leaving the class in deathly silence.

Her speech in the rest of the upper grade classrooms resulted in similar reactions, none more petrified than that of Monica Merwin, who listened to Sister's short announcement with a straight face, her hands folded on her desk, her eyes cast downward. Her backpack rested at her feet...inside its front pocket was the missing piece of the puzzle Sister Mary Grace kept in the plastic bag.

Eighteen

When Larry Jeffries finally managed to track down the would-be subject of his story idea, it was not without hitting a few roadblocks, in particular the stonewalling tactics of his contacts. Father Welker was not about to hand over personal information on a parishioner and friend to a reporter, if indeed the man on the other line was one, regardless of how sincere he sounded. He handed Jeffries off to Café Lisieux, whose phone number the priest did not mind distributing. It was in the Yellow Pages anyway.

If this Larry Jeffries truly was a reporter and researching an article for *Catholic Monthly*, Father decided, perhaps he could do Lola a favor in exchange for help with finding Rosie and encourage the young man to write a restaurant review to boost further publicity for the place. Surely a man who wrote for a national magazine could sell a simple review to the local papers.

If the old priest came off as evasive to Larry, then Lola was practically militant, turning around the conversation by asking him all the questions.

"What do you want with her?" Lola had the phone receiver wedged between her ear and shoulder as she rolled silverware into cloth napkins.

"Please," begged an exhausted Larry. "I only want to talk to her about a possible interview. I write for the *Times*, but I also freelance for various publications, including *Catholic Monthly*."

"Have you written anything for *Our Sunday Visitor*?" she asked. When Larry said he had not, Lola added, "Well, if you did, I'd have heard of you. Maybe you should write for them."

Larry could not help but laugh. "If I can just get a hold of your rosary-making friend, I'll try to make her a cover girl." He had never heard of *Our Sunday Visitor*. "Will you help me?"

Still skeptical, Lola gave him directions to the café and vaguely described Rosie's dining regimen. "I can't guarantee she'll be here, I don't control my customers," Lola said. "You want to see her badly enough, you'll make the drive."

She hung up before Larry could thank her. Her hands shook and she prayed a silent plea that she had not done something wrong. I'll be here, too, thought Lola, just in case. She had seen on news magazine shows how con artists operated, devising creative methods of scamming the elderly out of large sums of money. Who knew if this Larry Jeffries person was not going to try that with Rosie? At the café, she and Pre could keep a close watch on things.

By five o'clock, the early dinner crowd began to trickle inside and many were browsing menus when the lanky, longhaired fellow entered the café. Rosie, seated in her usual spot by the large front picture window, looked up for a moment from her tea glass and a glimmer of recognition spread across her face. Larry spotted her almost immediately as well and started toward her, only to be intercepted by Pre. Lola had given Pre the run down when the manager reported for work an hour earlier, and the young woman eyed him with instant suspicion.

"Can I help you?" Pre hugged an oblong laminated menu to her chest, ignoring the young man's smile.

"Oh, yeah." Larry stepped back, taken by Pre's abruptness. He noticed the steel in her bluish-gray eyes and smiled again, hoping to soften them a bit. "I'm just meeting my dinner date over there."

"Really? That's odd, because that woman sitting by the window has been eating here regularly for three years and I have never seen her dine with a companion. Don't tell me you're her son, just returned from the service, because I know for a fact she's childless." Her hands moved to her hips now, and Larry suddenly had a vision that this pretty lady before him was going to slap him silly with the menu then throw him out of the restaurant like a nightclub bouncer. He grinned. Not that he would have minded it.

Rosie watched the commotion from her table and called out to Pre. "It's okay, Pre, I know that man. Come, sit." She beckoned grandly to Larry, who casually slipped around Pre to the vacant chair at the two-top wooden table. Pre stalked behind him slowly, easing the menu down in front of Rosie's guest.

"Separate checks, I presume?" Pre eyed him warmly. She did not know how much money Rosie had tucked away, but darned if this guy was going to try for it.

Larry nodded and gave the menu a quick once-over. "Yes, and in fact, I'm just going to have the Caesar salad with a sweetened iced tea." He flipped the menu back to Pre and noted her unchanged expression, while Rosie ordered her usual Thursday dinner of steamed vegetables with brown rice.

"Be just a few minutes," Pre said, casting a "yell if you need help" glance at Rosie before heading back to the kitchen.

Rosie chuckled. "You'll have to excuse my friend, Mister...Jeffries, wasn't it?" Larry nodded, happy that she remembered him, and the old woman continued. "Pre's a lovely girl, and she can be quite protective of her friends."

"That's a wonderful quality to have in a friend."

"Absolutely." Rosie flicked the lemon wedge clinging to the rim of her glass into the cloudy brown liquid. "You give her time, she'll warm up to you."

I hope so, Larry thought with a glance to the swinging kitchen door.

"I noticed you don't a have a wedding band on your finger, Mr. Jeffries."

Larry unconsciously held up his left hand. "It's Larry, please, Mrs., uh ..."

"Barbara Fitzgerald, but call me Rosie."

"Okay. Uh, no, you're right. I've never been married." He shifted in his seat, thinking of a way to segue into the interview proposal. After all, he was the reporter, but she was making the inquiries.

"Interesting," said Rosie. "Pre's single, too." She bowed her head and looked at him from underneath her eyelashes. He was handsome, even with all that long brown hair bundled up in a ponytail behind his back. If his personality easily matched his looks, what a wonderful match he would make for Pre, thought Rosie. Their children would be just beautiful!

Rosie swirled the lemon and melting ice in her glass. She was getting ahead of herself.

Larry shook his head. "Oh, I'm not thinking that far into the future, Rosie. I just want to finish graduate school first. Besides," another glance toward the kitchen, "I've only known your friend for about sixty seconds, fifty-nine of which were not all too pleasant."

"Pish." Rosie waved the comment away. "I told you she's just very protective of her friends. I'm sure she'd do the same for you when you become her friend." The twinkle in her eyes caught Larry off guard and he laughed.

"Hey, now, I'm the reporter here! You think I can have a turn at giving the third degree? I'd love to discuss my ideas for an article about you."

Rosie appeared astounded. "An article about me? Why, who would want to read about an old woman who spends nearly all of her time praying?"

"People liked to read about Mother Teresa."

Another twinkle lightened the old woman's eyes. "Touché."

Larry pulled the handmade rosary from his shirt pocket. "It's because of this that I got the idea in the first place," he said. He intertwined his fingers with the strung beads and leaned closer to Rosie, outlining his proposal for the article. He would profile her as a fixture in the Hampton Roads pro-life community, emphasizing her silent devotion to prayer and her rosary ministry, regardless of the weather or other hostile conditions.

"You'd be shocked to know how recognized you are in the area," Larry told her. "Especially the other day. I managed to get a hold of some area businesspeople near the clinic; you're practically local color, a beacon of calm in the storm of the abortion controversy."

Rosie giggled. "Is that going to be the opening line of your article?" she asked. Her demeanor suddenly stiffened slightly. "Now, really, I appreciate the thought, but..."

"Hey, if you appreciate the thought, I think you'll appreciate the article when I actually write it," Larry interrupted, squeezing the rosary in his fist. "Would you be willing to grant me some time? I promise that if you're not satisfied with the completed writing, I'll tear it up and we can forget it."

"Well, Larry," Rosie said, "I don't object to being interviewed. I'm pretty straightforward when it comes to my faith and my views on abortion. I've argued my position to many a stranger on that street by the clinic, and given away scores of rosaries as well, sometimes to the very people with whom I've argued!" Larry smiled at this.

"So you'll do it?" He swelled with hope.

Rosie nodded. "What the hey. I don't see myself as being any more interesting than other subjects covered in *Catholic Monthly*, but if you think they will want the story, well, I suppose it would be nice to have fifteen minutes of fame."

"Don't worry, this'll definitely get published. If not *Catholic Monthly*, then somewhere."

Pre arrived, practically sneaking up on the duo with two large plates filled with food and a bottle of soy sauce for Rosie. She offered to refill drink glasses as eager hands lifted forks. "Anything else I can do for you?" Pre asked them both, but looking only at Rosie.

"We're fine, Pre," Rosie answered pointedly. "But I notice some empty tea glasses around the room. Really, I don't need a bodyguard."

Larry looked up from his salad. "I, on the other hand, could use some of that cracked black pepper on my salad," Larry said, nodding at the wooden pepper mill sticking out from the pocket of Pre's apron.

"Certainly." Pre wrenched the mill aggressively over Larry's dinner until he signaled her to stop, but for good measure she cranked it twice more. "Enjoy your meals," she added politely and retreated to the front of the café to refill drinks.

"Some waitress," Larry muttered.

"Actually, Pre's the manager, and the lady with the foot bandage who is also keeping surveillance is Lola Marquez, the owner." Rosie pointed to Lola, who was still sitting at the bar. She caught Rosie's stare and quickly ducked behind a swatch of newspaper.

"Maybe if I can win them over with my endearing charm I can convince them to supply some quotes," Larry mused. "Which, by the way, will be useless unless I get serious and start writing." He pinched a crouton from his salad and popped it in his mouth. "How about we discuss a time we can get together for an in-depth interview? When is best for you?"

"Why not tonight? I don't live far from here. We could have coffee and you can take notes or tape record or whatever it is you do."

Larry agreed and Rosie changed the direction of the conversation back to him - his background, family, and interests - to satisfy the rest of dinner. Larry's answers were pleasant but brief as, he explained more than once, that there was not much to tell. He was just a twenty-six-year-old masters' degree student in journalism at Old Dominion University, living with his older brother until his tuition debts were paid, and interning at a Norfolk/Virginia Beach daily.

With what free time he had, Larry scored portfolio fillers through freelance articles. Not much to tell, but at least fifteen minutes to tell it, thought Rosie. What she did hear, though, she liked, and knew Pre would like it too, if Pre would ever listen.

"Doesn't that put a crimp in your social lives, living together?" Rosie asked slyly.

"Hm?" Larry swallowed a mouthful of lettuce and garlic. "Not really. Roy is widowed, and he hasn't dated since his wife died. Hasn't shown any interest in it either. As for me, who's got time? Commuting from home to school to work and back puts a serious dent in my day, not to mention all the stuff I do in between trips."

"What about Roy? What does he do?"

Larry tore off a chunk of breadstick. "My brother runs a shop in Ghent. He sells antique furniture, mostly stuff obtained from estate sales. Heavy oaks and cherry, some fixtures, too."

"Did I hear you right?" Larry felt a hand brush his back and grasp his chair. Lola had hobbled over to the table. "Does your brother deal in bulk orders for businesses? We're due for some more tables and chairs to replace some older sets."

"He's done it before," Larry smiled. "He also restores and finishes, too, if necessary. Here," Larry took a business card and pen from his shirt pocket and scribbled a phone number and address on the back of the card. "Here's his work phone. I'm sure he can help you with whatever you need."

86

Lola took the card from Larry and examined the neat, sharp pen strokes, then flipped it over to see *Larry Jeffries, Freelance Writer* embossed in script font with a phone number and e-mail address in raised black letters. Her initial suspicion of Larry was fading. She had been searching all over Hampton Roads for a deal on tables and chairs.

"Thanks. Do you get a commission for referrals?" she joked. She spotted Pre weaving around tables with a pitcher of tea and waved her over to replenish Rosie's empty glass.

"I wish."

Rosie leaned over and playfully slapped Lola's hand. "Larry is going to write an article about me for a Catholic magazine, Lo. Isn't that exciting?"

"Well, it's not a done deal," Larry said. "I still have to call the editor and..."

"We're meeting at my house after dinner for an interview," Rosie broke in. "It's too bad you and Pre couldn't tag along. You both know the Catholic community here so well, and I know you could provide some insight for Larry."

"Insight for what?" Pre asked, joining the group and refilling the glasses.

"Rosie wants to know if we could help with this man's ..." she checked the card again, "Mr. Jeffries's article on her."

Larry laughed uneasily, feeling that he was about to lose control of his own project. "Whoa, Nellie! I didn't say that exactly."

But Lola ignored him. "Say, Pre, the crowd looks light tonight, I'm sure Bill, Jesse and I can handle the table and bar. Why don't you knock off early? You could escort our new friend here," she squeezed the back of Jack's chair, "to Rosie's house."

Lola cast a knowing glance at Pre, who refilled Larry's glass with a saccharine smile. Suspicion might have been gone, but what harm was there in having a chaperone? "I don't mind if you don't mind," she told him. "Do you mind, Mr. Jeffries?"

"Call him Larry," Rosie insisted.

Larry capitulated. Pre certainly was pretty, anyway. "No. Not at all."

Nineteen

"So she just blurts it out, right there in front of your class?" Chris Merwin nearly choked on a bite of fried chicken as CJ related the high points of his school day. "She did this in your class, too, Therese? Monica?"

Monica nodded quietly, scooping up a bite of macaroni and cheese. Her day had been miserable, and her mood remained sullen. All throughout lunch her friends chattered animatedly, speculating as to who would have been so bold as to actually use a pregnancy test urine stick at school!

Jennifer and Becky, huddled together in the courtyard with their regular lunch clique, even started a list of the most well known campus couples for a means of debate and discussion. Football heroes courting cheerleaders, seniors and their semester sweethearts...every pair the two girls could conjure between them went on the list. Becky was certain some of the couples were engaged in some stage of carnal knowledge. Monica glanced over her friend's shoulder occasionally, visibly disinterested until Becky penciled in the names of Monica's brother and his girlfriend.

"What the hell are you doing?" Monica demanded, pushing Becky with her shoulder. "Why did you write down CJ's and Nina's names?"

"Puh-*leaze*, Nic," Jennifer sighed. "They've been going together for almost two years! And didn't you tell us yesterday that CJ was having second thoughts about leaving the state for college?"

"Only because he didn't think he could get a scholarship, and he believed he could save money by living at home and going to W&M."

"Which is where Nina is going," Becky sang.

"And CJ's like at the top of the senior class," Jennifer added. "He'll probably get valedictorian. Of course he'll get scholarships!

The real question here, Monica, is why all of a sudden CJ feels the need to start saving money."

"Baby clothes and diapers?" snickered Becky.

"Stop it!" Monica slammed down her Coke can in disgust. Brown droplets of carbonated liquid sprayed the concrete table and open notebook. Monica leaned over it for a better view. "I don't see your name on here with Greg, Jen."

"Because Greg is scared of trying anything for fear his daddy'll rip his thing off," huffed Jennifer. "It's not like I haven't tried to get some action," she added with a giggle.

"Yeah, and Jennifer wouldn't be stupid enough to take a pregnancy test at school, where anyone could walk in and see. Duh!" Becky made a face. Monica's heart fell to her stomach and she tightened her lips together. Would Becky piece together her lengthy stay in the bathroom the other day with the pregnancy test? She hoped not.

"What would Jennifer have done?" she asked. "Since you seem to be such an expert on pregnancy test-taking etiquette."

Becky shrugged. "Skipped school, gone to Newport News or Norfolk to a free clinic and taken a test under a fake name. My sister Doris had a friend who did that once. Lucky for her it turned out to be a false alarm."

"I bet that scared her into waiting 'til marriage," Monica laughed awkwardly, tearing into her sandwich. Why couldn't they talk about something else, she thought. Talk about the weekend or make fun of the nuns like they used to do during lunch.

"No. She got pregnant about a year or so later. I think she's up to two now. Different fathers. She's working at Captain D's."

"I wonder if the test that came in the box they found turned out negative," Jennifer mused aloud.

No you don't. Monica balled the wax paper sandwich wrapper and stuffed it in her lunch bag. "How do we even know it belonged to a student here? How do we know somebody didn't come in from off-campus to use the ladies' room?"

"Who's going to do that, one of those yokel tourists?" Jennifer asked incredulously. "Enjoy our colonial streets, don't forget to pee in the cup? That's a bit far-fetched, don't you think?"

"It can't be any of the faculty, either." Becky munched on a taco chip. "They got their own toilets."

"Ooh!" Jennifer's hand flew to her mouth. "What if it belonged to one of the *nuns*?" she squealed between splayed fingers. "Wouldn't that be a hoot?"

"Sure, Jen," Becky was not convinced. "Who? Is it the MG herself, trying to throw everyone off track with her speech? Or maybe it's Sister Claudine? The average age of the nuns here has got to be well over sixty. Well past menopause."

"No, Sister Claire is only in her mid-forties."

Monica downed the rest of her soda and tuned out the bantering, thinking desperately of a prayer to ease her troubled mind and soul. Beyond the morning and afternoon rituals at school and weekly Masses, she had not prayed spontaneously in a while. She saw no reason to beg the Lord's pardon outside of church, thinking she already had everything she needed and wanted.

Now she thought of nothing else but doing just that, yet her guilt of asking God to clean up a mess she made nettled at her brain. Who was she to pray and expect His help, when every attempt came off as selfish? *Dear God, I had sex with my boyfriend and got pregnant. It was the wrong thing to do, though I tried to cover my tracks with protection that ultimately failed, and I don't want to accept the responsibility of carrying a child when I'm still a child. Could you get rid of it for me, pretty please? Send it sliding out of me in a delayed menstrual blood mass, regardless of how far developed it happened to be? Amen.*

She could promise the Lord never to touch Jack again - in fact, she was doing a good job of it now since they appeared to keep missing each other - but could she really guarantee that? She could ask Jack to take the same oath, but he might not agree to it, and what if she fell prey again to his insistence? What if he tried to force himself on her?

Now, at dinner, she pondered a second, albeit unappealing, option - abortion. Her family sat around her, engaged in the day's events and enjoying a nice hot meal while she considered ending a life before anyone could be made aware of its existence.

"Monica? Monica!" Laura tapped her daughter's shoulder. Monica nearly hit the ceiling.

"I was just going into the kitchen for more chicken and green beans. Do you want seconds on anything?"

Monica nodded. She was still working on firsts but asked for another drumstick. Unlike CJ, who was making do with the vegetables and macaroni, Monica and the other children had not chosen to abstain from meat the entire forty days of Lent.

"Are you okay, sweetie?" Laura asked. "You haven't been yourself at all lately."

All eyes were now on Monica. *God help me. Please please please...*

"I'm sorry. I guess I was just off in my own little world there."

Joshua giggled and plunged a finger into the tiny mountain of macaroni and cheese on his plate as Chris reprimanded him.

"Probably that nun got you all upset," he grumbled. "Very poor method of handling a delicate situation."

Laura returned with the chicken and extra napkins for the younger children. "Hon, I don't think this is the time to be discussing this." She crooked her head toward Judith and Joshua, who was now nibbling on his macaroni one elbow at a time.

"Why not now? We teach our kids morals every day of their lives. They should be made aware of these things so they won't be doomed to imitate." In a lower voice he added to his wife, "Why didn't she just address a general letter to the parents? She's probably shot herself in the foot by going to the student body first. How much you want to bet that whoever took that pregnancy test is working to cover her tracks this very minute?"

Worry creased Laura's face. "Poor thing. She's probably considering abortion out of fear."

"The gossip mills are running non-stop around campus," CJ offered. "Anyone who's had a date in the last two months is suspect."

Therese's eyes widened. "Yeah. There's even a list going around with possible parents. My friend Lisa saw it on the bus. Said a whole bunch of seniors' and juniors' names were on it."

Chris dropped his knife on the floor. Laura bent to retrieve it but was stilled by her husband's stern glare. CJ shot his younger sister a look that said, "Thanks a lot."

"I should certainly hope that there is no reason why you, any of you, would be lumped into that category," Chris said calmly, twisting his fork in his hands. Heads around the table shook with worried faces. Chris rarely got angry, but when he did he could raise the roof to the moon with his temper.

"It's also my hope," he continued, taking Laura's hand in his, "that if any of you ever get into trouble, you will come to us first. There is nothing, absolutely nothing, you can do that will make us stop loving you."

Chris took a deep breath, then reached down for his knife. Monica watched her father's reddened face drain into a healthy pink and the veins in his throbbing forehead subside. Was it really that simple, she asked herself. If she had just announced to the table that it was her pregnancy test, her baby, Jack's baby...would that make her parents love her less? Lessen their expectations of her? Would they just pat her on the head like nothing really happened? She opened her mouth to speak, but Therese beat her to the clock.

"Daddy?" she asked meekly.

"What is it, punkin?"

"I-I think I blew my lit quiz today?" she cringed, testing the waters for a potential explosion. Chris was a stickler for good grades.

"Did you study, or did you spend all last night listening to music and thumbing through those cheesy romance novels of yours?"

"I studied!" Therese was indignant. "Just not enough," she added meekly.

"Well, now you know the consequences of that, so next time you'll apply more time to studying and not fooling around." Chris polished off his water and poured another glass. "Now, was that so difficult, everyone? I'm sure Therese feels better that she got that off her chest."

Therese and Judith giggled, but little Joshua looked rather somber.

"Daddy?"

"Yes, son?"

"I just spilled green beans on the floor."

The table erupted in light laughter. Even Monica could not contain herself. It was the first laugh she had enjoyed in nearly a month.

Twenty

The only message left on Rosie's answering machine was ten seconds long - nine of silence and the last a deep sad sigh before the clunk of the receiver. Pre was standing over the old woman's shoulder, holding a tray of steaming coffee mugs.

"Do you get calls like that often?" Pre asked, concerned.

Rosie nodded. "Once in a while. I'm sure it's just a wrong number. I don't leave my name or number on the outgoing message, so I can expect a few of them now and again."

"But, Rosie, that call ...it just unnerves me to get calls like that. If that had been a wrong number I'd think the person would have hung up sooner. How do you know someone's not casing your house?"

Rosie took two mugs from the tray. "Because I have faith in people, Pre. If I lived my life with a paranoid nature, I wouldn't have much fun, would I?" she teased with a wink.

"I'm not paranoid, if that's what you're implying," Pre frowned. "I'm only concerned for your safety, Rosie. Crank calls, people coming out of the woodwork for interviews...I'm sorry, but when I think of you being in this big house alone..."

"I've been alone in this big house for three years and nothing bad has happened yet, Pre." Rosie started toward the living room. "Faith, dear. Why worry when I have the best security system around. I have the Lord, and she who has the Lord has everything. Nothing is wanting to those who have God. God alone suffices."

Pre, recognizing the excerpt quote from St. Teresa of Avila, could not argue with that. But still...

Larry was waiting for them on the sofa, entranced by the numerous rosaries hanging from every corner of the room. "Man, I wish I had my camera," he said. "A shot of you surrounded by your handiwork would have made a great complement to the article."

"Which doesn't exist," Pre mumbled, suddenly wishing she had not opened her mouth when she saw Larry eye her with a bemused look.

Rosie handed Larry his mug. "Oh, you want we should postpone this? There's no reason why you can't come back with a camera. I don't have any film in mine, else we'd use it."

"Oh, no, it's not a problem," Larry said apologetically, waving a hand. "I'd prefer we just go ahead while the questions are still fresh in my mind." He extracted a miniature tape recorder from his jacket pocket and checked the buttons to work at voice command. "I always carry it with me," he explained to the ladies. "One never knows when a story happens, so I was told once in a writing class."

"Okay." Rosie took a seat in her favorite plush rocker, leaving Pre to take the other half of the sofa. "If you like, Larry, I'm sure somewhere around here there is a picture of me you can have. Or we could ask Pre to stage something for you." Rosie gestured to her surprised friend.

"Oh?" Larry asked, idly playing with the recorder strap. "Are you the local Diane Arbus?" His tone was light.

"If Diane Arbus filled rolls of Kodak film with blurred close-up shots of her thumb, then I'd say yes," Pre retorted.

Rosie chuckled. "Pre, you're too modest, you do good work." She leaned back and pointed behind her. "See this picture of the shrine of Guadalupe in Mexico, Larry? Pre shot this last summer on her vacation."

"I did see it, it's very nice," said Larry, bending forward and squinting to see the small framed photo hanging above the old woman's chair; five other pictures of the same size surrounded it in a star pattern. "What about the rest of them?"

"That's my Marian wall," Rosie said with a touch of pride. She turned her torso and gave Larry a quick tour. "These are all photos of places where the Virgin was believed to have appeared: Fatima, Lourdes, Knock, Garabandal, and Conyers, Georgia. The Georgia photo is my doing, the rest were given to me by friends fortunate enough to have made the respective pilgrimages."

"Rosie sends a package of rosaries with everyone in the parish who make these trips," Pre added. Larry aimed the tape recorder toward her. "Feasibly her rosaries are being used around the world."

"That is my hope, anyway," Rosie said. "I'm really curious to know exactly how many people pray with them or simply take them for the sake of having something for free." She shifted back around to face her friends. "Which reminds me, I need to get another package together for the Wilsons, a nice young couple at the parish. They're going to visit Avila in March."

"When did you start making rosaries?" Larry asked.

Rosie closed her eyes, pulling the memory from the recesses of her mind. "I learned from my mother when I was about five or six, about a hundred years ago."

Her guests snickered. "Of course I exaggerate. Mother was a member of her parish's sewing guild in West Virginia. We belonged to a small parish in Fayette County, St. Luke's. Fifty or so families, many with five or more children, and once a week the mothers of the church met to stitch together quilts and clothing for the area needy, and there were many needy in those days. Children of the coal miners and primitive mountain folk were the more common recipients of the tiny smocks and sweaters they made.

"Mother also took in seamstress work while my father and his brothers worked in the mine to earn their keep and feed all of us: six kids in my family, and another eight between my uncles. Mother mended shoes and jackets for Sunday, usually for free or trade since people could rarely pay her."

She sipped her coffee and looked around the living room, momentarily losing her train of thought and searching for it within the walls. "Making rosaries was the idea of our Pastor, Father Maher. A giant Irishman who sang all the hymns in a bold bass voice, he was. He seemed to stretch into the clouds.

"Anyway, a friend of his from seminary worked as a missionary in Africa, preaching Gospel to the people there and helping them to improve their quality of life - sort of a forerunner to the Peace Corps. Father's friend was unable to find any Catholic supplies on the continent...all he had to teach with were a few worn Bibles and catechisms, no rosaries. So, he sent appeals to every contact he could remember asking for help.

"I remember this all happened right around Lent, because Father put up the suggestion that parishioners, as part of their Lenten sacrifice, give up one hour a day making rosaries from the plastic beads and cord the church would supply. My family, being very dedicated to the parish, naturally volunteered, and during those forty days seven rosary makers huddled in the living room for an hour of family bonding and knot-making.

"I made my first rosary with red beads strung together for the decades and black Our Father beads, not too different from the cord rosaries I make today. We didn't have centerpieces, so we had to make do with tying the ends of the decades together and stringing the five beginning beads and plastic crucifix on the remaining cord.

"Come to think of it, the whole thing looked rather crude, just like a five-year-old made it," Rosie chuckled. "But to me it was the most beautiful thing in the world, the best present I could give to the Lord and His mother."

"Do you have any of those first rosaries?" Larry asked.

"Goodness, no!" Rosie set her mug down on the floor next to her chair. "The thought of taking one for myself never crossed my mind. These rosaries were going to little African children who wanted to learn about Jesus and Mary and the history of the Church. I didn't know much about Africa, but I figured then that if they didn't even know about Jesus there, what else were they without? To take something away from them before they could get it was no different than stealing, and I knew stealing was wrong. My mother would have taken the switch to my hide if she saw me taking a souvenir of my work, too." Her eyes widened in mock fear.

"What about these?" Larry gestured to some of the fancier rosaries made of silver centers and crucifixes, some with semi-precious stones that glittered in the light of the chandelier above. "Did you make these, too?"

"Yes," Rosie answered. "Every rosary and chaplet in this house was made by me, with the exception of..." the old woman paused and rose, tottering down the hall to a back room. Pre and Larry sat quietly, staring at each other with puzzled looks. In the distance a light switch snapped, and the two heard some muffled activity, but neither dared to investigate.

Another snap of the switch followed seconds later and soft footsteps hailed Rosie's return.

"I've had this rosary since my First Communion. I was eight then." Rosie stood over her guests, a frail strand of tiny faux pearl beads dangled from her wrist. "You can see the beads are worn with use and the joints in the brass chain have rusted, as have the center and cross."

She scooped the swinging crucifix and cradled it in the palm of her hand so Larry and Pre could see it better. The *corpus* was faceless and smooth after sixty-plus years of being clutched and fondled during countless recitations.

"You've never replaced it?" Pre blurted out, who owned a few rosaries herself, though they were seldom used. "Not even with one of your own?"

"Why would I? The Lord doesn't care how old your rosary is, or even if you use one at all. The prayers are the same. I couldn't part with this one anyway." Rosie gingerly slid the beads into her shirt pocket. "My parents gave me this rosary, bought from a jeweler's shop in Charleston. Mother shaved a bit every day from the dairy money for a whole month to pay for it; I was the oldest, and that was the only time they ever did anything like that. When it came time for the other kids to celebrate First Communion, they received rosaries handmade by Mother, which were equally special, if not more. But this," she patted her pocket, "was mine."

"I learned to make these fancier strings," Rosie gestured to a pair of amethyst rosaries with sculpted brass crosses, "not long after finishing high school. I took a job behind the counter of Fitzgerald Jewelers in Beckley. Miles Fitzgerald was a forever happy, rotund beet of a gentleman who lived in Beckley with his family. They were quite well to do yet socially they were almost considered pariahs because of their Catholic faith - not to mention their Irish background. That never seemed to bother any of them, though, as they were largely accepted by the parish, to whom Mister Fitzgerald was a great benefactor."

"Uh, Rosie, I hate to interrupt," broke in Larry, "but when you say 'Fitzgerald,' you're not talking about Rose Fitzgerald's family, are you?"

The old woman had to ponder that question a moment. "Oh," she brightened, "you mean the Kennedys? No, no, there was no relationship there, at least none that I am aware of. For what it's worth, if there is a connection, I'm sure it's quite distant. I don't expect any invitations to Hyannis Port anytime soon."

"Being the only Catholic jewelers in the area," she continued, "Fitzgerald and Sons was the only place that sold precious stone rosaries with silver and gold chains and crucifixes, as well as fancy Miraculous Medals and the like. Mister Fitzgerald let me practice with an old pair of jeweler's pliers and some nickel wire."

She looked at her hands. "At night while the house was still I'd be crouched in a corner of the bedroom I shared with my sister, squinting in the dim lantern light as I bent the wire to and fro, trying to form perfect loops to connect each bead. I can still see the cuts and welts on my fingertips from pinching that coarse wire." She rubbed her fingers together as if, after a half-century, they were still throbbing from that first set of wire and pliers.

"You eventually married into this family," Pre observed, pleased that she was allowed the opportunity to eavesdrop. Very little of her friend's history was known to anyone in town, including Father Welker, to whom Rosie often confided. Rosie preferred to live in the present and look to the future, for despite God's power, prayers were just not effective in changing the past.

Rosie nodded. "I married Danny when I was nineteen and he was twenty-one. A chronic back problem resulting from a football injury kept him out of the war, leaving him plenty of time to court me. We stayed in a small apartment in Oak Hill for ten years, until my mother-in-law passed away. From there we moved into the big house to help care for Mister Fitzgerald. He lived another seven years with us, then pneumonia took him from us. Bless his heart." *Keep his soul,* she added in an aside to God. *Mother Fitzgerald and Danny, too.*

"In that time I made rosaries for the shop, colorful and bold ones. There were Tiger's eyes, black onyx, faceted glittering birthstones ...if there was a stone that could be polished and linked, you can be sure I used it. We had customers come as far north as Wheeling, even Ohio, to see what we had for First Communion and wedding gifts.

"I continued stringing the missionary rosaries, of course, for the church, but not only for Father's missionary friend but for anyone in town who couldn't afford one of our nicer sets. Occasionally, a parishioner would take a trip to Pennsylvania or Ohio and inadvertently evangelize to the Amish and Mennonites in the area, and they would request several to send that way. I think it was that word of mouth publicity that increased our customer base in the tri-state area in the first place, because we would get people in our store inquiring about the free rosaries. Later on, they would return to make generous purchases."

"So how did you come to Williamsburg?" asked Larry, quickly flipping the half-used miniature cassette over to resume recording. Given Rosie's history and detailed memory, he marveled at the potential for a great magazine article, perhaps even a series of articles, with Rosie's tale as the anchor. "Do you have family here?"

Pre leaned forward, equally interested. Rosie put a finger to her lips, a worried look spreading across her face. Pre thought for a moment that her old friend appeared ready to betray somebody's trust and reveal a deeply buried secret.

"I had some family here, briefly," Rosie said finally. "Danny and I were never able to have children of our own, so all of our paternal affections were transferred over to some of the parish children and our nieces and nephews. Danny kept the store running in top shape for the next thirty-nine years of our marriage; his nephew George took over when Danny passed. When that happened, this was about three years ago, I decided it was time to move forward. I didn't need that huge house, either, not while George and Linda were trying to rear four children.

"Danny had seen to it before he died that I would be able to live comfortably, plus I get a bit of Black Lung compensation as my father's beneficiary, which covers the cost of rosary supplies. I also receive donations from time to time to offset printing costs and postage, but I'm getting off track here." Rosie chuckled.

"I followed my sister's daughter here. The plan was for me to live with her and her family, a husband and two young boys. She likes to work and it keeps her out long hours, something of which I have never approved, but she didn't want to hire a nanny. Not the ideal situation for me; then again, I was raised in medieval times and wasn't 'with it,' as I've been told once too often, so what did I know?"

Pre scoffed at this. "Rosie, you'd be surprised to know how many woman are full-time mothers now, especially in this town."

Rosie sighed. "My niece isn't like other mothers. In fact, she and I disagreed on many points, including abortion. They were what we conservatives call 'cafeteria Catholics,' picking and choosing the tenets of the faith most agreeable to their liberal points of view. Even before I considered moving here I'd visit and get locked in some argument with them, especially her husband. My niece was usually quite complacent in speaking to me, out of respect for family, I suppose. But, uh, him," she caught herself before mentioning Neil by name, "Oh! He would constantly disparage the Pope and Mother Teresa and look upon everyone who disagreed with his position with scorn, like he had this air of superiority..." her voice cracked trying to finish the sentence. She bent over to retrieve her coffee mug and saw that the liquid was now tepid.

"I suppose I started sitting at the clinic out of my own selfish pride at first, I'm ashamed to say more to spite my niece's husband than for my concern for the unborn. God eventually forgave this stubborn old heart; at least, that is my hope, and my true compassion for the young girls entering the clinic grows stronger."

Another deep sigh, then a pause.

"I didn't know my two great-nephews very well, but I loved them, though because of the constant bickering in the house I knew I could not stay in that environment. I bought this house on a lark, got a great deal on it by having it zoned as a residence. Looking back, however, I realize that deciding to live alone may have been a foolish thing to do, considering..."

The old woman's voice faded into a whisper and her eyes followed the hypnotic swinging of a gilt crucifix attached to a rosary of blood red crystal beads, which hung from a nail over the doorway entrance to the living room like a mistletoe sprig. The short bursts of air produced by the ceiling fan caused the cross to twist slowly from the triangular centerpiece, and all Rosie could do at that moment was imagine Jesus, nailed to His Cross in Calvary.

There were no winds to comfort Him from the dry heat of the desert that bubbled His skin and warmed the trickles of blood brought on by the pricks of the woven thorn crown planted in His most sacred Head. Despite all that pain, Rosie knew, Jesus was not so selfish as to think only of Himself and His pain. From the Cross, He arranged for His own mother's care. "Behold your son," He said, indicating beloved disciple John, with whom Mary would then live. "Behold your mother," He told John.

Jesus would not have let the constant butting of heads drive him away to a big empty house, Rosie mused, but she let it happen. She could have stood her ground.

"I'm sorry, I guess I didn't realize how tired I was," she gasped. "You'll have to forgive me, interviewing sure takes a lot out of you." Pre raised an eyebrow. Time was not the only thing beating her friend into exhaustion, she guessed. Whatever memories she retained over the past three years were reemerging painfully. How sad, Pre thought, to let ill will eat away at your stomach like that, feeling that you have no recourse to vent.

She patted her abdomen unconsciously, her barren cocoon which would never shelter new life, and suddenly she empathized with Rosie. How often had she felt the same way, choosing to keep her own pains a secret as well?

Larry looked at his watch. "Oh, Jeez, it's nearly eleven! I didn't intend to keep you so late." He leapt from the couch, causing Pre to rock in her seat. "Rosie, I'm terribly sorry to have kept you so long. It's just that I don't think I have been taken by such a story before."

Rosie smiled. "Perhaps it's a good thing. Who wants to work on something for which he doesn't feel passion?"

"Like you and your rosaries," chimed in Pre, bending over to kiss her friend's cheek. "Go get some sleep. We'll see ourselves out."

The trio exchanged farewells as Pre led Larry out the front door. The reporter took note of Rosie's phone number and agreed to schedule a time to complete the interview. "Perhaps we could meet halfway, like at the coffee shop by the clinic? I could bring my camera and get a picture of you in your element."

"That would be wonderful," the old woman replied, and Rosie explained how she had recently lost her regular ride to the clinic.

Pre opened her mouth to say something, but quickly closed it again, unwilling to begin a fresh discussion that would only take more time away from her friend's much-needed rest.

Her guests finally gone, Rosie reached into her pocket and retrieved her childhood rosary, holding it as if it were an ancient relic. She headed straight for her bedroom and knelt on a small threadbare throw rug, facing a double portrait of Jesus and His Blessed Mother, shown in the celebrated Catholic poses of the Sacred and Immaculate Hearts.

"My Lord and my God," glassy eyes looked upward as if hoping to catch a glimpse of Heaven. "I have sinned against You this evening. I beg of You to forgive my simple, stubborn pride and pray that, as You showed Your loving Mercy upon the thief dying next to You on Calvary, I too may be able to swallow this pride and show mercy for my loved ones, maybe bringing myself to call them.

"Take care of my little grand-nephews. They do not deserve the tragedy that befell them. Thank You for giving them a strong, competent mother to see them through this time."

Rosie continued with the Joyful Mysteries of the rosary, rolling every bead between her aching fingers and enunciating calmly each prayer, stressing in particular the latter half of each of the fifty-three Hail Marys prayed. "Holy Mary, Mother of God, pray for us sinners, now, and at the hour of our death. Amen."

More than ever before, Rosie was certain of the need for Mary's blessed intercession in prayer. So many days she had spent in front of the clinic, letting decade after decade slip away as she implored Mary to be her advocate in Heaven, pleading alongside of her to God to protect the not-yet-born babies carried into the clinic.

There would be times where she would wonder how many changes of heart and mind attributed to her constant prayers occurred in the confines of the abortuary. Not once did she think of approaching any of the patients, she figured enough emotions were spent making these trips to and from the clinic - not to mention the invisible shields put up to protect them from the barbs of less couth pro-life protesters. She felt there was no need to add to their burdens. A kindly face and an extended hand could be misinterpreted, so Rosie would just stay in her seat and let the girls approach her, if they so desired.

Of all the women and teenage girls who did pause before her, eyeing curiously the inviting box of rosaries and the intense concentration of their maker, Rosie asked neither for their names or reasons for being in the area. She studied each face greeting her for a degree of remorse or melancholy, almost always berating herself silently for rushing to judgement in every case. They needed her prayers, and nothing more.

Her purpose there, she had to remind herself, was to offer herself spiritually to the Lord on their behalf to show through her own example that God would not abandon them regardless of what they did or would do. She reminded herself often that to pray without pride was most effective, far be it for her to take credit for the consequences of her prayers. That glory belonged only to God.

She launched into the Divine Mercy chaplet immediately after finishing the closing Hail, Holy Queen prayer of her rosary, skipping the introductory prayers of the Apostles' Creed, Our Father, and Hail Mary and starting instead with the meditations revealed to Saint Faustina Kowalska. Had she been in church and overheard by the parish's more meticulous members, she might have attracted a few disappointed glances. But Rosie felt a sense of urgency pushing her to complete the set, and she reasoned that the opening prayers of the chaplet were basically the same as in the rosary.

Of course, the rosary and Divine Mercy chaplet were, as a whole, prayers that required melodic repetition, but Rosie had her mind on other things, hence breaking prayer protocol. Her knees were sore at her final Sign of the Cross, and Rosie hoisted herself back to a standing position. She ached all over; it seemed as the years passed and the weather got cold, she was having a more difficult time kneeling for prayer, or bending down for any reason, for that matter.

"Thank you, Mary, for praying for me this night. Thank You, Lord, for listening."

She sat on her bed and kicked off her shoes before swinging her legs the rest of the way up. Per her nightly ritual, she removed her watch and wedding band and placed them in a heart-shaped box on her nightstand, next to her alarm clock, princess phone, and reading lamp. But before moving on to prepare for bed she tentatively lifted the phone off the hook, the droll humming tone audible from an arm's length away.

With shaking fingers, she punched three buttons and waited. Suddenly, she realized there was no pen or paper with which to record the number revealed by the static emotionless voice on the other line.

As it happened, there was no need, Rosie realized as she listened to the numbers being chanted. The last call to the house came from a cellular phone belonging to her niece, Carrie Masterson.

Twenty-One

Monica felt her heart leap against her rib cage and quiver when the phone rang. Probably Nina calling to talk mushy to CJ, she thought, looking at her watch to see that it was well after nine. Though Chris and Laura allowed their two oldest children to stay up until eleven provided that all homework was completed, they frowned upon calls past nine o'clock.

Monica sat in the kitchen at the breakfast table, an array of open library books and note papers spread before her in crooked fan patterns. Therese had retired to bed early, complaining of a headache, and Monica did not feel like watching television with CJ and her parents, opting instead to get ahead on a research paper for history class that was due the following month.

Next month. She wondered if her stomach would begin to bulge then, preventing her from being able to wear her nice slim-legged jeans or even the pleated plaid school jumper she despised. She looked at the refrigerator in the corner of the kitchen, laden with colorful magnets pinning crayon masterpieces and Chinese restaurant menus to the freezer door, and thought of the many different bizarre food combinations she would crave in the coming months. Pickles and ice cream, fried chicken with maple syrup, Oreo cookies drowning in butter pecan cake frosting...Monica could not decide which made her more nauseous - the prospect of eating that kind of food or having to make public her condition.

Footsteps thundered on the floorboards toward the kitchen. Terrific, Monica thought, it was for her. Maybe it was Jennifer or Becky, either one wanting her input on what had become known in the space of one day in the upper class circles as "The List." Therese revealed to her after dinner that the version she saw numbered more than fifty couples.

Chris's head appeared above the western-style double swinging doors. "Phone," he said blandly, his face creased with a frown. "Don't be too long now."

"Okay, Daddy."

"You doing all right in here?"

"Yeah." Monica stood and headed for the wall phone. "Just up to my elbows in Eleanor of Aquitaine."

Chris smiled. "I suppose that's better than being up to your neck in something more unpleasant. I'm going to bed. G'night." With that, Chris turned on his heel and disappeared into the hallway.

"'Night," she called after him, lifting the phone off the receiver and waiting for the click from the other phone before speaking. "Hello?"

"Hey," came a tired, deep voice. Jack.

Monica froze. Several words dissolved in her throat before she could return her boyfriend's greeting. "Hey yourself. What's up? Long time no hear." How stupid did that sound, she asked herself, when she really wanted to ask why they had not spoken in complete sentences to each other in the last couple days.

Jack laughed uneasily. "Yeah, I'm a real rat bastard for not calling the other day. It's got nothing to do with you, it's just been real crazy over here. Seems all I do is fill out college apps and write entrance essays and other samples. Waste of time if you ask me, I'll probably end up at William and Mary or ODU anyway."

"Umm." Normally a sense of encouragement would have inspired her to speak further, but now problems of selecting a college seemed so minimal to her. She could care less about entrance exams.

"Anyway, I know I'm calling late," Jack continued, "but I wanted to make it up to you with dinner tomorrow night at Café Lisieux. We can go early and then see that Shakespeare flick at the Naro."

"Sure."

Jack sounded disappointed at Monica's less than enthusiastic answer; a quick rejoinder assured him that it was just fatigue, not boredom, coloring her voice.

"Oh, okay, fine," Jack said cheerily. "Hey, what's up with The List? You seen it yet?"

Monica sighed. She thought herself too much of an optimist to think this conversation would not eventually steer toward that stupid list. "It's just a bunch of names, Jack, no big deal. The way Jennifer talks, there's a valid argument for everyone in school involved in a pregnancy."

The distant roar of the television lowered in volume. Laura was on her way upstairs while CJ flipped channels. "Uh, Jack," Monica added. "I better get going now. What time do you want to go to dinner?"

"Six okay?"

"Sounds fine."

"Great. See you tomorrow, Nic?"

"You know you will," Monica half-laughed. "Love you, bye."

"Nic, wait."

Monica felt the anxiety in her boyfriend's voice. "Yeah?"

A deep breath followed. "Jen didn't put us on that list, did she? I mean, there's no reason why she would, right?"

Monica did not answer.

"Nic?"

"No, I mean, I don't know, Jack. I'll see you tomorrow, okay?" Monica hung up quickly. A full minute passed before she released her grip on the phone.

Twenty-Two

"She's quite a lady, huh?" Larry pinched the collar of his jacket around his throat as he and Pre walked, their heads lowered into the wind, back toward the café to their cars.

"Rosie is priceless," Pre agreed, her eyes glued to the sidewalk, her breathing in time to her footsteps. "She's the highlight of every dinner shift."

"Does she really eat at the café every single night?"

Pre diverted her gaze upward and connected the stars. Cold aside, it was a beautiful, clear night. "Seven days a week without fail," she said. "Well, that's not entirely true, because she did miss Fat Tuesday, and she actually called to let us know. It was so weird, you know, like a student calling in sick to school."

Larry grinned. "Maybe she figured you and Lola would come looking for her, thinking she was being held hostage by a rebel band of phone scam artists."

Pre wrinkled her eyebrows. An urge to shove Larry into the street came and went quickly, and to do so would have meant exposing her bare hands to the cold. "Okay, I guess we deserve that, but you have to see things from our point of view. Rosie often sits protest at a health clinic where one of their doctors was recently assassinated. Nobody knows who's responsible or whether or not another murder is going to happen..."

"Hey, wait a sec," Larry interrupted, serious. "You don't think Rosie is in any danger, do you? Come on! Who's going to try and hurt a little old church lady with absolutely no motive?"

Pre shrugged. They came to the corner of the block and waited for a pickup truck to turn onto Richmond Road. "I believe that violence begets violence. There's no telling what could happen in the next four or five days in the wake of that man's death. What if some nut decides to mow down every bystander in the neighborhood in retaliation for the doctor's killing? Would you want to see that nice old lady caught in the crossfire with only her rosaries to protect her?" Pre was almost shouting now; a light illuminating in the second story window of a bed and breakfast inn prompted her to lower her voice.

"She does have a strong faith in God," Larry said wistfully. "Don't you?"

Pre bolted across the street; Larry broke into a short jog to catch her. "Wait up!" he called.

"I have faith," she said over her shoulder. "But I'm not without my issues, either."

"Such as?"

Pre laughed. "I'm not about to go into my life story freezing my butt off in Colonial Williamsburg with a guy I just met. Save your interviewing skills for the governor."

"Fair enough. How about going into your life story over dinner at Freemason Abbey in Norfolk tomorrow night?" They rounded the mall to the back lot. "I'll leave the recorder at home."

"There's my car." Pre fished inside her purse for her keys.

"That's a rather abstract answer to a request for a date," Larry said, amused.

Pre didn't look at him. "I work tomorrow night."

"Saturday, then?"

"Same," she lied.

"Sunday brunch?"

"That's our busiest shift," Pre lied. Lola closed the café on Sundays.

"You can't work forever, Pre."

"I like to work."

"So do I, but I also like to eat and breathe and enjoy other people's company." He moved closer to Pre. "Don't you?"

"I-I, uh, Lola needs me at the café. Her foot, you know."

"What happens when it heals, Pre?"

Pre became flustered and nearly dropped her keys; she could not understand why this man was making her nervous. She was not attracted to him, she knew, or was she?

She shook her head and backed away from Larry. No, no, she thought. I can't let this happen. I'm satisfied with the single vocation God willed for me ...why would this guy want to go out with me, anyway? What if the first date spawned several? I couldn't string him along like that, if he ever wanted to consider something long-term, something I can't give him.

Pre fiddled with her car keys until she found the one that unlocked the door. "I-I'm really sorry. I just can't right now..." *Or ever.*

Her door key secured between her thumb and forefinger, Pre hurried over to her car and slipped inside after a false start with the key. The motor was already running before Larry could say anything more.

"Pre! Wait a sec, for crying out loud!" Larry tapped the passenger side window. "What's the matter with you?"

Pre pretended not to hear. She slowly backed the car into the alleyway behind the restaurant and darted around the strip mall building, rolling through the stop sign and screeching out into the night toward the colonial downtown area. All Larry could do was watch her drive away and scratch his chin in bewilderment.

Twenty-Three

Sister Mary Grace O'Leary had expected an influx of phone calls from concerned parents following her class visits regarding the discovered pregnancy test package. What surprised, and for a while embarrassed, her was the fact that many of the parents she spoke to that night appeared more irritated with her than at the fact a student, possibly their own child, might either be pregnant or responsible for impregnating a girl.

The situation should have been handled more discreetly, many reasoned to the old nun, and as night wore on Sister Mary Grace realized her hasty actions could yield dire consequences. Three teachers had reported that the rumor mills were churning in the courtyards at full speed - dozens of names were being bandied about but no student had yet come forward to claim ownership of the box and its contents.

Nor did Sister Mary Grace expect anyone to say anything, as she was now certain her visits likely stifled any hopes of solving the mystery. What person was going to dare to admit she may be pregnant or he may have gotten someone pregnant if the entire student body knew about it? A pregnant female student would certainly have to withdraw from classes...could that be accomplished in a discreet manner now? Would the student in question choose to remain silent and seek a secret abortion to avoid odd stares and murmured accusations behind her back?

Sister Mary Grace may have been in her late sixties, ancient by the standards of the student body, but for all her errors and ignorance of the latest teen mentalities, she was not completely out of touch. Friends who worked at the local Catholic Charities had confided to her that some women's health clinics in the area were rather flexible in offering their services. A teenage girl in her first trimester could conjure a false name and age without providing proof, pay for the suction procedure in cash, and be back at home watching music videos on television like nothing ever happened, with her parents clueless.

The girl, if she desired, could also undergo a pelvic exam at the same clinic and obtain a long-term supply of condoms or birth control pills to ensure another abortion would not have to happen. Such was the "culture of death" as coined by Pope John Paul II: abortion, contraception, pre-marital relations. If only she had remembered all of that before she opened her big mouth, the old nun sighed to herself.

Young adults today were deadened to consequence, Sister Mary Grace knew. America was now the land of the quick fix, with responsibility giving way to convenience. Hungry for dinner but unwilling to cook? Pop a frozen dinner in the oven, high sodium content and chemicals be damned. Need to lose weight but unwilling to spend the time exercising and eating right? Pop a few pills in your mouth and watch the pounds melt. So what if all that caffeine speeds up your heart and frazzles your nerves? You'll be thin!

Too self-absorbed and busy in your career to raise the child you conceived? Abort! It's not really a child anyway...Sister cringed at such propaganda, and the mere thought that she might have inadvertently pushed somebody into taking that terrible option made her sick to her stomach. She felt so sick that she contemplated taking a day off for prayerful reparation and handing the reins over to the vice-principal, Sister Mary Charlotte.

"No, no, I can't do that," she muttered to herself after the convent's early morning Mass before a quick breakfast. The first bell for classes would chime soon. Sister Charlotte was blameless, and Sister Mary Grace knew she would only worsen matters if she disappeared into her room, leaving the school office to field more angry and upset calls. God would not turn the clock back for her and allow her the opportunity to relive the past day, so she prayed for His guidance in proper damage control.

It seemed to her that the Lord answered her almost immediately when Father Welker tapped her shoulder after Mass and offered his assistance in the matter.

Sister Mary Grace was shocked. "Has news of this already traveled around the county?" she asked, red-faced. Father Welker had not been on campus during the incident, nor had he even been in contact with the convent, as he normally did not celebrate Mass with the nuns. How could he have known?

"We have parents in the Hibernians," he answered. He explained that St. Vincent's monthly meeting of their chapter of the Ancient Order of Hibernians, an organization of Catholic preservation comprised of members of Irish descent, sparked a rather heated discussion between some concerned fathers. It boiled to a point so hot that the priest had to suggest a break in the meeting so some members could compose themselves.

"I'm not one to gossip," Father Welker continued, "but I dare say Chris Merwin in particular was quite incensed over the whole thing. It didn't help matters any when another man in the group intimated that Chris's own son might be one of the culprits."

Sister Mary Grace shook her head. "Oh, Gary. I've made a mess of things," she said on the verge of tears. "You'd think somebody like me would know better, but because of me a new life might be denied." The old nun put her hands to her face.

"Sister, please, take a seat." Father Welker eased Sister Mary Grace into a cushioned chair in the back of the small chapel used by the convent for morning Mass and Eucharistic Adoration. He produced a paper tissue from his pocket and handed it to the nun, who used it to dab her eyes. "There's no point in rehashing what was done, because it can never be changed. What we need to do now is find some aspect of the incident and turn it into a positive."

"I'm open to suggestions," Sister Mary Grace sniffled.

Father Welker took the chair next to hers. "Tell me exactly what you told each class, and I'll see what I can make of it."

Sister Mary Grace repeated almost verbatim the short, impassioned speech she delivered, noting also the reactions of students in the senior grade - one or two per class registered shock, but many more appeared tickled, like it was all one big joke.

The priest was silent for nearly half a minute after the nun finished speaking. "That doesn't sound too bad, Sister. Guessing that your demeanor did not stray into something harsh, you may have had a positive effect on the more sensitive students," he said.

"The idea here is that nobody should try to correct the situation by becoming forceful or threatening. We need to keep the best interests of the student and child - if there is a child; after all, we don't know what the test said or even if it was used - in mind."

"Like I said, I'm open to suggestions," Sister Mary Grace repeated.

"Who is celebrating Mass today for the upper grades?"

In addition to holy days, the lower school celebrated Mass every Friday morning and the upper grades in the afternoon. "Father George," answered Sister Mary Grace. Father Joseph George handled the youth ministry at St. Vincent's and was a favorite among the students, largely due to his being much younger than the other clergy in the parish.

Father Welker nodded. "I believe he has been appraised of the situation as well," he mused, standing to leave.

Sister Mary Grace folded the tissue into filmy squares and nervously pressed it into the palm of her hand. "I feel so terrible that you have to take time out of your day to help me," she said weakly. "How can I begin to repay you?"

"Pray," the priest answered bluntly. "The only thing any of us can do is pray, for the two young people, whoever they are, who thought that they were mature enough to control their lives the way they wanted."

He turned to leave again, looked down at Sister and smiled sadly. "Now there might be a third life in their hands. If so, we must pray without ceasing, as the Bible tells us."

Twenty-Four

The first call Carrie fielded in the early morning came from her sister, who was already aware of her older sister's habit of rising at five each new day to prepare for a day's work before seeing the boys off to school and Neil to work. So when her cellular phone chirped at seven-fifteen, Carrie was already fresh, as fresh as a grieving widow in the middle of a murder investigation could be.

Her children were becoming restless. They wanted their parents, Melissa Jordan told her sister, talking over the piercing cries of the newborn girl clasped to her breast. When could they go home, they asked repeatedly. Carrie's brother-in-law wanted to know as well. The stress of having to care for the baby, his wife, and two young nephews was starting to take its toll, and all Carrie could do was listen with horror as her sister revealed that Derek Jordan nearly lost it the night before and spilled the beans.

"It happened at dinner," Melissa whispered over her child. "He nearly told them, you know, about Neil. Carrie, I know it's been rough for you, and this is not the best time to bring this up, but the boys are just going bonkers here. The novelty of their stay has worn off, and I don't know how much longer I can keep them in the dark."

Carrie rubbed the bridge of her nose. "Yeah, I figured that would happen. I'm sorry for having to dump them on you like this."

"Don't apologize, Carrie. Nobody planned for this to happen."

Nobody except the killer, Carrie thought. "I'm waiting for a call from the police. I should know then when I am able to return to the house and claim Neil's body from the coroner. Then I guess I'll have to finalize the funeral arrangements. Neil's parents are flying into Norfolk this afternoon to help with other things," Carrie said with a yawn. She had only managed three hours of sleep. "His mother plans to stay on longer to help with the kids, so I should be back in Richmond around dinnertime tonight to collect them."

"Oh, Carrie, I don't know what to say..."

"Just say thank you," Carrie smiled, "and get some more rest, because you'll need it for the baby. Oh, there's one more thing I wanted to tell you."

"Yeah?"

Carrie swallowed. "I saw Aunt Barbara the other day."

Melissa let out a cry of elation. "That's great! When did you see her? How's she doing? How did she take the news about Neil?" A soft cry wafted in the background. "Oh, jeez! I need to talk to her myself, let her know about the baby. It's been a zoo around here..."

"Hey, whoa! Easy," Carrie tried to get a word in edgewise. "I only saw her on television, during the news. There was some coverage of a demonstration at Neil's clinic and the camera panned across the crowd to Barbara. She was sitting in front of some shop with her head down making those freakin' rosaries of hers." Carrie cracked her knuckles, a habit of hers whenever she became frustrated or angry. Recalling her aunt's obnoxious piety only reminded her of her own lack of it and how the old woman would look at her with disappointment, clucking and twisting her precious beads through coils of nickel wire. To think she had the nerve to bring that stuff with her when she visited!

It was a miracle that the old woman never sliced her fingers, Carrie thought, wondering suddenly how many rosaries were prayed by Aunt Barbara for her, or for Neil.

"Carrie?" Melissa inquired cautiously. "You still there?"

"Mm."

"Why don't you give her a call? Maybe she could help, too, with the kids and stuff until the initial stress dies down. Neil's mom can't stay forever, and Aunt Barbara does live nearby."

Carrie reached for the glass of water on the coffee table. "Oh, no. I couldn't do that. I'm in enough pain now that I don't need to open up any old wounds..."

"Carrie, she only disapproved of Neil's job. It doesn't mean she wished him dead," Melissa argued. "Besides, Aunt Barbara isn't the kind of person who's going to lecture you in your time of grief.

She's going to be more concerned with you and the boys and your welfare."

Carrie let her sister's words sink in, yet she still felt reluctant to make that first move toward possible reconciliation. "I don't know, Melissa. What you just said is probably true about her, but how can I really be sure? I haven't spoken to her in, what, three years? Her name was taboo in the house, and the boys might not even remember her. What if they don't feel comfortable around her?"

"You're making excuses," Melissa warned her. "The boys will be fine. I know you'll be fine with her too because the last time I spoke to Aunt Barbara, she was saying how much she missed you."

"When?"

The baby howled. Carrie heard Melissa set her down somewhere with a gentle shush. "When what?"

"When did you speak to her?"

Melissa shrugged. "A few weeks ago, I guess. She was planning to come up after I had the baby."

Carrie gasped. "I didn't even know you were still speaking to her."

Melissa was suddenly confused. "Why wouldn't I speak to her? I'm not the one she fought with. I love Aunt Barbara, don't you?"

Carrie did not answer immediately, but when she did her voice was small. "Yes, I do." She was not lying, but at that moment Carrie wondered if she hated her aunt's ideals more than she loved her aunt.

On the other side of town, meanwhile, an old woman knelt beside her bed for her morning prayers and thought the same thing with regards to her niece, whom she did miss dearly.

Twenty-Five

"Therese!"

Therese Merwin was halfway through the courtyard, walking toward her class with a small throng of friends when she turned around to see a tall, svelte, senior girl with red hair cut in a pageboy and pale, freckled skin jogging in her direction.

"Therese, wait up!" The girl waved a compact disc in the air. Morning sunlight cast a bright shock of white from the clear plastic jewel box.

"Hey, Nina," Therese called, flashing CJ's girlfriend a friendly smile. She liked Nina Simmons, and thought her a good match for her older brother - both were level headed, studious, and blessed with a light-hearted sense of humor, which easily explained the compact disc in Nina's hand. Therese never mentioned it outright, in deference to her parents' opinion that their children should wait until after college to marry, but she believed Nina would make a terrific sister-in-law.

Nina flopped over to the group of eighth graders, her smile lined with pink chapped lips. "Cold enough for you guys?" she asked nobody in particular, receiving a chorus of affirmations from everyone, many of whom shivered in dark gray cardigan sweaters and matching knee socks over blue legs.

"Therese, here's your 'Weird Al' CD back. Thanks for letting me borrow it, it was hilarious." Nina slid the music disc in the open pouch of the young girl's backpack.

"Not a problem. I got more if you want to listen to those, too."

"I'd like that, thanks." Nina nodded to the group awkwardly for a few seconds before excusing herself. "Well. Don't want to be late for Calc. Bye!"

Christina Thomas, Therese's best friend, leaned into Therese's ear and commented how nervous Nina had just appeared. Another, albeit softer, chorus of "yeahs" followed.

"Where did you pick up a thing like that?" Therese wanted to know. Nina may have come off as shy or halting in speech, but that's just how she was. What reason was there for Nina to feel nervous among a group of thirteen-year-old girls, anyway? She was ranked in the top ten of the senior class and was hence very well known.

Christina twitched her nose, thinking of how to put her next thoughts into words that would not cause an outburst from her friend. "Haven't you seen The List? CJ and Nina are, like, the first couple on it."

In the short space of three school hours yesterday, two handwritten copies of The List, aside from the original composed by Monica Merwin's friends, passed through several hands until one reached a senior male who spent his study hall hour in the afternoon aiding the school secretary. In addition to his usual duties of filing and delivering referrals to students from the dean's office, this student managed to find a few seconds to himself and made some unauthorized copies on the school's Xerox machine.

When the last bell rang, over fifty copies of The List had been distributed among the students, and some were even altered. One featured a few additional names pencilled in at the bottom margins and on the back of the page, while another was marked with crosses and checkmarks and question marks in a unique system of guessing the possibility of each listed couple being the culprits.

Christina's copy, given to her on the bus ride to school and already worn with excessive handling by a host of students, was streaked with a bright yellow highlighter pen. Next to each name was a different pair of initials. She unfolded it from her sweater pocket and held it up as Therese and everyone else in the clique gathered around her to look.

Therese scanned the names and saw that Christina was not being truthful; Chris and Nina were couple number seven, and beside their name were the initials 'BQ'.

"What's this mean?" she asked, pointing at the tiny script.

Lori Jenkins giggled between splayed fingers, which wrapped around her chin. "It's part of the baby pool, Therese. What you do is chip in five bucks and pick the couple that turns out to be the one expecting a little bundle, and the winner gets the bundle of cash!"

"I know what a baby pool is, Lori," Therese said hotly. She felt a ripple of nausea as Lori drew attention to her own initials next to a junior football player and his sophomore steady.

"By the way, 'BQ' is Barbara Quentin, you know, from Drama Club? You want in, too, Therese?" asked Lori.

"No!" Therese cried in disgust, snatching the paper and crumpling it into a ball. She wanted to rip the sheet into shreds. No, not shreds, she thought, but tiny specks to let loose in the wind like confetti; anything to erase the sight of seeing her brother's name lumped into an alleged list of...of what? Sexually active teens? Would-be parents? Proof that some people had nothing better to do than create and spread idle, and likely untrue, gossip?

"How do any of us know that the pregnancy test was positive, or even used? It might have been a practical joke, for all we know!" Therese cried. The notion of The List seemed amusing to her before, but now its reality bothered her. These people listed were made targets of cruel humor. CJ and Nina were now victims!

"What if a girl is pregnant, but not by the boy she's paired with, what then?" she demanded. "Who'd get the jackpot?"

Therese's friends stared at her as if she were about to break down. The warning bell rang above their heads, and some departed reluctantly to get to class. The prospect of seeing Therese Merwin explode into a serious hissy fit appealed to them more than going to school.

"Come on, Therese, we're just having a little fun," Christina chided. "Don't be such a stick in the mud." The loss of her copy of The List did not bother her, which surprised Therese, who was unaware that her friend kept an extra copy of the paper in her binder.

Therese stalked into her homeroom. "Easy for you to say. It's not your brother you're hoping knocked up some girl so you can make a few lousy dollars," she muttered. Whatever the turnout of The List's results, Therese knew one thing for sure: it would be a long time before she would ever speak to Barbara Quentin again.

Twenty-Six

Therese's prayer journal entry had been brief that morning, not straying once from the novena intentions offered through the Little Flower's intercession. Now, as she sat rigid in her desk as Sister Mary Regina bellowed the roll call, she wished she had known more about The List, in particular the inclusion of her brother and Nina, so she could have added more intentions to her petitions.

Quickly she removed a fresh sheet of loose leaf paper from her binder and slid it underneath her opened Spanish textbook, exposing the top half to allow for a stolen word or two to be written in between recitations of Spanish verbs.

She dated the paper in the top left hand margin and wrote slowly, her eyes darting between her work and Sister Regina, careful not to appear too engrossed as to attract the nun's attention, and a reprimand.

Dear Therese, my mind is so troubled that I do not know how I can write these words without bursting into tears. Recently a discarded container for a home pregnancy test was found on campus, spurring many arguments among the student body about its owner.

It hurts me to learn that there are friends of mine who are making light of all this, using it as an outlet to gamble and gossip.

She chewed on her pen cap and responded in kind to a group pronunciation of Spanish keywords.

What bothers me the most, dear friend, Therese continued, *is that some people, like Barbara Quentin, are willing to bet money that my brother CJ might be a father, and Nina a mother!*

She turned a page in her textbook in unison with her classmates. Sister Regina introduced a new lesson story starring textbook characters Pablo and Maria as a couple going to the movies. Their actions were explained with conjugated Spanish verbs and a new list of vocabulary words decorated with tildes and accent marks. Therese chimed in with her class in repeating each word after Sister Regina before resuming her petition.

Could there be truth to these rumors? CJ and Nina have been dating steadily for a long time, and I do not believe I have ever seen my brother so far gone over a girl like he is with Nina. It makes me wonder about a lot of things. For one, there's CJ's sudden decision to stay in Virginia for college - is Nina a factor in this decision? My parents never officially told CJ he couldn't get married after high school. Of course, he'll be eighteen then and can do what he wants. But will it happen, though? Will it happen for a reason that nobody wants to accept?

I must also add two more names to my novena intentions this week, dear Therese: CJ and Nina. I pray that this frustration I feel will turn out to be for nothing, and that Nina will not be pregnant or have reason to be so. If she is, however, what shall I pray for, Therese? Could I be so selfish to ask God to let Nina miscarry, when so many people want to adopt? How can I make a true petition if I don't really know what's going on?

Therese skimmed her letter quickly and resisted the urge to crunch it into a paper ball. She saw only a jumbled mess of words and was concerned if even Jesus could decipher it. She wished she could just cry out and scream until the doubts inside her dissolved, and all of the anguish burning in her stomach could be expelled in a gush of air.

She clutched her abdomen as a sharp pain tore through it. Was she getting her wish? Did God answer her?

She flipped the letter over when Sister Regina turned her attention to another student while going over the previous night's homework. Therese decided against rewriting the letter and tried to pray.

Lord Jesus, she began silently. *Please forgive my babbling and confusing words. I fear I may be coming off as frantic. The truth is, You know better than I do what is happening between CJ and Nina. You know who brought the pregnancy test to school and what the results were. Everything that has happened here, You know, and it is Your business. It is not mine.*

I pray through the intercession of St. Therese that a swift solution to these mounting problems will come. I pray for the girl, whether or not she is pregnant - whether or not it is Nina - that she will think of the safety of her child. If there is no child, may Your Love and guidance come to those who need to know that sex is not a game.

I never once thought it was possible that CJ would be having sex outside of marriage, and I hope the rumors are not true. He's a smart guy, Lord, and it would kill Mom and Dad if it were true.

Please give me a sign that CJ and Nina are okay, Lord. I would be so grateful for one. I don't think I could ask either of them outright for the truth. Let Your Will be done. In Jesus's name I pray. Amen.

She thought a moment, and added, *St. Therese, thank you for being my advocate in Heaven. Keep praying.*

Therese folded the paper width-wise into a long rectangle and tucked it into the back of her Spanish textbook. Sister Regina called upon her at that exact moment to provide an answer for number twelve on the homework assignment.

"Um," Therese fumbled with her binder as voices around her tittered, amused to see one of the legendary straight-A Merwins caught off guard. Another pain exploded in Therese's stomach before she could speak and she doubled over in her desk.

"Miss Merwin, are you all right?" rang the prim voice of the middle-aged nun. Stifled giggles morphed into murmurs of concern as the girl, now blanched, shook her head.

Sister Regina snatched a green clipboard with the room's number and her name written on it in black block letters - the makeshift hall pass. She handed it to a student in the front row. "Miss Ely, would you please escort Miss Merwin to the ladies' room? Do not dally, either."

Marsha Ely, a plump, toothy girl with a shock of pitch-black hair nodded and held the door open as Therese, clutching her abdomen, sped past her.

"Go straight to the nurse's office if you feel too sick to return to class," the nun called after the retreating pair. "Miss Ely, you return immediately after that." Class resumed as Sister Regina prayed a silent Gloria for Therese, guessing that womanhood for the young girl was about to painfully bloom.

"Where does it hurt?" Marsha asked Therese once they were in the stark, beige-tiled girls' restroom. Therese grimaced, the place smelled like disinfectant and stale urine; she looked up at the tiny windows near the ceiling, which were propped up to ventilate the enclosure. They were not working.

She plodded into the farthest stall, not even bothering to check to see if the toilet looked clean enough to use. She hated using public restrooms, even at school, having inherited her father's paranoid concern for catching germs and anything worse.

"It's my stomach," she told Marsha. "It feels like somebody stuck a butcher's knife in it."

Marsha winced. "You're not going to puke, are you?"

"I just need to go to the bathroom. Maybe I'll feel better," Therese said.

"I should go, too. Who knows when I'll get the chance again," Marsha said as she disappeared into a stall. The clicking of door locks reverberated throughout the room.

Seconds later, a low moan erupted from Therese's stall. Marsha bent over and peered underneath the stalls, seeing Therese's loafers tapping the tile floor. "What's the matter?"

"I got my period," Therese whined. "These pains are menstrual cramps!"

"You didn't know your time of the month was coming?" Marsha asked. Her own cycle began six months ago and she had learned to track it down to the minute to avoid accidents.

"It's my first one."

"Oh."

"What do I do? Should I just line my underwear with TP?" The girls' restroom did not have a hygiene product dispenser. Therese made a mental note to bring that up at the next student council meeting.

"That never works, I tried it once so I know. Hold on a sec." Therese heard a flush and a loud click, then a retreating footfall as Marsha, hall pass in hand, exited.

"Stay there!" she shouted. "I'll go see if the secretary has pads."

Therese, sitting on the toilet with the elastic waistband of her shorts cutting into her calves, asked aloud, "Where am I going to go?" to the ceiling, receiving her echo as a reply. Her cramps had yet to subside as well. She sighed, her mother had warned her to be watchful for this, as her period could have started any day. Laura even bought extra supplies but Therese never thought once of slipping a pad into her backpack for such an emergency.

There was a Bible verse, Therese recalled, that illustrated somewhat the menstrual cycle. It was in Deuteronomy, though she could not recite it exactly - something about how when a woman was not "purified" she had to do all sorts of stuff, like hide away until it was over.

So now she was a woman, Therese mused. It was not the most glamorous rite of passage, she decided, but having it happen in the midst of the school's pregnancy test mystery gave her an odd feeling. She was a woman, but would she also be an aunt very soon, too?

"Ugh!" Therese squeezed her eyes shut, enduring another cramp. Where was Marsha so she could get out of the stall? She squinted into the sunlight streaming through the tiny windows and wondered if Mary experienced the same kinds of pain and cramps during her monthlies. She was a human, no different from anyone else save for being conceived without original sin and giving birth to Christ, yet Therese still would have liked to known for certain if perhaps God decided to spare Mary this one aspect of womanhood.

It hurts so much, God, she prayed. *Mary, if you can sympathize, pray for me to get through this.*

The bathroom door finally squealed open. "Marsha?" Therese called.

"Um, no," came a static reply.

Therese bent down to see a pair of feet moving toward her. She recognized the scuffed saddle shoes. "Nic?"

Silence. Then, "Therese?"

"Yeah, whatcha doing?"

"What's it look like?" Monica stepped into the adjoining stall to do her business. She had to urinate frequently these days, another wonderful aspect of pregnancy.

"I got my period just now," Therese said.

"Wow. I don't know whether to congratulate or pity you."

Therese laughed. "Do you have a pad on you? I don't think Marsha's coming back. She's got the hall pass, so for all I know she went to the Trellis for a late breakfast."

"Sorry, squirt. It's not my week. I don't have any."

Therese frowned. "Yes it is. You were complaining of cramps a few days ago."

Monica froze. *Oh, God*. Did she just slip? "When did I say that?"

"In our room, the other day." Therese's voice echoed in Monica's ears. "Don't you remember? I thought you were sick."

Monica felt ready to hyperventilate. She was thankful Therese could not see her face, or she certainly would have aroused suspicion. Think of a lie, she thought. What's another lie in a life of lies?

"Oh, that was the last day of it. Flowing stopped the next morning."

"Oh...okay," Therese said, faltering and sounding disappointed. Monica hoped she was not thinking too much about it.

Monica finished her business, flushed, and left the stall. "How are you feeling?" she asked. Best to keep the conversation directed toward Therese, she decided, as she tried to think of another topic to discuss.

"Awful. I can't believe I'm going to have to go through this every month for the rest of my life."

"Not really," Monica said over the flow of the faucet as she washed her hands. "Only until menopause, which comes much later. Of course, when you're pregnant you don't get periods, either."

Pregnant. Dang it, thought Monica. Why didn't I just stop at menopause?

"Great," Therese moaned. "Hey, look out the door and see if there's a short girl with black hair coming this way."

Monica pretended to look outside. "Is she wearing a plaid jumper?"

"Well, duh!"

Eventually Marsha did make an entrance with the needed bounty. "I gotta go, Therese," Monica called through the closed stall door.

"Okay, Nic. See you at Mass."

Finally finished, Therese quickly cleaned up and hurried with Marsha back to class. Judging from the varied looks of boredom on her classmates' faces, Therese figured she had missed little.

The rest of the morning progressed smoothly, with Therese thinking about her sister and hoping that the saint for whom she was named was making progress in delivering her petition to God.

Dear God, I hope Monica's feeling better, she added. *She sounded so odd just now, like something was bothering her.*

The bell rang, and slowly students filtered out of their classrooms to go to their next classes. Therese followed suit, not giving Monica another thought until after lunch.

Twenty-Seven

The second call to Carrie Masterson came from Detective Mark Skinner, but not before a brief debate with Neil's family.

Per Carrie's request, her late husband's body had been released to the funeral home of her choice to be prepared for a brief service, followed by cremation. To prevent another media circus and a possibly violent demonstration, Carrie opted for an exclusively private service, limited to Neil's immediate family, on funeral home grounds.

Simple as the plan sounded, Carrie found herself suffering more anxiety over handling Neil's body than she did about worrying about the search for his killer. Neil's parents, Sarah and Jim Masterson, were both devout Catholics, and they blanched when Carrie explained the cremation process.

Jim, visibly upset at the thought of his son's body burned like kindling, left for the solitude of the hotel suite he and Sarah rented, leaving Carrie at the mercy of her mother-in-law. Sarah had less restraint and came out swinging, pointing out that cremation violated the precepts of the Church. Why, by the way, was Neil not going to receive a proper Catholic funeral Mass, she wanted to know as well. Sarah had good mind to bolster her claims with the catechism, but she did not bring hers and she knew very well that Carrie did not have a copy handy, either.

"Do you honestly believe for a moment that a Catholic priest is going to preside over a funeral Mass for a doctor who performed abortions?" was Carrie's tart reply. Sarah had no answer for her, but asserted that theirs was a church that preached forgiveness, founded by the Son of God, a God of eternal mercy. God would show mercy for Neil, she believed.

"I don't think it would be a problem. My friend Myrna's grandson committed suicide last year, and our church held Mass for him." Sarah paced Carrie's hotel room.

"Whatever," Carrie added, "but the Catholic Church does allow for cremation in special cases. I checked, believe it or not."

Unwilling to create further tension, Sarah Masterson, speaking for her and her husband, conceded to the plans as made by their son's widow, but the pending burial continued to unnerve her. "If it's a matter of money, Carrie, Jim and I would be more than willing to cover the cost of a plot or crypt," Sarah Masterson pleaded. "At least think of your sons. They're going to want a grave to visit in the years to come, something concrete to memorialize their father." Sarah wiped her eyes; the prospect of witnessing the cremation greatly disturbed her, as did Carrie's intention to dump the remains in the James River. She imagined her grandchildren might be traumatized as well.

"More traumatized than having to watch their father sealed inside a giant steel coffin and lowered into the ground, forever?" Carrie countered. "Sarah, I am thinking of my boys, that's why I'm doing this. I believe that in the long run it will be less of a hassle for them."

"How much of a hassle?" Sarah was confused. "We'll buy a plot outright in a perpetual care facility, one for you too if you like. The boys will only need to visit and pray."

"And what if I bring them one day to visit and Neil's grave is desecrated by some rabid pro-life activist, or, worse yet, dug up and his body stolen?"

Sarah's eyes widened in horror. "Who would do a thing like that? Really, Carrie, don't you think you're letting your imagination run away with you? What more harm could anyone do to a dead man?"

Carrie sprang from the hotel sofa and padded to the miniscule kitchenette area for some water. "You would be surprised to learn how far people will go to drive a point home. Some whack nut might decide to scare other doctors into rethinking their careers."

She turned to face her mother-in-law, whose face burned deep red.

"Not everyone who disagrees with your position on abortion is a 'whack nut,' Carrie," she said coldly.

"Sarah, you know I didn't mean it like that."

"You're wrong," Sarah said plainly. She was not having any more of her daughter-in-law's grief, even if Neil was not yet fresh in his watery grave. "I don't know what you believe anymore, because suddenly you are not the same person who married my son. The Carrie Watters I knew wasn't this paranoid. Sweetheart, it worries me."

Carrie whipped a tissue from a nearby box and blew her nose. "My husband, your son, is dead," she stated. "Killed by someone who likely subscribes to radical pro-life beliefs. Pro-life! How can you say I'm the one who's mixed up?"

Sarah sighed. "All I'm saying is don't judge an entire group of people because of a crime committed by one person. Would you brand all twelve Apostles as evil men based on the actions on Judas Iscariot?"

"No. Then again, I haven't given much thought to anything biblical."

Sarah stood. "Well, maybe it's time you thought of releasing some of your burdens to God. He's only too happy to help you."

Is He? Carrie wanted to ask. Where was God when Neil was lying on his back bleeding underneath his assassin? "Sarah, Jim probably needs you, and I should be fresh when the police call..."

Sarah understood and left quietly, leaving Carrie more upset and grateful for the day when her in-laws would return home.

Detective Skinner whistled after hearing Carrie's abbreviated narration of her clash with Sarah Masterson. "You going to be okay with them around?"

"Don't worry about me. I'll get through this fine," Carrie answered, exhausted. "I'd feel even better if I knew you caught the person who started this whole chain of events."

"So would I," Mark said soberly. "Not a print to be had from the scene, none that matched anything in our database, anyway. All of the others that were adult-sized were identified as either yours or your husband's."

Carrie looked down at her fingertips; she volunteered to be printed for the search. It must have taken at least an hour to wash away the ink.

"A tour of your neighbors' homes yielded zilch as well. Apparently you live on a street filled with sound sleepers."

The news came as no shock to Carrie, and she nodded politely. As long as they had lived in their home, she and Neil just never seemed to get around to meeting their neighbors. There were no children on the street to socialize with the Masterson boys, and Carrie often wondered if perhaps Neil's line of work prevented her from opening her door.

No, Carrie shook her head, looking away from the phone, imagining that Mark Skinner could see her through the receiver. I wasn't that ashamed, not to the point of alienating myself.

"We've had a few phone tips," Mark added quietly, thinking at first that he should not have said anything for fear of raising Carrie's hopes. "All dead ends, though. I'm sorry. Then there's the occasional call from somebody claiming responsibility..."

"None of those panned out?" Carrie interrupted.

Mark was glad Carrie could not see his grim countenance. "No, we've traced all of them. They're frequent callers; these clowns have claimed to be behind everything from the Olympic bombing to the Nicole Simpson and JonBenet Ramsey murders, among other things."

"It doesn't make sense," Carrie mused. She had read of other accounts where such an attack, like Neil's murder, was immediately followed by a bold declaration from some reactionary group or individual, perhaps a follower of a fringe activist organization who wrote missives using letters cut out of magazines. Why had nobody come forward to boast this time?

"Could be completely unrelated to groups like that," was the only explanation Mark could offer. "At any rate, the governor's been quoted in the paper this morning as saying how adamant he is about seeking a conviction for this creep. He's thinking death penalty."

Carrie recalled the article, still folded facing up on the coffee table, and had to admit that she had not thought that far ahead of the game. Naturally she wanted to see the killer brought to justice, but given how long it took to bring a criminal to trial, not to mention the years spent fighting appeals to stop an execution if that were indeed the verdict, she wondered if it was worth all the trouble.

Heaven forbid there should be any concern for the welfare of Neil's children amid all the drama of a trial, Carrie thought. That was, she knew, if a trial happened. Two days had passed, and Neil's killer could be in Europe or hiding in the Carolina mountains like that guy who was suspected of bombing an Alabama abortion clinic. Eric Rudolph, Carrie remembered, snapping her fingers. That was his name. "Could he have been behind this?" she asked.

"We considered it," Mark told her, "but the MOs don't match. It was never proven that Rudolph singled anyone out in particular."

"I better make this short," Carrie said. "My cellular phone is ringing. You'll call the second you have new information?"

"Of course," Mark said. He wished Carrie well and rang off just as Carrie answered her other phone.

"Carrie Masterson." Her voice was staid and lukewarm. She hoped it was not another reporter. She did not even know how the ones who had called before got her number.

"Hello, Carrie." The voice on the other line crackled and faltered. "It's Aunt Barbara."

Carrie caught her breath. "Hi."

"I-I guess I'm returning your call," Rosie began. "I have Call Return on my phone service and checked the number."

"I see." Carrie's palm sweat as she gripped the phone. Why did she not use the hotel's phone when she called her aunt, Carrie thought. That number would have been harder to trace, and Carrie was not yet ready today to begin a dialogue with her estranged aunt. Sarah had been plenty for one day.

"I wanted to say how sorry I was about Neil," the old woman said quietly. "He did not deserve to die like that, shot like an animal. So barbaric."

"Thank you, Barbara. I appreciate the call." Carrie cringed at the comparison.

"Is there anything you need? I can help watch Neil Junior and Jacob while you tie up some loose ends."

Carrie checked her watch. "No need, thanks for asking. Jim and Sarah just checked in, and the boys are still with Mel in Richmond. I'm leaving to go there in a few minutes, actually, to pick them up. They, uh, still haven't been told."

"Ah." Rosie found that odd, then figured that her nieces and nephew-in-law must have gone to great pains to shield the boys from the outside world. All the better to cushion the shock, she guessed. "Well, I guess that answers my question of whether or not you'd like to meet for lunch."

Carrie sighed. Her aunt was extending an olive branch, and she was flying right past it to do a million different other things. She thought about her earlier chat with Melissa. She misses you, her sister had said.

"I'm sorry, Barbara," Carrie said. "I'd suggest dinner, but I'm going back to the house tonight and it's going to be crazy with Neil's parents and having to deal with the boys."

Carrie hated to hear the sigh of disappointment exhaled through the receiver. "Unless," she hastily added, "you would like to join us there. I probably won't cook. I don't think anybody will be in the mood to eat, anyway. I realize that I'm going to need all the help I can get when I tell Neil and Jacob, and they love you like a grandmother." She bit her lip at that; the boys had not seen their great aunt in three years and it would be a miracle if they remembered her.

Rosie smiled, her heart fluttering. She knocked, the door opened, and a hand stretched to greet her. "Of course I'll be there to help. I'll see you tonight."

Twenty-Eight

Roy Jeffries preferred to begin work early in the morning, as the rest of the city was busy shuttling from home to the coffee shop to work. Walk-in business came into the store in short trickles during this time, and Roy generally left people to browse freely through the stacks of furniture. Many people who walked in his store that early were usually jobless folks killing time before an interview or bored housewives not ready to return home after dropping their children off at school.

Occasionally Roy would saunter down the rows with them, appearing as one of them. People like that rarely, if ever, bought anything from him, as his prices tended to be steep. Such was the market for antique cherry bedroom sets and heavy oak buffet tables, and Roy was certainly not going to waste his time on somebody who could not pay.

Direct orders with local and state businesses made up most of the business at Jeffries Furniture. Restaurant owners adhering to ragtime era themes were especially loyal customers. Leave it to Roy to supply the perfect antique bar fixture to accentuate all the eatery walls decorated with junk found deep in some grandfather's shed and yellowed posters of films long forgotten. It amused Roy, yet somewhat saddened him, to think that a polished maple bar counter once used in an eighteenth-century aristocrat's home could now become nothing more than a catch-all for local flyers, coupons, and wallet-sized basketball schedules from Hampton University.

Then the check would arrive, and any guilt eating away at Roy's stomach would quickly subside. Such restaurants were apt to either branch into franchised establishments and hence require more fixtures or recommend Roy's services to other businesses.

Since Norfolk was a city rich in history, finding the objects was simple. Estate sales were always ripe for the picking as Roy purchased items from people only too willing to unload Grandma's treasured three-hundred-pound dresser, unaware of its true value. Whenever possible, Roy would tip off other area dealers to suddenly available antiques, thereby cementing a network of people dependent on each other for the best deals.

While absent-mindedly polishing a dusty china cabinet with his sleeve, Roy spied a fortyish woman sporting a thick foot bandage underneath a worn sneaker hobbling towards him. Her gaze was directed elsewhere, examining a stack of old framed stained-glass windows that Roy had acquired from a recent demolition in the Ghent district. Her arms were folded as she scanned the mountain of furniture crammed in the storefront as if she were looking for something in particular.

What the heck, Roy thought. At the very least, maybe she would take home one of the frames. They were priced at sixty bucks each, a steal compared to other shops.

"Can I help you with something?" he called to the woman. His hands and clothes reeked of turpentine and suddenly he felt self-conscious about approaching his customer.

Lola Marquez, dressed plainly in a button-down blouse and navy slacks, looked up and hobbled closer to Roy. "Are you Larry's brother? I met him last night at my restaurant, and he mentioned that I might find something here."

"Uh, yeah. I'm Roy." The referral from Larry surprised him; his brother usually did not advertise the store. "I might as well write ad copy," Larry would say with a sour face, having suffered through a marketing course in school.

He wiped his hands on a rag he kept stuffed in his back pocket before extending one to Lola. "You'll have to pardon my appearance. I was in the back stripping and refinishing a piece earlier, and I smell like a gas station."

Lola laughed and gladly took Roy's hand in a hearty shake. "That's quite all right, Mr. Jeffries. I can sympathize. Not a day goes by when I don't come home smelling of the catch of the day."

"That kind of stink I could tolerate more than what's in my workshop," Roy said. He disliked small talk, preferring to just get down to business. This woman, however, did not appear to be in a hurry, and maybe she was in the mood to spend.

Lola introduced herself and explained her need for a specific style of dining table - perfectly square with thick, sturdy legs and drop leaves that pulled out from under the tabletop. "Our café is quite busy, especially during the summer tourist season, and I believe with some creative placement I can fit a few more tables in the dining room without violating the fire code."

Roy rubbed his chin. "I think I have what you're looking for." He twisted his torso and pointed behind them to a staircase partially concealed by a large wooden door off its frame. "I keep a lot of stuff on the second floor, including old kitchen tables. I've got Formica and wooden tops, and some matching your description, too. You're welcome to take a look."

Ignoring the dull feeling in her bad foot, Lola slowly made her way to the staircase and disappeared from sight as she ascended. Roy could hear her, however, with every squeaking step. "Careful where you step," he called up after her, remembering her swollen foot. The stairs were old and warped, and certainly no longer meant to withstand heavy footfalls.

"Don't worry," Lola called back, her eyes upward the entire time. The dim light provided by the overhead chandelier lent an eerie feeling to the short trip and Lola involuntarily shivered. She feared with each step that one of the wooden planks would give way, plunging her down into a dark, filthy abyss within the recesses of Roy's store.

Lord Jesus, I know this might sound silly, Lola prayed, *but please protect me from this aging building. I'm afraid the second floor will turn out to be as uninhabitable as the first.*

Lola was right. While the second floor did not house as much heavy furniture, it appeared to have the most dust. Lola could see particles dancing in the light of the wide windows lining the far wall like a myriad of tiny sprites. The floorboard creaked also with every step, announcing her presence upstairs to everyone perusing the furniture on the ground floor.

Hurriedly she found two tables that met her criteria and made a mental note of their exact locations before making a slow descent downstairs. Roy's office was situated about ten feet from the corner stairwell, cordoned off from the rest of the store by two glass-paneled walls concealed with closed blinds. Unable to see Roy wandering the store, Lola wobbled straight to his office.

"Hello?" Lola tapped the glass window of the door lightly, causing it to open a few inches wider and offer a grand view of the back of Roy's head as he stared intently at his computer.

He swiveled around in his chair to face her. "Found something?" he grinned, already hearing the jingle of the cash register.

"Y-yes. The two twin tables in right-hand corner, next to the yellow metal stove caddy." Roy nodded in agreement; he knew the tables. "I think they may need some touching up," Lola added.

"Okay," Roy said, leaping up and brushing past Lola. "I know which tables they are, so that'll save the trouble of you going back upstairs. Wait here, and I'll be right back with an estimate."

"Thank you."

Lola turned back to the office when Roy left and noticed that the man's office bore similar qualities to the rest of the store - it too was coated in dust, overstuffed, and ancient, except for the computer equipment.

Stacks of paper invoices leaned against each other on one desk by the right-hand corner. The desk next to it held Roy's Macintosh and a litter of inked Post-it Notes which stuck to the monitor, motherboard and even the back of Roy's chair. Lola giggled at the sight of it. It was a rather archaic and disheveled message system, and she guessed that if just one of those neon pink squares were plucked from its place and moved somewhere else, Roy would be completely lost.

She and her husband ran the café using a similar method for the first year until Mother Marquez suggested taking a night course in time management and organization. Lola wondered if Roy would be offended if she recommended the class to him. He seemed like a nice guy, like his brother.

She glared at Roy's computer screen; a World Wide Web browser was opened to a website displaying bold white text against a camouflage background. Hardly an appropriate design for an antique dealer's Web site, Lola thought, unless Roy was just goofing off in cyberspace. She could relate to that, having caught her son several times browsing sites unrelated to his studies on their home computer while he claimed to be doing "research."

Tempted as she was to decipher the words on the screen - Lola had left her reading glasses in the car - she remained frozen instead in her spot. Roy could return any second, she knew, and she was certain her idle curiosity could spiral into a sin. Spying was wrong, and despite her best intentions, Lola gave in to her curious nature and leaned forward, straining her vision to see the headline "BOMB-MAKING MADE SIMPLE" lining the top of the screen.

Under the headline ran a paragraph written in print too small for Lola to see from the six-foot distance. She noticed that it ran the length of the screen.

Oh, my. She hoped she was reading the screen wrong.

Heavy footfalls thundering down the stairs signaled Roy's approach, and Lola rubbed her eyes, her head aching. She looked again at the screen, but the site had disappeared, replaced by the image of a flying toaster from the computer's screen saver.

"Well, now," Roy said, wiping the dust from his hands. "I can give you those two for one eighty-five each, and, because you're a friend of Larry's," he winked, "I'll throw in the finishing at no extra cost. Delivery is extra, though, unless you want to pick them up yourself." He looked down at Lola's foot and hoped at least for the extra charge.

"Thank you, how very generous," Lola's smile was genuine. "I can get a truck here when it's time to collect. No problem."

"How's Wednesday morning sound?" Roy eased into his office and beckoned Lola further inside.

Roy took his seat and produced a blank invoice from his desk drawer. Lola stared over his shoulder, trying to think of a way to nudge the computer mouse and bring back the website.

"Eh?" Roy said, looking up from a handful of carbon papers.

"Oh." Lola snapped her attention back to Larry. "Wednesday is fine."

"Great." Roy was still disappointed at the loss of the delivery charge, but a sale was a sale. He found a clipboard and attached the invoice to it, handing it and a pen to Lola. "I take Visa and Mastercard," he said as she filled out the necessary boxes. "Cash, of course, is always welcome," he added with a wide smile.

"How about a check?"

Roy nodded slowly. "Two forms of ID. I suppose it'll do. I don't expect you'll be trying to escape on that foot."

"No," Lola tried to chuckle but her voice sounded too nervous. Her mind was still on the computer. "Not for a while."

Twenty-Nine

Therese was given permission to call home during her lunch break for emergency supplies, and Laura, quickly packing Judith and Joshua into the van for the unscheduled trip, arrived at school just as Therese was finishing her sandwich. Mother found daughter in the courtyard, bundled in a coat and scarf. Why the girls did not just eat in the cafeteria and stay warm with the younger students baffled Laura, but she knew from her older children that only the upper-class students had access to the courtyard, hence it was the place to be seen…even in the cold.

Laura knelt beside her daughter, who sat at one of the round stone tables with a few classmates, and handed her two nondescript paper bags.

"Nic left her lunch, I noticed as I was leaving," Laura said. "I know it's hers because CJ doesn't like those fruit-filled granola bars she's always eating." She leaned in closer to Therese. "You need any help with the, ah, other thing?"

"Mom!" Therese was mortified. Her friends, all of whom had already experienced first menses and the ensuing motherly fawning, looked on with varying expressions of sympathy and amusement.

Laura smiled. "Oh, sorry." A bit louder, she added, "Don't want to embarrass you in front of the whole school." A smattering of giggles erupted around the table.

"See that Nic gets that, please?"

Therese said she would. Monica's lunch period began right when hers ended.

"Good. See you later." Laura started back to the courtyard entrance toward the parking lot. "And don't get those bags mixed up!" she added, calling over her shoulder.

Thirty

Jack Nixon slept fitfully the night before; his exhausted appearance corresponded perfectly with his mood. In a word, he looked terrible. His brown mop of hair clung to his skull as if he patted it flat with baby oil, and his wrinkled shirt was not tucked in the front or the back. His socks, though both dark in color, did not match, an observation that become more apparent whenever he attempted to cross one leg over his knee.

Miguel Marquez immediately knew something was wrong the second Jack slumped into the desk next to him for math class. Jack always kept a tidy appearance, even in the worst weather. Jack would never walk into any room looking this disheveled, Miguel thought, but he kept quiet. Sister Bernadette watched over the seniors like a hawk. Even an involuntary whisper from the back of the classroom could be detected and greeted with a stern glare.

Both boys, after completing their math exam a good ten minutes before their next class, were asked by the middle-aged nun to courier a stack of ten extra textbooks to the media center, or, as Miguel often joked, "The Media Center Formerly Known as the Library." Each young man hoisted five thick tomes, carrying them just below their torsos with the top of each stack just below eye level, out the door into the courtyard.

Neither one being in a hurry to return to class, Jack and Miguel took small, leisurely steps.

"Say, Jack?" Miguel prodded.

"Yo."

"You know," Miguel began, faltering. Tender heart-to-heart talks were not his forte. "If there's something bothering you, you know, just spit it out. It might help you feel better."

"What makes you think something's wrong?"

"Dude, you look like crud. You're usually so *GQ* when it comes to clothes, even in the uniform." Miguel personally did not take to the school's dress code. The shirts itched like crazy.

Jack laughed uneasily; to Miguel it sounded more like a scoff. "It's that obvious, isn't it?"

"Your parents still on the outs?" Over the past year, the Nixons' marriage was slowly deteriorating. Nearly every conversation between the couple ended with at least one of Jack's parents slamming a bedroom door or storming out to the backyard to regain composure. Jack dreaded having to come home from school, unsure of what night would bring.

"Yeah, but that's not what's bothering me now. Funny, it seems that's more like the least of my problems."

"Well, it can't be Nic, 'cause you two are going out tonight."

Jack sighed, casting his vision to the cracked spine of the textbook on top of his stack.

"You are going out with her, aren't you?"

"Yeah, but..." Jack skidded to a halt. Doors along the hallway opened, and second period lunch students were flooding the hallways around them. Jack and Miguel nodded to respective acquaintances as they passed; Jack did not speak up again until he spotted the familiar duo of Jennifer and Becky approaching. Monica was nowhere to be seen.

"Hey." Jack nudged Becky with his elbow as she walked past him toward the courtyard soda machine. She turned in surprise, remarking that she did not recognize him for the books.

"Hey, Miguel," she breathed, waggling her fingers in a dainty salutation to the other boy. Miguel grunted an awkward hello.

"Where's Nic?" Jack wanted to know. "She usually eats with you guys, doesn't she?"

Becky looked over to a faraway concrete table, where Jennifer and two other junior girls were setting up their meals. "Oh, Nic forgot her lunch today, so we each lent her a dollar to get something from the cafeteria. Knowing her, she'll probably get a Little Debbie snack and a Dr. Pepper." Becky rolled her eyes; suddenly the tuna sandwich sitting at the bottom of her lunch bag did not appear as appetizing.

As if on cue, Monica emerged from around the far-left corner across the courtyard, where the school cafeteria was situated, holding a plastic container and a paper cup. Becky waved grandly, trying to catch her eye, but Monica continued on to Jennifer's table, not looking upward.

"Nic! Over here!" Becky yelled, and Jack suddenly lowered his head behind the textbooks, which to him felt heavier; he planted his feet farther apart to support the load.

Monica looked up and quietly beckoned her friend over to the table, not seeing her boyfriend; that is, until Miguel made a sudden beeline to the library.

"Jack, we're gonna be late if we don't unload these and get back to class," Miguel said, a few steps ahead of his friend.

Jack watched as Monica waved back at Becky then turned back to her lunch, leaning over to speak to Jennifer, her eyes still gazing upward toward them.

"Yeah, you're right," Jack agreed out of Miguel's earshot. He asked Becky to relay a message to Monica before setting off behind Miguel. "Later!"

Becky found her lunch clique well into their meals. She eyed Monica's choice of lunch with mild suspicion. "Salad? Ugh. Since when do you start eating rabbit food?"

Monica shrugged. "Just thought I better start watching my figure. I read in *Cosmo* that the average college freshman puts on fifteen pounds in the first year." She looked uneasily at the small bowl of greens before her, ripping open a packet of dressing.

"Oh, Nic," Becky waved a hand. "That's two years from now. Live a little."

"Yeah, and like that bleu cheese dressing isn't going to cross out all the nutritional value you're supposed to get from lettuce," said Jennifer wistfully. "And what's up with Jack? He didn't even say hello to you. Just whimpered off with Miguel."

"He's going to drop off some books and come right back," Becky said in his defense. To Monica she added, "All the same, he's been acting weird today."

"So have you," Jennifer broke in. "Are you two splitting up?"

Monica shoveled a large bite of drenched salad into her mouth, allowing for a few seconds to think of a good answer. Technically, they were still together, but Monica knew that the status quo could change very soon, if Jack already had decided to call it quits.

He had to know by now, she thought. Her abrupt goodbye after last night's call betrayed her, and she spotted his scraggly figure loping into homeroom earlier that morning. Jack was liable to freak out if they ended up alone together ...

What was she saying, of course Jack would freak out! He was months away from graduation, looking forward to a college career on a wrestling scholarship, not to mention being free from the tension between his quarreling parents. Did he see himself as suddenly becoming like them, Monica wondered, with her?

Did he hate her now, or was he afraid of her, afraid that the growing bud in her belly could at any second burst forth and clasp a slimy grip on Jack, chaining them together for life? She nibbled on a carrot disc as her friends conversed about other things, her eyes on the hallway where Jack and Miguel were soon to appear.

When the young men finally did so, Monica quietly excused herself from the table and joined them. Miguel, rehashing the excuse that they would receive nothing but grief for missing the first part of catechism study, bolted ahead.

"I'll walk with you," Monica offered. Jack plunged his hand in his pockets; Monica took the gesture as a sign that he did not want her around.

"So, when were you planning to tell me?" Jack demanded when he believed they were alone. "Like, maybe sometime after the kid enters preschool?"

Monica huffed. "Give me a break, okay? You think this has been easy for me? At least you're not the one who's gonna bloat like a parade balloon."

"So it is true." Jack felt his heart plummet to his stomach; a mixture of fear and horror bubbled in his throat and he felt suddenly ill. He was going to be a father...Monica was pregnant...sweet Monica, who trusted him wholly and implicitly, who believed him when he said nothing could happen the first time, especially if they did it a certain way. He had believed it, too. How many of his friends also making love like playing the roulette wheel assured him of that?

He berated himself silently. I am such a moron, he thought, Lord, you would think I would know better, with all the talk of AIDS and disease. He did not think of that, however - nothing of that sort applied to either of them, so he believed. He and Monica were virgins, expressing their mutual love as adults truly should.

An eternity of silence passed between the couple until Jack cleared his throat to speak. He felt as if his voice box were about to fall from his mouth. "What are you going to do?"

"Don't you mean we?" Monica glared at him.

"Huh? Uh, yeah, right," Jack stammered, wringing his hands. "Sorry. Does anyone else know?"

Monica shook her head. "I can't tell anyone around here. It'll be all over the school by the end of the day. And what with that freakin' list going around..."

"Yeah, but our names weren't on it. Were they?" So many copies were floating around campus now.

"That doesn't mean anything," Monica replied hotly. "That list is nothing more than idle speculation of people who just can't grasp the situation we're in."

Monica started to cry, and Jack drew her into an embrace. "In a way, I'm relieved," she told him. "I've wanted to tell someone, but I couldn't bring myself to say anything. It's not exactly what my parents expected of me."

"So, what are we going to do?" Jack asked again, this time more softly.

Monica blinked as Jack stroked her cheek. "I don't know. What, we're gonna get married and keep it?" She tried to laugh, but nothing would come. "This was just such a mistake, we can't handle a baby. We can barely handle ourselves, much less each other. And you need to go to college."

"So do you," Jack said. "Have you thought about adoption?"

"Yeah, but that would mean having to tell everyone." Monica eased away from her boyfriend's touch. "Face it, I can't hide a pregnancy with bulky sweaters either. I can already feel thousands of eyes staring at me in curiosity and shock, like I'm some kind of freak."

"Hey," Jack countered, spotting a group watching them from the courtyard. Instinctively, he lowered his voice. "You're not a freak, and you're not the first teenager to get pregnant either. We'll get through this."

"It just wasn't supposed to happen to me, though," she whined. "Other girls get pregnant...it only happens on the news, or in other cities, far away from me." She lowered her head, realizing she was now a statistic she had often seen in newspaper articles, the kind of girl her parents would speak of in disdainful tones. "We are so blessed to have stability in this flock," Chris Merwin would often say to his wife.

Right, thought Monica. Now his blessed child was expecting a blessed event.

"Look, you better get to class," Monica said, wiping her eyes. "We'll talk tonight at dinner."

Dinner. The money spent at dinner might be better saved for the future, Jack thought, but for what?

Jack pecked Monica on the lips, an act considered taboo on campus, and disappeared around the corner toward Sister Bernadette's room to retrieve his books. Monica hurried back to her table, passing off her conversation with Jack as intimate small talk while choking down the remainder of her wilting salad.

As Jack rounded the corner he kicked a discarded paper bag containing a neatly packed lunch sitting near the door of the ladies' room. Somebody must have dropped it, he figured, or maybe brought it to school to humor his or her parents before deciding to trash it in favor of a slice of pizza from the cafeteria.

Seeing nobody to claim the bag, Jack picked it up and carried it with him to class, unwilling to waste a perfectly good lunch. He was unaware that the girl who dropped it was crouched in a stall of the ladies' room, doubled over with menstrual cramps and the shock of discovering through an accidental eavesdrop that she truly was about to become an aunt, but not by the sibling she suspected.

Thirty-One

"Another first," Pre murmured to herself, smiling and waving to Rosie, whose thick-haired head, framed by ear muffs, filled the small window of Café Lisieux's front entrance. Pre quickly set a clean coffee mug next to her own before unlocking the door for her friend.

"Come inside for some tea," she offered the old woman. "I just came early to catch up on some receipts, and I don't have anywhere to be until we open."

"Thank you, a cup of tea would be just fine." Rosie removed her muffs, coat and gloves. She was dressed in a bold violet pantsuit; Pre guessed that had not changed after Mass. "I'm so sorry to keep you from your work. Usually when I pass by here I can see Lola through the windows, flitting around like the busiest butterfly."

Pre laughed, filling Rosie's mug with hot water. "She's quite the perfectionist, I'll give you that. Picky, too. I couldn't tell you how many times I've come here to find her checking each shaker to see if they have equal amounts of salt and pepper in them." She brought forth a mahogany tea chest and displayed an array of tea bags to Rosie, who selected a packet of chamomile.

"Where is Lola, by the way?"

Pre mentioned Lola's trip to Norfolk in search of extra tables. "She only stopped by here long enough to let us inside. I think she said something about trying that store owned by Larry Jeffries's brother. She had his card with her when she took off. I wish she had at least let me come with her, I can't believe she's driving all over Hampton Roads on that foot."

Rosie batted two white packets so the sugar inside would clump at one end before she tore them open. "Oh?" she commented. She knew better than to say anything more; when Lola got an idea she did not let anyone change her mind. "I hope she can get a good deal. I've heard those antique stores in Ghent can be expensive."

"Not as expensive as the ones in Yorktown," Pre pointed out. "Once I saw an end table no bigger than a TV tray that I thought would have looked nice with my living room set," Pre lowered her hand to her thigh to mark the table's height. "Two thousand dollars they wanted for it!"

"My!" Rosie's eyebrows shot upward. "Did George Washington set his beer on it once?"

Pre stirred her orange pekoe. "Even if he did, that's still too much. Maybe if St. John of the Cross set *his* beer mug on it when writing *Dark Night of the Soul*, I might have considered financing it." She shrugged. "Oh, well. Some congressman's probably using it as a remote control caddy right now."

Rosie choked on a mouthful of hot tea. "Pre, you're incorrigible," she declared, wiping her chin with her hand as she coughed. "You should be touring night clubs. You have such a great sense of humor."

"Nah, I like it here." Pre idly drummed her fingers on the bar. "Were you looking for Lola earlier?"

"Yes, I couldn't quite get to her after Mass. I wanted her, well, both of you, to know that I won't be dining here tonight either."

"Again? That's twice this week." She flashed a bright smile. "You didn't get a microwave, did you?"

"Ha, ha. What makes you think I don't have a date?"

"Because you would have brought him here."

Rosie put a hand to her mouth to keep from laughing out loud. "As it happens," she said, regaining her composure, "I am expected for dinner elsewhere. It's not a date, just a family affair, but don't worry about any more absences. I'll be back with a vengeance tomorrow night."

Pre nodded, remembering Rosie's tale the night before about her estranged niece. Could a reunion be in the works?

"Oh, the vegetables!" Pre then said suddenly, slapping her head. She needed to check storage to see if there were enough ingredients to make tonight's dinner special of chicken pot pie. Lola could come back from Norfolk any minute now to start baking the pre-made piecrusts. As busy as Lola was handling the day-to-day activity of the café, from paying the bills to overseeing the staff, she tried to get in the kitchen to cook as often as possible, creating sweet pastries and simmering soups as an artist would a visual masterpiece.

Pre tried to take as much of the business load from her boss as possible to allow Lola the pleasure of cooking. For this Lola was grateful, as were the many regular customers of Café Lisieux who had the privilege to sample the fruits of her culinary skill.

"Well, we'll certainly miss you tonight, just like on Tuesday, Rosie." Pre looked back toward the kitchen, feeling guilty for slacking.

Rosie drained her tea mug and handed it to Pre for the dirty dishpan under the bar. "I'll see you next time, then, unless you're otherwise occupied."

"Why would I be occupied? I'm almost always here, but I always find time to visit in between customers."

Rosie's mind danced around the words she really wanted to say, hoping not to get Pre too upset. "I figured you might have other plans this weekend. I know eventually you do get days off from work."

"What kind of plans?" Pre grew ever suspicious.

"A date..." Rosie wheedled. "With Larry Jeffries."

Pre's heart skipped a beat. Had Rosie followed them outside last night? "What makes you think that?" she asked in a playful tone, all the while dying of embarrassment.

"Well, I might have intimated to Larry that you were single, you know, planted a bug in his ear, suggested he take you out one night," Rosie waved the comment away as if she betrayed a dark secret of Pre's and showed no remorse for it.

"Why did you do that?" Pre cried amid a sudden clatter of pans coming from the kitchen. Both women jumped slightly from their stools. Pre rushed to the kitchen door and saw a head dip down to collect the cookware. Bill tripped over the broom handle again. She watched him clean up while Rosie explained herself.

"When you went to use my bathroom, Larry and I talked. He said you were a pretty lady."

"You're a pretty lady, too, Rosie. You go out with him."

"Oh, come on, Pre. He likes you. Besides, it's not as if I made you out to be a desperate spinster in the works," Rosie countered defensively. "I might have mentioned, though, that since Lola's accident you were working yourself to the bone and that you could use a nice dinner out, or even a movie."

Pre returned to the bar and leaned on the counter. "You didn't happen to mention my finger size in case he wanted to stop by Bailey, Banks and Biddle, did you?"

"No, but I did mention that you like yellow roses and chocolate-covered espresso beans," the old woman smiled.

"Who's the incorrigible one here, now?" Pre rubbed her temples, a dull pain throbbed above her eyes and she thought she could almost dent her skull trying to get to it.

"Rosie, as much as I appreciate your concern for me and my single status...really, I am happy with my life as it is."

"You are?"

"I am."

Rosie frowned. "You don't look it."

"I don't look it now because I'm aggravated that somebody," Pre leered at her old friend, "doesn't think too much of me that I can't make my own decisions as to whether or not I want to date or work. I enjoy working, that's why I do it so much."

Pre gasped for air. Rosie eased a full pitcher of ice water toward her and the young woman snatched it and filled her mug to the rim.

"So you don't like it," Rosie ventured carefully, "when people try to speak for you and pre-judge your intentions." Pre answered with an enthusiastic nod.

"Well," Rosie smiled. "Now you know how I feel."

Pre let that last comment sink into her consciousness; at first she was puzzled by the remark, but a sharp glance from Rosie sparked memories of last night's dinner shift, of she and Lola keeping an obvious vigil over the old woman and the reporter. What they did, Pre realized, was no different from what was happening to her now.

"Oh, dear God," Pre blurted out.

Rosie's mouth gaped open. "Pre! I was only trying to prove a point. It's certainly nothing to break the second Commandment over," she exclaimed.

Pre hastily blessed herself. "I didn't mean to do that at all, any of it," she insisted. "I swear, Rosie, we were only looking out for you. If it turned out that we were harsh..."

"Pre!" Rosie rolled her eyes. "What's past is past, and I'm fortunate to have friends like you and Lola. Don't worry anymore about it, I won't."

"Huh." Pre sipped her water. "I feel like such an idiot."

"You're not an idiot," Rosie said firmly, and as the two women looked at each other a light bout of laughter erupted between them. A good half-minute passed until either woman could catch her breath to speak.

When that happened, it was Rosie who piped up first. "Pre?"

"Mm."

The old woman wrung her hands. Another explosion was likely to explode, but to her the risk was worth it. "Why won't you go out with Larry? He's a nice enough fellow, and I know he'd loved to take you out to dinner."

I know, too, Pre thought. "You're just not going to let this go, are you?"

"Not until you're walking down the aisle in a white dress," Rosie gestured across to the church across the street, "to be wed to your significant other or to Christ."

"I don't like to wear dresses."

"So wear pants. Just choose a vocation. Be happy."

"I've chosen the single vocation. Can't a girl be happy with that?" Pre rested her hands on her hips. "I have a good job, great friends, and I'm never lonely."

Rosie tapped her temple. "True, but I know there must be days you wake up and think how nice it would be to roll over and hug your husband."

"Rosie!" Pre flushed deep pink.

"Hey, I'm old, I'm not dead. I was married once, you know. We didn't exactly spend all those years playing cards."

Pre shook her head, wondering how long the vision of Rosie and her faceless husband in the throes of passion would linger in her mind. She squeezed her eyes shut to expel the image from her brain.

"One dinner with the man isn't going to kill you," the old woman continued. "If it turns out that you and Larry are not compatible, you don't have to see him again. It's your choice."

"Doesn't sound like I have a choice about the first date," Pre mumbled.

"If you go I'll never bug you about not getting married and becoming an old spinster whose only enjoyment is derived from watching those courtroom shows on television while surrounded by cats." Rosie batted her eyes. "Besides, you might actually discover that you like the man. He's not Catholic, but he holds the same principles as you do, plus he's gorgeous!"

That's not what I meant, Pre thought sadly to herself, that I would have a good time. That I will like Larry, perhaps grow to love him, and be loved in return. I can't let that happen, it wouldn't be fair to him.

Larry reminded her too much of the type of man tired of trolling bars and longingly eyeing personal ads, Pre thought, and she fought back the desire the reveal this theory to her friend. That would mean having to explain her medical woes, something about which not even Lola knew.

Larry had the glow of fatherhood; Pre could certainly see the young man pushing a stroller or engaging in a rowdy football match with a giggling miniature likeness of himself, tumbling in the grass and behaving silly and making faces just to hear his child's laughter. Pre was certain Larry wanted the picket fence with all the trappings, and she could never give that to him, or any other man.

"Pre?" Rosie was clutching her purse. "What do I owe you for the tea?"

Pre shook away from her reverie. "Nothing," she said. "It's on me." She noticed the old woman slide off her stool.

"Leaving already?"

Rosie nodded. "I've a few errands to run before my niece picks me up tonight."

"Really?" Pre was dying of curiosity to meet this woman. "Why not bring her by one night to eat?"

"Sure, I promise to." If there is a next time, Rosie then thought, and I hope there is. She looked at Pre to say goodbye, bewildered suddenly by the look on the young woman's face.

"Something wrong, Pre?"

"Hm?" Pre looked up. "Oh, no. I've just got a lot on my mind."

"Need any help? I don't have to leave just yet." Rosie quickly prayed a silent Hail Mary for her friend.

"That's okay, it's something I kind of need to do on my own."

Rosie chuckled. "You'll never do anything alone, God will always be with you." Cocking her head toward the church, she waved a quick goodbye and charged out the door into a fresh gust of late-winter wind.

Thirty-Two

Not five seconds after Rosie's departure did the phone ring, and Pre answered to an earful of static from Lola's car phone. The café's owner was speeding down Granby Street - as quickly as one could speed through an off-kilter system of stoplights - toward the interstate ramp with one hand on the wheel.

"Lola, what are you doing?" Pre admonished. "That phone is for emergencies only." Images of her friend losing control of her car and crashing into a concrete piling swelled in her mind, while her own miseries of life and love instantly dissolved. Pre hated car phones; she lost count of the instances where she had witnessed potentially fatal accidents, all because of someone gabbing on one while not giving his full attention to the wheel.

"This is an emergency, of sorts. I found the two tables we need," Lola declared. Pre held her receiver away from her ear about an inch to muffle the loud noise.

"That's great, but how is this an emergency?"

"I need to get a truck by Wednesday to pick them up." Lola's car drifted to the broken line, nearly sideswiping a Chevy Camaro, and she jerked her car back into the left lane. "Who has a truck we can use?"

"Can't we talk about that when you get back here? I don't want to keep you on the phone any longer than is necessary." Pre heard very well the horn of the angry Camaro owner over the line.

"Just as well, I'm about to hit the tunnel. Listen, I have some other things to do, so I won't be in 'til two. See you then. Bye."

Lola rang off with an explosive crackle that left Pre's ears ringing. Leave it to Lola to volunteer a truck that neither of them owned for such an important task, Pre thought, wondering why her boss just did not pay the extra money to have the tables delivered. Lola was good for it, the café was turning a healthy profit.

Pre racked her brain, mentally listing the names of everyone she knew who owned a vehicle large enough to haul two dining tables from Norfolk on an hour-long drive fraught with narrow, busy roads. Who would be willing to put his truck through that, for free, no less? Maybe Lola could reward the kind soul with a complimentary dinner and dessert, Pre mused silently, deciding to speak with Father Welker when she saw him next. His skills for flushing out volunteers in the parish were impeccable.

"Buy why wait?" she asked aloud, surprised by the sound of her voice. She picked up the phone again and dialed the St. Vincent's office, but the parish secretary informed her that Father Welker was not keeping office hours today so he could celebrate Mass at Holy Name Academy.

"Thanks," mumbled a disappointed Pre. Since when did Father Welker say Mass for the school? "No message."

Pre folded her arms on the bar and lay her head down upon them. *Lord,* she prayed, *I know You don't operate a truck rental service, but Lola and I are going to need some help in that department. There must be somebody out there with a truck and some free time to spare who is willing to help. Please send that person to us, Jesus.*

Oh, and St. Anthony, she added to the patron saint of the lost and found, *I could use your help, too. Pray for me, and ask Jesus to send us a truck.*

She blessed herself absently and finished off her water, unaware that somewhere in the Hampton Roads Bridge Tunnel, Lola Marquez was making a similar request to Jesus through St. Anthony's intercession. Her left index finger was bent through a metal one-decade rosary ring, with the tiny beads cutting into her skin.

Thirty-Three

Larry Jeffries sat hunched over an open textbook, poising a neon yellow highlighter pen over a page that explained ethics in journalism. He enjoyed studying in the coffee shop of the Barnes and Noble bookstore in Newport News; sometimes total quiet could be unnerving to him, hearing nothing but the tinnitus buzzing in his right ear while trying to read or write an assignment was enough to send him scaling the walls.

Here, amid homemakers relishing a mid-morning break while rifling through home and garden magazines and business people sneaking out of the office for coffee, Larry found a good balance of white noise that eased him into a comfortable mood without becoming too distracted. Plus the coffee was always good and hot.

He skimmed a few pages lazily, staring at the words but not really reading any of them. He had been up since five cramming for a theory in journalism class that afternoon, despite the fact that he knew all the material backwards and forwards and upside-down. He had hoped the extra bookwork would take his mind off Pre, but it was a task proving to be fruitless.

He reached into his backpack and pulled out a hastily scribbled transcript of his interview with Rosie. He detected a faint odor of vanilla - he noticed that a customer sitting at a nearby table was drinking flavored coffee - and smiled. Rosie's house had smelled of vanilla, too, from a large unlit pillar candle on an end table.

Pre had smelled nice as well that night, a delicate herbal scent, probably from shampoo. Very feminine, Larry thought, and very attractive.

Larry studied his writing, throwing around potential introductions for his article in his mind, yet nothing he deemed powerful enough to grab a reader's attention came to mind. Though he had yet to pitch the story to *Catholic Monthly*, he wanted at least a rough draft written - something to present to Rosie so she would not think he was merely wasting her time.

Pre might be interested as well, Larry figured, especially if she agreed to contribute a quote about her friend. He wanted to ask without having her misconstrue it as an advance. Then again, he did want to ask her out again...why did she say no the first time? Rosie had told him that Pre was unattached, and if Pre had thought him not to be her type, why was she not up front about it?

Idly he picked up his coffee spoon and checked his distorted reflection on the concave side. He was not an unattractive man; many of Larry's female classmates and co-workers had at one or another complimented his long hair and style of dress - he had an air of professionalism yet did not appear to take himself too seriously. "Laid back" was often the term his friends used to describe him.

Did Pre not like "laid back?" Larry did not think so, judging from what little information Rosie was only too happy to provide. "I've never met a woman before so in love with life...and her work," the old woman confided the night before just seconds after Pre excused herself to the bathroom. "So unselfish, too. Do you know that when Ephraim Marquez died Pre took on the entire operation of Café Lisieux so Lola could handle the funeral arrangements and just cope with her husband's death? Only twenty-two, just out of college, she was!"

Larry leaned over in his seat, worried that Pre might be listening from some hidden air vent. "Was she planning to quit her job for a career related to her degree?"

"Lola mentioned something about Pre wanting to work as a book editor, or some kind of job in publishing. She's even mulled over going back for her master's, but she's so set in her routine with the café. I don't know if that will ever happen. Lola tries to lighten her work load so she can at least go to night school, but Pre won't hear of it."

Larry remembered thinking then how dedicated and trustworthy Pre appeared to be - her friends were lucky to know her, and her husband would be equally blessed, if not more. Not that Larry was contemplating getting that far with Prefontaine

Winningham; just a simple dinner and a show at the Naro Theater would suffice for now.

It was after this revelation about Pre that Rosie suggested that he offer his expertise in the publishing field to the young woman. "You're a professional writer, at least the most professional one I know," she said. "There must be somebody you know in the business who publishes poetry. Pre writes such beautiful verse."

Larry glanced behind him at three poetry shelves bordering the massive paperback fiction section and recalled his reply to the old woman: he would look into it. Truth was, his experience centered on news reporting, and he did not know Robert Frost from Jack Frost, much less the proper steps to take in querying and submitting poetry to literary journals.

His stare panned farther left toward the rack of magazines spanning the store's east wall. Maybe he would pick up a copy of *Writer's Digest* or *Poets and Writers* and peruse them for a point of reference in the event he saw Pre again, which he hoped was soon.

Why not now? Boomed a voice out of nowhere. Larry started, looking left and right for the source of the voice. Seeing only two other tables occupied by little elderly women and a lady of about twenty manning the cappuccino machine, he became even more confused.

Am I losing my mind, he thought, or is my conscience's voice finally breaking into a manly bass? He opened his backpack again and fished blindly for a pen to correct his notes when his fingers grasped hold of a familiar object.

He pulled out the rosary given to him by his new friend, the prayer beads strung in Mother Teresa's habit colors in honor of the late founder of the Missionaries of Charity. Rosie admitted to being an avid admirer of the late nun. Larry shuffled the note papers in front of him to find the quote by Mother Teresa offered to him by Pre as a possible staccato lead for his story.

"It is a great poverty to decide that a child must die that you might live as you wish," he read to himself.

Larry clutched the beads. Why *not* now?

* * * *

"What now?"

Pre answered on the third ring to Larry's warm salutation. Her heart caught in her throat, but quickly dislodged itself so she could speak.

"Hi there," she greeted Larry with an enthusiasm that surprised him, given her abrupt getaway last night from Café Lisieux's parking lot. "It seems I owe you an apology."

"Oh, really?" Larry was glad he decided to call the café first instead of bothering Rosie for Pre's phone number. Yet, as he leaned against a pay phone stand outside of the bookstore, tapping his feet in the cold like a child needing to use the bathroom, Larry felt suddenly nervous. Why did this woman make him shiver, more so than the cold?

"You'll never guess what I'm holding in my hand." Pre's voice was low and strained through the worn pay phone receiver.

"I dunno. You're at the café...I'm guessing a spatula?"

"Funny," Pre smirked. "I'm flipping through the September/October issue of *Catholic Monthly* from last year. There's an interesting article in here. 'Who Speaks For Those Who Can't Speak At All? Pro-Life Organizations of the Southeast,' have you read it?"

Larry imagined an impish grin spread across that shining, pretty face. "Not only have I read it, but three months ago I could have recited it you word for word," he laughed.

Pre curled the small magazine in her hand. "I found it in the back office, they're from the church. Father Welker keeps a subscription for the parish, and his secretary must have lent Lola a few back issues when she was over there this morning for Mass."

"I commend the priest's good taste in Christian journalism, but what did you think of the story?"

Pre traced the image of Our Lady of Perpetual Help on the cover with her index finger. "Actually, I haven't read it yet," she answered sheepishly, "but it's a nice title. The pictures look good, too. So that's why I'm apologizing, I guess. You really are a freelance writer."

"Apology accepted. I'm a freelance writer and photographer. Most magazines pay extra for graphics, which is partly why I take pictures. I also like to enhance my writing in the event it doesn't turn out like I want it, or if something must be cut to meet length requirements." He wondered if Pre was going to bring up their parting last night; he certainly was not planning to do so, lest he upset Pre and weaken his chances of securing a date.

"Hey, you wouldn't happen to have a pickup truck, would you?" she asked. "Large enough to hold two tables?"

Larry nodded to Roy's forest green Dodge dual-engine truck; his brother allowed him to use it today while his own car sat in a parking lot at Pep Boys, waiting to be serviced. "I know where I can get one. Are you moving?"

Pre explained Lola's recent purchase and the subsequent need for a delivery vehicle. "Great!" Larry exclaimed. "I'm glad Roy could help her out. Yeah, I could probably get him to lend us the truck; we've hauled twice as much cargo in the bed of that monster."

"You're sure he won't mind?"

"Of course not. I'll just tell him it's for a friend."

"I can't thank you enough for this," said Pre. "Café Lisieux owes you a free dinner. Stop by anytime. You can even sign the article for the church, if you like."

"My first autographing," Larry mused. "Okay, I accept, but perchance does this dinner include a companion for conversation?"

"Could be. Rosie is always around."

"That's not what I meant," he chided.

"I-I don't know," Pre stammered, blushing. "I have to work."

"You'll have to eat eventually. Surely Lola gives dinner breaks to the staff?"

Pre sighed. What was the use in fighting both Larry and Rosie? What was one dinner in a lifetime of dinners?

"Is seven tonight okay?" Larry pressed.

"Sure," Pre answered, defeated. "I'll be here." They hung up simultaneously.

Larry exhaled deeply, thanking God for giving him the strength to see the call through. Twenty-five miles away, Pre Winningham thanked God for getting her a truck.

Thirty-Four

Monica sat through the Scripture and Psalm readings like a stone statue, motivated only as the congregated upper class stood in perfect unison for the Gospel reading by Father Welker. A low chorus of adolescent voices buzzed with curiosity before services as the older priest joined Father George for the procession to the altar. Now heads turned to each other questioningly as he read the words of St. John. Everyone was confused that the Gospel being read was not the selection listed in the schedule passed out before Mass. Something was afoot, and nobody in the makeshift chapel needed to ask the reason.

Father Welker, attired in his pristine priestly vestments, read succinctly from the lectionary resting on the podium, his deep voice booming throughout the enclosure and enveloping the congregation with his passionate rendition of the Gospel. Father Welker loved the Bible; he studied nearly every translation ever published, including the Latin Vulgate and Greek texts, and he could cite book, chapter and verse with the best of any fundamentalist Christian who dared to challenge him in apologetic arguments.

Which was why, in planning his impromptu homily for the afternoon Mass at Holy Name Academy, the good priest did not have to do much research to find the appropriate Scripture verses to precede it.

"A reading from the Gospel according to St. John," he announced.

"Glory to You, O Lord," responded the students and faculty in kind.

Father Welker's large hands gripped the edges of the lectern, his gaze directed to a point in the back of the building near the door, an old habit of his from his early days as a seminarian when public speaking still unnerved him. "Jesus went unto the Mount of Olives," he began, quickly darting his gaze to the front row and the puzzled look on Sister Mary Grace's face. He threw her a wry smile and continued.

"And early in the morning, He came again into the temple, all the people were coming to Him; and He sat down and began to teach them.

"And the scribes and the Pharisees brought a woman caught in adultery, and having set her in the midst, they said to Him, 'Teacher, this woman has been caught in the act of adultery, in the very act.

"Now, in the Law Moses commanded us to stone such women; what do You say?'

"And they were saying this, testing Him, in order that they might have grounds for accusing Him. But Jesus stooped down, and with His finger wrote on the ground.

"But when they persisted in asking Him, He straightened up, and said to them, 'He who is without sin among you, let him be the first to throw a stone at her.'"

Father Welker intentionally cleared his throat, hoping that last statement of Christ's was sinking into every student's head. If the Gospel was having any effect on them, he could not be certain of it; the sea of faces before him registered varying expressions - from interest to ennui. He lowered his eyes and continued reading.

"And again He stooped down, and wrote on the ground.

"And when they heard it, they began to go out one by one, beginning with the older ones, and He was left alone, and the woman, where she was, in the midst.

"And straightening up, Jesus said to her, 'Woman, where are they? Did no one condemn you?'

"And she said, 'No one, Lord.' And Jesus said, 'Neither do I condemn you; go your way. From now on sin no more.'

"Again therefore Jesus spoke to them, saying, 'I am the light of the world; he who follows Me shall not walk in the darkness, but shall have the light of life.'"

Father Welker held aloft the lectionary and bowed his head. "The Gospel of our Lord," he declared.

"Praise to You, Lord Jesus Christ," came the unified response; a shuffling clatter ensued as the entire upper class student body and faculty took their seats. The priest fumbled underneath his vestments for a moment to retrieve a folded sheet of paper, a gesture noticed by Father George, still seated behind the altar, and altar servers CJ Merwin and Miguel Marquez. Father Welker was not one to use crib notes when delivering a sermon; this was indeed a very unusual occasion.

"I couldn't help but notice the smattering of voices out there, when you saw me rise to the lectern instead of Father George," the old priest began. "I don't normally condone chatter in the Lord's house, but in this case I will let it slide. Shows you all are paying attention."

Light laughter erupted. Therese Merwin, sitting in the third row alongside her friends, forced a smile. Jack Nixon, meanwhile, sat in the very last row in the far right corner, squirming and silently cursing the stuffy air in the building. He leaned forward to see the row of girls seated on the opposite side the building and searched for the back of Monica's head. It did not take long to find that familiar purple "scrunchie" holding her dark brown hair in a ponytail. She looked completely frozen and unsmiling.

"I also hope," Father Welker continued, "that you don't mind my taking the liberty of altering the readings today. I realize that according to this liturgical year we are not supposed to contemplate the Gospel of John today; however, given the current climate of this campus, I thought it more appropriate to address the concerns conveyed in the writings of this particular evangelist.

"In this Gospel, John reiterates the Lord's command from an earlier version of Christ's life, namely the Gospel of Matthew, which should be familiar to you all: 'Judge not, that ye be not judged.' It presents Jesus living an example of His preaching; a woman has sinned, she is displayed by her fellow townspeople, and many are eager to stone her.

"You know, sometimes as I study this passage I try to place myself at the scene. I can clearly see Jesus huddled in His corner, boring Aramaic characters in the sand while a pack of salivating wolf-like men stand at attention surrounding this poor woman, palming smooth, heavy stones in their sweaty hands. They wait with baited breath, thinking of how her skin will bruise and break under the force of pelting rocks.

"The more I think about it, though, the more I realize I need not travel back in time to get the full understanding of John's Gospel," he said, "because I can see the same thing here today."

Jennifer leaned over to Monica and whispered, "Here we go." Monica did not budge.

"How many of you like to read those tabloid newspapers?" Father Welker asked. "You know, the kind you see at the checkout stand of the supermarket, with the bold headlines and pictures of movie stars?" A few hands, some from even the faculty, slowly crept upward. "I imagine every one of us at one time or another has picked up one of those papers while waiting for the little old lady at the head of the line to write a check in the cash-only lane. I'm guilty of doing it myself."

He chuckled warmly, and many of the students responded in kind and relaxed. "By virtue of curious human nature, we're attracted to bold headlines bearing gossip - be it a famous actress checking into a rehab clinic or a rock singer believed to be a closeted homosexual. We read these snatches of yellow journalism and opinions form in our minds...we judge these people by the news we read in the tabloids, regardless of whether or not it is true. We revel in the misery of others when it is discovered that they are suddenly bankrupt, perhaps because we envy their fame and beauty, and in doing so we become no better than that circle of townspeople in Jesus's day who wanted to stone that woman.

"It isn't right for any of us, any of us, to act that way. Christ does not want us to behave this way."

Father Welker held up the sheet of paper in his hand; a number of heads in the back bobbed up and down for a better look at it. Therese and her friends, however, could see it fine. It was a copy of The List.

"Some of you may have seen something like this circulating around campus, and one or two of you might even have had a hand in its creation. I don't know myself, for this only came to my attention this morning as I prepared this sermon. Look at this closely," he waved the paper higher in the air, "and ask yourself one question. 'What do I see?'

"The obvious answer would be that it's a sheet of paper, or a list of names, wouldn't it?" After a few more heads up front reluctantly nodded, he continued. "I think differently, though. I see a stone. Or rather, I see a stone meant for every name on this list. When I read the names written on this sheet of paper, which is disconcerting to me because I recognize several students's names written here, I see judgment being passed on many people who do not deserve it.

"Some of you students wear jewelry or t-shirts bearing the initials WWJD - What Would Jesus Do? Well, I can tell you one thing He would not do, and that's mark His initials next to a couple's name to secure a bet, which I see has been done on this copy." The old priest counted set of initials. "Seven people on this one."

Father Welker noticed a female eighth-grader to his extreme right lose her smile and bow her head. At least one person was listening as well as hearing him, he thought. He set the paper down and leaned forward on the lectern, the small reading light casting a black shadow across his face.

"Jesus Christ was born and crucified that we might be saved, and during His time on the planet He lived that we might learn from His example. His example involved showing mercy on others, not passing judgment on a person just because he proved himself capable of error, or, other words, of simply being human.

"Now, getting back to the woman the crowd was eager to stone to death, does this excuse what she did? It does not. She did commit a grave sin, and that cannot be erased with a wave of the hand."

Monica, still frozen in place, lowered her eyes to her abdomen. You're not kidding, she thought.

"Yet, as Jesus teaches us, sins may be forgiven, and when Christ commands us to 'go and sin no more,' we have no choice but to do so if we want His saving Grace. With regards to the popular subject of conversation these past two days, well, who among us can really pass judgment if none of us knows the full story? How much damage can be caused with our speculations; if indeed there is somebody on this campus who is, ah, in the family way, does anybody here believe that idle gossip, stones of gossip, will not affect that person? Will idle gossip lead somebody to delve further into sin, abortion perhaps?"

Jack swallowed hard at this. Had Monica considered abortion? If he had not learned of the pregnancy, would she have had one and never told him?

"My brothers and sisters in Christ," said the old priest, "as we go forth to enjoy our weekend let us remember Christ's command to 'go and sin no more.' Let us not worry ourselves with one who may have left a questionable item in a school restroom or who may have committed a questionable deed. Christ also taught us not to point out a splinter in our brother's eye until we have removed the large wooden beam from our own eyes. Let us be conscious of our own mortal sins before we make light of those committed by others, if any at all were committed.

"As members of the Church founded by Christ, we aspire to be close to Him through the Sacraments. Remember that sin keeps us from Christ, and only through confessing our sins can we redeem ourselves in His eyes," he said. "Remember that, I implore you all, the next time somebody hands you a list made of stone."

The priest leaned back; not a word emitted from the congregation, not even a heavy breath. Therese was holding hers, taking in every word of Father Welker's homily, suddenly guilty for recent thoughts. Farther back in the building, Monica was again close to tears. When she finally bowed her head, it was to her right, just in time to see Jennifer mockingly deliver a wide-mouthed yawn. Monica frowned.

"Now, let us stand for our profession of faith," Father Welker announced, jumping into the Nicene Creed as everyone stood and recited with him. Father George too stood, and the older priest eased control of the Mass back to him with the reading of prayer petitions. The remainder of the service progressed uniformly through the Eucharistic prayers, the Our Father, the sign of peace, and the consecration of the Host.

Father George turned to Miguel first to administer the Sacrament. "Receive the Body of Christ," he whispered, sliding the Host onto the boy's tongue. When he moved to CJ, he was met with an unexpected gesture.

CJ folded his arms across his chest and bowed his head, staring at his shoes, a sign that he would not receive the Blessed Sacrament but would instead gladly accept the priest's blessing. Father George, a bit surprised but pleased nonetheless that CJ would not commit sacrilege, obliged him before descending from the altar to offer Communion to the congregation.

A ripple of gasps washed over everyone's heads at the sight of CJ; Therese looked on in shock. She guessed that CJ must have been harboring a serious sin to warrant his decision not to take the Eucharist. She never felt more proud of him in all her life; a lesser person would have accepted the Sacrament. Don't ask, don't tell. God, however, knows, and that matters the most, she thought. Therese was happy to know that her brother took that notion seriously.

Father Welker, to be sure, also took notice of the young man's actions with strong, silent approval. Regardless of whether or not CJ Merwin was involved in the pregnancy scare, the priest was happy to see such conviction in faith in someone so young. If only more young people thought and felt the same way, he thought. The young people were the only hope for keeping the Catholic Church strong in the next century.

Monica could only stare straight ahead, wondering how her brother could have committed a greater sin than her own. Jack, too occupied with Monica to pay attention to what was happening at the altar, sighed loudly and buried his head in his hands.

"Hey, who's CJ going with?" whispered a girl sitting behind Therese, unaware that the sister of the altar boy in question was within earshot.

"Nina Simmons. She's on the student council with me," came a hushed reply. Therese recognized neither voice and did not dare turn around in her seat. Sisters Bernadette and Charlotte were pacing the outside aisles on either side, patrolling the students for idle chatter.

"You think Nina will do that, too, what CJ did?"

"You think it means he got her pregnant?"

Therese tried to block out the dialogue. It was as if nobody listened to a word Father Welker said; the gossip prevailed, in God's House of all places!

167

She stood up with her row to receive Communion. *St. Therese, my Little Flower, pray for me, please*, she pleaded silently. *Jesus, what do I do? How do I battle the gossip and ill will toward my family without stooping so low myself? Teach me Your Mercy and dignity, Lord. I need You now!*

Therese stepped slowly along with her row, hands pressed together in prayer, eyelids half-closed, with the Jesus Prayer reeling continuously in her mind. *Lord Jesus Christ, Son of the Living God, have mercy on me, a sinner*. Over and over and faster she prayed until the words blended into a mush of syllables.

She had sinned, sinned greatly, she was sure of it. As often as she and Monica clucked over possessions and privacy, Therese had never experienced such boiling anger with her sister as she did earlier that day. Hate...for her own sister, who only days ago was her choice to be her confirmation sponsor! Add another oft-quoted "deadly sin" committed today - vanity, Therese knew, for she was already embarrassed at the thought of an unwed pregnant woman standing behind her as the bishop anointed her - and Therese realized she was slowly barreling downhill.

She saw the girl in front of her receive the Eucharist and shuffle to the left to receive the Blood of Christ administered by Sister Mary Grace. Therese looked up to see Father George, his left hand supporting the paten, dipping his right hand to select for her a Host.

Therese could only stare at him, then at the perfectly round, white Host rising up from his fingertips, suddenly glowing like a full moon. She was looking at the Body of Christ - that was the Catholic belief of transubstantiation - and wondering if she was worthy of Him. A look of urgency in the young priest's face told her to come forward and receive, as the line behind her growing and not moving.

Abruptly she instead mimicked her brother's gesture, leaving Father George no recourse but to return the Host to the paten and bless the young girl. Therese uttered a quiet word of thanks and ducked past the principal back to her seat, where she knelt immediately and prayed.

Had she turned back after Father George's blessing, she might have seen a few mildly interested faces, including those of the two girls previously chatting behind her. She missed also the concerned countenance of Laura Merwin, who was leaning against the back wall of the building, having arrived late for Mass with her youngest children in tow.

Thirty-Five

"Hey, Tim," Roy Jeffries bellowed from his office, leaning back in his chair with his feet propped up on the desk.

Tim Leland appeared in the doorway, his beige work shirt spotted with deep brown varnish. "Yeah?"

"How's it look out there?"

Tim shot a glance over his shoulder. "We got two ladies checking out the writing desks, but I don't think they'll be taking anything home. I overheard one of them grumbling about not missing the next show at the Naro."

Roy nodded. "What all do you guys have left to do?"

Tim reported that they were nearly caught up with all of the store's restoration orders. "Me and Will were going to start on those dining tables upstairs next."

"Well, being that it's been slow today, I've been thinking of just closing early," Roy said. "If you're caught up, the tables can wait another day. You want to head up front and turn the sign around?"

Tim almost burst with joy. He was not going to argue with the boss, it was his store. "You mean it? You feeling alright, Roy?"

Roy grinned, playfully pitching a paper ball at his employee. "Yeah, I'm fine. I just need to get some paperwork finished up before I give it all to Lori," he said, referring to the store's accountant. "Everybody gets paid for the full day. Tell 'em all to go home."

The last two customers left five minutes later - five minutes too long for Tim, who was eager to take advantage of the three free hours given him - and five minutes after that Roy's two other employees grabbed their coats and keys and literally ran out the back door. Roy hollered his farewells from his office.

Finally alone, Roy tapped the spacebar on his computer keyboard, and the screensaver flying toasters quickly popped out of sight, giving way to an open World Wide Web browser window displaying the home site of his electronic mail server. Roy entered his e-mail nickname - VIGIL316 - and password, finding six new messages since last checking the mailbox six hours ago.

Messages one through three were unsolicited junk. Earn five thousand dollars in five days, save money on copier machine toner by buying bulk, forward this petition to save *Sesame Street* from funding cuts...Roy deftly moved his mouse pointer to the delete button to trash the unwanted mail. He drummed his fingers on the desk as his low-megabyte dinosaur of a computer struggled with the Internet connection. He was anxious to see the fourth message, which was a reply to a query posted late last night to a private message board service operated by a militia website Roy often visited.

A person using the moniker NIGHTHAWK included a bracketed excerpt of Roy's original post in his reply message, along with his answer to Roy's pipe bomb question. *Everything you need, you can get at any hardware store*, the note read, followed by a list of everyday raw materials one would think belonged to a construction worker. Roy studied the necessary bomb ingredients - nails, steel piping, epoxy, among other things - mildly surprised with how easy it was to procure this information.

Larry was on the wrong track, he thought as he scrolled down to the last page of the e-mail, skimming Nighthawk's good luck message - FIGHT THE GOOD FIGHT blared in bold capital letters. Here was the perfect exposé for his journalist brother: vigilantism on the Internet and the potentially dangerous information one may find on the screen of some ten-year-old's computer, as simple as typing the word 'bomb' in a search engine.

Roy would wait, of course, before sharing such a suggestion with his brother. He needed all the help he could get.

He pointed the mouse to the print button and clicked once. Within seconds the rickety second-hand bubble-jet printer to Roy's right churned out Nighthawk's e-mail message. Roy erased the original onscreen and disconnected the modem, folding the printout into quarters, pondering where to shop.

He pulled out his wallet from his back pocket, opening it to reveal a snapshot of a thirty-something woman with light blond hair and bronzed skin smiling under a floppy sailor's hat. Roy caressed the photo with his thumb, wishing at that moment to trade everything he had to have Diane back with him.

"Don't you worry, baby," he whispered hoarsely. "I'm gonna get the people who took you away from me, you and little Roy." Soon, he thought, there would be others joining Dr. Neil Masterson on the slow, painful journey to Hell, forced to meet the faces of those who might have been. Thousands, no, thought Roy, millions of faces, like blades of grass in an open field, would come into focus for these monsters - children who might have become artists or teachers, doctors or scientists or social workers, all healing the world through new ideas, words, and music. Roy hoped everyone involved in the death factory that took Diane and little Roy would soon see the generations denied, and then explain to them why they had to die, just before being cast into the Lake of Fire.

He tucked the list in his wallet and shrugged on his jacket, whistling as he locked the front door of the shop and ventured out into the cold toward the bus stop.

Thirty-Six

Four rings, five, six, then seven dissolved into silence. Roy did not keep an answering machine at the shop, much to the annoyance of his regular customers and younger brother. Larry called around three that afternoon to confirm a time to pick Roy up from work; from there they would trek to the garage to retrieve Larry's car.

"Dadgum it, Roy, where are you?" Larry cursed into the phone. He let the stale ringing last another fifteen seconds before slamming down the receiver. He sat alone in the employee lounge of *The Norfolk Times* building, balancing a steno pad on his knees and nibbling on a bag of pretzel sticks. He preferred the lounge to the cramped office space requisitioned to him for the duration of his internship. He could lie flat on the lounge's soft-cushioned couch without his feet or head hanging over one end and work if he so desired - a more comfortable option than the cold, metal chair that accompanied his matching gray desk.

Larry was fuming, he did not need his brother's elusiveness today, of all days. Barring heavy traffic streaming out his end of Norfolk, Larry hoped to get to the shop within the half-hour. Then, tacking on another hour to get the car, get home, shower and change, he would have considered himself fortunate to be on time for dinner with Pre. He hoped nothing was wrong at the antique shop; Roy never liked to let the phone go more than three rings without an answer.

He kept Tim Leland's pager number in his day planner, and quickly punched the proper sequence of numbers to get the man's attention. People milled in and out of the lounge as Larry replaced the receiver and waited; he acknowledged everyone with a polite nod.

"Working hard or hardly working?" chided one young man from the layout department as he breezed toward the soda machine.

"You doing anything later, Jeffries? There's a group of us heading down to the Duck-In after work, you know, to have a few beers. Want in?"

"Can't. Got a date tonight. Maybe next time."

The young man stopped dead in his tracks, spilling drops of root beer on his knuckles as he opened the aluminum can. "You?" he asked incredulously. "A date? Man, that's bigger news than anything on the front page." He waved abruptly as he left, and Larry was fighting the temptation to respond with an extended middle finger when the phone rang.

"This is Tim Leland," responded a bored voice. "I was paged from this number."

"Tim, this is Larry. What's up at the shop? Nobody's answering the phone."

"Oh, hey, Larry!" Tim relaxed and his tone cheered considerably, and Larry detected that Tim perhaps had been drinking. Tinny sounds of jukebox cowboy music and midday revelry sizzled in the background as Tim relayed the events of the last two hours, coloring in more details of his own extracurricular activities rather than news of Roy.

"So you don't know where Roy went after he closed up shop?" Larry asked. Terrific, Larry thought. What would compel Roy to just send everyone home and leave himself? How did he expect to get home from Norfolk?

"No, man, like I told ya, me an' Will done left before Roy did. He said he had paperwork to do, so I figured he'd still be there."

Larry was relieved that phones were not equipped with olfactory equipment so he would not have to smell the liquor on the man's breath. "Whatever," he said. "Look, if Roy pages you, tell him I just left to go home."

"Yeah, no problem. Hey, don't worry about your brother, guy. He's resourceful, he'll find a way home."

"Right." Larry rang off without saying goodbye, wanting badly to hurl the phone against the wall opposite him. What was wrong with Roy? It was one thing to claim a store holiday to catch up on paperwork, but to just spontaneously close in the middle of business hours? That was not Roy's nature at all, Larry knew, and exactly how much paperwork was there to be done? Why did it warrant sending people home, when Roy could have just worked in his office alone? His brother certainly was acting weird lately.

Larry stood and stretched. What work assigned to him at the paper today was not due until Saturday evening, and that he could churn out and send to his supervisor through the e-mail after dinner tonight. Or perhaps tomorrow morning, he thought with a smile, if Pre would agree to a nightcap somewhere. He bolted out the lounge before anyone could tackle him for extra work.

Thirty-Seven

Therese begged off dinner, which for Lent amounted to very little that she liked to eat - linguini with clam sauce and broccoli. She complained of cramps and asked just to lie down in her room. Laura, sympathetic for her middle child's plight, agreed to keep a plate warm for her in case Therese was feeling hungry.

"Oh," Laura added. "If you put some heat directly on your stomach it will alleviate some of the pain. Get the heating pad from the hall closet." Therese nodded and disappeared upstairs, leaving only five at the dinner table, as Monica was also upstairs, preparing for her date with Jack.

Monica assumed that dinner at Café Lisieux was still happening; Jack had not called to confirm or cancel, so she called him. Mrs. Nixon was pleasant enough on the phone, and Monica wondered briefly about her current domestic problems when the older woman explained that she was running errands around the time Jack would have normally come home. "I thought he was already headed your way," said Sharon Nixon, pausing a second before speaking again. "Monica, is everything okay between the two of you?"

"Never better," Monica lied, crossing her fingers. She listened half-heartedly as Jack's mother expressed concern over her son's recent depressed behavior and how he went through last night with very little sleep.

"We haven't been fighting, if that's what you mean," Monica said. "If there's been any tension between us, it's probably got to do with Jack going off to college soon, especially if he leaves the state." She took a deep breath, hoping Jack's mother would buy the excuse.

"I understand completely," responded a very worried Sharon. As much as she liked Monica, she did not want Jack to be led by his heart when it came to important decisions like college. If a scholarship from an out-of-state school were offered to him, she would expect Jack to take it without any reservations. Girlfriends came and went, but education was forever, and if after graduation Jack and Monica were still able to forge a strong relationship, then they could marry. She would not object, so long as Jack and Monica understood the magnitude of such a commitment.

"I'll let you know if he comes home," Sharon told Monica.

Now, Monica stood before her vanity mirror, lost in thought, unsure if her date was still a go and whether or not she should continue applying her makeup. Her trance was broken when Therese stumbled through the door, fidgeting with the cord of the heating pad.

"Oh," Therese looked up, surprised. "I didn't know you'd still be up here." This was a lie; she had seen Monica bolt upstairs following the deathly quiet ride home from school and knew she had yet to emerge. Jack had not arrived, and Therese wondered if he would.

Therese crossed behind Monica and caught her reflection in the mirror they shared, hovering over Monica like a disappointed guardian angel.

"Your mascara is clumping," she mumbled before diving underneath her bedcovers with the heating pad. Lying on her stomach on top of the pad, Therese reached over the head of her mattress and inserted the plug.

Monica leaned closer to the mirror and jabbed at her eyes with her mascara brush, trying to thin out the tiny blobs of black collecting on her lashes. "Thanks," she said, then turned around to look at her younger sister, now a floral-print hump. "How're the cramps?"

"Bad."

"You need any Midol?" Monica rummaged through the vanity drawer and pulled out a small pill bottle, rattling the few tablets inside. "I got a few left you can have."

"You sure you don't need them?" Therese's words were covered with frost.

Monica was taken aback by her sister's unusually curt attitude, but surmised that the cramps were really talking. "Oh, I don't get cramps this late in the week," she covered.

"I thought your period ended." Therese sat up, looking directly at Monica's face and curious to see how her older sister was going to talk her way out of another lie.

"It did." Monica spoke calmly, wishing instead that she could scream. Therese had to know something was wrong by now, with the way she kept contradicting herself. Memories of the morning encounter in the girls' restroom at school haunted her, and Monica wished she had just fought off the urge to urinate then.

"Sometimes I'll get cramps even when I'm not menstruating," she added. "Ask Mom, she'll tell you the same thing. It's not unusual to get cramps after a period."

Therese frowned. Why wouldn't Monica just admit it already? "So how come you said 'this late in the week,' implying that you still have your period? I'd think you would know for certain if you're having your period."

"Look, you want the Midol or not?" Monica asked, exasperated. Her brain was too scrambled and preoccupied with Jack to have to construct a more concrete alibi that Therese could not challenge.

Therese, meanwhile, sulked back under the covers, clutching the heating pad to her stomach. "I'll live."

"Fine." Monica tossed the pills back in the drawer and huffed out of the room, electing to wait for Jack downstairs. Therese curled into a fetal position and thought of Monica's womb swelling into the second and third trimesters, trying also to picture what her niece or nephew would look like. She prayed for the baby's health, and for Monica, until she fell asleep.

Thirty-Eight

"I told the boys this morning," Carrie said sullenly as Rosie greeted her at the front door. She noticed blotches of red covering her niece's cheekbones, and surmised that was the reason why Carrie was wearing sunglasses despite the overcast sky.

Carrie politely declined her aunt's invitation to wait inside, her excuse being that she did not want to dally, as the boys were still visibly devastated. She wanted to get back to them quickly, she said.

In truth, however, Carrie just was not ready to come face to face with the old woman's decor; she knew in her gut that rosaries still hung from the rafters and that the old woman's walls were covered in New Testament scenes and Marian paintings. It would only remind her of past wounds, and tonight was about trying to heal them, not to irritate them.

"Fine, then, I understand," came the gentle reply. "I'll just get my coat."

They drove past Café Lisieux on the way to John Tyler Highway. Rosie leaned forward in her seat and waved at Pre, who was setting up the sandwich board with the night's specials on the walkway. Pre looked up in time to see the familiar silver-curled head grinning at her from a strange car, and she waved back enthusiastically, happy to have caught at least a glimpse of the mysterious niece.

"Friend of yours?" Carrie inquired as she steered right onto Jamestown Road.

Rosie nodded. "Pre manages the café. I eat there often." She raised her eyebrows; that was the understatement of the year.

"Hmm." Carrie appeared uninterested in the bit of trivia. "I'll have to try that place sometime," she added absently. "I've been by a few times but never thought of stopping in to eat." She frowned;

she caught herself almost saying 'we' instead of 'I' and was unsure of why she used the singular. Neil was dead now, but that did not mean that he never existed. Why was she acting like she wanted to completely disassociate herself from him?

The Masterson house was situated just outside the town limits of Williamsburg in an upscale neighborhood bordering a semi-private golf course and clubhouse draped elegantly in twisting vines and accented by white gazebos and a fountain pond. A pretty place for a wedding reception, thought Rosie, thinking momentarily of Pre and the young woman's reluctance to marry, much less date. True, Pre was still relatively young, and people these days were waiting longer to marry, but at least those marrying late in life were actually looking for potential mates.

Rosie shook her head, trying to focus on the rows of magnificent houses streaking past as Carrie drove deeper into the community. She prayed a silent Gloria for her young friend and then a Memorare for herself, that she might have the patience to last through the evening.

"So, how are Melissa and the baby doing?"

"They're both fine," Carrie answered woodenly, a bit peeved that her sister wanted the boys out of the house - she still thought it was too soon to tell Neil and Jacob about their father. Given the circumstances, however, she knew she really did not have a reason to be angry.

"What have they named the baby?" Rosie had yet to receive her announcement.

"Loretta Ann, after his grandmother."

A thin smile brightened Rosie's face. "I'll have to call tomorrow morning. I wouldn't want to wake the child by calling late tonight." She turned to Carrie, who kept her eyes on the road. "How did the boys take the news?"

Carrie slowed the car, turning with a sharp jerk of the steering wheel onto her street. "Neil Junior is taking it harder than Jacob, maybe it's because he's older. I don't know. They're both quite inconsolable."

"They don't know the magnitude of their father's murder," Rosie ventured, "or the investigation surrounding it?"

Carrie shook her head. "I'm finding it rather difficult to explain that somebody in cold blood put a bullet between their father's eyes possibly because of his work. I only told them that Daddy was shot." "Surely they'll learn the whole truth, Carrie," Rosie said, concerned. "If not from the news, then from somebody..." Rosie trailed off, noting the pained expression on her niece's face. She then wished she had not said anything at all.

Carrie's car ambled up the Masterson's driveway; all ominous signs of a police investigation - the yellow tape, the chalk outlines - were gone. Carrie was not sure how long the trappings of criminal activity were to have remained, but she was relieved anyway that her sons did not have to come home to a scene straight from an episode of *Unsolved Mysteries*. The town car rented by her in-laws was parked along the curb; Rosie noticed Sarah Masterson's sunglasses resting on the dashboard.

Carrie yanked the parking brake with force; Rosie thought at first the stick would break off in her niece's hand. "Look," the younger woman snapped, "if it comes up anytime soon, or if either of my boys start asking questions about what really happened here, then I will sit with them and talk, but not before then. They're going through enough pain right now without my having to add to it."

"Okay." Rosie folded her hands in her lap, unbuckling her seat belt only when Carrie quieted the engine and sent her own belt flying upward to its case. Don't press it any further, she told herself. Picking at a wound does not help to heal it.

Sarah and Jim Masterson greeted Rosie from the living room. They had ordered Chinese food and told Carrie to expect the delivery person in the next ten minutes. "We've got it covered, too," Jim said, patting his wallet. "Barbara, I hope you like Cantonese."

Rosie said that Chinese food suited her fine, though she was apt to spend most of her meal isolating the peas from her fried rice. "You and me both, dear," replied Sarah, laughing for the first time since she received the news about her son.

"Where are the boys?" Carrie asked, following her mother-in-law's now forlorn gaze up the staircase. "I should get some plates," she then said, retreating hurriedly for the kitchen. Rosie, gently excusing herself, made her way upstairs.

She found her grandnephews sniffling together on one of the twin beds set perpendicularly against the far right corner of the large bedroom. Neil Junior hugged his younger brother tightly around the neck, while Jacob hugged a pillow sheathed in a *Star Wars* pillowcase. A quick survey of the room revealed to Rosie that the entire room was decorated in a similar motif - bed sheets, curtains, and posters.

"Hello there."

Rosie noticed a faint glimmer of recognition in the older boy's eyes as both looked up at her. It surprised her, for three years was a long time for a child, especially someone as young as Jacob. He appeared to have grown at least a foot since she saw him last. Neil Junior had changed considerably as well; his once flaxen hair was darkening around his crown like a halo, and nearly all of his baby fat had melted away to reveal a more wiry boy with a long, handsome face, an eleven-year-old version of his father.

"My, have you grown, both of you! I haven't seen you boys in three years," Rosie gushed, stepping cautiously inside as the Masterson boys watched uncomfortably. "Do you remember your Great-Aunt Barbara?"

Only Neil Junior nodded, tentatively at that. Jacob clung tighter to his pillow and blinked his red-rimmed eyes, which were glassy wet and sore from crying. "My daddy's not coming back," he whispered.

"I know, and I'm so very sorry for that," the old woman said. "This is a very nice room. You keep it clean, I see."

"We have to," Neil Junior said, annoyed, as if cleanliness was the one thing in the world that perturbed him. "Mom and Dad told us that if we stepped on any of our action figures and broke them that they wouldn't buy us new ones," he said, his voice numb. He looked at the collection of figures perched on the windowsill, bent in various attack poses with miniature assault weapons, and appeared ready to cry again. His father would never buy him another toy again, and Rosie realized Neil Junior made that connection as the words came out of his mouth.

The boys scooted over a few inches on the bed to let their great aunt sit next to them. "I know you're going to be hurting for a long time," she said, "and there's always going to be an emptiness in your hearts that nothing else can fill." Little Jacob sniffed new tears at this.

"But as you move forward in your lives the pain will not ache as much, as long as you hang onto the memory of your father and remember the good times you shared with him," she said.

"Is Daddy in Heaven now?" Jacob asked, chewing the corner of his pillow. Neil Junior, knowing their mother had been trying to break her youngest son of the habit, gently pulled the pillow away and tossed it on the other bed.

Rosie scratched her chin. A simple question in need of a simple answer, but none came immediately to mind. Some people might have averred one way or the other, forming their answers based on Neil Masterson's relationship with Christ, which was unknown to probably everybody except Neil Masterson. Knowing it was not her place to speak for God in such matters, the old woman usually avoided that topic of discussion.

Jacob, however, looked up at her with heartbreaking eyes, desperate to know his father's spiritual fate. Rosie prayed a silent yet quick plea to the Lord for help and slapped her thighs lightly, indicating for Jacob to come sit on her lap. He complied, and the old woman reached her arm around the older boy, who inched even closer.

"It is my hope," she began, supporting the weight of Jacob's body with a half-hug, "that your father is in Heaven with Jesus and Our Lady. Jesus wants nothing more than the salvation of everyone here, regardless of how we live our lives on Earth. You do know what Jesus taught us about getting to Heaven, don't you?"

"Grandma gave us a Bible," Neil Junior murmured, bouncing off the bed to fetch a small, black leather-bound book from the opposite bookshelf.

"Thank you, Neil," Rosie noticed the Bible was the King James Version, used primarily by Protestants. She thought it odd that the Mastersons, devout Catholics like she, would present their grandchildren with this translation. Then again, Rosie's own house was filled with Bibles, from the KJV to her tattered Douay-Rheims to her father's own copy of the Latin Vulgate, which she continued to read to keep her knowledge of the ancient language fresh.

Rosie saw no problem in keeping the King James Bible; at least Carrie and Neil did not discourage their children from reading Scripture, but as Rosie opened the book she noticed the spine and pages were flawless, rarely touched.

"Neil, honey, would you read this for me?" Rosie flipped ahead to the New Testament, specifically the Gospel of St. John, chapter five.

"Verily, verily, I say unto you,'" the boy's voice quivered, "He that heareth my word, and believeth on him that sent me, hath everlasting life, and shall not come into condemnation; but is passed from death into life.'"

The old woman whispered in Jacob's ear, "Do you know what that means?" The boy made a noise of indifference. "It means that if you believe in Jesus and that He was born to the Virgin Mary and lived on Earth and died on the Cross for us, then you will have eternal life in Heaven. If you receive Christ's sanctifying Grace."

"How do we know Daddy has Grace?" Jacob asked. He could not bear to think of his father anywhere else right now but with God.

"Well, Jacob, honey, that's where faith comes in. We must have faith in Jesus that He has shown mercy on your father, and we must hope for your father's sake that before he died he reconciled himself with God. I wish I could tell you more, but it's really not my place to decide who goes where after death. That task belongs to Jesus alone."

Jacob bowed his head. "What if we asked God to take Daddy to Heaven. Would He?"

"Grandpa said Dad might be in Purgatory," Neil Junior added. "I've heard of it, but I don't really know what it is. Is it like Hell?" Jacob's eyes grew wider at the thought of his father damned in Hell and his sobs grew louder.

Rosie felt a knot tighten in her stomach, surprised that neither of her grandnephews were familiar with the Catholic teachings on Purgatory. For all their personal conflicts with the Church, had Carrie and Neil not even allowed their children exposure to just some of the basic Catholic beliefs? Did Neil Junior and Jacob's involvement with their faith end with Baptism?

If neither of the boys were familiar with the Church's teachings now, Rosie knew there would be no question that they may fall away from the faith altogether as adults, perhaps learn to even hate it. The most vocal anti-Catholics she ever met were former Catholics; some would harass her in front of the clinic as she made her rosaries, unwilling to listen to her defenses. Closed minds, closed ears.

"I think I can find some passages in here that might explain Purgatory for you. Ah!" Rosie held up the Gospel of St. Matthew to Neil Junior and asked again for him to recite.

Neil stared at the tiny red words, the words of Christ. "'Agree with thine adversary quickly,'" he recited verse twenty-five of the fifth chapter, "'while thou art in the way with him; lest at any time the adversary deliver thee to the judge, and the judge deliver thee to the officer, and thou be cast into prison. Verily I say unto thee, Thou shalt by no means come out thence, till thou has paid the uttermost farthing.'"

Jacob frowned. "What's an adversary?"

"An adversary is like an enemy, somebody who is always against you," Rosie answered. "For instance, the Devil is our adversary because he believes in doing evil."

"Did Daddy have adversaries?" Jacob pronounced the new word slowly.

"If you mean enemies...I really can't say." *Lord Jesus, forgive me for that little white lie,* she prayed. "There were people who disagreed with him on certain matters, as people often do, but enemies...people wanting harm to come to him...I really don't know."

"Somebody must have hated him." Neil Junior clenched a fist. "Or else he'd still be alive."

"And we won't have any answers to why that happened until person who did this is caught," Rosie assured him, "and he will be caught, he or she." Inside, the old woman's stomach flipped over and over. What if the killer was never found? What if a suspect was never named, and the case remained open indefinitely, until the passage of time soured any hopes of finding fresh clues?

"Anyway, we were talking about Purgatory," Rosie had the boys turn their attention back to the Bible. "What you just read,

Neil, is one of the few Bible passages which Catholics use to support the existence of Purgatory. Purgatory," she took a deep breath, searching her mind for the easiest explanation, "is like a holding cell, of sorts."

"Like jail," Neil Junior stated.

Rosie nodded slowly. "In a manner of speaking, yes. But here on Earth not everybody who goes to jail is eventually set free. The Bible states that nothing unclean enters Heaven, in other words, souls still tainted by sin. As Catholics, however, we believe that there are instances where some of these souls are still worthy of eternal life, yet are not quite ready to enter Heaven.

"Jesus says here," Rosie pressed her thumb on the Bible passage, "that one can't come out of this prison until he has paid the last farthing, or last penny, right?" Both boys mumbled in the affirmative. "The Church translates this passage like this: Purgatory is the prison, and the payment is repentance on behalf of the prisoner, or sinner. When the repentance is finished, the soul is set free and allowed to go to Heaven."

"How long do they stay there?" Jacob asked.

"I don't know, sweetheart. Time has no meaning beyond this earthly life, and it's really up to Jesus to decide which souls are cleansed and ready to be set free. But we can help here by praying for the souls in Purgatory, asking Jesus to set them free."

Jacob appeared to like the idea of praying for his late father, but Neil Junior was still skeptical. "How do we really know if Dad is in Purgatory, or ...somewhere else?" He swallowed hard on the lump in his throat. "What if we ask Jesus to take somebody out of Purgatory, and it turns out the person was in Hell the whole time anyway? What good does that do?"

Rosie could see the anguish flaring in the young man's eyes, wishing she could offer him a straight answer. God, however, was not about straight answers. "We just have to have faith, Neil. Without faith in God, we have nothing."

"I want to pray now for Daddy," Jacob wriggled away from his great aunt.

"I think that's a wonderful idea," Rosie told the boy as he sank to the floor in a kneeling position. She then looked at Neil Junior with pleading eyes. After a few seconds he took his place next to

Jacob, if only to please his younger brother and humor the old woman.

Rosie began to cross herself, but caught a glimpse of white blouse slip past the open doorway. She moved outside, leaving the two boys to whisper their silent prayers.

She found Carrie leaning against the wall just outside the door. "Dinner's ready," she said.

"I'll usher them downstairs now." Rosie started back inside but was stilled by Carrie's hand.

"Let them finish first."

Rosie turned slowly back to her niece. "Yes, of course. Carrie?"

"Yes, Barbara?"

"How long have you been out here?"

"Not long," Carrie shrugged. "I was coming upstairs to announce dinner when I heard Neil reading, so I...well, I just kept quiet."

"I see," Rosie smiled.

"I-I don't," Carrie added, sucking in air between her teeth, "I don't want my children thinking that their father was a bad man."

"Neil was not a bad man, Carrie. He loved his family, and I'm sure in public he was pleasant to others, as he was to me in the beginning."

"However," the old woman's expression darkened. "I can't lie to you, Carrie. There are people who believe your husband did bad things, myself included. Not everyone is able to disassociate the person from his actions, though."

"What about you?" Carrie demanded quietly.

"I can, I can now," Rosie said after a moment's thought. "It's a shame I was not able to say that when Neil was alive."

Fresh tears threatened to fall. "I just don't want my Neil to be in ...I'm sorry." Carrie wiped her eyes and covered her face while her aunt drew her into an embrace. A spontaneous prayer for her niece flew through Rosie's mind, as did one for her grandnephews and for the man whose soul could be anywhere - it was not her place to say.

Thirty-Nine

"How's your pasta?" Pre pointed her fork, which had stabbed on its tines a floret of cheese-covered cauliflower, at Larry's overflowing bowl of pasta primavera before devouring the steaming hot vegetable.

"It's delicious, and abundant," Larry said as he spun a long strand of fettuccine around his own fork, dipping the pasta into a puddle of light cream sauce and scooping up a zucchini slice to eat with it.

"To tell you the truth, though," Larry whispered, leaning in closer so as not to be heard by Lola, who sat at the bar pretending not to spy on the couple, "I've been craving a nice cut of filet mignon all day."

"Ah, ah, ah," Pre sang. "You won't be getting any meat at the café on Lenten Fridays, whether you observe the season or not." She munched on a forkful of tofu and rice. "So I guess for one night you'll have to suffer like the rest of us," she added jokingly.

"S'alright. We can go to Dog and Burger tomorrow when I take Rosie out to the clinic for pictures."

Pre arched an eyebrow. So confident, she thought, to think that there would be another outing. "Really?" she asked slyly. "I wasn't aware that I was making an excursion tomorrow. Good thing that my audience with the Pope isn't scheduled until *next* weekend."

Larry's face was a straight line. "Don't you want to see Rosie's first photo shoot? She's pretty pumped up about it."

Pre had to laugh at her dinner companion's choice of words. She found it difficult to imagine her septuagenarian friend "pumped up" over anything. Athletes and teenagers, like the one approaching to refill water glasses, were "pumped up." But Rosie? Pre shook her head.

"Are we enjoying dinner tonight?" Miguel asked in his most convincing concerned waiter voice.

"I'm fine," Larry answered pleasantly, "but Pre won't go out with me to Norfolk tomorrow morning. I wish I knew what to do about it."

Pre hid a smile underneath a napkin as Larry carried on like an innocent crime victim.

"I don't know, Miguel," he sighed, "I've tried to be charming and sincere, sensitive, you know, all those kinds of mushy qualities the ladies dig these days." Pre snorted at this. "But nothing works. Can you help me out, guy? I'm drowning here; you gotta have a line or two that works at school for you."

Miguel drew circles in the dew forming outside the water pitcher. "Buddy, you're asking the wrong guy. At least you got a date tonight instead of busing tables and refilling water," he said in mock despair. "But I don't know why Pre won't go out with you tomorrow," he added, looking at the café manager. "Mom's giving her Saturday day off."

"Really, now?" Larry brightened, and Pre turned then to Miguel and politely informed him that he was fired.

"Uh-uh. I'll appeal to a higher court," he retorted, gesturing to his mother, who, Pre saw, was making a hasty retreat to the kitchen after viewing the exchange from afar.

Pre blushed, avoiding Larry's gaze. "I have laundry to do tomorrow."

"You do laundry, Pre?" Miguel asked playfully before joining his mother. "Have fun tomorrow!"

Pre sighed, shoving another yellow squash disc in her mouth. Like rats deserting the *Titanic*, she thought. She looked up through her eyelashes to see Larry enjoying a hearty laugh.

"So," he began casually, winding another strand of pasta. "Dog and Burger for lunch tomorrow? My treat."

"I gave up meat for the whole forty days this year."

"Have a hot dog. They don't really count as meat, do they?"

"I'd just as soon avoid them anytime of year."

"Then get French fries. Or watch me eat."

"You're sure you want to venture out that way?" Pre steered the subject toward Saturday's other destination. "The big protests may be over, but you never know what will happen by the clinic."

"No more than the usual demonstrations before Masterson's murder," Larry replied with a shrug. "Anyway, Rosie wants to go. Maybe it's withdrawal or something, but she really wants to be there for herself. Even if it's just to take pictures."

Pre nodded reluctantly. "Then I'll go, for Rosie. Besides, I suppose somebody should be around for when all that cholesterol and fat stops up your heart and you have to be taken to the emergency room. Rosie doesn't drive."

Larry smiled and opened his mouth to deliver a flirtatious retort when he noticed Pre's attention suddenly diverted to the front entrance. A teenaged couple unzipped their jackets and waited patiently to be seated.

"You know them?" Larry cocked his head toward them.

"I know the boy is CJ Merwin. He's Miguel's friend," Pre said. "I think that's his sister, I'm not sure. It's been a while since the Merwins brought all their kids in to eat. I know it's not his girlfriend, because I've seen her with him before."

"Pretty girl." Larry admired the young lady's long dark hair and the graceful way she brushed several strands of it from her face.

Her face, it looked so melancholy, he noticed, with her eyes downcast and her lips pursed together as if a series of angry words stuck in her throat, wanting to break free. So puzzling, he thought, that somebody so obviously blessed with good looks, a thoughtful companion, and the opportunity to enjoy a nice meal could seem so sad, especially when millions of people around the world had much, much less.

Millions more would not even be born to enjoy such things, is what Larry figured Rosie would opine if she were at the café tonight. Millions of unborn children, denied life, would be denied a view of a sunset, a bite of chocolate, the feel of snowflakes light and wet against the face.

"Amazing what we take for granted," Larry mumbled.

Pre sipped her water. "What's that?"

"Oh." The thought bubble encasing Larry burst and he blinked, returning to dinner. Pre waved her hand in front of his face.

"Anybody home?"

"Sorry. Brain meltdown," Larry said, rearranging the last four bites of his meal on his plate. "So, what's for dessert?"

Pre quickly recited from memory the night's dessert list, as the selection changed regularly. "You're welcome to anything, but dessert's on my Lent list, too," she said. Larry chose the strawberry shortcake.

Pre rose from her chair. "I'll get it for you, my dinner break is almost over as it is. Coffee?"

"Thanks, I'll take it black. Is popcorn on your forbidden food list as well?"

"No, why?" Pre asked, confused.

Larry grinned, showing a full set of strong, white teeth. "We could catch the late show at the Williamsburg Theater when you're shift's over. I mean, if tomorrow's your day off, then there's no reason to head straight home. You can afford to stay out a bit late, can't you?"

"I don't know." Pre was wary. Dinner with Larry was nice, but a movie? The night was turning into a date, just what she did not want, and she was still on the clock!

"I'm not as young as I used to be," she added. She took a step back and bumped into Miguel, who nearly toppled his tray of soup bowls. Coached by his mother, the boy had been straining to eavesdrop on the couple every chance he had. This time, however, he could not let himself pass by without a comment.

"You're not old, Pre! You couldn't be if you were born during Munich."

Larry shook his head, his interest piqued. "What?"

"Ask Pre, it's a great story." With that, Miguel slipped away and wove around the busy table towards the kitchen.

Larry turned to Pre, expecting a more elaborate explanation of the young man's cryptic remark.

"I'll get that cake," Pre said instead, already halfway to the kitchen. Lola, sitting at the bar, nicked Pre on the shoulder as she walked past and winked.

CJ Merwin, having finished his salad, watched the playful exchange between Pre Winningham and the mystery gentleman with the long hair and glasses in the sports coat and blue jeans. He looked to CJ like a college professor, a possibility he then quickly nixed, seeing as how the man looked too young to have gone through graduate school and a doctoral program. Unless, CJ thought, the man was one of those child prodigies, finishing his higher education while still in his teens, but what were the odds of seeing somebody like that in Williamsburg?

At any rate, CJ thought, to see Pre with the young man - any man, for that matter - warmed his heart. He did not know the café manager well, just a few meetings whenever he joined Miguel at Café Lisieux for lunch, but seeing any couple happy together was a blessing. It reminded him of the strong love he felt in his own family, and CJ never neglected to thank God for giving him to stable, loving parents.

He felt something brush his folded hands; Monica was reaching for the sugar packets. She ripped open a white one and a pink one and poured the contents into her iced tea. "You didn't have to do this," she said, her voice cracking.

"Hey, don't start with that," CJ warned. "No guy who stands you up is worth the tears." Anger flushed his cheeks as he recalled seeing his sister curled on the couch, gazing out the living room window for a glimpse of Jack's car. She looked pathetic, like a soulful-eyed dog pining for his absent master, waiting on hinges for his return. He did not tell her so, however, for she would only cry more. Between Monica's previous heartaches and Therese riding out her first menstrual cycle, CJ decided there was enough misery in the house.

So, when the clock chimed seven and Jack was nowhere to be seen, CJ called Nina and altered their plans.

Nina. CJ smiled. She understood perfectly and agreed to postpone their date an hour or so, meeting at his house to catch a later movie, giving them an hour, at least, to be alone before Nina's curfew.

"I told you, I'll be fine," Monica moped, lying through her teeth. She wondered why Jack did not at least call and cancel dinner. That would not have devastated her as much as the feeling she had now that Jack had deserted her. Did he plan to avoid her entirely for the rest of the school year, hopping behind pillars in the school courtyards as she passed by? Would he be conveniently in the shower or on his way out the door every time she called his house?

"Jack was going to bring me here tonight for dinner." Monica's voice was small. Miguel appeared with a basket of bread and another Sprite for Monica, still perplexed at seeing the brother and sister together on a Friday night.

"We got your food coming up in a sec," he told them. Just as he said that, a waiter arrived with appetizer plates of hummus and raw vegetables and hot polenta. Neither CJ nor Monica felt hungry enough to order full meals, so they agreed to split appetizers.

Monica liberally spread a dollop of the spicy chickpea spread on a triangular slice of pita bread. "What if Jack had an accident," she suggested, grasping at every straw, "and he's lying on some gurney in a hospital and we don't know it, not even his parents?"

CJ rolled his eyes. "I really doubt that happened."

"Well, what if he did?"

"Nic!" CJ tapped the handle of his butter knife on the tabletop. "The only thing that happened is that Jack was a no-show. Whether your date just slipped his mind - which I doubt because Jack has a memory like Rain Man - or whether he decided he doesn't want to see you exclusively anymore, I can't say. Just start breaking away from him, Nic. He's not worth it if you're going to do nothing buy cry and mope around."

He buttered a slice of rosemary bread and took a large bite. Monica, meanwhile, rubbed her stomach. Earlier when she used the bathroom she detected a strange sensation: a soft, sifting noise, like a gelatinous sandbag was resting inside her. She guessed it was part of the pregnancy, her body was creating the protective sac wherein the baby would grow. Jack's baby.

"Maybe you and Jack have run the course," CJ suggested, still chewing. "He'll be going off to school in a few months, so maybe he's just trying to drift apart to make it less painful."

Monica lowered her head. Her brother could not have been more wrong - she and Jack were bonded for life, regardless of whether or not they spoke again. They were bonded together for the life of their child.

"You seem to have much wisdom in the relationship department," she countered hotly. "I suppose your own high school fling has a shelf life as well?"

"There's hardly a parallel between me and Nina and you and Jack," CJ replied evenly. "At least when I ask her out I show up."

"Oh, that's right. You love Nina. You love her so much you're willing to give up a top college so you can hang around here at some community college with your *girlfriend*...."

Her rant was far from being finished, but when Monica saw the hurt expression on CJ's face she trailed off into an inaudible murmur. She poked a polenta cake with her fork, chastising herself silently for exploding. Who was she to know the machinations of her brother's heart, much less his motives for wanting to stay close to home?

For all she knew, maybe William and Mary offered him scholarship money, or an opportunity to enter a particular degree program other schools did not offer. Part of her felt guilty for bad-mouthing Nina as well, and Monica had to admit that she was a mite jealous of her brother's girlfriend.

If it was Nina, and not her, who was pregnant, Monica mused, what would CJ do? Take off running in the other direction, as it appeared Jack had done? Marry her and quit school to support his new family? Stand by Nina and screen potential couples willing to adopt?

"I would never treat Nina the way Jack treated you tonight," CJ added matter-of-factly. "Supposing that Jack did have an accident, he would have ID on him, and his mother would have called. Mom would do the same with Nina if I was in a wreck."

"I guess you're right," Monica mumbled. "I didn't mean to snap at you, either. It's just..." she saw Miguel approaching with the water pitcher and shut her mouth.

"Anything else you need?" Miguel asked, setting down CJ's water glass.

A miracle, thought Monica, that's what I need. Just to have this baby disappear so I can patch things up with Jack, and salvage the rest of my life.

"We're fine," CJ smiled. "What are you doing later?"

194

Miguel sighed. "Closing up, going home, catching Conan O'Brien before I completely pass out. On the bright side, I got paid today, so next weekend will be more exciting." He explained that weekends for him would be free once again as soon as his mother's foot healed.

"I couldn't let her down," he added before drifting toward other tables. Monica thought it sweet of Miguel to sacrifice his Friday night and all prospects of hanging out with his friends or a date to help his mother.

That, however, also made her feel all the more depressed. Lola Marquez and Nina both had dependable young men, and she did not. Where was Jack, she wanted to know. What was he doing now?

She and CJ ate in silence, taking in the activity around them, but Monica's gaze kept locking on a small green scapular hanging from the ceiling to the right of her brother's head. She was familiar with scapulars in other colors, which represented different Catholic devotions - brown for Our Lady of Mount Carmel, blue for the Immaculate Conception, and white for the Blessed Trinity - but this one was different. Most scapulars Monica had seen were constructed of two wool rectangles connected by cord. The green scapular looked more like a cloth pendant.

Squinting into the light just above the dangling sacramental, Monica saw an outlined figure of the Virgin Mary sewn into the green panel. The air vent along the wall, however, made it difficult to see for certain, as the air tossed around the light wool object, twisting it around rapidly. Monica made a mental note to ask her mother about it; Laura Merwin knew everything about Catholic devotions.

CJ's eyes were glued to the professor clone, now sitting alone at the small table against the far wall. A plate of shortcake crumbs rested near his hands and a cup of coffee gone lukewarm. CJ judged him to be in his mid-twenties, a year or so younger, perhaps, than Pre, who was close to thirty herself.

He watched the gentleman stand and stretch, then reach into his coat pocket for some bills, which he slipped into Miguel's palm as the young man walked past to say goodnight.

"...still salvage this night."

CJ tilted his head back to his sister. "Huh?"

Monica sighed. "I said I was going to use the pay phone to call Becky to see if she wanted to rent a movie tonight. She said she was going to stay at home and be bored, so I figure why not be bored together?"

"Sounds like a plan," CJ said absently, watching Larry Jeffries banter with Miguel. "Go ahead. I gotta wait for the check."

In the kitchen, Pre helped the cook garnish dessert portions with powdered sugar and chocolate sauce swirled in circular patterns on plate edges and folded crepes. Each order also included a bulging strawberry cut lengthwise two-thirds the way into the fruit about five times, with the slices spread apart like playing cards. Pre admired her handiwork, a bit reluctant to let each dessert creation be served, knowing they would be reduced to crumbs without a second glance.

"Jason, order up!" she called over her shoulder to one of the waiters, arranging her orders of crepes and a slice of peanut pie in a triangle on a large oval serving tray. Her stomach rumbled like a dying motor, and the pungent aroma of cocoa and sweet corn syrup tickled and taunted her into breaking her fast from sweets. *Lord, please help me in this time of temptation*, she prayed, unsure if she should add Larry Jeffries as a temptation.

She scooped some whipped cream that gelled on the counter with her forefinger and sucked the digit clean, hoping the quarter-sized dollop would quell her cravings until Easter Sunday. Jason, hurry up and get your order, she thought to herself, or else my cravings will cease because I will have eaten everything.

As if on cue, Jason materialized, with Miguel in tow. The waiter gladly whisked the desserts away while the busboy lingered.

"What did Larry say to you before he left?" Pre asked. She had seen Larry slip the boy some money and wondered if Miguel would do the honorable thing and place the bills in the café's tip share till.

Miguel winked. "Only that he felt lucky to know us all, and that he has a date with you tonight."

"Get out of here!" Pre flapped a hand towel.

She watched Miguel rush out of the kitchen, and, through the small door window, watched as he hastily bussed some freshly vacated tables. Shifting her gaze, she noticed that Larry had not yet left. He was standing behind CJ Merwin's friend, waiting for the pay phone.

Whomever he called did not stay on the line very long, for after about a minute Larry hung up the phone, scanned the breadth of the dining room and exited. He would be back, this Pre knew, even though she did not vocally accept his offer for a date. A date, how silly, she thought. Dates were for teenagers!

Miguel's words, regardless of whether or not they were true, still weighed heavy in the young woman's mind. Maybe Larry is lucky, Pre thought with a smile. Maybe I am too.

Forty

For the first time in her pregnancy, Monica awoke with a powerful urge to vomit. She barely made it to the toilet as her mouth swelled with the remnants of last night's popcorn and Oreo cookie binge with Becky, and no sooner than she fell to her knees did she let go.

The taste left in her mouth repulsed her - like spoiled tomato soup and salted butter. It took several rounds of teeth brushing to alter the feeling inside of her; she brushed until she thought her teeth would crack from the pressure.

Laura tsk-tsked and only scolded her daughter for gorging on junk food, not to mention all the virgin Piña Coladas she drank using the mix Becky brought to the small party. "It's all that coconut milk that did this," she told Monica, handing her daughter a bottle of toilet cleaner.

"That stuff probably ate through your stomach lining...I can't drink it either."

Monica watched the discolored chunks of digested food expelled from her stomach disappear with a flush, spinning clockwise like obscene spin art - Oreo black, dull orange, colors she could not even name. That's about how I feel, she thought, exhausted, her head throbbing in time to the rhythm of the movie's soundtrack from last night.

Becky was thrilled to receive her phone call, and she rushed over to the Merwin house with a worn copy of *Titanic*, a box of tissues, and a bag of goodies. "Get ready for an orgy of the senses," she had squealed, and for the next three hours the girls gobbled junk food, giggled, cried, and acted like teenagers. Monica felt grateful for the reprieve from her woes, not thinking once of the baby, Jack, or anything else the rest of the night.

Now, she wished she too could just slip uneventfully down a drain, and not have to worry about what happened with her ...what? Boyfriend, or ex-boyfriend?

Still kneeling, she sprayed blue cleaning fluid in the toilet bowl. If only there were a way to wash this pregnancy away just as easily, she thought. She pressed her finger into her gut - that squishing sensation was still there. Somewhere underneath that, an evolving fetus grew.

A short, sharp rap on the door startled her. Joshua danced on the other side, badly needing to use the bathroom. Monica obliged and opened the door, tussling her baby brother's hair in a morning salutation.

"Are you sick, Monica?" Joshua's blue eyes - the only evidence of Chris Merwin on the boy's face - looked up with concern. He squeezed his knees together to keep the dam from bursting.

"I'm fine," Monica said with a smile, then urging her brother to do his duty. The bathroom did not need another near miss.

Rousted awake by her sister's impromptu retching, Therese stretched her thin, sore torso and grabbed her prayer journal from the edge of her desk. Like Monica, her night's sleep was restless and nauseous, but for different reasons. Not surprisingly, the first words written after *Dear God* were *please help me!*

I can't bear much more of this, she scribbled in slanting letters along the lined pages, her vision still clouded with sleep. *I understand that, as a teenager, I am subject to all the aches and pains of womanhood, but do they have to be so intense? I've taken pills, applied heat...my last resort is prayer, Lord. Please relieve me of these cramps, I have enough pain overloading my senses this week.*

Dearest Therese, Little Flower, she continued, *I apologize for what appears to be my monopolization of your spiritual favors. I imaging there are hundreds of thousands of people around the world calling on you to pray for them, begging you to ask Jesus for help...why should my petitions be any more urgent than theirs? For all I know, there are people requesting your intercession who are in desperate financial straits, seeking relief from severe illnesses, looking for jobs. I'm nearly halfway finished with my novena, and I've changed my requests so many times that I would not be surprised if you didn't know what to ask Jesus for!*

Monica plodded into the room and dove back into bed without comment. She did not catch the look on Therese's face, a mixture of sympathy and scorn.

I love my sister so much, she wrote, *but lately I can't look at her without wanting to spit venom. I see her stomach swelling and I wonder why she would put herself knowingly in this predicament - after everything we have been taught about STDs and other consequences...why would she do it anyway?*

But, did she do it willingly? I still don't know, and I'm scared to ask. Was she raped, or did Jack threaten to dump her if she didn't comply? Worse yet, was it Monica who initiated everything?

Therese tapped her pen against her chin, reading and re-reading her lament, thinking it nothing more than babble. "What am I doing?" she muttered, slamming her journal shut. Monica rumbled underneath her sheets, but Therese did not care if she was disturbed.

Lie there, Therese thought, glaring in disgust at the lump across the room. Lie there like the liar you are. What are you going to do, she wanted to ask, when are you going to tell Mom and Dad? Will you tell them at all, or find an easier solution?

Therese turned over on her back, counting the pockmarks on the ceiling. *God, fix this,* please, she prayed. *I don't want to be angry with Monica anymore, and I know it hurts You to see me sin. I don't want to sin anymore. Please don't let the baby die, either.*

Forty-One

Father Gary Welker saw the paltry number of bodies spaced apart in wide gaps in the wooden pews of St. Vincent's and sighed heavily. A far cry from the Church of yesteryear, when lines of people waiting for their confessions to be heard snaked around the nave and down the aisle, when people accepted everything about the Catholic faith instead of picking and choosing the doctrines and traditions that suited their lifestyles.

Of course, many churches in the United States did little to maintain life support of the sacrament of reconciliation, cutting public confession hours to one, maybe two, per week. St. Vincent's regularly scheduled confession hours were relegated to Saturday mornings, but most parishioners likely did not even know that. If they did, they were probably too busy running weekend errands or sleeping late or convinced that reconciliation meant nothing in the post-Vatican II age.

The old priest sulked in his chair in the draped confessional, really a tiny anteroom in the back of the church with the two chairs divided by a filmy beige curtain that one could slide back to the wall if one preferred not to accept the sacrament anonymously. Only one such room existed, therefore only one priest could hear confessions at the appointed time; anyone missing out on the two-hour block was welcome to make an appointment, but if that ever happened, Father Welker knew, it rarely happened with him.

As it was, he was the only priest to occupy the confessional in the last year. Father George begged off duty, citing his heavy workload with the college campus and high school ministries. Father Hans Schwarzlöse, a visiting Jesuit from Munich, also conveniently disappeared on Saturdays to visit neighboring parishes and monasteries.

Father Walker usually brought a book or stack of magazines. to read in between hearings; on occasion he could polish off an Agatha Christie mystery or half a year's worth of *Reader's Digests* without receiving one soul. But often he used the time for prayer, pleading with God to soften the hearts of the lukewarm congregation and guide them fully back into His Church.

He prayed that His priests may be given the opportunity to "loose what had been bound" among their flocks so that the Holy Eucharist could be received with clean consciences and clean bodies, the way Jesus Christ intended when He told His apostles to "do this in memory of Me."

The door opened softly as the good priest was skimming a chapter of *The Way of Perfection* by St. Teresa of Avila. A tall shadow fell on the curtain as the body behind - breathing heavy, nervous and trembling - dropped to the kneeler provided.

"In the Name of the Father, and of the Son, and of the Holy Spirit," intoned Father Welker, folding the book in his lap and signing himself as the shadow mimicked his gesture.

"Bless me, Father, for I have sinned." The voice was deep, male, and a bit uncharacteristic for the thin frame the priest could make out in the slightly waving curtain. He guessed it was a poor attempt at voice disguise.

"It's been about four months since my last confession," the man added, his head bending down into the armrest of the kneeler. The priest thought the voice sounded familiar.

"What sins have you to confess today?" he asked gently.

Another deep sigh, then a tremor in the voice. "I've taken the Lord's name in vain a few times, unconsciously. I've missed Mass once, but that was because I was on the road, visiting schools."

"Well, if there was no way you could make any services..." reassured the priest. So, he thought, he was at least a senior in high school, likely a Holy Name student, preparing for college.

"Oh, I know, Father," the young man interrupted. "But I realize I could have made a better effort at finding a church to attend."

"Very well." Father Welker still did not recognize the voice, but he admired the boy's candor. "What else have you to confess?"

"Well, I-I ..."

The shadow fidgeted; the priest envisioned young palms sweating and sticking together. "Don't be afraid to say what you must," he assured the boy. "Remember why you're here. This is not a process for meting out punishment, but a time to reconcile your sins and ask for Christ's forgiveness. There is nothing you can do or have done that would cause God to turn away from you. Am I making sense?"

"Uh-huh," the shadow stammered. "But this is pretty big."

The priest shrugged. "Maybe it is, but maybe only in your mind."

A pause, then another sigh. Then, "I had sex with my girlfriend and now I think she might be pregnant."

Father Welker felt his heart thud against his chest. So here was one half of the couple responsible for the pregnancy test. It had to be!

The priest swallowed hard; everything he knew about the situation, unfortunately, was born of rumor and speculation. He had to keep the boy - whoever he was - calm so he would not abruptly leave.

Because of the seal of the confessional, however, he could never reveal to anyone what transpired here, either. At least Father Welker had the chance to talk to the boy and hopefully influence him to do the right thing, not to correct a wrong with another act of wrongdoing.

"You don't know if your, eh, girlfriend is definitely pregnant?" he ventured, resisting an urge to tear the curtain away, keeping instead his hands tightened together in a ball. The boy wanted anonymity and that was how it was going to be. *Lord Jesus*, the priest prayed, *give me the strength to do the job You have for me.*

"Well, she took one of those home tests, you know, the stick that turns blue ..." the voice fizzled into uncomfortable silence. "But, I've heard those things are not always accurate, and she hasn't seen a doctor, so I guess I can't say for certain. We only did it, er," the shadow shifted anxiously, "had sex, just that once, and that was about a month ago, so if she were pregnant she wouldn't be showing yet."

"Umm," the priest nodded and scratched the back of his hand. "Well, your girlfriend is not here to defend herself or confess, we are here today for you, to confess and repent your sins - your part in this particular sin, too. Have you done anything to remedy this situation?" Father Welker hoped sincerely that the subject of abortion would not be breached.

"As far as I know, none of our parents know yet about anything, but it won't be long. We can't keep this secret forever," the boy started. "I don't even know why we did it anyway. I'm lying, I know why ...I guess maybe we both thought we were mature enough to handle it. Now I can't even look at my girlfriend without wanting to freak out. She doesn't know that, though."

"I can't understand how it happened," he added. "We used protection."

Father Welker cringed. "The only method of birth control that is one hundred percent effective is abstinence. Were you not taught that?" he asked, wanting to expand on the fact that the Church not only frowned upon extra- and pre-marital sex, but any form of artificial birth control used with the intent to stifle pro-creativity. He wished now he could remember a pertinent quote from Pope Paul VI's legendary encyclical *Humanae Vitae*, or *On Human Life*, to share.

"Yeah, I was. I knew, but I guess I didn't think about it then," the shadow answered at last.

"I know," Father Welker continued. "We rarely see the consequences of our actions ahead of time. I attribute that to our own arrogance. At times we tend to think of ourselves as infallible that we forget our mortality."

"There's more, Father."

"Come again?" Father Welker did not normally take kindly to being interrupted but he let this instance pass without comment.

"I want her to have an abortion. I'm guessing that it's proper to confess a sin before it is committed?"

Father Welker felt as if the boy had just kicked him in the stomach. Abortion? This was the young man's answer to resolving his actions?

"What kind of solution can be considered acceptable if a life is sacrificed?" the old man gasped.

"I can't take care of a baby, much less an entire family," the boy vented defensively. "I'm not going to ask N-, er," the boy stopped short of revealing his girlfriend's name, "that is, m-my girlfriend to endure a pregnancy, and I sure as hell can't give up college."

"Young man, do I have to remind you where you are?" Father Welker was stern but not yet to the point of boiling over.

"Sorry." A meek whisper.

The priest loosened his collar, as the temperature in the tiny room seemed to rise with the heat of the conversation. He asked the shadowed boy if the girl in question had agreed to the abortion, and the young man admitted that he had yet to broach the subject.

Thank You, Lord, the priest prayed. *May that awful word never pass this boy's lips into his girlfriend's ear.*

"I don't see what the big deal is." The priest saw two wiry arms fly upward in an exaggerated arc. "If she's only a month along, then how much harm could possibly come of it?"

"An abortion is a big deal." Father Welker was stiff. "It is a risky procedure for the mother, and naturally it is fatal for the life inside her. A woman undergoing an abortion could contract an infection or bleed internally to death. Would you rather your girlfriend pay such a price so the two of you won't have to look bad in front of your family and friends?" The old priest tried his best to contain his anger, but listening to this young man - this child - rationalize a death. A feticide!

"How can the Church be against abortion?" the young man asked. "There's no mention of abortion in the Bible?"

"Do you believe in the Trinity?"

"What?" The shadow turned its head toward the door, its owner contemplating an escape. Where was this going? "Of course I do."

"Really?" Father Welker crossed his legs. "The word 'trinity' is not mentioned in the Bible, either. It is through the Church's traditions that we are guided in matters not covered in Scripture, traditions handed down from Christ to His apostles through Peter, all the way down the line to today." He then offered to back up his statements with some Scriptural quotes, but the boy declined to hear them.

For a fleeting moment the good priest pictured a small yet worried line of parish elderly, curious to know when their turns would come, if at all. He pushed the thought out of his mind and strained to see through the loose threads of the curtain, hoping to catch a glimpse of some sort of feature - the shape of the boy's nose or face, the haircut - that he might recognize.

But the shadow did not budge, muddling any chance for the priest to decipher it. The boy stood. "I didn't think you could understand. I-I shouldn't have said anything." With that, he bolted out the door, leaving a quick breeze behind him to brush back the curtain, revealing patches of denim and short dark hair. He looked to Father Welker like half of the students at Holy Name.

"Wait!" Father Welker leapt from his chair, but the disadvantage of advanced age became all too apparent as he reached the threshold of the anteroom. The young man was already out of the church, probably halfway down Richmond Road.

Marlene White, one of St. Vincent's more devout and known dowagers, noted with concern the harried look on Father Welker's face as he staggered to the church door, greeted only by the swaying pine trees in the yard across the street.

"That boy, er, teenager, who was just in here," he demanded before she could speak. "Did you see his face? Do you know who it was?"

The white-haired woman shook her head slowly, muttering an apology, and the priest slid an inch down the doorframe. It was a fruitless question to ask of her anyway, as Marlene White's children were grown and long gone. Her involvement with the high school ended when her youngest graduated twenty years ago.

Father Welker's hands fell slack to his side. Whoever that was, wherever he was, the priest knew, he needed help, as did the young life he helped create. *St. Jude, patron of lost causes, pray for that boy*, he pleaded silently. *Ask the Lord to keep them safe.*

Forty-Two

The funeral service of Dr. Neil Masterson was an intimate, private affair, short on platitudes and heavily emphasized with prayer. Only immediate family members were invited and only immediate family showed. Carrie and her two sons, Rosie, Neil's parents and siblings and their nuclear families sat staidly in folding chairs with cushioned seats in the chapel of Westwood Funeral Home, all dressed in varying shades of black and dark blue.

Carrie opted for a closed casket to be displayed during the service; the cremation would follow later that afternoon with only her present. She felt Neil Junior and Jacob might have panicked at seeing their father's pale, lifeless body lying in a box ...better to see just the coffin than watching their father being swept into an urn as a pile of charred remains, she thought. The closed casket, she hoped, was the least traumatic choice for the service, and Rosie was more than willing to escort either or both boys outside in the event their first funeral became too unbearable.

That did not happen; Neil Junior and Jacob sat side by side in the front row between their mother and grandmother, both fixated on the unadorned casket surrounded by two large bouquets of lilies - gifts from the staff at the clinic. Carrie chose not to have a casket viewing as well - the less publicity the better, she thought, and she wanted the whole thing over with as soon as possible. She wanted time to mourn properly, without the watchful eye of a news anchor.

Occasionally little Jacob would glance upward at his paternal grandmother, watching with sad eyes the tears streaming down the older woman's cheeks underneath the black veil that covered her eyes. His gaze would then fall upon a sparkling chain of crystal beads intertwined with her fingers. An impulse to reach for the dazzling string rose in him, but when his older brother nudged him in the side to pay attention, the little boy obediently turned back to the service.

"Can I see that thing?" Jacob asked his grandmother as they left the funeral home with Rosie in tow. Neil Junior padded softly behind them. Carrie stayed behind to oversee the cremation, while the rest of the party shuffled away to their own cars.

"What, this?" Sarah Masterson held up her rosary. Jacob marveled at the multicolor reflections shining from each crystal starburst bead and tugged at the intricate silver crucifix, its top and sides flared into arrows.

"How come you're not wearing your necklace, Grandma?" he asked. "Is it broken?"

Sarah laughed nervously. "No, sweetie, it's not a necklace. This is my rosary. See?" She unraveled the long loop of beads and, spreading then out form a giant circle, held it higher for the boy to see the five beginning beads at its base.

The next question out of the boy's mouth surprised both Sarah and Rosie. "What's it for?"

Sarah and Rosie looked at each other, then down at the little boy. Neil Junior also looked on, equally curious to know the purpose of the prayer beads but unwilling to admit his ignorance of them.

"Your mother never explained to you the rosary devotion and the prayers that accompany it?" Sarah asked incredulously. Both boys shook their heads, and Rosie closed her eyes. Why would her grandnephews know about the rosary, or any Marian devotions, for that matter? A child could never learn his Catholic faith if his parents did not practice it. What other aspects of the faith did they not know?

Rosie rested her hand on Jacob's shoulder. "Jacob, Neil, didn't your mother teach you how to pray the Hail Mary, how to ask for Our Lady's intercessory prayer to God?"

"We know the Hail Mary," said the older boy dully, as if implying that he and his brother were not entirely ignorant when it came to spiritual matters.

By now Jim Masterson had emerged from the funeral home, blowing his reddened nose in a wrinkled paper tissue. He unlocked the front doors of the rental cars and wordlessly sank into the driver's seat.

"We're going back to the house, Barbara," Sarah said, ushering the children in the back. "Everybody else will be stopping by eventually, too. Are you coming with us, or do we need to drop you off somewhere?"

"My home is fine," Rosie replied as she lowered herself into the back next to Jacob. "I'm expecting company."

"Not a problem," Jim spoke at last, turning around in his seat and resting his arm behind Sarah's neck. "It wasn't the best of circumstances, but it was good to see you again," he added as an afterthought.

Rosie smiled a small Mona Lisa smile. "Thank you, Jim." With that, she pulled her own rosary from her purse and explained the devotion to her grandnephews on the drive back to her house.

Forty-Three

Normally the drive to Newport News from Williamsburg was short. At worst it took twenty minutes, notwithstanding traffic snarls and road construction, which was fast becoming a staple along the interstate toward Virginia Beach. For this reason, Pre suggested the time-consuming, albeit smoother, commute down State Road 60. Plus, Pre told Rosie as she set the cruise control, the change of scenery might be nice.

"My eye," Rosie scolded. "You're stalling."

Pre fiddled with the radio. "I'm not stalling," she insisted. "Why would you think that?"

"Did your date last night not go well?"

"How did you know I had a date?"

Rosie looked out the window. Apollo's Chariot, a sprawling roller coaster housed in nearby Busch Gardens, loomed in the distance, all curves and sharp plunges. "Lola," she said lightly. "She told me this morning after Mass that you and Larry left together after closing."

"We went to a late movie," Pre said, "and you weren't at Mass today. Lola told me when I saw her this morning that you weren't there, so how could you possibly know about my date?" Skipping nights at the café, now morning Mass. Pre bit her lip, worried. Something was going on with her friend.

"So, where were you, if you don't mind my asking." Pre slowed to a stale red light.

"Oh, I was with my niece this morning. She doesn't usually attend morning Mass." It was not a complete lie, except Rosie knew that the Lord might have raised an eyebrow at the word "usually." Carrie never attended daily Mass, and judging from her sons' lack of knowledge where simple Catholic sacramentals were concerned, she reasoned Sunday attendance was not a regular occurrence as well.

"Ah." Pre did not know whether to apologize or not for her behavior, but the itch of curiosity still nettled. "So," she asked slyly, "you didn't answer my question. How did you know about my date?"

"It's this amazing contraption my niece has," explained the old woman with a straight face. "It's called a telephone. I think."

The two women looked at each other and burst out laughing. "You sneak!" Pre accused. "All this talk about me prying into your beeswax, and you're making clandestine phone calls like a spy!"

"I'm old. I'm entitled." Rosie was firm. "There's never anything on television, I have many years left to spend on this planet and I need some method of passing time."

"You could pray more," Pre offered.

"We all could do that," the old woman nodded.

They drove in silence the rest of the way to Roy Jeffries's house, breaking intermittently to confirm the directions given them. Pre reasoned that driving to their house would have been easier than taking two cars to Norfolk.

Pre steered her car into Roy's driveway behind the large pickup truck and parked, taking her time to apply the parking brake and undo her seatbelt before killing the engine. Rosie, on the other hand, was nearly to the front door. "Hurry up!" she called to the cowering figure in the car.

Roy Jeffries greeted the ladies barefoot and sleepy-eyed, clad in an olive drab tank shirt and black running shorts. Rosie stifled a gasp upon seeing him. "Come in," he waved the two inside, rubbing a hand towel on his face and balding pate. "You caught me coming in from my run. I don't normally look this casual."

Pre smiled politely. If the man looked any more casual he would be naked. She was surprised he wasn't blue from the cold, and figured he must have worn a sweatsuit on top of those thin clothes. "I'm not blocking you, am I? Because I can move my car."

"Oh, no. No, no." Roy flittered anxiously about his living room, idly straightening stacks of newspapers on the coffee table and picking up his discarded, soaking socks. "Not necessary, not at all.

I'm not due to leave for another thirty minutes. I open late on Saturdays."

Pre nodded, not completely believing Roy Jeffries. For someone in no rush to leave the house, he seemed to be all over the place; he looked how she felt, flustered and unsure. She noticed the man's hand shook slightly when he gestured both women to the sofa.

"Larry's getting his shi-, er, *stuff* together," Roy tittered, ashamed suddenly for nearly letter a four-letter word slip by the presence of the old woman. "Can I offer either of you some coffee while you wait?"

Both Pre and Rosie said thank you, no, and Roy apologetically excused himself to the shower. Neither woman minded; in fact, both were relieved to see him go. His jittery demeanor only heightened Pre's, while Rosie tapped her chin, certain she had seen the man before.

She was about to mention this to Pre when Larry burst from his room, juggling a thick spiral notebook and soft zippered camera case. "I'm ready, I'm ready," he said, acting as jittery as his brother did. "Just doing a double check for film here ..." He unzipped the pack and fished through its contents.

He then looked up and saw Pre, cross-legged on the sofa in a William and Mary sweatshirt and jeans. "Hi there," he said softly.

"Hi." Pre did not look directly at him but grinned quietly to herself. Rosie threw them both a questioning look. Apparently Pre enjoyed her date last night more than she let on to her.

"Larry, your brother rushed out of here to his room so quickly that I didn't have time to tell him how much Lola appreciated his letting you use his truck to deliver her tables," the old woman said, stepping gingerly around the room toward him. She paid particular attention to the books slanting spine-out on the shelves of the entertainment center against the left wall facing the couch. Many titles were classics, with a few mystery novels and journalism theory books interspersed in between. A miniature travel clock rested on the edge of one shelf, while the top one was filled with various knickknacks.

She saw an unopened Coca-Cola bottle with the William and Mary logo emblazoned on it, one of those tacky souvenir walnuts with glued-on google eyes, affixed to a base reading *Myrtle Beach* in silver letters, unopened mail. These were the clues at Rosie's disposal, and they did not tell her much.

"Yes, that's right," Pre added, snapping her fingers. "We owe Roy a free dinner as well. Just tell him to stop by any time. Lola will remember him."

Larry pricked up his ears toward Roy's room and heard the shower run. "I'll be sure to tell him," he said. "In fact, I might just come down with him to eat."

He slung the bag over his shoulder and winked at Pre. "Provided the wonderful service and food are the same."

Pre blushed.

"Why not tonight?" suggested Rosie. "Surely if your brother is keeping short hours he'll be able to come."

"Dinner rush is usually around six," Pre said, inspecting a photo of the president on the cover of a news magazine on the coffee table. "But if we know you're coming, Lola will hold a table."

Larry patted his jeans pockets for his keys, then leaned toward Roy's room. "Hey, Roy, we're taking off now. I'll call you later at the shop!"

"Okay!" came the faint reply, muffled by running water.

Larry held the front door for Pre and Rosie. "I think Roy has plans, but I'll ask later. If he isn't able to come tonight, I will anyway. If you don't mind, that is." He looked directly at Pre as she passed.

"I'm not one to turn away paying customers," she replied coyly. "Of course, I won't be working tonight."

"But you have to eat," Rosie pointed out.

Pre tried to laugh, wishing she could just shrink into the carpet and disappear, she was that embarrassed. Why doesn't she just hand over a list baby names and caterers while she was at it, Pre wondered.

She knew why not, Pre then thought, because Lola would want that job.

The Hampton Roads Women's Clinic kept short operating hours on weekends as well; a point most onlookers guessed irritated the pro-life contagion only slightly. In actuality, protestors could not have been more upset; abortion did not take the weekend off, not even Sundays, as if to spit in God's eye. Despite the

213

bitterness toward the clinic, however, protestors were few on the weekends.

Despite also the light activity outside and inside the facility, Pre still was forced to negotiate cramped parking lots, finally settling on a metered stretch of curb two blocks south. Saturday shoppers strolled down both sidewalks bordering 21st Street, quick-stepping into boutiques to avoid the cold.

Pre exhaled white blasts of cold, watching the world from the driver's seat. Quite a difference between now and the scene broadcast across the state three days ago. Dr. Masterson's assassination appeared to have little staying power in the community as an initial outburst of rage subsided into a static routine...public interest waned once the television vans drove away to pursue more timely events. Such was the fickle nature of the media and those who kowtowed to it.

Meanwhile the plight of the unborn remained the same, and the murder appeared to dissuade neither the staff nor any new patients. Thank goodness people like Rosie cared regardless of publicity, Pre thought.

"Why don't we set up by the coffee shop, where I saw you originally?" Larry took the old woman's arm and guided her across the street during a break in traffic. Pre made a move to follow but was sidelined by a sudden stream of cars just released by a changing traffic light.

Larry looked back, as Pre called to him that she would catch up soon.

Hands in her jacket pockets, Pre ducked into the wind and started up the sidewalk toward the clinic, bobbing from stately women toting shopping bags and the occasional jogger wheezing a well-tread route. She spotted Rosie chatting with the Norfolk Coffee Company manager as he set out a chair for her, and watched as Larry slumped against the shop wall. Long strands of hair fell over his face as he bent over to adjust his camera lens.

Her skin prickled, and instinctively she crossed her arms and rubbed the bumps away. She was not cold, however. She was not sure why she felt this way.

What is that, she asked herself, feeling her heart speed up to a rhythmic throb as if she had ran the length of 21st Street instead of walked. Briefly she tucked her nose and mouth inside her zipped-up jacket, the once strong scent of Larry's cologne lingered from last night's outing within the threads. Wouldn't Rosie like to know how it got there, Pre thought.

"I take it you're not the kind of girl who kisses on the first date?" Larry asked her late last night as they exited the Williamsburg Theater in the colonial district. Both shivered, adjusting to the sudden drop in temperature as they left the overheated building, with Larry instantly moving closer to Pre to block her from an onslaught of wind.

Pre, taken aback by the gesture, shied away and skipped around a nearby lamppost to avoid his touch.

"Oh, come on," Larry slapped his arms down in frustration. "I'm not going to molest you. It's cold out here!"

"I-I know," Pre stepped cautiously closer. "It's just that, that...it's been a while since I went out on a date. I guess I'm a bit rusty."

"So, no kiss then, huh?" Larry asked, disappointed.

Pre shook the small popcorn container she brought with her, extracting bits of edible white puffs from the pile of burnt husks and unpopped kernels. "I'm an old-fashioned girl. No kiss, sorry."

"You know, I just thought of something," Larry said as he rubbed his chin. "This could be considered our second date."

"How do you figure?" Pre asked, trying to dislodge a speck of popcorn stuck in her teeth with her tongue.

"Well, we had dinner tonight at the café." Larry bounced onto the steep steps of the Laura Ashley boutique and flipped his jacket collar up around his neck. "Then I left, end of date one."

He leapt back down to Pre, who watched him in amusement. He looked like a pogo stick bundled in wool, hopping madly to keep warm.

"Then," he rubbed his hands together, "I return to the café to take you to the movies. Date two."

"Please," Pre scoffed, tossing the container in a nearby trash can. "One night, one date. Or at least consider this Date One-B." She tossed Larry an authoritative look over her shoulder.

"Ah, ah." He wagged a finger at her. "Time had elapsed. One event was long finished before the second one began. Therefore one could be compelled to call two separate outings two dates, hence a kiss right now isn't out of the question."

Pre's mouth gaped open in mock surprise. "One lousy hour passed! That's hardly an appropriate gap between dates."

"Is there a minimum time gap? Why wasn't I informed? Who made you boss to decide these things, anyway?"

Pre stamped her foot. People were still exiting the theater and the couple attracted some curious looks. Pre tried to smile back at them but her lips cracked underneath her breath.

"I would think at least half a day should pass before the next outing qualifies as a *bona fide date*," she replied. "I see the movie as a continuation of dinner, argue it any way you like. One date."

"Date One, Act Two," mused Larry. "What does that get me?"

"A friendly handshake," offered Pre timidly, extending a clammy hand. When Larry did not take it, she withdrew it into her jacket. "Two dates is a kiss," she insisted.

"Five is hand-holding, what is ten?" Larry moved suddenly close to Pre that he stood over her; his cool breath brushed her face and erupted goose bumps on her flesh. "Unlimited phone calls after eleven at night, all-day excursions hunting for antiques, cozy nights on the couch sipping wine?" He took her hands from her pockets; strangely she did not resist.

"Ten is what, Pre? I'd like to know, because I'd like to stick around for a tenth date, and a fifteenth, a twentieth, a hundredth."

Pre looked away. Was it the cold that reddened her face? "I- I was going to say ten was a free toaster...you know, as a joke." But Larry did not hear her, or he was too busy drawing Pre into a gentle embrace, bending his face down to hers.

Watching Larry now focusing his camera for a clear portrait of Rosie, Pre recalled the kiss, trying to remember the last time a man had touched her in such a way to make her completely melt. She had always taken extra precaution not to become too attached to any man she dated, rare as dates were with her. It only seemed fair, she reasoned, given her condition. What man thinking of a long-term relationship, perhaps marriage, would want to pursue a barren shell like her? In Pre's eyes, she was doing men a great service by remaining aloof.

Why was it so difficult, though, to be that way around Larry Jeffries? Their dinner conversation last night had been lively, the most fun she enjoyed without Lola or anyone else at the café, and the movie was just as nice. She felt so at ease with Larry, and when his lips met hers, she did not want to break away, and that worried her.

Is this what you want for me, God? she asked of her Creator. *Then why can't I be a complete woman to complement a complete marriage?*

"Hey there!" Larry waved to her from across the street. "What are you waiting for?" He beckoned to her as the traffic hit a lull.

Rosie continued to string her beads, alternating aqua and white to complete the first decade, then securing a knot before adding a white bead for the Our Father. A Saturday shopper paused to admire the old woman's completed handiwork, about a dozen rosaries left in her bag which she draped over the arm of her chair, looping each crucifix through the longer strand of beads to keep them from falling.

Rosie noticed the woman admiring a pink clear crystal rosary and offered it as a gift.

"Thank you." The woman held the beads, interlacing them in her fingers. "That one you're making looks like it's going to be pretty."

"It's a pro-life rosary," Rosie explained as she began the second decade, alternating red and white beads. "Each decade is set in multiple colors, with each color representing some special prayer intention for the pro-life cause."

Larry snapped pictures of the rosary maker interacting with the woman, then alone in intense prayer as her fingers pinched the cord to cordon off the location of the next knot. "There's a pro-life rosary?" he asked, his mind abuzz with creating a sidebar to his article, now in its first written draft. "How does it go? I could use the info as part of the story."

"I keep a few pamphlets on the pro-life rosary in my bag." Rosie pointed downward but was unable to reach the bag's straps without risking beads spilling from her lap. "Pre, there you are. Reach into my bag for the pamphlet envelope, would you please?"

Pre complied, flipping through several Xerox copies of rosary and chaplet instructions, colorful holy cards, and apologetics leaflets in the large manila packet before finding the correct brochure and surrendering it to the reporter.

"The prayers are the same as with a traditional rosary," Rosie explained, "but there are additional prayers to the Lord in reparation for abortion."

"The red beads," she indicated the second decade strung, "symbolize the blood of every unborn child spilled as they are aborted."

She paused for breath. Just thinking about the suction procedure performed on early-stage fetuses unnerved her. To have to need a pro-life rosary saddened her, and her only hope was that people accepting the rosary were willing to recite the prayers attached to it.

"For the next decade I will add black and white beads," she continued. "These represent prayers for the medical community aiding the pro-choice movement." She meant to say 'pro-death' movement. The unborn had no choices. "Anyway, it's all right there for you. Use as much as you like."

"Thanks." Larry folded the pamphlet into his back pocket. "I'll want to include an address, too, assuming you have these rosaries to give away."

"I do and I will. I keep a post office box for mail requests. You may use that."

Larry allowed a break for a group of four to pass through, while Pre offered to spring for coffee or cocoa. When she emerged from Norfolk Coffee Company with three piping hot paper cups, Rosie had distributed three more rosaries while Larry set his camera to rewind the film he had taken.

"Will you be taking any shots of the clinic, too? For contrast?"

Larry thought a moment about it and agreed. "People might want to see what we're up against."

He unzipped his bag and produced a second loaded 35-MM camera, and immediately fired off several shots of the building from different angles. He shook his head. "I should have brought my camera the other day, when the square was packed," he muttered. "There's no real drama in a static photograph."

Pre and Larry looked out over the building and surrounding areas. Only one other protester was visible today: a plump woman in an electric pink coat holding a homemade post reading *Abortion Kills.*

"Why not close in on her?" Pre asked, pointing to the woman.

"I'll need her permission first." Larry had already secured vocal consent with the woman who accepted Rosie's prayer beads.

Pre shrugged. "I can't imagine why she would refuse, if she knew what the picture was for. Besides, she has the guts to stand in public and espouse her beliefs."

Larry wound the camera after a shot of some distant nurses entering the building. As long as they were not posing, he did not foresee a problem using the picture, but likely it would end up in his slush pile. "True, but there's a big difference between local and national exposure. Maybe global, who knows? She might feel skittish about that."

Larry was right. The woman cowered behind her sign as the two approached her, unwilling to become immortal on Kodak paper, as if she believed the flashbulb screaming from Larry's camera would diminish her soul. Pre had never before seem anyone so adamant about not wanting a picture taken.

Though not persistent, Larry's polite manner managed to scare off the woman altogether, sending her running down the street to an ancient Volkswagen Rabbit parked along the curb, leaving Larry and Pre to look on as she drove away.

"Weird," was all Pre could say.

"No, just cautious," Larry said. "She can't really be certain why we're here."

"I just find it interesting she would be here protesting in the first place if she did not expect to be confronted." She sighed. "Well, I'm out of ideas for a photo subject."

Larry turned back to her. "I'm not," he said in a low voice.

Rosie enlisted the help of Chuck, the coffee shop manager, and within minutes Pre was planted in front of the clinic, holding a poster board bearing a similar anti-abortion sentiment scrawled in black marker.

"Perfect!" Larry exclaimed, snapping more photos.

Rosie distributed a few more rosaries to passersby and packed up her supplies before crossing the street to join her friends. "Larry,

I want a copy of this photo for my wall," she said. "I don't have any pictures of Pre at all, and I won't pass up the opportunity."

Larry looked questioningly at Pre, who explained the she did not like to stand in front of the camera.

"No?" Larry tucked his camera in his bag. "That's a shame. You're quite photogenic. I wouldn't mind having a copy of this for myself."

Pre's mouth dropped open, but Larry cut in again before she could speak. "For my portfolio, thank you very much." An unused frame in the hall closet of Roy's house came to mind as well. After all, Larry thought, it was his film, and he would be developing the film in his basement. He could make as many copies as he wanted.

"Okay. I have everything I need. Thank you, Cindy and Claudia." He bowed comically to both ladies. "Now, who's up for Dog and Burger? My treat."

"That's kind of you, Larry," Rosie said. "But I'm off meat for the Lenten season."

"So you'll sit and watch," chorused Pre and Larry, who looked at each other and laughed.

"What was that?"

Pre calmed down quickly. "Just an inside joke."

"I see."

Forty-Four

"Crud!"

Detective Mark Skinner clicked on the button of his computer mouse once, then five, then twenty times in rapid succession on various spots on the screen to no avail. His Internet connection had winked out on him yet again in the middle of downloading a file. He closed his World Wide Web browser window to discover that he had managed to retrieve only fifty percent of the file he wanted.

In other words, he had jibberish.

Four days following the Masterson murder, leads were still non-existent - no one person had stepped forward to claim responsibility, nor had the *motus operandi* matched other recent attacks on abortion clinic employees in the tri-state area. Mark leaned back in his chair and fired up the Internet connection again; he sorely needed to find a better service provider.

He got up and stretched; three straight hours in front of the glowing monitor was numbing his mind and his rear end, and a quick glance outside the window nudged his guilt. There were a million places he could have gone today, his only day off, and a million things he had to do.

Stacks of bills waited unpaid for him on the corner of the desk, dangerously close to due dates, while piles of dirty laundry multiplied on his bedroom floor and in his bathroom. As a result, the only clean clothes he could find when he woke up that morning were a pair of jeans and a black turtleneck, no socks. It was not that Mark was not motivated enough to clean the blossoming sty in which he lived, but he felt compelled to make some headway in the Masterson case first. He wanted to have something to tell Carrie Masterson on Monday morning, something besides, "I'm sorry..."

He got a Coke from the kitchen, and by the time he returned to his PC a high-pitched wail announced his re-entry to cyberspace.

Next to his keyboard was a list of newspaper archive websites provided by a friend, beautiful red-haired Nancy from two doors down. Nancy worked in media acquisition at the Old Dominion University library, and managed to get for him passwords for each of the website addresses on the list.

Mark did not have the time to waste browsing through acres of minuscule microfiche, and therefore was eternally grateful for the school's passwords, which were generally used by the staff to provide research articles for students. Mark had promised Nancy a nice dinner at the Trellis in Williamsburg in exchange for her slight indiscretion. She heartily accepted; the Trellis was expensive.

"This had better work," he muttered, hunting and pecking the letters of the password for the *Washington Post* online database with both of his forefingers. He was not about to blow half a week's salary on food for nothing. Well, he recanted silently, Nancy was not exactly nothing.

A search option menu materialized on the screen underneath a large newspaper masthead logo - he was in. "Yes!" he whispered.

He typed in the word 'abortion' first, curious to see what files would be indexed. Sixteen lines of data scrolled downward before him, all linking to various articles covering some aspect of the topic, in particular the ongoing partial-birth abortion debate in Congress. He saw nothing related to the Virginia Tidewater area.

Searches using 'pro-life' and 'pro-choice' yielded identical results to the first query, but nothing new. 'Neil Masterson' yielded zilch.

Next site was the Richmond daily, a graphics-heavy website that slowed his connection to a snail's crawl trying to load the front page. Mark rubbed his eyes and waited patiently, downing his soda in two deep gulps. What did one expect to find here, he thought, on the Internet, where rumor was king, where few people killing time in chat rooms made themselves known as the people they truly were in the real world? Mark wondered if perhaps he should have just gone outside and enjoyed the day.

Masterson's murder was quite a hot topic of conversation on the information highway, he did discover in his virtual travels. Archived discussions of the murder could be found on various message boards on pro-life websites and elsewhere on the Internet.

Mark recalled the many missives he had read that evoked sympathy for the Masterson family, as well as others that praised the killer.

Through reading the information he found, Mark slowly came to one theory that Masterson's murder was more of a personal vendetta than a political statement. Carrie Masterson could name no visible opponents aside from the usual protesters and pulpit speakers, and just about all of their alibis checked out.

Finally the website loaded in its entirety, and Mark punched in the necessary password. A search with 'abortion' resulted in fifty articles, with thirty-seven of them about the partial-birth procedure. Mark skimmed the titles, certain he was about to hit another dead end.

"What's this?" he asked himself, pointing his mouse to open an article with an intriguing title. As it appeared on his computer, Mark learned that the story was one of a series that dealt with how abortion affected specific area families. Luckily for Mark, the article contained hyperlinks to parts two through four in the series.

Ten minutes later, while perusing part three, Mark hit pay dirt.

This article concerned one Diane Jeffries, a Newport News resident and wife of antiques dealer Roy Jeffries. Six months before the genesis of the article, Mrs. Jeffries was blissfully enjoying the end of her first trimester, agonizing only over whether to decorate the baby's room in a Winnie the Pooh or *Rugrats* motif. However, this bliss was short-lived, as a routine visit to her doctor revealed tumors on Diane's uterus, polyps that were determined to be malignant.

Diane's doctor, Mark read, wanted to operate immediately to avoid the spread of cancer. Since radiation therapy was certain to threaten the welfare of the unborn Jeffries, terminating the pregnancy was recommended.

Naturally, the couple was devastated at the news; they had tried since their wedding night to conceive, and now instead of anticipating a blessed event, people were telling them to forget it, get an abortion, get surgery and try again later. A worse scenario saw Diane having trouble conceiving after the possible operation, meaning that the child she was carrying might have been their only chance at a baby, a chance they were encouraged to let pass!

Mark scrolled further downward, skipping briefly over a blurred color photo of the Jeffries couple, taken obviously in happier times, until he spotted the magic word: Masterson.

Bingo.

Through husband Roy's point-of-view, the ensuing year of events unfolded into a macabre soap opera with the revelation of a heated argument that forever changed his life. Diane, Roy was quoted as saying, was reluctant to abort, yet considered the procedure as a life-saving measure; they could adopt later if childbearing was no longer possible, she reasoned. Roy, however, wanted a son of his own and was a practicing Christian, and in his opinion there was no option that involved sucking the fruit of his loins out of his wife seven months premature.

Enter Dr. Neil Masterson of the Hampton Roads Women's Clinic; insert a few sinister, incidental chords here, Mark thought. The husband of a former co-worker of the worried lady, he read, Masterson agreed to a consultation. This was done, according to Roy, without his knowledge, and the only way he found out in the first place about the appointment was through a discarded memo Diane had written to herself and thoughtlessly tossed away.

Masterson himself contributed nothing to the article and neither confirmed nor denied meeting Diane, Mark saw as he skipped further ahead, so whatever transpired between Masterson and Diane remained a mystery.

Roy Jeffries claimed it was Masterson who convinced his wife to have the abortion. His theory was that the doctor filled the anguished mother-to-be's head with 'what ifs,' convincing her that allowing the child to die far surpassed the option of riding out the pregnancy, thereby possibly speeding up her own mortal clock. Jeffries never could pinpoint the exact day Diane entered the clinic because the procedure was also done in secrecy, but what happened afterward, Roy Jeffries said, would be forever burned in his memory.

The irregular bleeding began on a Thursday as Diane doubled over in pain. Mark skimmed more of the article, glancing briefly at the gory details of what Diane's husband and family thought was a natural miscarriage. They soon became suspect, however, when the pain would not subside. Diane was rushed to Mary Immaculate

Hospital in Newport News two days later, where she hemorrhaged for hours and died with a twisted look of pain on her face.

An autopsy pointed to an infection developed following an abortion, news that sent Roy Jeffries reeling, so said the source himself. Mark squeezed his eyes shut, hoping to offset eyestrain, before reading on to learn that Roy claimed he could never prove his wife actually visited Masterson's clinic for the abortion, as her name did not appear on any of their records. Masterson, when confronted, claimed doctor-patient confidentiality and refused to identify Diane through photos.

Masterson himself just might have slipped through the situation entirely had not his wife, Carrie, called the Jeffries home to offer her condolences. A bouquet of lilies sent to the funeral home came with a card that read, "With sympathy, Dr. and Mrs. Neil Masterson."

Mark sighed. Way to go, Carrie. Maybe sending the flowers hoped to alleviate guilt, or maybe Carrie was just sending her sympathy to the widower of a former co-worker, but Mark guessed that Roy took the message the wrong way. Seeing Masterson's name on the card must have been a slap in the face, he thought, wondering if Jeffries decided to retaliate with bullets.

Mark twisted in his chair. Anxious as he was to solve the Masterson murder, he seemed to be losing sympathy for the victim; he felt as if somebody had slipped him a Novocain pill to numb his heart. Imagine, he thought, sending flowers to memorialize a woman you might have been responsible for killing, if it could be proven. Flowers fade in time, and Masterson could have done much more to alleviate his guilt, assuming he suffered any, given that he had emerged from the tragedy unscathed. Until last week, Mark thought.

Then again, Mark asked himself, can the reader truly determine the entire story behind Roy Jeffries's actions? Just how angry did he get with his wife? If he killed Neil Masterson, he had to be brought to justice.

Mark printed out the article; it was not exactly a full fingerprint, the murder weapon and a map to the assassin's home, but it was something to take to the DA's office with the hope of securing a warrant to search Jeffries's house and place of business.

He watched the printer cartridge glide across the paper in the printer. Was Jeffries his man? Thinking as a regular guy, he could understand why Roy Jeffries would want to blow the doctor away. Thinking as a cop, however, he wondered how he could link Jeffries to the crime scene. The article now in his hand was a year old - showing possible motive - but God only knew how many people Neil Masterson might have ticked off since then.

He looked at his watch - two o'clock. He switched off his Internet connection just as his phone rang, which would definitely have bumped him offline anyway. Nancy was home from shopping.

"Found a great dress for half off in Ghent," she purred. "Perfect for dinner at the Trellis."

Mark was glad Nancy could not read his mind. Seeing Nancy in a dress half-off was worth full-price. "You called at a most opportune time, my dear, because I'm in the mood to celebrate."

"Any luck with the Internet?"

"I'll tell you at dinner. I'll call now and see if I can't get us a late seating. Call me back in a few?"

Nancy whooped with delight. "Tell Marcel to save us a Death by Chocolate," she said before ringing off to shower.

Mark chuckled and reached for the phone book, flipping to the restaurant listings, then changing his mind and retreating toward antique dealer listings, jotting down the address of Jeffries Furniture on a scrap of paper.

Forty-Five

"Hey, I know that chick."

Monica twisted around in her seat, staring as Rosie, Larry and Pre shuffled into the line at the Dog and Burger counter. Jack pointed at Pre with an unwrapped straw.

"That's Pre. She works for Miguel's mom at Café Lisieux," Jack told her. "She made lunch for us last week."

"I know who she is," Monica shot back. She recognized Larry also from last night, curious to know what brought them this far from Williamsburg. The older lady brushing past them to the enclosed seating outside looked familiar too, but Monica could not place her.

"Anyway, I-I'm sorry about last night," Jack whispered, lowering his eyes. "I guess I just freaked."

Monica crammed a few French fry shards in her mouth. "Yeah, you said that already." About every ten minutes since you dropped by the house, she wanted to add.

"Uh, yeah." Jack tapped on the table. He had driven out to the Colonial Parkway the night before instead of coming home and parked at a scenic view stop to think, inadvertently falling asleep in his car, or so he told Monica when he appeared on her doorstep that morning, disheveled and morose. CJ wanted to punch him square on the jaw when he saw him, but Monica called him off, agreeing to hear out Jack.

Now, considering all the events since getting into Jack's car, she wished she had unleashed her older brother.

Jack's throat dried, and he sipped his cola. "I should've called you, I know. I didn't mean to worry anybody, least of all you and Mom."

"I was hurt," Monica said pointedly. "Scratch that, I am hurt! I didn't do this by myself, you know."

"I know, I know," he shushed her, "but what's done is done and I want to take it back but I can't."

Monica held up a hand. She had enough. "There are some things I want to take back too but can't."

"Hey, we talked about this, and you and I both know there is no other option." Jack was indignant. "What do you think's going to happen if we tell our folks? We'll be grounded for life, and that's not even the worst of it!" He leaned forward in his chair. "That is, we'll be grounded if we don't get kicked out."

"My father would never do that."

"Maybe not, but they'll never look at you the same way again, that's for sure, and damned if they'll let you date anymore, me or anyone else."

Monica reached for the salt but withdrew her hand. Bad for the baby, she decided. Then again, what was the point? "Right now that doesn't sound unreasonable."

Jack's eyes widened. "Nic, you know I love you."

She nodded.

"And I'm trying to be an adult here, and do something that will be better for us in the long run."

Again, a nod.

"It's just not the right time."

"I know."

"So," he wolfed down the remaining two bites of his cheeseburger. "What did the doctor say?"

Monica looked away from him. Recalling the whole scene in the clinic gave her the chills. She half-expected to wind up in a darkened room filled with display cases for needles and grotesque machinery attached to hoses used for collecting fetal remains. An abattoir for humans, or a scene from a Stephen King novel, that was what she expected instead of the pink wallpaper and landscape paintings walling her inside the examination room, décor that made her feel uncomfortable all the same.

She felt like she was at the dentist's office - get a tooth extracted, get a baby extracted. Even the *People* and *Cosmopolitan* magazines in the lobby were current issues, and soothing tepid Musak blared from unseen speakers; "Like a Virgin" buzzed overhead in soft piano and trombone. How ironic, she remembered thinking.

"They can do it as an outpatient procedure," she reported. Out, out, damn patient, out of the womb! "Since the baby's still in the first trimester, it will only cost one hundred and fifty dollars."

"Only?" Jack cried. Where was he going to get that kind of money? Even raising half the amount seemed impossible to him. Neither he nor Monica worked, and Jack knew he could not ask his parents for that kind of a loan without arousing suspicion.

Still, he thought, it beat having to shell out for medical bills and other expenses for the next eight months and beyond.

"Okay, I can try for half of that. You can get the other half?"

Monica felt her lunch rumbling in her stomach, threatening to retreat upward. "I guess," she finally answered, though she did not know where to begin looking for seventy-five dollars. She had four fives tucked away in a coffee can in her closet - mad money saved from babysitting for movies and CDs. She kept no secret hiding place for abortion funds.

"I think I can sell a few things to make up the difference, add it to what I have," she added.

Jack nodded. "I could take my Nintendo to the pawn shop. I never play it anymore."

"You think you'll get more than fifty for it?" Monica could not believe her ears. They were actually planning to pay for an abortion!

"If not, I'll find a way to get the rest. So," he interlaced his fingers into a ball. "When's it going to happen?"

"They said they can take me late Tuesday afternoon."

"I have a match at Catholic High -" Jack began to protest.

Monica wanted to throttle Jack. "I know, Jack. Let me finish." She rolled her eyes, wishing it were Jack, and not her, who was going to lay on the cold examination table and be prodded and poked with gloved hands. Men had it so easy, she thought. Things like this just seemed to roll off their backs.

"Well?"

Monica wrinkled her forehead and pressed her hands, palms down, on the table. "So, that will be our cover. I'll tell my parents that I'm going with you to see the match and that we'll stop for dinner afterward." Her voiced choked and she coughed, "Instead of going to the match, however, I'll go to the clinic. You'll drop me off on the way to the match and come get me when I'm...it's done."

"Sounds like a plan."

Monica wiped her hands on her lap. "I don't want to do this, Jack."

Jack reached for her, but Monica shied away, leaning back in her stool. He caught a glimpse of Pre and Larry, enjoying a lively dialogue over French fries coated with nacho cheese, and wished their conversation could be as light.

"Nic, what are you going to do? Have the baby? Be a mommy?" he chided, bordering on mean-spirited. "You think your folks are gonna let the kid bunk with Josh and Judith and be homeschooled with them, while you go off and do your thing?"

"I would not dump my baby on them like that," Monica replied. "Besides, did I say anything about keeping the baby? I just want to consider other alternatives, is all."

"We discussed that to death," Jack sighed, exasperated. "If we put this off any longer, it's gonna cost more money to do this, plus it might put you at greater risk to wait. Monica," he stretched out to her from across the round table, wanting badly to touch her, to wipe away the pain, the fear, and the anxiety, all with one embrace. Monica was the best thing to happen to him ever, and now he was probably going to lose her, thanks to his bursting libido.

"I don't want to lose you," he sniffed back tears. "I always hoped we'd stay together, and that you'd come up to visit me at whatever school I ended up. I know I made a mess of things, but we still have a chance to correct things, and nobody will be the wiser. I promise also that we don't have to have sex again until we marry, if that is in our future."

Monica tried not to look at Jack's face. His cornflower blue eyes were her downfall every time; now glassy with tears, they were certain to melt her reserve. She fixated on a dried spot of ketchup on the table. "I still think this is wrong, what we're doing. But you're right about my parents, as much as they love me, I don't think they'll understand."

"So, Tuesday then?"

She turned back around. Larry was helping Rosie shrug on her sweater while Pre grabbed a copy of the free arts weekly tabloid from the wire stand by the back door. "Tuesday," she said aloud woodenly, while inside her heart she cried out to God for mercy, begging Him not to send her to Hell for this.

Forty-Six

"Hey, Larry?" Roy tossed his keys on the occasional table by the front entrance. His brother had to be home, for he saw the car parked along the curb to allow Roy's truck to take the driveway. Larry kept odd hours and liked to keep his own car unblocked so he could come and go as he pleased.

He checked the kitchen. "Larry?" No answer. Then his brother's bathroom and the backyard deck, where Larry sometimes curled up on the bench rocker to read. No Larry. Roy struck gold in the basement, finding the door to Larry's darkroom closed and the *Do Not Disturb* sign hanging from the knob.

"Hey, Larry!" He rapped sharply on the door. "You alive in there?"

Roy heard an abrupt knocking noise, like something being dropped, then, "Yeah?"

"When did you get back?"

"A while ago." Roy heard some more banging and shuffling on the other side. "I'm going to be another hour or so. I wanna finish this roll I took today," Larry added.

Roy nodded. Good, he thought. Larry could easily kill several hours in the darkroom if he really got into his work. Larry was a perfectionist when it came to photography, and it was not uncommon for Roy to come downstairs to do laundry and discover his younger brother had spent the night meticulously playing with grayscales and brightness.

"What about dinner? You want I should call the Chinese place?"

"Nah. I'm meeting Pre for dinner tonight." Silence, then another loud clunking sound. "I'll be outta here by five so I can shower and change." Asking Roy to take the café up on their free dinner offer did not enter into Larry's mind; he was thinking only of getting over there to see Pre.

One hour, thought Roy, glancing down at the rolled-up bag clutched in his hand. Not enough time, but no matter. He could get to work after Larry left. Considering how crazy his brother was over this new lady, Roy was certain Larry would be out until very late. Everybody wins.

"Alright," Roy called. "Have fun. I'll fend for myself."

"Okay." Larry listened for his brother's footsteps as they squeaked upstairs before resuming his work. The first snapshot of Rosie in front of the coffee shop turned out slightly blurred. He slammed his fist on the table in frustration, spraying developer fluid on his hands and wrists. He hoped that the rest of the roll did not turn out as badly.

The article was nearly written now, if only still in the first draft, composed on scraps of napkins from Dog and Burger and purloined hotel stationery found around the house. To have at least one decent portrait to accompany the words would be a blessing.

Fortunately the remainder of the roll showed promise. One still shot with Rosie and the woman given the rosary looked great - Larry felt he captured the brilliance of the old woman's eyes as her wrinkled hands held up a finished strand of knots and beads, her work for God, her love.

The shots of Pre were equally good, even in black and white tones her beauty shone. If only she could see for herself how pretty a smile she had, how it lit up the day around her and became infectious, without putting herself down so much. At last he had proof. Larry hung two pictures to dry on a clothesline, souvenirs to pass along at dinner.

The clinic pictures and landscapes were very much what he had expected - dry, cold, and imposing. Without the sign in view, the clinic might have looked like any typical modern building, alive with business. Unfortunately.

He concentrated on a photograph featuring a dark-haired female figure exiting the double doors; the stenciled letters on the clinic doors were obscured in the shot, but it was the only shot of the clinic that had any element of action in it. Very little action at that, Larry thought, but it was still an image too powerful to ignore.

Larry noted the girl's lowered head, the hands closing the coat lapels together under her chin, as if worried somebody she knew would spot her. He imagined her mind racing in fear, desperate to concoct an excuse in the event one was needed.

"Criminy," he sighed. What's a nice-looking girl like you doing in a place like that? He lifted the developed photo from the tray, trailing tiny drops of fluid on the table and floor. So young to have to deal with so serious a problem, Larry thought as he held the snapshot closer to his face. Something looked odd, but he could not quite figure out what it was.

He reached below the tabletop for the built-in utility drawer, feeling through rulers and inkless pens for his magnifying glass, which he centered on the young girl's face. A perfect reproduction of a face he had seen before enlarged instantly. Still beautiful, still melancholy.

"God, no ..." he whispered.

* * * *

The numb feeling stayed with him - during his shower, while dressing, and on the drive to Williamsburg. He worried Roy with his robotic movements around the house and was encouraged to at least swallow a few aspirins before the long drive.

With some unconvincing words of assurance to his brother, Larry took off, his mind still on that girl he photographed leaving the clinic. It was the girl he saw last night at Café Lisieux, he knew it had to be her. Maybe Lola or her son could provide a name; the pictures were tucked away in a manila folder on the passenger's seat, and suddenly Larry was quite disturbed, thinking of the most delicate way for them to see the light of day.

Roy watched his brother pull away from the curb outside their house and disappear down the block toward Jefferson Avenue before marching back to his workplace with similar robotic steps. He kept a writing desk in his bedroom, on which was littered unchecked invoices and customer requests. These were brushed aside to make room for the paper bag containing items all purchased legally from a nearby hardware.

234

He extracted a thick aluminum pipe from the sack as the remaining metal objects inside clinked loudly together. He thought fleetingly of his brother and his new lady friend. Pre, was it, he asked himself. Unusual name for a woman, he decided, then again people these days strove for nonconformity. Life was nothing more than a competition between parents to give their children the most bizarre monikers ever conceived, it seemed.

He fumed. Those who bothered to have their babies, anyway.

"Have fun, Larry," he muttered. Marry your weird-named chick and live on your journalist's salary while she waits tables occupied by fat Yankee tourists. Have lots of children. Just pray Pre - pray Pre, pray pretty, pretty Pre, Roy chuckled at the alliteration - doesn't treat your son like a disease, like a wart with a heartbeat that nobody seems to mind excising.

He held up the pipe to his eye as if looking through a telescope. Of course, he reminded himself, she would soon not have anywhere to go if something like that happened.

Forty-Seven

Monica opened the back kitchen door to the smell of fried catfish and hush puppies; the aroma assaulted her with such force that she had to sit down immediately, lest another wave of nausea tint her face green and send her spewing. Everything, it seemed to Monica, made her sick now - food, Jack's cologne, even the simmering wisteria wax potpourri her mother kept on the kitchen windowsill, bubbling on the highest notch of the dial to counterattack to stench of cooking fish.

"Hey, you," Laura said over her shoulder, lifting a fillet from the frying pan with her spatula. "How was the movie?"

"Fine," Monica lied. "I think I got a headache from reading all those subtitles."

"Yeah, foreign films will do that," Laura cackled. "I used to hate having to watch all that Fellini for film class back in college. It wasn't enough that I didn't know what was going on, but to have to read everything, oh! Even then, we were still clueless."

Laura whirled around and set a plate of cooked catfish on the table in front of her daughter. Monica held her breath.

"I saved a few cuts and cooked them with lemon pepper marinade." Laura cocked her head back to the stove. "The guys all voted for fried, but I know you and Therese don't want all that grease."

Monica shifted uncomfortably in her seat. "Thanks."

"Did you and Jack talk? Is everything okay?" Laura's face creased with concern.

"Yeah, we straightened everything out. We're okay," Monica answered. She looked up into her mother's eyes, which were too light to be called brown. Bronze, maybe, Monica thought, like shining hard candy. "We've made a date for dinner after his wrestling match on Tuesday, you know, to smooth more things over."

Laura tightened her grip on the oily spatula in her hand. "Jack isn't pressuring you to do something you don't want, is he?"

"No!" Monica shot back, too quickly for her own judgment. She hoped her face did not reveal her lie, and searched her mind for another direction in which to steer the conversation without crashing. The powerful aroma of catfish, however, clouded her senses.

She put a hand to her stomach, feeling the baby turning cartwheels inside her, dancing with the butterflies. In three days the baby would be gone, and the butterflies would morph into slugs...

"Uh, Mom?" Monica twisted away from the platter of fish and inhaled deeply. "Have you ever, um, kept a secret, you know, even from Dad?"

"When I was little, but eventually everything leaked out. From your Dad, though, I keep nothing." Laura scanned the cabinets for a bottle of Tabasco sauce. "Comes with the territory when you get married."

Laura craned her neck and eyed her daughter with interest. "Why? What secrets are you keeping and from whom? Jack?"

Not anymore. "No, it's just that I was sworn to secrecy about something, but it's something that probably should be told for the welfare of the person involved..." her voice trailed away; Monica wrung her hands, thinking herself crazy for taking the risk. Why not just hand Mom the aftercare pamphlet given her by the doctor, while she was at it, she thought.

"This is about that mystery pregnant girl, isn't it?" Laura asked as Monica sighed, knowing better to assume that her mother would not figure it out. Eventually everything leaks out. "You know who it is."

A reluctant nod was Laura's answer. "She made me promise not to tell anyone, Mom. She's really frightened and doesn't know where to turn. I guess she let it slip to me 'cause she figured I wouldn't freak out."

Laura shook her head and prayed a silent plea to God through the intercession of St. Gerard, patron saint of mothers-to-be. "It was going to be discovered anyway, Monica. Your friend can't hide a swollen belly, didn't she think of that?"

The second the words came out, however, a darker realization dawned as she saw Monica cast her eyes downward, and Laura stopped short of breath. "Dear God," she whispered. *Dear God, watch over Your unborn, especially this one.*

She reached into the oven with a black mitt and retrieved a cookie sheet filled with broiled fillets, setting it down with a loud bang on the stovetop. Monica, jarred by the noise, clutched her stomach again.

"She's going to do it, have an abortion?" Laura demanded. "Right after a doctor who performed them was gunned down in his own home?"

Monica blushed deep red. "She said they stepped up security there..."

"There's no security for that baby," Laura grumbled. "Nothing is ever one hundred percent safe, Monica. Your friend should have realized that before she started having sex."

I'm sorry, Mom. I was stupid. So stupid.

A loud bang from the front door signaled the arrival of Chris, Therese and Judith, back from an excursion to the video store and hungry for dinner. Laura poked her head over the swinging door and announced a five-minute warning for the family.

"Nic, honey," Laura motioned her daughter to her feet. "I need the table set. We'll finish this later, okay?"

Monica nodded, her head already in the open refrigerator browsing rows of half-empty condiment bottles. Later, they would discuss this later. What was one more hour piled upon the weight crushing her chest?

* * * *

Correction, ten dollars, Monica told herself, forgetting about the tube of lip balm and, of course, the pregnancy test she had purchased. Only sixty-five more to go.

She looked around the bedroom, seeing absolutely nothing for which a pawnbroker would shell out that kind of money. Her shelves were lined with ticky-tacky junk holding more sentimental than monetary value - a gold-plated debate team trophy, knotted tassels from elementary school graduation, and a Catwoman action figure still encased in its blister package. This was Monica's net worth.

Monica considered the possibility that a trophy shop might buy the marble base screwed to the plastic cup, as well as the alleged increased value of the toy that could interest a comic shop proprietor. Both items combined, however, would not come close to covering the cost.

Where to find sixty-five dollars?

"I'm only getting my book!"

Therese was a sudden gust of wind, inside the room in a millisecond, taking one long stride to her desk for one of her dog-eared romance novels. She did not dare look in her sister's direction.

"What'd you guys get from the video store?" Monica asked her.

"Some dumb Jim Carrey flick Judy and Josh wanted to see. I'm just going to read."

Monica slumped to the floor in a cross-legged position. "You can read up here. I'll be quiet, in fact I'll be reading for school myself."

"S'kay. I was going to have some cookies and milk in the kitchen." Therese retraced her steps, anxious to get away.

"That sounds good. Maybe I'll come down in a bit, too."

"It's a free country," Therese retorted, already out the door and past her mother as she trod downstairs.

"What's with her lately?" Monica asked herself out loud as Laura took a seat on Therese's bed. "I don't remember my first period making me that cranky."

Laura harrumphed. "Amazing what the mind represses. I seem to recall a certain pre-teen who once locked herself in the bathroom, vowing not to emerge until the week was over." She threw her daughter a pointed look. "If you weren't cranky then, I know you made the rest of us that way."

"So, maybe I was a bit self-conscious," Monica tittered, amused briefly with how much more that statement applied to her today. "It's not like hitting adolescence automatically turns sweat into perfume."

"Honey, you were bending over every thirty seconds to check for stains! That's not a bit self-conscious, that's borderline maniacal vanity."

Monica sighed. Vanity, she thought, one of the seven deadly sins. How many was that for her now?

"Hey," Laura playfully swatted Monica's knee. "I'm just yanking your chain." Her voice softened. "How are you holding up?"

"Fine. What's that in your hand?"

"This," Laura explained, handing the sheaf of printed papers to Monica, "is some stuff I want you to give to your friend, assuming it's not too late." She looked at Monica, who involuntarily shuddered at her mother's worry. "It's not too late, is it?"

Monica slowly shook her head, blanching at the thick stack of papers resting in her lap. "You want her to read all of this?"

"She can just skim over the encyclical. The Pope wrote this not too long ago - *Evangelium Vitae.*"

She saw Monica wrinkle her brows, puzzled. "It means 'The Gospel of Life.' It was written to address various issues threatening human life - not just abortion, but also euthanasia and artificial conception. This other thing," Laura bent forward and shuffled the papers in Monica's hands until she found the proper page, "is a collection of articles I found on Blessed Gianna Molla."

That name was new to Monica; she marveled at how her mother was able to keep track of the growing list of deceased declared either Venerable or Blessed by the Church, while she still had trouble naming all of the twelve Apostles. A fleeting glance at the first paragraph of the top article, abutting a picture of a fresh-faced brunette cuddling two babies, revealed everything Monica needed to know about the late woman.

Wife, mother, and physician, Gianna Molla achieved immortality within the Catholic community, Monica read, through her firm pro-life beliefs, refusing to perform abortions and refraining from one herself when a cyst threatened her fourth and final pregnancy. Days after giving birth she passed away, prompting those who knew Gianna to hail her as a role model for all mothers, expectant and experienced.

"Whoa, Mom," Monica said. "I don't think it's as serious as it was for this lady. It's not like, uh, my friend, has cancer. It's not a life or death matter."

"Tell that to the child growing inside your friend," Laura replied dryly. "Everybody wants to argue for the pro-choice side; I say, let there be another choice, a different choice. Your friend should know that, too."

"She's really afraid of how her father will react," Monica hinted. "How can she think about alternatives when she's worried she'll have to find an alternate place to live?"

Laura paused; the words were becoming harder to organize in her mind. "I don't know who your friend is, and I respect your decision to keep her anonymous. Therefore, I can't tell you what would happen with that family. I would think her parents would be willing to help preserve the life of both children involved."

"How would you react?" Monica asked, going for broke.

Laura half-smiled. "That's a day I hope I never have to see." Monica's heart fell at this. "I'd be angry, definitely, and hurt, disappointed - probably more with myself for not being the best mother I should have been. But," she sank to the floor opposite Monica, "after the smoke cleared, I would be here to see to it that the baby was delivered safely to a loving adoptive couple."

"You wouldn't want to keep it?"

"I wouldn't mind another baby in the house," Laura said truthfully, "but if you or Therese or CJ were to bring in a grandchild, that baby would be my responsibility, and don't try to argue about it. I just can't see any of you ready to take on child rearing...your eye will be on the baby but your mind will be on going to mall with your friends. A baby is not a pet, Monica."

"However," Laura struggled to stand, bracing herself on Therese's bed, "I would gladly take in a baby any day of the week than have any of you experience an abortion. We would find a solution that doesn't involve death."

"'Our body is sacred: it is an instrument, together with the soul, for doing good ...surround the body with sacrifice and your purity becomes freedom,'" Monica read from a highlighted sentence on one of the pages. Wow.

She did not feel so free anymore; the baby sat like a miniature cannonball in her stomach, getting heavier with each passing day. That was nothing, however, compared to the burden of her silence.

"Uh, Mom..." Monica faltered, her palms itching with sweat and sticking together as she clasped them together in a last-second prayer for courage. *God, help!* "I -"

"MOM!"

Both women gasped in surprise as Monica's bedroom door exploded into the bookcase behind it, rumbling all of Therese's paperbacks and trinkets. "Judith!" Laura admonished loudly.

"What have I told you about barging into rooms?" She righted the door away from the bookshelves, checking the particle board for dings. "What if somebody had been behind here?"

Judith, still in the threshold, stamped her foot, acting much younger than her nine years. "But mo-*oom*," she whined. "Stupid Josh won't stop bugging while I'm trying to watch the movie. He keeps repeating the words and singing."

"Your brother is not stupid," Laura said sternly, "and where is your father? Why isn't he handling this?"

"Daddy's out in the garage with CJ changing the oil in the van."

Laura let out an audible, exaggerated sigh. If only she too had an escape pod like Chris's coveted garage. "Okay, I'm coming down there." She started out the door after Judith, now elated and imagining a torrid punishment for her baby brother. "Give those to your friend, please?" she asked of Monica, nodding toward the papers. "Pray for her, too, and her baby. I intend to keep her in my own."

"Right, Mom." We'll talk later, she added silently. Always later. Monica inched upward and lay on her bed, reading the multi-chapter thesis of the Holy See. What was one more hour? Or one more day?

Forty-Eight

"This," Larry gestured to the large glass jars in front of him, "is a dietician's worst nightmare."

He and Pre stood in the tiny bar area of the Trellis, one of Williamsburg's best known restaurants, famous for its seasonal menus and rich desserts, notably the world-renowned Death by Chocolate. Not feeling adventurous enough to want to tackle the sixteen-ounce per slice treat, however, Larry gazed instead at the three types of chocolate cookies in the jars, still unable to decide when the bartender appeared for their order.

"We'll take one of each," Pre told the wine-vested server, who smiled and produced three small bags from underneath the bar. "We can go halfsies on them," she added to Larry, reaching for her wallet to pay.

"Hey, hey, now." Larry stilled Pre with a hand as she tried to pay; she felt her skin prickle at his touch. "I got this.

"Oh."

Pre slipped her wallet back in her purse and rubbed her hands, enjoying the warmth of the restaurant. She thought it unusual to see such a light dinner crowd on a Saturday - standing at the bar allowed her an excellent view of all dining area, and on any other night when she came in to buy cookies the place was practically bursting to capacity.

"You know what?" Larry asked as he was handed his change. "I like you better this way."

"What way is that?"

"Your face to me, and not turned in the other direction while running for your car." He brushed back a few strands of hair that had escaped his ponytail. "Is this the start of a new trend, one hopes?"

Pre's mouth was dry. Standing close to the bar provided a grand temptation, but she knew not even a shot of one hundred proof anything could give her the courage to break the news to Larry. She was a jellyfish.

"Tell you what, Mr. Jeffries." She sidled past Larry toward the exit. "Let's go find something to drink with these cookies and we can discuss the latest trends."

Larry grinned and followed her around the partition to the door, unaware of the pair of cold blue eyes boring into his back. Detective Mark Skinner stood not fifty feet away, awaiting his bar order.

Forty-Nine

On Sunday, the seventh day, Café Lisieux and her staff rested. Ditto Roy's shop.

Rosie appeared at Mass in her usual spot in the second pew, giving herself a good twenty-minute interim before the seven-thirty service. Plenty of time for praying the Joyful Mysteries and the Divine Mercy Chaplet, she surmised.

Added to her regular list of intentions for the rosary were prayers for the continued success of the Jeffries brothers' careers, and for God to continue guiding Pre and Larry closer together.

I haven't been to a wedding in years, she told the Lord, *but of course You are aware of that. I wouldn't mind so much to receive a handsome, embossed invitation in the mail this Christmas, or sooner. Let Your Will be done.*

She added her late nephew-in-law to her growing list of deceased relatives and friends, all of whom she hoped had long since achieved Heaven, but could not say for certain, hence the prayers. What harm could prayer do them anyway?

She clasped her fingers around her First Communion rosary so tightly while thinking of Neil during the decade of prayer meditating on the birth of Christ that the beads left red indentations on her hand. They stayed like that for most of the morning.

The message light blinked on her answering machine when she returned home. "Sorry I missed you," crackled Larry Jeffries's voice on an oft-used cassette. "Will try again later."

Larry and Roy left seconds after the call for services at their church in Newport News, the former with his mind on Pre and the latter with his mind on chaos. Both asked God for reassurance in their individual endeavors.

A message awaited them when they returned from breakfast. "Sorry, Larry," a recording of Pre's voice croaked. "I will miss you..."

Fifty

Jack Nixon attended midday Mass with his mother, while his father opted to mumble an Our Father or two in between chip shots with his friends from work. He sat motionless in the middle of his pew, distracted by the various cues to stand and sit, his posture warped and his expression bored. Please forgive me were the only three words running through his mind, from the celebrant priest's greeting until Jack received the Eucharist in his trembling, clammy hands, his gaze spinning around the church looking for Monica. She was nowhere in sight.

Monica Merwin spent the day flipping idly through a library book while watching television, paying attention to neither and keeping absolutely still. She was certain there was some movement inside her regardless, and she made a mental note to consult some reference texts the next time she was at the library and look up how soon into gestation one could feel a moving baby.

During the family's pre-Mass Rosary that afternoon, with everybody gathered in the den with heads bent and voices low and pious, Monica let her mind wander. Her breasts were starting to feel sore, and that made it less comfortable for her as she knelt next to her mother in the half circle of people around the coffee table. She guessed it was part of the pregnancy process, the swelling to produce milk for the baby that would never be.

What happens to the milk, she asked herself, if it goes unused? Will it slosh around inside me as a reminder, or harden into little benign stones?

A nudge from Laura's elbow jarred her back to the prayers and Monica joined in the closing Fatima prayer of the third decade. She was to lead the fourth decade of the Joyful Mysteries, following her parents and CJ in this daily family tradition. Therese would lead the final decade and Judith would recite the Hail, Holy Queen prayer, ending the Rosary.

Monica sighed. She did not feel like reciting anything right now, there was enough to distract her as it was, and she was not sure that prayer could do much to help her at this point. If God was listening, she thought, He did not seem to be in any hurry to answer her.

"Our Father, who art in Heaven, hallowed by Thy Name." She cleared her throat. "Thy Kingdom come, Thy Will be done, on Earth as it is in Heaven."

The rest of the family murmured the rest of the prayer at varying speeds, with little Joshua's voice being to loudest and by far the most enthusiastic. She remembered being that excited about prayer when she was the same age; she used to imagine herself sitting on Jesus's lap, not unlike with Santa Claus at the mall, telling Him everything she wanted and how much she loved Him and how she would never make Him sad.

Nice job, Nic, she told herself.

"Hail Mary, full of grace, the Lord is with thee," Monica began the first of ten Hail Marys. I wish I was full of grace instead of something else, she wanted to add. "Blessed art thou among women, and blessed is the fruit of thy womb, Jesus." The fruit of her womb should be so lucky.

She looked down the line to her left, then right. Calm and thoughtful faces floated all around her. CJ's, she noticed, appeared to be damp around the eyes. Was he crying? Why?

Dinner for the Merwins would be late. The family opted for the final Mass of the day, a lively folk music service held primarily for the William and Mary students but open to everyone. The family of seven filled and entire pew in the middle of the main nave, one row behind Lola and Miguel Marquez, who acknowledged everyone with a smile.

"Dinner was terrific Friday, of course," CJ whispered in the café owner's ear during the Sign of Peace.

"Thank you," Lola whispered back, her hands covering his. "Come back soon, and bring that pretty Nina with you."

"Uh, sure." He turned to Miguel and held his fist to his ear as if holding a phone, mouthing *call me* to his friend. Before Miguel could respond, a melodic acoustic guitar strummed the beginning of the Lamb of God hymn and the congregation joined voices as everyone knelt for the Consecration of the Host.

"Move," Therese growled to Monica, who had inched close to her sister so as not to straddle two different kneelers in the pew. The older sister bowed her head, wincing in pain as Therese pressed Monica's knee toward the gap in between the kneelers, causing Monica to lose her balance.

"What is with you?" Monica hissed, ignoring the warning glance on her father's face. Therese only stared straight ahead.

When Therese crossed her arms and bowed her head for the priest's blessing in lieu of Communion, Monica became more concerned for her sister. She could not gauge her parents' reaction to her sister's gesture because she stood in front of them, but she was curious all the same. What kind of sin could Therese be harboring to prompt her not to receive the Host - tonight and at school?

If it was as mortal a sin as Therese believed, then why did she not go to Confession at the appointed time yesterday? Chris or Laura would gladly have driven her to the church. These thoughts nettled in Monica's brain, so occupying her that she did not realize that she had received the Eucharist until after Father George had placed it in her cupped hands, extended to him out of habit.

Monica tried to object, tried to lift her hand cradle to the priest and ask him to take the Host back, but the words would not come. Instead she stayed rooted to her spot before the priest, staring at the perfect circle in her hands. The Body of Christ, nestled between her life and heart lines.

Slowly she started back down the aisle, encouraged by an urgent, pleading look from Father George. She was halfway to the Merwins' pew when Laura tapped her shoulder.

"Nic, what are you doing?" her mother whispered, horrified. Monica looked down and saw the Host still in her hands, clutched like a prized quarter.

"Oh, right," Monica muttered, slipping the Host in her mouth.

She reentered the pew, stepping over lowered kneelers and falling to a heap next to Therese, who looked on with disdain. Monica rested her arms on the pew in front of her and concealed her reddened face in the crooks of her elbows. She deserved that look from her sister, Monica decided, thinking it a good punishment for showing disrespect for Christ in His Church.

Fifty-One

Pre curled up in her recliner and stayed put the entire evening, pushing her remote control channel buttons and watching the screen flip from show to show. The phone rang intermittently throughout the day, her machine peppered with messages from Larry which escalated from calm to worried to exasperated.

"Dadgum it, Pre! Pick up the phone!" blared his voice through the pinholes of the machine's tiny speaker, sounding less forceful than he likely intended. Pre hovered over her handheld phone gloomily, resisting the urge to press the talk button.

"I-I just don't get you, you know," he said, his voice tempering. "We had a great time last night, or so I thought." A deep sigh followed; it sounded harsh. "Whatever. Look, I'm not giving up until I get a clear idea of what the story is. You can't hide forever." A rumbling noise, followed by a sharp beep, signaled the end of the call, the last one of the night.

Just like a reporter, she thought sadly, not satisfied until everything is in boldface banner headlines. I CAN'T DO THIS ANYMORE! See page two for details.

"Argh." She switched off the television and replaced the remote in its caddy, snatching the one for the stereo and turning on the compact disc already inside. Steel drums and Jimmy Buffett singing soon filled the darkened room; Pre padded to her kitchen for a drink.

"Oh, Larry, Larry, Larry..." she moaned. "I did have a good time last night." Scratch that, she added silently, a wonderful time. Which is why I can't subject myself to any more wonderful nights, she decided. Too many wonderful nights might overload my system and cause me to fall in love with you, Larry, if that hasn't already happened.

* * * *

Larry spent the rest of his Sunday on the back porch, snoozing on the bench swing with a crushed beer can in his fist, many more on the dirt before him. Roy threw an afghan on him when the clock struck ten and he did not come inside. Larry would eventually, though, so Roy just left him as is and retired to his online chat session. His home connection was, like the one at work, very skittish, but Roy was patient with it. He was not going anywhere, not for a while.

Fifty-Two

Jacob and Neil Junior were bathed, brushed, and tucked into bed by the time their grandparents returned from dinner. Carrie, close to tired herself, set down her John Grisham paperback and rose from the couch to make coffee.

"Oh, don't bother, honey," Sarah shed her coat and glided into the living room. "We'll be off to bed ourselves in a few minutes." The Mastersons were now staying with their daughter-in-law for the duration of their visit.

"This early?" Carrie glanced at her watch. Eight-forty.

Sarah slipped off her flats and rubbed her left foot. "Oh, this town! You have to walk everywhere on those cobblestones. No, we decided that we'd head home early; Jim managed to trade in our tickets so we could leave tomorrow afternoon. I'm sure by now you've had enough of us, and besides, you and the boys need the time alone to sort things through."

"Sarah, no." Carrie fell back in her seat. "You two are no bother to me at all. What about Neil's will? You're not going to stay for the probate?"

"Why?" Sarah asked. "Surely your lawyer will handle all of that, and anyway we really do need to get home."

But Carrie was not hearing it. "Sarah, you and Jim are retired. What's the rush?" she snapped, rubbing her eyes.

She caught Sarah's surprised face and immediately apologized. "I guess with all the people in the house it's been easier for me to get through this. If you and Jim leave tomorrow I don't know..." she turned away, her eyes filling with tears at the sight of the front door. Neil opened that door six days ago to gunfire...she and the boys would be entering and exiting the house through that door for years to come, and the mere thought of stepping on the same concrete that soaked in her husband's blood gave her the chills.

"Carrie." Sarah leaned closer to her daughter-in-law, tucked her left leg underneath her. "I appreciate that you want us to stay, but you knew this day would come. We can't stay here forever." She then stood and moved behind the couch, glancing down the hall for her husband; she caught sight of Jim's shirt flap flying as he wandered from the hall bathroom to the guest bedroom. "It'll take some time, but you will be fine. The boys, too. As long as you're strong they will be, too."

Carrie nodded. "Even with the boys here, I still feel alone, unprotected. I keep wondering if whoever did this is going to come back for the rest of us."

"I don't think that will happen," Sarah replied firmly. "I've yet to hear of a case like this," she noticed Carrie cringe at her husband's death being referred to as a case, "escalate to that level. If you're still uncomfortable, well, I suppose you could move."

Carrie shook her head. "I don't know if I could do that, even with all the stigma attached to this place now. Neil loved it here; we put so much into this house, and we're near all the boys' sports clubs and Cub Scouts and all that."

"A security system, then. Or get a guard dog."

Carrie wanted to laugh at that. The boys had been pestering her and Neil for a dog for years. If only the circumstances were happier.

"And you won't be completely alone," Sarah continued. "You have your sister in Richmond, and of course Barbara is close by."

"Yeah, I suppose she is." Carrie stifled a yawn. "Well, I better not keep you. Jim's probably already in bed. I'm headed that way myself."

"This early?"

Carrie twisted her lips into a wry smile. "Funny."

They made brief plans for breakfast in the morning and Carrie went upstairs to bed. She still expected Neil to join her. One more thing to which she had to adjust.

She lay on her back and fixated on a small light shadow cast on the ceiling from an outside lamppost, wishing the hours to speed up so she would not have to spend too much time alone in bed. Both boys stayed with her the night before, which helped a bit, but Carrie knew that it could not become a habit. Jacob and Neil Junior had to be brave, and so did she.

"Are You there, God, it's me, Carrie Masterson," she said quietly with an awkward smile. She hoped He had a good sense of humor. "How long's it been since I last did this? You probably have a better idea than I do. I'm not very good with dates."

She coughed. "I'm sorry for having neglected prayer, especially during the time I believed You existed, which must include now since I'm talking to You. I wonder if You groan and sigh whenever someone like me comes to You only in times of crisis, then forgets all about You once they've hit the jackpot. I hope You'll listen to me anyway."

"I just want my sons to grow up happy," she said, inhaling deeply. "Happy, healthy, and responsible. Please, just be with them, Lord. Whatever happens to me, let it be done, but please don't let my boys wind up like their father."

"God," she added shyly, "Thank You for Barbara. I don't appreciate her as much as I should, and if anything positive comes of this, I know she'll have something to do with it."

Fifty-Three

Help me! Help me! Helphelphelphelp...

Therese was quickly becoming more disappointed with herself. She had been writing pages and pages of eloquent prayer in her journal in the two years that she owned it, and to record a novena to St. Therese, she thought at first, did not seem difficult. This morning, however, her mind was a blank slate, much like the blinding white page in her line of sight.

"St. Therese, pray for my family," she muttered, keeping a close eye on the door. Monica was in the bathroom per her usual lengthy pre-school routines; Therese fought the urge to kick the door down in hopes of catching her sister throwing up or suffering some other side effect of pregnancy. What good, however, would that do, she asked herself. Monica was fast becoming an expert at explaining away the unusual.

So here Therese sat, at her desk, tapping her pen.

"Nic! Therese!" called their father from downstairs. "Breakfast in five. Let's move!"

"Coming!" Therese hollered back as Monica exited the bathroom and rushed into the room to throw on some clothes.

"Better get in there before CJ does," she said off-handedly, her head in the closet.

"Right."

"How's your period?"

"Not so bad now." Therese uncrossed her legs and started for the bathroom. "Seems to be getting lighter."

Monica selected a clean white blouse and plaid jumper from her half of the cramped closet. "It'll do that. Sometimes on the last day you won't flow at all, but it never hurts to wear protection, anyway."

Should have told that to Jack, Therese wanted to retort, but instead said. "I heard you don't flow at all when you're pregnant. Come to think of it, you told me that."

Monica looked up from buttoning her shirt to see that same look of her sister's face from last night's Mass, the scowling disapproval that darkened Therese's eyes. The stare was menacing as it bore down upon Monica, as if Therese were trying to communicate telepathically. *I know what you did.*

"Therese," Monica began. Therese stalked into the bathroom and slammed the door shut.

Fifty-Four

The knocks on Pre's door rained down like thick hail. *Thumpthumpthumpthump...*no stopping to rest. The noise rattled Pre off the couch, where she had slept through the night in front of a television screen lit with electric snow.

"I'm coming," she grumbled, swallowing the pungent aftertaste lingering in her mouth. She considered a quick brush, but the knocks progressed into incessant, annoying doorbell rings. She ran a finger over her top row of teeth before checking the peephole. Lola's distorted face filled the fisheye lens.

She did not wait for Pre to invite her inside. "I don't know whether to be relieved or furious," she cried, flopping down on Pre's recliner, exhausted, looking as if she ran straight from her house, a good five miles away.

"Lola, hello," Pre smiled weakly. "Come in. Sit down."

"Don't get smart," Lola huffed. "I drove seventy through the school zones to get here, thinking I'd find you lying unconscious on the bathroom floor."

"What?" Pre could not believe her ears. Why had her life suddenly become an episode of *Rescue 911*, and who was directing it? "What made you think a thing like that? You want some coffee? I know I could use some." She backpedaled into the kitchen.

"I didn't see you at Mass last night," Lola called amid the din of slamming cabinet doors. "When I saw Rosie at church this morning she said you didn't show in the morning either. I called to check on you last night and got your machine."

Pre tore into a fresh bag of automated drip coffee, taking a second to savor the vanilla nut aroma before scooping a few servings of grounds into a filter. "So?" she called back. "Maybe I went to a different Mass. There's only four every Sunday, two held simultaneously in the parish hall and church. I could've been anywhere."

"Like lying around on your butt watching Cartoon Network while everyone who cares about you worries themselves sick?" Lola joined Pre in the kitchen, leaned into the sink and snatched a Dixie cup from its holder. "Don't try to deny it, either. I know your routine, what you do when you get moody. I bet if I checked the garbage I'd find an empty Ben and Jerry's container," she added slyly.

"Nope." Pre thrust open the top door of her refrigerator to reveal a frosted pint of Butter Pecan ice cream resting in the door shelf. She stuck out her tongue; it felt fuzzy and numb inside her mouth. "Besides, if you were that worried, why didn't you come over last night to check on me? I was here all day."

"So you did skip Mass, I knew it! Are you sick?"

"No," Pre shot back. "At least, not physically." She fiddled with the coffee machine, which emitted a wild hiss as the pair retreated to the living room.

"That's not like you, to intentionally miss a Sunday obligation," Lola said, concerned.

"I will make amends." Pre threw herself lengthwise across the sofa. *Bless me, Lord, for I have sinned. It's been a long time since my last Confession. I think Princess Di was still alive. I'm waaay overdue.*

Lola marched back into the kitchen for coffee mugs. "This sickness you, er, claim to suffer..." she poked her head around the wall, "it wouldn't happen to involve a certain young man of mutual acquaintance now, would it?"

Pre covered her face with a throw pillow. She knew Larry would come into the conversation eventually. "He called you."

"He called Rosie, but not initially about you, just to do some fact checking for his story. She asked how things were going, he said things weren't going anywhere, and this morning as I'm leaving church she corners me in my pew."

Pre smirked. She heard it through the grapevine. Not much longer would my secrets be mine.

"Doesn't Rosie know it's a sin to gossip?"

"It's also a sin to blow off your Sunday obligation," Lola pointed out to her friend, "and if I'm not correct, I swear I saw a few more Café Lisieux coffee mugs in your cabinets than what I gave you originally." Pre rolled her eyes at this. "So think before you start sifting through the dirt for rocks to throw."

Pre sat up, grasping the arm of the sofa as her head throbbed. "I just don't understand everyone's fascination with my personal life, is all. I go out on a few dates, big deal. Marriages have lasted fewer hours."

"I agree some of us have been a bit overexcited when you and Larry started going out, once we all got to know him," Lola nodded, recalling one comment made by her son about how somebody as attractive as Pre managed to stay single for so long. "I guess we were just hoping this was, you know, the one." She emphasized this with a thumbs-up gesture.

Pre dabbed at her eyes. No tears yet, she noticed but the day was just beginning. "Lola, there will never be a one for me."

"What are you saying? Larry's crazy about you. He said as much to Rosie."

"Oh dear." Here they come, Pre thought, one drop at a time. Why had she led him on, let him kiss her, and laughed at his anecdotes over chocolate chip cookies? "I so didn't want that to happen."

"Why, Pre? Don't you feel the same way about him?" Lola's voice was gentle, albeit puzzled. "When I saw you with him at the café the other night, well, I got that impression."

"You're right, I'm nuts about him," Pre finally admitted out loud. "Maybe I'm just plain nuts."

"That I've always known," Lola joked. In the kitchen the hissing and percolating from the coffee maker faded into an inaudible simmer, and Lola ducked back to fetch coffee. "You're making no sense at all."

"Lola, I can't have children."

Silence. Then a conspicuous clunking sound followed as a ceramic mug fell against Pre's Formica counter.

"Lola?" Pre called just as her boss appeared in the doorway.

"For real?" was all the ashen woman could say.

"For real." Pre moved closer. "That's the first time I've said it aloud. The first time since I found out, anyway."

"How? When?" The questions came out in brief gasps; Lola's hand fluttered to her heart. Pre was the daughter she never had, though she constantly neglected to say as much to the young woman, for fear, perhaps, of sounding too sentimental. She knew Pre was not comfortable with such sappy talk. That aside, Lola could not help but feel neglected herself for never being informed of something as important as this. Pre was normally very open with her.

Pre gestured Lola to the sofa, sans coffee, and delivered an annotated version of her tale: the diagnosis, the surgery (a revelation which shocked Lola, who had believed Pre was getting her appendix removed), and the painful aftermath that stayed with her. "I've never told anyone, though I think some people have their suspicions, like Laura Merwin for one, judging from what we talk about and what she sees in my reactions, I suppose."

"I've pretty much accepted it, being barren, that's not the problem," Pre added. "I guess I cope by believing God has another purpose for me, though I'm sure I'm taking my sweet time in finding it..."

Lola appeared to be more upset over Pre's barren nature than Pre was. "I just don't get it. You think Larry's going to forget about you simply because you can't have children? How do you even know he's thinking of marriage? Really, aren't you being just a bit premature?"

She stood and paced the compact living room, with Pre's eyes following up and down and back again. "We've only known him barely a week! That's hardly enough time to forge a committed relationship, and even if marriage is Larry's intent, he has other things to consider. He's still in school and doesn't have a permanent job, and he doesn't seem to be the type of person who would jump headfirst down the aisle without making some preparations."

"Which is why I want to make a clean break now," Pre said, knocking her fists together. "Before he starts entertaining these ideas...before I..." she sniffed back the first tears to no avail, "...before I am unable to walk away."

"Does Larry know about this? What am I saying, of course he doesn't, not if you're behaving like this!" Lola sat back down on the sofa; Pre did not look at her. "Well, at least tell him, because I believe he has a say in this matter. You might be surprised, Pre, he might not care. You could be fretting for nothing."

"I already know the answer," Pre argued softly, her memory flashing back to the night before when she and Larry browsed a late-night bookstore after enjoying their dessert, to the look in Larry's eyes when a stroller rolled past them. Inside, a drooling, happy toddler violently shook a Winnie-the-Pooh rattle and burbled in infant code. Pre could not begin to describe to Lola the light in Larry's eyes. A yearning, that was the best word she could use.

She remembered watching on helplessly as Larry waggled a few fingers in reply to the baby, asking the mother for his name and could he take him home? The mother chuckled wearily, and Pre tried to join in the merriment. No man who did not want kids would have acted that way in public, she decided, and she relayed this thought to Lola, who scoffed.

"Larry likes you for you, not for how well your reproductive organs work. I can't believe someone as intelligent as you could behave so childishly."

"I'm sorry to have disappointed you," Pre said dully, abruptly leaving the couch. "That coffee's probably ice cold by now."

Lola remained still, continuing to digest everything revealed to her, not wanting to be completely convinced. "You're sure there's nothing you can do? There's no medication or operation available to you?"

"Nope." Pre was quick to answer, as she had asked those same questions years ago to much discouragement. "Nothing within reason that doesn't go against the Church." Both women were aware that the Church frowned upon artificial means of conception, but those options were closed to Pre anyway, as long as her own internal equipment was useless.

"What about adoption?"

"Lola," Pre commanded, gripping the counter for support. The aroma of vanilla coffee now made her nauseous. "Just drop it, please? I know you mean well, but I've already made up my mind. There's nothing more I can do about this."

Lola reached for her purse. "You're wrong," she told Pre, extracting her rosary. "You can pray."

"I already have a rosary." Pre waved away the proffered beads. "Several, in fact, including one from Rosie that looks just like that." Where that particular rosary was, Pre knew, was an entirely different matter; to Pre, rosaries were like ballpoint pens, scattered about the house in a myriad of unknown nooks. On the rare occasion the young woman did pray a set of mysteries, she kept track on her fingers. She knew she could not lose them.

"So much for the theory that no two rosaries look alike," Lola said with a giggle. "Or is that snowflakes? Whatever, take this one anyway, as a loaner. I have several, too." With that, another string of beads appeared from the purse. "We're going to pray together, for guidance."

Pre's eyes widened. "Now? Here?"

"You don't pray?"

"Of course I pray. What kind of question is that?" Pre shot back. Just this morning, in fact, Pre finished her daily regimen of silent meditation and the requisite Our Father. Normally a day would be peppered with additional short missives, with big prayers saved for emergency situations like help for ailing relatives or the threat of natural disasters. Not an effective way to lead a prayerful life, she figured, but Pre complained little about results. Most of them, anyway.

Now, as she watched her employer struggle to a kneeling position, Pre asked herself if this situation merited the lengthy devotion. "I doubt God will see fit to plant a fruitful uterus in me, Lola," she said.

"Kneel," came the stern reply. "Pretend you're Michael Jordan and shoot. If you never shoot, you will always miss. I'll start with the Creed and opening prayers, then we'll alternate decades." Lola closed her eyes and was halfway through the Sign of the Cross when Pre objected again.

"Lola."

"Do this for me or you're fired." Lola opened one eye and glared at Pre with it. Pre, who saw easily past the threat, complied. The sooner we do this, the sooner it's over, she thought.

Fifty-Five

Lunchtime arrived almost immediately after first bell, at least Monica believed it did. The day was moving rather quickly past her. Either that or she was floating in a post-sleep haze.

Sister Charlotte's lecture during history class droned on at her usual monotone, prompting many elbows to prop up heads in desperate attempts to stay alert. Monica, however, sat straight and stared at the chalkboard, fixated on the nun's loopy cursive until the letters started to squiggle and contort into psychedelic curlicues. Her mind replayed the last seconds of the morning before breakfast.

*I heard you don't flow at all when you're pregnant...*over and over it echoed in her mind like a skipping compact disc. Therese's eyes were daggers, poking at her conscience.

As class let out Monica caught her young sister's eye as they passed in the hall; she was on her way to eat while Therese headed toward the library for independent study.

"Wait!" Monica breezed past a block of lumbering students milling into various classrooms, bag lunch in hand. As she reached the corner pillar of the courtyard near the library, a dull cramp struck her abdomen and Monica sucked in a gust of wind, steadying herself against the concrete column. The pain felt like a typical menstrual cramp, she thought. Was that normal for pregnancy?

She pressed a hand to her gut. That squishy sensation was still there, and her head felt dizzy. Maybe the running was too much for the baby.

Therese was just outside the library doors when she finally turned around. "What is the matter with you?" she cried angrily.

"I-I'm just out of breath. Why didn't you just stop when I called you?"

Overhead the late bell chimed, and Therese cocked her head toward the din in response. "That's not what I meant anyway and you know it," she snarled, bursting through the entrance.

"Wait up!" Monica ignored the look on Sister Mary Edith's face as she pushed through the library turnstile, breaking a cardinal rule of the building by toting her lunch bag. Instantly she closed her mouth and concealed the bag in her arms, as the old nun ruled the library with iron will and a countenance to match. Even mild coughing in a spurt of book dust was taboo.

Monica felt her larynx tighten in the overheated building as she approached her sister in the nonfiction shelves. "Psst!" She beckoned Therese to a remote corner, far from the watchful scowl of the elderly nun. Therese snatched a coffee table-sized book from a row of upright spines before grudgingly following her sister. "You know?" Monica asked in a low whisper.

Therese nodded slowly, a thousand accusations filed away in her mind, yet she decided to keep her words to a minimum. No amount of berating could turn back the clock for Monica.

"Have you told anyone?" was Monica's next question, and it was asked in a shaking voice.

Therese thumbed through the page-sized color prints in the book. "No. It's not my problem, so it's not my responsibility either. That's your job."

"Me?" Monica heard her voice hit a high note and immediately she checked between the shelves for a flash of blue veil. "Me?" she repeated, hushed. "You know Mom and Dad will freak."

"If you know that, then why did you do something that would make them freak in the first place?" Therese countered haughtily. Her face then fell slack with worry. "Jack didn't force himself..."

Monica shook her head. How easy it would have been to lay the entire blame on Jack, but she had lied enough. "No. It just ...happened. I wasn't thinking at the time, at least, not with my head. Plus it was just that one time."

Therese snorted. "Once is enough. Once is too many, and I can't believe you actually did it! You!" Her voice bounced off the metal shelves, and Monica tried to shush her, to no avail. A distant rustling from behind the desk signaled bad news: Sister Edith would soon find them and brand them with a cold stare and a pale, wrinkled finger pointing to the door.

Therese, however, did not appear to care. She was already free from the shelves and walking toward the circulation desk, library card in hand, before the nun could comment. Monica loped behind as Sister Edith checked out the book and sternly bade both sisters a good afternoon. Translation: *Get out of my library.* Both left unsmiling.

"I suppose Jack wants you to have an abortion."

Monica felt Therese's voice fill with venom as her boyfriend's name was spoken. She remained silent, answering the question with a downcast gaze.

"You're going to compound sin on top of sin," Therese gasped, suddenly disgusted. "Who are you and what have you done to my sister?"

"Therese, please. Try to see it from my point of view," Monica begged, regurgitating Jack's spiel from a few days ago, the same words she did not want to hear then. Therese, however, was less convinced than she.

"Here's a thought." Therese stuck her finger between the closed pages of the book and pried the tome open. "Why don't you try to see it from another point of view." She flipped page toward the front of the heavy book, her left wrist buckling slightly from its weight. Monica saw hundreds of fleshy beings with veined eyelids whizzing past as Therese searched.

"How far along are you now?"

"Huh? Oh, about a month. Maybe a little more."

Therese found the page she wanted and thrust the book at Monica. "Here."

Monica looked down at a black and white photo of something resembling a gelatinous blob issued from a powerful sneeze, or perhaps a clump of cells she might have seen once underneath a microscope in biology class. "What?"

"This is what your baby looks like now," Therese explained as Monica winced slightly, not from the photographs but from the possibility that somebody was eavesdropping. "Within three weeks, your baby will have developed organs and limbs; that is, if you allow your baby to live that long."

Monica stared balefully at the book. That little glop of transparent white, no bigger than her fingertip, was a baby in progress. "It's so little," she breathed. "What could it possibly feel so soon? It's not as if I would be doing anything like one of those partial-birth deals, where the baby is practically ready to be born." She heard the words yet had trouble believing that they were coming from her own mouth. She looked at the picture again.

Were those the beginnings of arms she saw on either side of the elongated "body?" Monica berated herself silently for not paying much attention in health class to this particular unit, else she may have been more adept at deciphering the object before her, this pre-fetus, and therefore have a clearer idea of what she was about to do to the one inside her.

"A baby that early in growth is already developing a spinal cord," Therese said, tracing her finger along an illuminated line that resembled the vein of a cooked shrimp. "Blood cells are being produced, too, Nic. This is alive, in you!"

She snatched the book and slammed it shut. "You really think you can live the rest of your life knowing you had your baby flushed down a toilet like it was a useless piece of doo?"

Monica recoiled at her sister's strong language. "I just can't believe something so tiny -"

"Insects are tiny," Therese interrupted.

"What?"

"Insects are tiny. You don't think they have the ability to feel pain like we do?"

"Therese," Monica rolled her eyes. "There's no point of comparison. Insects are not people."

"So would you agree that babies are not insects, too? Babies not yet born, even?" Therese hoped for the sake of her nephew or niece that Monica would agree with her.

She turned away from Monica briefly to see her older sister's friends eating lunch in the courtyard, watching them from a distance. She handed Monica the book on impulse, praying a silent plea to Jesus. "I gotta go," she said. "I don't hate you, Nic, but if you go through with this...I don't think I'll like you for a while." With that, she sped away down the corridor.

"Therese!"

But Therese had already rounded a corner and disappeared, leaving Monica with a thick life science book and an uneaten lunch as her friends continued to eat and talk amongst themselves. She stepped into the courtyard toward them and grimaced as another pain tore through her. Maybe the baby knew what was going to happen, Monica guessed. Could nerve cells and intuition develop as quickly as blood cells? Could an unborn child scream without a mouth?

She palmed the book in both hands, gazing at the cover image of an unborn child in the third trimester, a smooth red orange thumb poised at the shapeless mouth. It appeared too large for the sac surrounding it.

It. She, Monica realized. It was a she, and this she on the book cover was already born, probably walking and talking and laughing and grabbing things with chubby fingers. Her child would never do any of those things. Twenty-four more hours to go...

"No, no, no."

She wanted to push the remorse away, squeeze it into a tight capsule and stomp it into the dirt. Remember, she told herself, why she was going to the doctor. What kind of life could she offer a baby at sixteen, with no degree, no true job experience, and no skills? How could she show her face if she decided to continue the pregnancy, knowing she had brought shame...

Wait.

She looked again at the book, then at the shadows of passing students slithering along the brick walls. What was shame, compared to salvaging a life? Therese was right, there was life inside her, yet Monica was too concerned with her own to think about it.

Oh, God in Heaven, forgive me, she pleaded silently. *I am so selfish. I have no valid reason to abort this child, only my own petty vanities and eagerness to cover up something that should never have happened.*

She turned her head to see an open door to her left - the upper school office lay within, where a two-foot high statue of Our Lady of Fatima perched on a stone pillow just inside. A gentle face radiating a Mona Lisa smile floated over praying hands wrapped with a black bead rosary. The white mantle with its numerous chips and yellowed spots betrayed the statue's true age, but Monica thought it lovely nonetheless.

Mary never cared about what others thought of her, when baby Jesus formed in her womb before her marriage to Joseph was a done deal. Mary must have been more tolerant than other women, Monica thought.

"Pray for me, Mary," Monica whispered, swallowing hard and entering the office, her knees quivering like thick jelly. Lunch period for her was about to end, and the friendly conversations over sandwiches she missed were winding down, plastic baggies and empty milk cartons were tossed in the trash, and her classmates were drifting back to class.

All, that was, except for Jennifer, who at the moment was barreling toward Monica.

"Wazzup?" she squealed, slapping her friend on the back. "Where were you for lunch? You're going to be late for fifth hour, you know."

"Yeah, well," Monica choked on her words. "I'll tell you later. I need to see the MG." *Go away*, she really wanted to say.

"Cool." A wad of contraband bubble gum crackled in Jennifer's mouth. "I'm working here for my study hall. Let's motor."

Monica followed Jennifer the rest of the way inside to Sister Mary Grace's office, suddenly too self-conscious to look up at the Fatima statue that greeted them.

"Miss Jordan's out the rest of the day," Jennifer giggled as if it were the most important news on earth. "That means I get a full hour of computer solitaire, cause when Miss Jordan's away, the MG usually holes up in her office with the door closed."

"She doesn't give you anything to do?" Monica asked, wondering what was the point of having a student helper around the office if no help was needed.

"Oh, I work, when Miss Jordan is here," Jennifer said, referring to the school secretary. "I think these nuns are lost without her, personally. Hold on a sec." She crept up to the principal's door and rapped a few times underneath the brass nameplate. No answer.

"She must be out too. Why did you need to see her?"

Monica flushed, and she inadvertently stepped back into the statue, rocking it slightly on its pillar. "Oh, I just lost something the other day, and thought maybe somebody turned it in."

"Ah," Jennifer nodded as a mischievous smile brightened her face. "Speaking of lost and found..."

She clutched the knob of the principal's door and turned slowly, easing the door open wide enough to slip inside. Monica peered through the slit to see her friend rush behind a cluttered metal desk and dip beneath a stack of papers.

"I-I don't really think you should be doing this," Monica protested weakly as Jennifer rifled through a drawer. She cast a worried glance behind her shoulder, keeping vigil for the nun's return. She already had her blood sister's anger weighing on her mind, and she did not need the wrath of a Sister, too.

Jennifer, however, ignored Monica's caveats. "I saw the MG store this away. I don't know why, though. Nobody's going to fess up to leaving it here."

She rounded the desk with sprightly steps, a plastic freezer bag hanging from pinching fingers. "Isn't it gross?" Jennifer asked, punctuating her question with a squeamish noise. "I wondered if they dusted it for prints."

Monica felt her heart stop as Jennifer waved the bag containing the discarded pregnancy test box in front of her eyes. "That's the box they found?"

"Yeah, and whoever used it obviously spared no expense. I've never seen a generic store brand one before."

Monica shook her head, hypnotized by the relic. "Neither have I," she told her friend. This time she was not lying.

Fifty-Six

Rosie, happy with herself for convincing Father Welker that tensions in the area had settled significantly, smiled at passersby down 21st Street, her hands busy with yet another rosary in progress. The priest, clutching a sample of Rosie's handiwork, prayed the Chaplet of Divine Mercy with a small circle of protesters a hundred feet away from her station. All heads, covered in knit wool, bowed and responded to Father's deep voice in sing-song unison - a scene difficult to ignore, one Rosie hoped would publicize the pacifist nature most pro-lifers embodied.

News of the investigation of Neil Masterson's murder became scarcer; after nearly a week, the doctor's assassination faded from a bold front page headline on newspapers across the state to a one-paragraph summary on section B of *The Daily Press* in Newport News. Still no leads revealed to the public, Rosie read that morning over breakfast. She wondered if any leads existed at all. She never thought to broach the subject to Carrie, who had yet to volunteer any information. Little ears were always within eavesdropping range, anyway.

"Have a nice day. God bless you," she said pleasantly to an elderly gentleman who pocketed a St. Anthony chaplet as he stepped into the coffee shop with nary a word or a nod to her. Rosie sighed. Maybe the glint of the medal attached to the thirty-nine-bead chaplet, when reflected in the morning sun, made it too irresistible to leave on the round patio table alongside rows of other rosaries and various chaplets made the night before. Maybe the man would actually make use of St. Anthony's prayerful intercession.

Maybe.

Business was slow that morning for most shops on the street. Rosie watched with concern as a nurse wrapped in a gray wool sweater rose with dragging feet up the steps to the clinic door, her head lowered timidly and her eyes darting left and right. Lack of news was definitely not a good thing for the clinic employees, Rosie guessed. No suspects recorded in custody meant that each stranger strolling past the building was a potential terrorist, scanning the area and keeping mental track of the comings and goings of everyone in the clinic.

Maybe the nurse thought the person who shot Neil Masterson was gunning for her next, visualizing red round bulls-eyes on her chest and face. The thought made Rosie shudder.

Would Larry know, she asked herself as she strung a red-beaded rosary decade, of any supplementary information gathered by a *Times* reporter on the police beat? She wished she had thought to ask him when he called last, but much of that conversation centered around his recent heartbreak. What was it with Pre? What caused that young woman to turn hot and cold around Larry, unpredictable and baffling?

Jesus, Rosie prayed silently, *I know I promised Pre I would let it go if she decided for herself not to pursue a relationship with Larry, but I just can't stand by while this poor fellow is miserable! Why is Pre acting so fickle?*

She fingered a just completed rosary - brown beads with a white plastic crucifix - rolling the strand in her palm. *I don't think she's being fair, Lord*, she continued, glancing to her left as the prayer circle broke and its members dispersed in different directions with their pro-life placards. *Was she abused as a child, or perhaps attacked by a drunken classmate in college? Does she just not experience...feelings for men as a whole? What is Your Will for her, Jesus? If Larry isn't the one, let me know and I'll drop it.*

She closed her plea with a silent Gloria and blessed herself as Father Welker approached with his now empty coffee cup.

"Refill?" he offered.

Rosie picked up her cup, swirling the last swallow of lukewarm cocoa, and downed it in one gulp. "Thank you, Gary, but I think that first batch has me plenty wired."

"Some water, then? Barbara?"

He followed the old woman's agape stare across the street to a balding gentleman in a long winter coat shiftily pacing the sidewalk in front of the clinic. "What's up?" Father asked, lightly nudging Rosie's shoulder.

"I know that man. Roy Jeffries. He's the brother of that reporter I've told you about." She rose from her chair and waved a hand, trying to catch the sullen man's attention and failing. "Hm. He's probably taking an exercise break. He runs a shop around here somewhere. Lola bought a table from him the other day."

The priest nodded. "He looks rather preoccupied, like he's waiting for something. Or someone."

As the priest made his observation, Roy extracted a rolled-up paper bag from and inside coat pocket and shoved it into a city garbage can on the curb and stalked away, turning the corner at Granby Street.

"Break time's over, it seems," Father Welker commented.

"Guess so." Rosie shook her head, while several hundred yards away Roy Jeffries strode back to his shop, whistling a happy tune and congratulating himself in advance for keeping his cool for when he would make the plant for real tomorrow.

Fifty-Seven

Roy nodded to a dark-suited man admiring the collection of discarded window frames and, not waiting for acknowledgment, sped to the back of the store. An urgent look from Will, however, diverted him from his intended destination - his office, where a backlog of busy work awaited him - to the workshop in the back room of the building.

"That guy was asking about you." Will cocked his head toward the front. "Sounded pretty serious to me, I don't know. I got the feeling he didn't want to talk about oak versus mahogany for sprucing up his dining room."

Roy's demeanor remained calm and disinterested. "I wouldn't worry about it, guy. It's not like we have anything to hide." He eased toward the doorway and peered down the pathway dividing mountains of used furniture - the man's charcoal jacket and pants were crisp and clean, with tiny strips of white cuff gleaming from both sleeves. Roy studied the firm jaw and aquiline nose, which supported mirrored sunglasses. The guy looked like a cop.

"What did you tell him?" Roy asked.

"The truth." Will wiped his hands on a soiled towel, his eyes watering at the varnish fumes. "You took a break, didn't know when you'd be back."

"And how many minutes ago was that?"

"Dunno. About ten?" Will danced nervously, shifting his weight from foot to foot. Roy understood the young man's discomfort, being well aware of Will's prior arrest record. Petty stuff, however, nothing that should not have warranted this much worry.

"Hey." He slapped Will on the shoulder. "Chill, all right? If he wanted you, he'd have asked for you now, right?" When Will nodded, Roy asked about his other employee.

"He's loading up a truck for Mr. Johnson out back. That china closet from two weeks ago."

Roy checked the clipboard, which hung from a rusty nail by the door, where a copy of the day's delivery roster was kept for quick reference. Edna Mercer, an elderly widow living off of Social Security checks in a high-rise condo near the Freemason area of town, was expecting a set of end tables to accent her Salvation Army cast-off living room sofa. She was next on the list after the Johnson china closet.

"Got my truck keys?" Roy held out an opened palm as Will surrendered said keys. "Right. Help me get the Mercer end tables in the bed. I'll take them out now."

"What about that guy?" Will peered over Roy's shoulder, cringing as the man in the distance impatiently checked his watch. Roy looked up as the man's sunglasses came off to reveal a full, determined face, one that looked very familiar, one Roy recalled seeing on the news offering a sound bite with regards to the Masterson murder.

Catch me if you can, buddy. Roy half-jogged out the back door. "Tell him the truth again," he said, turning to wink at Will. "You're good at that."

Seconds later, as the tables were secured and as Roy ignited the truck engine, Detective Mark Skinner poked his head inside the workshop, wincing as the sharp aroma of varnish fumes attacked his olfactory senses.

"Can I help you, sir?" Will pretended not to remember the man.

"Yeah, that fellow who walked past me a while back - about six foot, jeans and flannel top, heavy coat - he just disappeared. Was that your boss?"

"Y'mean Roy?"

"Yeah, Roy," Mark said, irritated and shouting over the engine of the retreating truck.

Will watched Roy's Dodge amble up the alleyway behind the store and turn a corner. "Just missed him. Went to make a delivery, but he'll be back -"

"In a few minutes, you don't know when, I know," Mark finished the young man's sentence and threw up his hands. An urge to flash his badge and perhaps scare the pants off the varnish-stained yokel passed quickly through Mark's mind. He had aroused enough suspicion already, and anyway he was not really sure what to look for at the store. Any potential bomb-making materials could easily be explained away as necessities for Roy's business, and he doubted the man was so stupid as to keep a weapon used in a murder at his workplace.

Sitting at the bottom of the Chesapeake Bay was a better hiding place for that, Mark thought.

"You want some coffee?" Will offered. "I don't think Roy'll be long."

"That's okay, I'll come back. You're open 'til six today?"

"Yup."

Mark waved a pensive good-bye and ducked around a pile of office desks, suspicious that Roy Jeffries might be on to him. Unlikely, though, he finally decided, as he never told Roy's employee that he was a cop. Perhaps antique sales and restoration was a fruitful business, more so than he first believed.

He eased back toward the workshop and noticed Will engrossed in stripping a tabletop. Tiptoeing a few steps toward Roy's office, Mark checked his surroundings again for prying eyes before slipping inside. He had no idea how long that table would keep the attention of Roy's bumpkin worker, so an out-an-out tossing of the office was dismissed.

A perfunctory inspection, however, presented nothing that interested Mark, with the exception of the computer. Mark leaned over the mouse and nudged it slightly with a gloved hand, waking the screen to an active Internet browser set to a search engine Web site. He pointed the mouse to the top menu bar and selected the 'Bookmark' option to reveal a list of World Wide Web sites Roy had marked for future reference.

"Hello." Mark's eyes lit up as he absorbed the names of various extremist and anarchist Internet organizations. He memorized all the names and let the mouse free, dashing out of the store before Will emerged from the workshop to make a phone call.

Fifty-Eight

"Give away many rosaries today?"

Rosie was hunched over in her chair, reaching into her canvas bag for a handful of beads. "Oh," she spoke into the bag, slowly lifting her torso upward, "about five or six so far. Not bad for a Monday. Oh!"

She looked up and saw her niece smiling tentatively at her.

"Carrie," Rosie greeted her cheerfully. "This is the last, er, that is to say..." She looked past Carrie at the clinic. "This is a surprise."

"Yeah, well," Carrie followed her aunt's gaze. "I'm not here long, just came by to pick up some of Neil's things."

"I see." Rosie let the beads fall into a pocket she had made with the tail of her sweatshirt. "If you don't mind my asking, why didn't you just have everything shipped to you? I mean, it's a long way to drive from your home, and considering what happened to Neil...and this place..."

"He was murdered, Rosie, it's okay to say it out loud," Carrie interrupted. "Maybe it was because he worked here that he was shot, maybe not. That still hasn't been determined."

Who am I kidding, Carrie thought, what other reason could there be for Neil's death? Carrie shoved her hands in her pockets, grateful at least that her aunt had yet to give her a look that said if Neil hadn't worked here, he'd still be alive.

Rosie could never say that out loud, this Carrie knew. Nobody could foresee a person's death.

"You're here," Carrie observed. "You've come a long way as well."

"I have my reasons."

"As do I," Carrie countered, exhaling a white blast of cold air. "I can't run away from what happened, and this building isn't going to hurt me."

"Well," Rosie arched an eyebrow, "not you, anyway."

"Barbara," Carrie warned sharply, wondering suddenly why her aunt felt she had to embed her opinion in every conservation they had. "Let me finish. I wanted to say that I'm not threatened anymore. I doubt there will be anymore violence in the wake of Neil's death, against me or anyone else, and that I'm getting better."

The old woman's eyes blinked. "Very nice, Carrie. You almost convinced me."

Carrie felt her knees weaken; butterflies danced in her stomach. "Really? I didn't quite believe it myself."

"Have you been inside yet?"

Carrie shook her head. Her past visits to the clinic were all brief and never extended beyond the lobby, just minute-long pleasantry exchanges with a nurse or two while Neil broke free for lunch. Today she was probably going to be led further into the bowels of the clinic, past examination rooms and patients holding urine samples in plastic cups or laying spread-eagled on cold tables while being probed and preparing for pap smears, among other things.

She knew what went on in the clinic, she had always known, and now the reality of perhaps spying something unpleasant unnerved her. Rosie could see that in her niece's face.

"You don't really want to go inside, do you?" Rosie asked gently.

Carrie shook her head again.

"So don't. Get somebody to deliver Neil's things." Rosie picked green beads out of the pile in her lap and strung them together in one decade.

"Too many ghosts in there," Carrie whispered, now feeling a bit self-conscious as Rosie's priest friend eyed her with interest. "I used to keep telling myself that if it was legal, then it was okay."

"And now?"

"Now...I don't know." Carrie shivered in a brisk gush of wind. "I guess I thought that if I came down here I'd have closure, you know? Get the stuff and get out."

"You'll have closure when Neil's killer is caught, and he will be caught. Count on that."

Carrie laughed woodenly. "That's what the detective said."

"Do you want me to go in with you? Would that help?"

"You?" Carrie noticed the serene look on Rosie's face, shocked that such a suggestion could be made. "That clinic stands for everything you despise, Barbara! Yet you want to go inside?"

"No, I don't." Rosie's voice was equally calm. "I want to help my niece get through a tragedy, and if I have to walk into that slaughterhouse to do it..." a pleading look from Carrie broke her train of thought. "All right, Carrie. I won't say anything, but I'll definitely pray. I know the building can't hurt me either."

Rosie carefully scooped up her beads and returned them to her bag along with the partially-made rosary. Taking Carrie's hand as a mother would with a child, the two crossed the street during a lengthy traffic lull.

Father Welker, leaning against the coffee shop with a fellow parishioner, watched the duo climb the steps with a gaping stare. What was Rosie doing, he wanted to know.

She's entered the Lion's Den, dear Jesus. Help her, and her friend, he prayed.

Fifty-Nine

To Pre's relief, Larry did not show his face at lunch or dinner. Both meal crushes trafficked smoothly in and out of the café with nary a misplaced order or unsatisfied customer. Lola's wait staff performed their duties with cheerful faces and nimble steps, all trying to outdo one another with regards to fawning over customers and keeping water and tea levels constantly high.

Pre had to smile; the time was nigh for Lola to select the Employee of the Month. Along with having a Polaroid portrait tacked to one of the bulletin boards, the lucky winner received a complimentary dinner for two with all the trimmings, something anyone on a waiter's salary would naturally desire.

Pre joined Lola behind the counter for a breather. "You slip pep pills in the break room watercooler?"

"Better." Lola folded her dishrag over her forearm. "I slipped a spinach lasagna in the oven. Everyone in the kitchen's been going nuts."

This did not surprise Pre. Lola's home cooking was enough to set the driest mouth watering. Pavlov would have been proud.

Pre noticed a couple stretching and shrugging on their jackets, and she darted to the cash register to settle their bill. Polite pleasantries of meal compliments and words of thanks flew across the register counter, all the while with Pre keeping a plastic smile on her face to mask her discomfort. Inside she was blubbering like a baby, regretting the events of the last few days and hating herself for not being honest with Larry.

The Jorgensens, more regular Café Lisieux customers, made matters no better for her when they inquired of that handsome gentleman with whom she dined the other evening. What a nice man he was, they commented, and how nice it was to see Pre enjoying his company.

Pre nodded sagely and flashed the smile, volunteering nothing more and wishing Mr. Jorgensen would just sign his credit slip and leave.

"You okay, Pre?" Lola asked as the café manager staggered back to the bar on quivering legs.

Pre clutched her stomach. "I don't feel so good, like I'm going to throw up." She held up her trembling hands. "I'm jittery all of a sudden, shaking. Look at me."

"You haven't had your break yet. When was the last time you ate something, other than sneaking sundae toppings from the pantry?"

"I don't remember. I had a handful of Chex Mix for lunch, before I got here..."

"That's substantial," remarked Lola sarcastically. She grabbed Pre by the wrist and pulled her into the kitchen. The smell of ricotta cheese and tomato sauce hung thick in the air, increasing Pre's nausea despite her now roaring hunger pangs.

Lola stood on tiptoes to fetch a loaf of white bread from a high shelf near the stove. "Get the peanut butter," she ordered of Pre as she snatched a clean butter knife from the utensil drawer.

Pre complied and slouched on a stool at the food prep counter while Lola prepared the sandwich. The thought of gooey peanut butter and squishy bread glued to her gums for the remainder of the evening did not appeal much to her, and the thought only kept the acid bubbling in her stomach.

"You'll feel better once you've eaten." Lola set the sandwich down on a paper towel. "What you do want to drink?"

Instead of answering, Pre twisted around to the refrigerator. No more ginger ale, both women noticed. "Just my luck," Pre muttered.

"I'll get you some Sprite from the soda fountain," Lola said, retreating the kitchen briefly, leaving Pre to nibble on her dinner while waiters pushed in and out to collect and drop off dishes.

"Rosie is here," Lola announced as she returned.

"Duh." Like that was not a common occurrence.

"She's with someone."

In a split second Pre's face filled the kitchen door window, her heart thumping wildly, then slowing down as she watched a dark-haired woman, her face obscured by passing customers, follow Miguel to Rosie's usual table.

"*Another* reporter?"

Lola shrugged. "Didn't ask, didn't even go over there yet. Finish your sandwich, I'll soon find out. Oh," Lola was halfway out the door when she turned and pointed to the walk-in freezer. "I just remembered, we do have some ginger ale in there."

"But we don't store drinks in the big freezer."

Lola winked. "Just take a look."

Pre found the green glass bud vase next to a carton of eggs. Sprigs of wilting baby's breath spilled over the rim and surrounded the single yellow rose leaning aft. A small white card was attached.

"Where you go, I will go," she read aloud in the coolness of the enclosure, "and where you stay I will stay." The quote was from the Book of Ruth, commonly quoted during wedding ceremonies, Pre knew.

She turned the note card over to see only a bold black question mark. Game on, her move.

"Oh, Larry," she muttered, replacing the vase so she could rub her arms. "You too, Lola." Why couldn't Lola just leave well enough alone? Why would she aid and abet this continued wooing, despite knowing why the relationship could never happen? She started out of the freezer to find out just that.

"Hey, Lola!" she called, but abruptly stopped short at the sight of Larry Jeffries, waiting for her with a large bouquet and a forlorn smile.

"I got the other eleven here, you know, for a matching set," he said, presenting the flowers to a shocked Pre. "I still don't know what I did to chase you away, but I figure there's nothing like a peace offering to start over on the right foot."

"You did nothing wrong, Larry, it's just -" From the corner of her eye, Pre caught a pair of eyes watching the scene. Lola's familiar brow was visible in the door window and, upon being discovered, disappeared.

Larry extended his hand to Pre; she noticed his fingertips quake slightly. "Hi there," he said. "I'm Larry Jeffries. I have about three hundred dollars in the bank and I haven't bought a new pair of shoes since I started grad school. I'm not looking for anything long-term just yet, and I don't want to be put in an uncomfortable position, but I'd like just to date and have some fun together."

"Okay." Pre took Larry's warm grip, her own hands like ice. "I'm Prefontaine Winningham. I co-manage a restaurant and I've never willingly entered into a relationship because I can't have children and I don't want to make empty promises to any man who would one day desire a family."

She paused, waiting for the reaction, be it a fifty-yard dash, a dramatic breakdown into sympathetic tears, a pat on the shoulder, anything. Instead she was met with silence. Larry's face was a straight line.

"Well, now," he said finally, "was that so difficult?"

Pre twiddled her fingers, trying to warm them. "Uh, no."

"Good." Larry handed her the roses. "You got a vase for these?"

"Huh?" Pre wrapped her knuckles around the stems, cautious of the occasional thorn the florist might have neglected to excise. "That's it? That's all you're going to say?"

"What do you want me to say, Pre? I am sorry, but I didn't think you'd want pity," Larry said, stepping closer. "For what's it worth, though, it makes no difference to me at all whether or not your reproductive organs work. It never did, and I don't why you didn't tell me sooner if you thought it was that important."

"How do you tell a person something like that when you just met?" Pre asked, frustrated.

"You tell them as a friend," Larry smiled softly. "The best relationships start from friendship, you know."

Pre looked down at the roses; one bud brushed her chin and she relished the scent of them. Suddenly the queasiness in her stomach had subsided. "That they do," she admitted, feeling Larry's arm slide around her shoulder. She did not push away.

From the other side of the kitchen door, Lola and Rosie strained to hear everything, simultaneously offering up a prayer of thanks.

Sixty

The cramps returned around midnight, rousing Monica from an already fitful sleep. She lay on her back, contemplating a trip to the bathroom, though she did not necessarily have to pee.

Still, there was that sensation, like she usually experienced whenever...

Oh, God.

She winced as the bathroom light flickered and she stubbed her toe against the bathroom scale. She bit her lip as she undressed; she did not need an audience this late at night.

The crotch of her underpants was a swatch of dark red blood. Monica gasped at the sight of it, for it looked twice a heavy as a regular menstrual flow. She crouched on the toilet and simply stared at the mess, her baby, Jack's baby.

Oh, Jesus.

She cleaned herself quietly and wadded up the soiled panties, tossing them into the trash. They were beyond the rinse cycle, and Monica smirked sadly at her own actions, thinking of all those photos of dead babies in garbage cans she had seen in various pro-life pamphlets. She should have been relieved, and part of her was, but she also felt miserable, as if in mourning.

She snatched a maxi pad from the cabinet underneath the sink and silently returned to her room, feeling around in the dark for her dresser and a fresh pair of underwear. An unintentional clink of a brass handle against its drawer woke Therese.

"Huh?" Therese's weary head rose from underneath her comforter, eyes peering into the light cast from an outside street lamp, then at the dark shape fumbling through clothing drawers.

"Go back to sleep," Monica hissed.

Therese sat up instead and switched on her reading lamp. "What's wrong?" she asked, then saw the dress shield resting on the edge of Monica's bed. "Why is that there?"

Monica tore off the adhesive strip and glued the pad to a clean pair of panties. "I've had a miscarriage. It's like getting your period, only bloodier."

"What?" Therese leapt out of bed but just as quickly sank back down, paralyzed by her sister's cold stare. "Shouldn't we call 911?"

"It's too late for that, the baby's gone," Monica croaked. "It's probably been going on for hours, and what's a doctor going to do, anyway? Shove it back in?"

"Well," Therese slid her legs back under her sheets. "At least go see a doctor afterward...in case there's something messed up inside you."

"Yeah." Monica crawled into her own bed, checking the hallway through the open slit in the doorway for any activity. Hearing nothing except for her father's rattling snore at the other end of the hall, Monica nestled deep into bed and closed her eyes.

The sound of sniffling from Therese's bed, however, prevented her from finding sleep. "What's with you?" Monica demanded. "I figured you'd be as relieved as me."

"Relieved? How can I be relieved that a baby is dead? My niece or nephew?" Her voice was a mild squeak.

Monica shushed her sister sharply. "You want an audience?" She could not understand Therese's sudden mood changes - anger to frustration to anger to sorrow. Maybe it was her own period making her act that way.

"Maybe this is God's way of telling me that He knows I'm not ready for this," Monica said quietly, hoping to calm Therese. "You and I both already know that."

"It could also be God's way of offering you the opportunity to right the wrongs in your life," Therese added. "Go and sin no more?"

"Sin no more," Monica repeated. That she could do, or at least try to do better than she had.

"What about Mom and Dad?" Therese posed. "And the Nixons?"

"They're married. They can have all the kids they want."

285

Therese did not laugh.

"I'm kidding, Therese."

"I'm not." Therese's face was a dark stone. "How can you crack jokes after what just happened? I'll bet you prayed for a miscarriage so you wouldn't have to tell anyone."

"I prayed for help," Monica said in her defense.

"Well, God answered you, and you're going to thank Him by doing nothing? You're not going to take responsibility for what you did, not even to claim that pregnancy test?"

"The test wasn't mine, Therese."

"What?"

Monica rubbed her eyes and stared at the ceiling. "Jennifer showed me the box. It wasn't the same one I bought."

A guttural noise, one expressing a combination of shock and disbelief, escaped Therese's lips. "You mean there's *another* girl at school who might be pregnant?"

"It looks that way."

Therese flounced wildly in her bed, trying to get more comfortable but her mind would not let her relax. She punched her pillow to no avail, her head sank into it like a lead weight, pushing the stuffing to either end.

"They need to know, Nic," she told her sister. "They said there was nothing we couldn't tell them, remember? The baby was their business, too, whether you believe it or not."

Monica lay flat and still, checking to see if she could feel the miscarriage happening, wondering if the fetus felt any pain or if God took it all away before allowing the mass to die inside her. The squishy feeling in her gut was still there, but likely not for very much longer, Monica realized.

"I can't tell them about this," she decided aloud. "This way Mom and Dad will still respect me."

"But you won't really respect yourself, will you?"

No, Monica thought, trying not to cry. She cried plenty over the past seven days. She would not respect herself, not as long as she kept silent. Maybe in a few years, she could tell her parents, soften the blow.

Until then, however, the pain she felt would probably hurt her more than the pain she was enduring now.

Sixty-One

CJ reclined downstairs on the living room sofa, his glazed eyes glued to a muted David Letterman, unable to sleep. The same horror show came into focus every time his eyes closed - blood smeared on skin, a shrill howling sound too big for the tiny mouth from which it originated, tiny fingers reaching out to grasp safety but failing. All this happened while CJ watched, doing nothing.

The television show did little to push the thoughts away, but CJ left it on regardless. The bright glow stung his eyes, and the moving, soundless lips confused him, though he did not dare turn up the volume. As soundly as his parents slept, there was always the chance he could wake Joshua, and nobody slept when Joshua was wakened.

Occasionally his stare would drift to the phone. So many times, so many times that he lost count, CJ wanted to call Nina and tell her not to do it. Don't go to the clinic, he wanted to say, it might not be safe. Alleviate my guilt.

Was Nina still awake now, he wondered, having any apprehensions like she did last month...until he assured her that every precaution would be taken. Then the uncertainty vanished, and Nina wanted to be with him. He did not force her. Goaded her, perhaps, but she supplied the condom, and she still got pregnant!

CJ kicked off the afghan covering his legs, as he was feeling too warm. God, I didn't mean for this to happen, he cried out in his mind. What if something goes wrong at the clinic, what if she can't have children later on, or what if she dies? I've heard that happens, God. I don't want Nina to die.

What about the baby, he asked himself.

He was reluctant to see the abortion through, he knew, but what else could he do? College was fast approaching for both of them, and even if he married Nina and they kept the baby, what kind of life could they give him? A vision of himself and Nina trussed up in matching fast food uniforms, reeking of grease and reconstituted onions as unpaid bills piled around their ankles flashed briefly in CJ's mind. He could not drag Nina into that kind of existence. Nina was a smart girl. She wanted to go into social work, to heal the world.

Heal thyself, CJ thought with a sad smile.

He looked down at the coffee table. Judith and Joshua had been coloring on vanilla paper and left the evidence of dull-tipped crayons and wrinkled works of art. One sheet depicted a sky full of clouds and hot air balloons, and from each basket there smiled a family of stick figures. The largest balloon carried a stick figure Virgin Mary into the vast blue crayon sky; she smiled underneath the WWJD logo, emblazoned on the balloon in dark green.

What Would Jesus Do? He sure as Hell would not agree to spring for half the fee for his girlfriend's abortion, CJ thought. He would never have put Himself in such a position in the first place!

"I'm not Jesus," he whispered to the television. I'm a weak, stupid little boy who couldn't wait to get into a girl's pants, he added silently, leaving much more there than I had at first.

Now Nina was scared witless of what was going to happen to her, and upset with him because he did not have to go the procedure. This was partially true, for CJ knew he would endure it on a different plane. This was his child, too, he reminded Nina as they finalized their plans. He was going to hurt as well.

"Take care of her, God, please?" he begged. "Take the baby to Heaven and please forgive us for what is going to happen. I wish something else could be done."

Inside his heart, a small voice echoed, ringing in his ears. *There is something.*

CJ sat up with a start, cautiously checking the noise level of the television set. He faintly heard the clattering percussion of a musical act, but nothing like the dainty female voice that seemed to speak directly to him. He shook his head, certain he was losing his mind, as well as his self-respect ...and his child.

He flopped backward against the sofa, and the remote control slipped out of his hand and down into the crevice between the seat cushions, falling hastily into the dark chasm where spare change and unwrapped peppermint pinwheels often disappeared for all time. "Damn!" he muttered, plunging his fist into the couch and coming with something extra.

"Huh?"

He stared down at the string of beads wrapped around the remote. They were dark red and worn with handling, fastened together with a medal which gleamed against the light from the television. Therese's Little Flower Chaplet, he recognized, the one he bought for her.

"How did you get down here?" he asked the beads. He knew Therese rarely took the chaplet out of her room.

Then the voice spoke again. *There is something.* CJ leaned over the armrest and peered up the stairs to confirm that he was alone. He was.

He palmed the chaplet, noting how some of the beads were starting to chip and discolor with age. Therese would never get rid of it, though, and he reminded himself to return it to her in the morning. For now, however, he decided to hang on to it. He knew the chaplet prayers, too.

Sixty-Two

"Nervous?"

Nina looked up from her clasped hands, which drained white with her dual vice grip, at the pleasant young lady bundled in a long green wool coat and matching beret. The woman's gloved hand curled around a brochure espousing tips for early venereal disease detection.

"So," the woman lowered into a mock Southern drawl. "What're you in for?" They were both sitting cross-legged in neon orange chairs in the waiting room of the Hampton Roads Women's Clinic, breathing in the scent of pine wafting from an unseen air freshener; an orchestral rendition of "Take the Long Way Home" by Supertramp played softly over the office Musak.

Behind a sliding pane of frosted glass, set square in the center of the facing wall, a bowed brunette head bobbed in and out of view, emerging from the porthole only to gather insurance information from those able to provide it.

"I'm sorry," Nina said politely. "I-I just don't feel like talking right now."

"Ah." The woman's head tilted back in an exaggerated nod. "You'll have to pardon my curious nature. I'm always sticking my nose where it doesn't belong, when it should just stay smack on my face."

Nina did not laugh at the backfired joke, opting instead to select a sorely tattered *Cosmopolitan* magazine from a pile and thumb through full-page cologne ads. She inhaled the strong scents of flowers and spice, which swirled together and evoked memories of one day when Nina, as a demure kindergartner, experimented with fragrances by mixing samples of her mother's perfumes in a Dixie cup, resulting in an odorous disaster. Why that thought in particular came to mind Nina could not fathom.

"I just figured you might be here for your yearly," the woman prattled on, nodding to an exiting patient. "You don't look too enthused to be here. Then again, who would want to anticipate lying on a cold table like a turkey about to be stuffed for Thanksgiving?"

Nina winced at the analogy and involuntarily squirmed. She had never experienced a pelvic exam before, much less set foot in a clinic that offered them, or abortions. She wondered if hers would be the only such procedure for the staff today, if hers would be the only unborn child to die. The secretary within the realm behind the frosted glass had thrown her a look of disinterest when she arrived, unblinking when she gave her name as Rosalind Russell, her mother's favorite actress. Perhaps the lady never saw any of Ms. Russell's films, Nina thought. Either that, or the nurse was used to dealing with pseudonyms; Nina imagined patient logs reading like a *Who's Who* of the world.

The woman removed her beret. Tufts of frizzing brown hair cascaded down her shoulders like a tangle of dark straw. "Yep, it's that time for me. Gotta make sure the gear's still ticking, so I can work another year on having a little rugrat."

A baby? "You're not concerned about what goes on here?" Nina asked her, forgetting briefly that she did not want to talk to anybody.

"I don't have insurance, so it's the only place I can afford. What's your excuse?"

"Same," Nina sighed. "And it's the only place nearby that -"

Realizing what was about to be said, Nina clamped her mouth shut. She tried so hard not to say it out loud...abortion ...I'm having an abortion. For some reason she believed that if she said nothing, the procedure would be nothing.

"Oh," the woman whispered after a thoughtful pause. "So," she flung a magazine from an unoccupied chair and moved closer to Nina, "you hear about what happened to that doctor here?"

Nina nodded.

"They still haven't found the guy who did it. You think maybe it was that guy who's hiding in the woods? The one everyone thinks bombed the Olympics in Atlanta?"

"I don't know." I don't care either, she wanted to add. I just want to get this done, end it now. Nina stared at the closed door leading to the exam rooms, wondering what was the delay in getting her to her appointment. Aside from the woman next to her, there were no other patients in the waiting room.

The woman, meanwhile, fiddled through her purse, brushing away makeup bottles and pens until she found a flattened pack of cinnamon chewing gum. Nina turned down the foil-wrapped limp stick offered to her, leaving the woman to shrug as she folded it in half and devoured it.

"Miss Russell?" A nasal voice blared from inside the office. Nina's attention remained enrapt in the magazine. It took a nudge from the dark-haired woman to remind Nina that she was Miss Russell.

"Miss Russell, is it?" the secretary inquired as Nina gingerly approached the window.

"Y-yes. Rosalind."

The lady smirked. "Loved you in *Auntie Mame*," she cracked as she pointed out a few omissions on Nina's medical form. Nina filled in the blanks without comment and returned to her chair, grimacing at the cackle behind her.

"You're not here for an exam, are you?" the woman in the wool coat asked. "Why would you use a fake name if you were? And, if you ask me, I'm surprised a girl as young as you could come up with that one."

"Well, I figured using Cher would have raised a few eyebrows," Nina retorted in a tone a bit nastier than intended. She quickly rejoined with an apology. "I'm just not in a good mood right now. I don't do this every day."

"Thank goodness for that," the woman sighed. "How nice it would be if no woman had to abort any day." She deflected a scornful glance from the face behind the frosted glass, an obvious eavesdropper.

"So why are you here, then? Why would you give your business to a clinic that does abortions, which you clearly seem to hate?"

"Who said I was seeking treatment here?" the woman asked, raking a hand through her hair. "I only said I needed a checkup, and that this was the only place I could afford. Never said I actually made an appointment, or that I was planning to have the exam here."

She leaned closer to the young girl and whispered, "Did I, Nina?"

Nina froze, the arms of her chair hugging her closely, constricting her. Who told this woman, she wanted to know. She worked for a month to cover her tracks - a closed lip leaked no secrets, leaving the rumor mill dry. CJ, too, had a stock in her discretion, and Nina knew he would never have said anything to anybody, not even Miguel.

She studied the woman's face. Nina did not know her, nor had she recognized the face from church or school. Many of the school maintenance workers were older, heftier and grizzled from years of hard labor - nowhere close to matching the lovely apple-cheeked face before her.

Pleasant, Nina noticed, yet passionate.

"How do you know me? Who sent you here?" Nina demanded of her. "Nobody is supposed to know about this. Nobody..." she choked on her words, taking deep breaths to calm a sudden fit of heaving sobs.

"Don't fret, dear." The woman stroked Nina's arm. "Your parents still think you're in school, and the school thinks you're out sick. A clever plan, though eventually your next report card is going to reflect the absence. No telling if your parents will notice it."

"If it ever came up I was going to tell them that CJ and I skipped and went to the mall," Nina sniffed. "No amount of punishment they give me for that will be as bad as this."

"You're paying in cash, too?"

Nina snapped open her clutch bag and flashed the corner of a fifty-dollar bill. She thought momentarily of her CD Walkman, which would forever be strapped to Miguel Marquez's ears. She could only guess what bauble CJ sacrificed to come up with his share.

The woman handed Nina a tattered Kleenex. "You know, that money could be better spent."

"On what, baby food? Tickle-Me Elmo?" Nina pushed the tissue away. "I can't keep the baby, my father will freak! And I can't

293

finish school with my stomach out to here," she extended her arms in front of her, "looking all bloated and gross."

"All I'm saying is give the baby a chance," the woman pleaded. "Your baby doesn't deserve to die this way."

"It didn't ask to be conceived, either," Nina blurted out.

"Exactly," the woman was firm. "You made that happen, so why punish the child?"

Nina started to quake, a wave of nausea swirling up inside her. She noticed several pairs of eyes watching her, judging her with mild stares. How did they see her, she wondered, as a tramp? A murderess?

"Go to Hell! You don't know what I'm going through!" she shrieked in the woman's face. "Leave me alone!" With that, Nina bolted for the door. The secretary called out for Miss Russell, but Nina's ears were pounding too loudly for her to hear anything.

Anything, that was, save for the explosion that occurred after she crossed the street to the coffee shop. A foot-long scrap of shrapnel sailed in an arc over the road and missed her skull by inches, denting the fender of a nearby car.

Nina turned slowly around to discover that a chunk of the clinic had been obliterated from the blast. Anguished screams vented from gaping hole by the front door, approximately where she had been sitting.

Sixty-Three

Detective Mark Skinner ordered an Italian soda and paused in front of the Norfolk Coffee Company window, sipping idly from the dewy transparent plastic cup and studying the clinic entrance. Having failed at securing a warrant - no judge in town was willing to offer him one based on "circumstantial theory" - he elected to simply tail Roy Jeffries himself.

Something was bound to happen, if not today, then soon, Mark decided. The other detectives on the force thought him paranoid when he checked out a bulletproof vest, certain that Mark was charging a windmill. Even after he had shown them the connections between Roy and the clinic he found on the Internet they shook their heads, all noncommittal. The man had neither any prior arrests nor even a speeding ticket, and no complaints filed against him at the Better Business Bureau. For all they knew, the man probably still called his mother every Sunday and ladled soup to the homeless.

The vest itched liked a bad case of poison oak, but Mark sucked in his discomfort. Better to be covered in rashes than gunshot wounds. In a few minutes he would head for the antique shop and check for Roy's truck, perhaps stake out the shop from the back alley.

"What are you planning, Roy?" he muttered to himself, averting his eyes from the clinic only briefly to inspect the sports section of the *Times* folded on a nearby table. Further delving into Roy's history brought forth the connection to the paper via his brother, Larry. Mark recalled feeling suddenly morose, thinking of the possibility of one brother reporting the other brother's crime.

His soda finished, Mark ambled outside, noting passersby on either side of the street, shuffling toward work or shopping or late breakfast. The usual protesters were nowhere in sight; then again, the clinic had only been open for about thirty minutes. Maybe the pro-life contagion liked to sleep late.

An eternity passed before the first sign of activity happened. The clinic doors burst open with force as a young girl emerged, running, it seemed, for her life. Maybe for two lives, Mark thought, paling at the sight of her. Auburn locks bounced with her every step, swinging in circular motion as she dodged a slowing truck. She could not have been more than sixteen, he decided. That face belonged in a teen magazine advertisement for skin care, not in the would-be line of fire. He had half a mind to approach her with his badge and ask her why she was not in school right now.

The bomb blast rattled his skeleton, and instinctively he ducked behind a parked car. "Get down!" he hollered to everyone within earshot, waving the young girl closer to him as she crouched low, confused.

Cries of surprise and fear filled his ears, while concrete hail rained heavy, creating large pockmarks on the roof of the car in front of him. Mark covered his head with his jacket and shrieked a request to dispatch for backup and a bomb squad on his cellular phone - who knew whether or not to expect another explosion?

That you, Roy? Is this your calling card? Mark tasted bile rising in his throat. How was a bomb supposed to solve everything? Were there any unborn children, nestled in their mothers' wombs, inside that clinic? Did any of them get hurt, along with other innocent people? Was it worth the hurt, Mark wanted to ask Roy or whoever else was responsible.

Slowly, gun in hand, Mark slid up the side of the car, inspecting initial damage through the windows. Causalities appeared to be limited; he noticed a cluster of people tending to a fallen pedestrian while many of the clinic staff limped out of the broken building. All heads craned eastward toward the wail of an approaching siren.

The red-haired girl was huddled in a ball beside the curb, stone-faced and clutching her stomach. "You okay?" he called to her.

The girl gently brushed away gravel from a bloody scrape on her knee and nodded silently. Mark gestured to the coffee shop and ordered her inside before he dashed across the street.

He studied every face floating past him, looking for the slightest hint of calm or anticipation, any expression but the expected reactions one would show in such a situation. Whether or not the perpetrator was dumb enough to linger and admire his or her handiwork was the only question Mark wanted answered. Help was on the way, and they could take care of everything else.

Mark found that serenity concealed under the brim of an Orioles baseball cap. Its owner quick-stepped through clouds of smoke toward the intersection of 21st and Granby, shooting a scornful smile at the crumbling wall of the clinic before turning.

"Roy Jeffries!" Mark bellowed, gripping his gun with both hands and brushing onlookers aside with a steely glance. The man he addressed slowly halted, then turned his upper body around to see the glint of the detective's gun.

"Police! Stay where you are!"

Roy cursed to himself, despondent as his alibi dissolved with the specks of clinic ash into the wind. "Hello, friend," he called to Mark. "Sorry I missed you at the shop."

"You're a hard man to track down, Jeffries," Mark bantered angrily. He inched closer to his suspect. "I trust you're not hurt?"

Roy slid his hand inside his denim jacket and lifted his .22 from an inside pocket. Mark caught the movement and cocked his own weapon.

"Drop it," he warned, aiming for the bird logo on Roy's cap. In all his years with the force, Mark had never used his gun outside of the shooting range, and for a fleeting moment he wondered exactly how quick on the draw he could be. Against a cardboard adversary, no problem, but this guy was flesh and blood and chaos.

Roy turned his head away from Mark, prompting the detective to order his hands in the air. Instead Roy jammed the gun in his mouth and pulled the trigger. More shrill screams filled the air as Roy's lifeless body slumped to the sidewalk, his head crowned with a halo of dark blood.

Sixty-Four

Nina sat at a small round table and tended to her wound with a few slivers of ice wrapped in a cocktail napkin. Thankfully, the wound did not appear to go very deep into her leg. Nothing that a dollop of antibiotic cream and a bandage could not heal.

Chuck approached with mug of hot chocolate capped with a pyramid of whipped cream. "On the house," he told her, "don't worry about it. You're sure you're all right?"

"Fine, thank you. And thank you for this." Nina's voice was small and frightened. She wrapped her fingers around the warm mug to keep them from shaking.

"Do you need to call anyone? Your folks?"

My parents, thought Nina. They would just die if they found out ...

"I drove here. My car's not far."

"Well, take your time, 'kay? You're in no condition to get behind the wheel."

Tell me about it, she wanted to retort, but instead silently turned to her cocoa and slurped a mouthful of cream. No condition to drive, no condition to think, she mused, because she was in a delicate condition. Had she faltered at the clinic she would probably be in critical condition.

All because she could not bear to hear the truth of why she went to the clinic in the first place, Nina realized. That woman in the green coat goaded her, and ...

Nina looked around the shop, then out the window at the scene as ambulances and police cars crowded the streets, waving calm into the frantic activity with broad gestures. She looked for the woman but could not find her. Had she perished in the explosion, Nina wondered, feeling nauseous. An innocent woman trying to help her, murdered by someone trying to stop abortions! It made no sense to her.

She reached for the mug and her hand brushed a small, velvety object. A red rosebud, its stem clipped of thorns, rested on the table.

Nina spotted Chuck wiping moisture rings from a nearby table. "Hey, did you give me this?" she pointed to the rose.

Chuck slid a pile of muffin crumbs into a curved palm, glancing at the flower as if he had never seen one before in his life. "Nope. Don't know who did, either."

"Huh." Nina plucked a round, red petal and squeezed it between her forefinger and thumb.

Sixty-Five

CJ could wait no longer. Three o'clock to him seemed an eternity away, and as his guilt ate away at his stomach he found that he could not keep down any of the veggie burger Pre Winningham had cooked for him as he sat at the bar of Café Lisieux. He pushed the plate away gently, feeling a volcano filled with stomach acid preparing to erupt.

"Something wrong, guy?" Miguel leaned over and nabbed a stray French fry from his friend's plate, as his own was nearly empty.

"I'm just not as hungry as I thought."

"You want some more Coke?" Miguel leaned over the bar for the soda gun. "Or some water? Soda's good for indigestion, though."

Miguel looked up at his friend, only to see an empty stool.

* * * *

He walked, then jogged, the rest of the way home, leaving his backpack at the café. His parents would be angry to see him home from school three hours early, CJ knew, but better to have it out in the open now than to let his secret burn his conscience forever.

He wished he could get in touch with Nina, find out how she was doing, if her procedure - he could not even bring himself to think the word 'abortion' - was successful. She told CJ that she would try to be back at school before lunch. No such luck, and that worried CJ, especially since there was no way he could get to a phone and call the clinic to check up on her.

He reached his front door and drew in a long, rippled breath. His legs wanted turn around and run, sprint down Jamestown Road to the ferry, swim across the river and keep going, past Surry to

North Carolina without so much as a backward glance. His heart kept him glued to his place.

"Mom? Hello?"

An eerie silence permeated the foyer - usually the house was alive with young, gay voices as Laura schooled her youngest children in the study. CJ poked his head inside the room and, seeing it empty, ventured quietly into the kitchen.

Both of his parents, to CJ's surprise, reacted mildly to his appearance. There were no stern looks, no nodding acknowledgments. Their eyes were fixed on the third person at the kitchen table - Monica, whose presence startled CJ as much as his father's. Why was his father home from work so early? He noticed her eyes were rubbed raw with tears and that she was barely able to speak as she saw her older brother staring at her with curiosity.

"CJ, whatever it is, let it wait in the den." Laura's voice was tense.

CJ, however, did not move. Seeing Monica upset, and noting the conspicuous absence of his younger siblings, led his thoughts to a possible death in the family. If that were the case, though, then why were he and Therese also not informed?

His query was met with a cryptic answer.

"You could say that," Chris answered, "but this doesn't concern you. Let us alone."

"Dad, this can't wait. It's really important."

"Damn it, son!" Chris flushed beet red; his daughter let out a heavy sob. "What the hell could be more important than your sister having a miscarriage?"

CJ looked from his father to Monica, his own saucer-wide gaze falling slack. "Trust me, Dad. It is."

Sixty-Six

The necessary papers were signed, notarized and filed with the county clerk's office at noon on the Friday following Nina Simmons's admittance to St. Mary's, which, after a grueling labor, resulted in the birth of a squawking baby boy bearing a shock of red hair. On Sunday, after the requisite examination proved the newborn healthy, Pre was permitted to pick up her son, Francis Xavier Winningham, and take him home. Lola opened Café Lisieux to a private celebration for the jubilant mother.

"So," asked Rosie, balancing a dish of assorted finger foods atop an empty Coke can, "when can we expect to add a 'J' to this fine young baby's monogram?"

Pre cradled Frank in the crook of her left arm and stroked his feathered hair, attracting smiles from all around the dining area. "February seventeenth, right after the wedding," she said between coos and caws directed to her son. "He'll be signing the marriage license and the adoption papers one right after the other." She nodded to a smiling Father Welker in passing; he was pleased to be presiding over the pending wedding and Frank's baptism.

"Then," Pre shifted Frank to her other arm, "it's down to Florida to visit Grandma and Grandpa. I wish they could come up for the wedding, though. I mean, I'm grateful for the time off, but I still worry about leaving the café for so long."

"Hey now, Lola ran this place fine before you, she'll be fine," Rosie remarked playfully. "Besides, I promise not to do too much of a bang-up job while you're gone." The old woman was looking forward to working as Pre's replacement for those two weeks, and was flattered that Lola proposed the idea. Rosie had been a faithful customer for almost four years, who else would know better how to satisfy diners than a regular one?

She turned momentarily to Carrie and the boys, huddled together at one table joking with each other over a platter of Buffalo wings. The last of their belongings were moved into her house that morning, with Carrie having closed on her own house the week before. Rosie felt relieved that Carrie did not harbor any reproach toward Larry when they met; in fact, Carrie appeared more sympathetic to the reporter's loss, something she never would have done nine months earlier.

The widow's initial reaction to the letter left by the late Roy Jeffries, which confessed his crimes and emphasized the fact that he acted alone, was swift and punctuated with angry words. It hurt that her husband's killer would never be brought to justice, though Rosie pointed out to her that that was not necessarily the case.

"God will judge Roy Jeffries," she stated plainly then. "He is the only one qualified to do so."

As the months wore on and Neil's case was officially closed, Carrie began to heal, emotionally and spiritually. Roy's hasty funeral and burial brought closure to her pain, and seeing a dark-suited Larry with Pre by his side as they bowed their heads before the polished coffin awoke in Carrie a flood of understanding for the young reporter. His brother had, in the course of hours following his suicide, been hailed a hero by some and editorialized as a coward and terrorist by others - she swore every euphemism she read in the papers had already been used to describe Neil. She knew she could not blame Larry for everything that happened.

Now, stepping gradually back into the faith in which she was raised, Carrie enjoyed the celebration of new life at the café with her aunt's dearest friends. She raised her glass of iced tea in chorus with the other revelers as Rosie proposed a toast.

"To Francis Xavier, the best Christmas gift a mother could receive," the old woman announced to a smattering of 'hear hears.' Baby Frank wiggled in his mother's arms, bubbling at the mouth.

Larry eased next to his fiancé. "Let me take him for a while, hon," he offered. "I need the practice, too." Pre gladly, albeit reluctantly, handed over the infant; her arm was starting to numb under the weight of him.

Miguel circled the room, refilling glasses. He arrived at a table full of Merwins, and grinned at Laura's obvious joy and CJ's relief that Nina made it through the delivery relatively unscathed. She was still in the hospital, feeling weak but not critically ill.

"So how's William and Mary treating you?" Laura asked Miguel.

"It's nice, but I'm glad for the break." Miguel leaned on the table. "I thought it was going to be easy, what with taking only four classes this term. But, man, I must have three times the homework I did when I took seven classes in high school!"

Laura chortled. "Why does that sound so familiar?" She mussed her oldest son's hair, shaking him lightly until a smile cracked his face. By virtue of Franciscan University's winter break, he was able to be home in time for the occasion, though he was not present for the boy's birth.

Once the initial shock of CJ's revelation nine months before settled, he and Nina decided, after conferring with his parents, that abortion could no longer be considered an option. The trauma of the clinic bombing had affected Nina that deeply.

"Is Nina heading back to the convent after she's discharged?" Miguel asked. The sisters at the high school welcomed Nina into a spare bedroom following her expulsion from her home, thereby allowing her to finish the school year through private tutoring. Dan and Elsa Simmons had yet to contact their daughter, and all the nuns continued to pray for a familial reconciliation.

Chris nodded slowly. "Far as I know, though we've offered her room at our place." He turned his head to look at Monica, who stood in the far corner chatting with Larry, her countenance still glum. Jack left for college after graduation with nary a word to anyone, leaving Monica to assume that despite surviving their near miss, their relationship was finished. No farewells, no apologies.

Monica was strong, however, this Chris knew. She got past her own problems through the Grace of God and the support of her family. She would get over Jack.

Rosie watched the exchange from her seat, her eyes following Therese, now a blossoming young lady, as she excused herself and slipped outside, where she parked on the stoop by the café entrance.

Therese twirled her Little Flower chaplet on her index finger, staring dreamily down the street at rows of homes decorated for the Christmas season. She zipped up her jacket as far as it would go and pulled the collar over her lips, moistening the metal zipper latch with her even breathing.

"You'll catch your death out here," Rosie, poking her head out the door, told her. She kept her voice soft so as not to startle Therese. It did not work.

"Oh!" The chaplet flopped onto the ground. Rosie noticed the beads were misshapen with wear, a good sign.

"It was getting stuffy in there," Therese said.

"I see," Rosie nodded as Therese scooped up the string of beads. "That chaplet's looking a bit ragged. I could make a replacement if you like. I have plenty of rose beads."

"Thanks, but I like this one. CJ gave it to me. Hey," the girl brightened. "You could make a rosary for the baby."

Rosie smiled, she was way ahead of Therese. An unfinished strand of large wooden blue beads lay curled on her worktable at home. The finished product was to be Frank's baptismal gift.

"Pre says I can come over to see the baby anytime I want, and that I can babysit," Therese added wistfully, hoping for many nights of work in the near future. She still thought of little Francis Xavier as her nephew. Pre said she intended to tell the child of his heritage as he grew older, and Therese debated with herself as to whether or not to let the boy call her aunt.

"How nice," Rosie commented, believing that one night of babysitting an infant dogged with colic or an earache could dissuade any teenager from considering an early pregnancy. If only changing a live baby's diaper was a requirement in every high school home economics class, Rosie thought, how many young people would find chastity all the more appealing?

"I can't think of more capable hands to care for Francis while the future Mrs. Jeffries is away," she added, stooping down to pat Therese's shoulder before retreating to the warmth of the café. "Don't stay out too long now."

She had just opened the door when Therese suddenly jerked her head upward. "Do you think Larry's brother's in Hell?"

"What?"

"Larry's brother." Therese's voice trailed away into silence. Out of respect to Larry and Pre and the Mastersons, the Merwin children were told by their parents not to broach the subject of Roy, the clinic, and other related topics. Therese hoped nobody was able to hear her as the door opened.

"I don't know where Roy is now," Rosie answered honestly.

"But he killed a man, and then himself. Isn't that a mortal sin?"

"It is. The Catechism says that suicide is contrary to love for God," she told Therese. "Any outsider might acknowledge that by taking his own life, Roy Jeffries showed disdain for the life given to him by God."

"As for whether he's in Hell or not," she continued, "I can't say. The Pope has said that we cannot even be sure that Judas Iscariot, of all people, is there. Only God knows for certain, and we don't know what was going through Roy's mind before he died. It's not right for us to speculate."

"Yeah, I read something in the paper a month ago where some teacher got in trouble for telling her class that Princess Diana went to Hell because of her sins, but we don't know that for sure. I mean, how did the teacher know that Di died unrepentant?"

Therese sighed. "I was just curious, because I didn't know if it was okay to pray for Roy anyway."

"I don't see why not," Rosie said with a shrug. "Prayer won't do any harm."

"I know, but...if there's the chance Roy is already in Hell, what good will prayer do? Once you're in Hell, you're there forever."

"Well," Rosie began, shivering in the cold. The snow drizzled down and thickened at their feet. "Only Jesus could save Roy's soul. We also know how strongly Roy felt about abortion, though his methods of expression were morally wrong. Perhaps through prayer we can help prevent further tragedies from happening. Pray for a peaceful end to abortion that doesn't involve the murders of others."

Therese tossed her chaplet into the air and caught it. "You know, back when Dr. Masterson was killed, I prayed a St. Therese novena. It started out being for my family's health but sort of turned into a petition for life in all respects. By the end of it, Nina's baby - Frank - was not aborted as she and CJ planned."

"Nina said later that somebody left her a rose, like when the prayer asks for a rose," Therese then revealed in a low voice. "I've heard of things like that happening before, you think St. Therese really gave it as a sign?"

"Could be. Could be also that there's another explanation. Life's full of coincidences, you know."

They pondered that thought for a moment in silence, until the cold weather got the better of the old woman and she opened the door again to a gush of warm air. "Coming, Therese?"

"Right behind you. Go ahead."

Rosie reentered the café as the crowd of partygoers oohed and aahed over an enthusiastic infantile squawk. Therese looked back at the scene until the door closed and concealed it.

God, thank You for answering my prayers through St. Therese's intercession, she prayed silently, rolling a rose bead between her fingers. *Please watch over Frank, and Nina and my family, and please repose the souls of Neil Masterson and Roy and Diane Jeffries. I'm hoping with this novena, prayed through the intercession of St. Therese, that once again my prayers will be answered with a rose.*

About the Author

Kathryn Lively is an award-winning author and editor whose work has appeared in numerous Web sites and magazines. She is also the author of *Pithed: an Andy Farmer Mystery*.

www.KathrynLively.com

Made in the USA
San Bernardino, CA
22 December 2015